D1206822
St. Olaf College Libraries
FRAM FRAM KRISTMENN KROSSMENN
SAINT OLAF COLLEGE
Gift of Richard G. Peterson

NKt
1327

R&S Peterson
December 1993

THE SPHINX
AND THE SYBARITES

By the same author

NOVELS

The Raining Tree War
African Horse
God Perkins
Light on a Honeycomb
Beloved Latitudes
The White Cutter
The Gardener
Stagg and his Mother

SHORT STORIES

My Organic Uncle and Other Stories
The Bunch from Bananas
(for children)

POETRY

Another Country

PLAYS

Music to Murder By
An Audience Called Edouard
Motocar
Richard III: Part 2
The Dream of Chief Crazy Horse
(for children)
Pride and Prejudice
(stage adaptation)
Beef
Master Class
Ploughboy Monday

NON-FICTION

Between Ribble and Lune

The Sphinx and the Sybarites

DAVID POWNALL

SINCLAIR-STEVENSON

First published in Great Britain 1993
by Sinclair-Stevenson
an imprint of Reed Consumer Books Ltd
Michelin House, 81 Fulham Road, London SW3 6RB
and Auckland, Melbourne, Singapore and Toronto

A CIP catalogue record for this book
is available at the British Library

ISBN 1 85619 225 3

Typeset by CentraCet, Cambridge
Printed in Great Britain
by Butler & Tanner Ltd, Frome

For my son Max

late come and welcome

I imagine his
face that is more the face
of a clock, and the time told by it
is now, though Greece is referred
to and Egypt and empires
not yet begun.

from 'At It' by R. S. Thomas

A mystery
Curdled in me and I could suddenly see
My self and my name as separate things.

from 'The General' by Dom Moraes

ONE

An emissary of the tyrant of Sybaris, that famously rich Greek city in Italy, spent thirty-four days in my house in the Iamidai lands of Elis pounding at me to accept work in state prophecy.

It was the most protracted period of bargaining that I have ever endured, and I (one who loves situations that take time to turn) got scant joy out of it.

The progress of the negotiations was often hampered by my silences as I emerged from my winter diathesis. The young Sybarite did not understand how I could shift between gloomy coldness and hospitable warmth within such short spans of time.

When I said yes, it was the beginning of my peaceful springtime self – sage not lover, seer not servant of desires. As the star Arcturus descended into the ocean we celebrated our hard-won agreement: hard for me because it had taken him so long to recognise my worth; hard for him because he had been forced to pay the original amount that I had demanded.

Ten talents of gold is a great sum. It could have been less if the emissary had been able to tell me exactly why I was wanted in Sybaris, but the tyrant had issued orders that I must not be given any such information.

In pitch darkness gold gleams brighter.

The fig trees on my farms were sprouting their first leaves as we embarked for Sybaris. I had rested for a summer, an autumn and a winter from my calling, not seeking any new venture. What I had earned for my last engagement had been enough to carry me through. But now I was in work again, all my faculties sharpened, and doubly so for my encounter with this mystery.

We left the coast of Elis at the mouth of the sacred Alfios, the river most beloved of Zeus. Not far from where the fresh water mingles with the salt is my home, tucked away behind hills of wild olive. It is an Heraklean land, strong and beautiful, but one that must be left at times or the religious claims it makes become crushing. However, on the morning of our embarkation I was not glad to go, and wept when saying farewell. My lands, my sons and slaves were so plentiful and my flocks were so increased with young, the pastures so thick with new grass, that it gave my departure the sensation of leaving bounty for emptiness.

The ship itself was a beautiful craft, built of bleached cedar, with gorgeous sails of black and pink made of a textile which could be worn next to the skin should one be short of a shirt. All the luck which the master enjoyed came from the same source as the aura which surrounded his ship – the wealth of Sybaris, the city with which he principally traded in his voyages from Miletos. The prices which he could obtain for his cargo there were high and steady. Also, the use of the city as an entry into the Tyrrhenian trade meant that he did not have to run the risk of circumnavigating Sicily, with its host of rapacious coastal city-states, nor to pass through the Straits of Messina, which are dominated by pirates and the whirlpool of Charybdis. Instead he was able to discharge his goods in safety, take his money and return home with metals from the Tyrrhenians without having to face any of these dangers – all thanks to the acumen of the Sybarites.

This exclusive traffic with the profitable Tyrrhenian market had made the other free Greek cities in Italy and Sicily jealous, and Sybaris was well hated for its success. Attempts had been made to steal away the Tyrrhenian trade, but these had been repulsed, not by war, but by Sybaris constantly demonstrating that it was a reliable and fruitful trading partner, plagued by no ambition other than to remain secure in its prosperity. While its enemies gnashed their teeth in envy, Sybaris worked smoothly on, multiplying its wealth.

What problem could such a city have? When the master asked me this question I could not answer him.

I love the sea when it is smooth: it purifies, soothes and steadies.

Although I was affable and outgoing to the master and the emissary, within myself I was drawing new strength from resting aboard ship, often in a vibrant trance as fresh energy flowed into my winter-wasted flesh, untwisting the warped sinews in my heart, unpicking the stiff knots in my spirit. To sit and stare at the surface of the sea and feel the gentle motion of the hull beneath is like a return to childhood for me, and the salt air is motherly. Also it opens me up, frees my bowels, breaks the wax in my ears, loosens every muscle and tendon.

But should the wind start to blow and the waves mount! Then I suffer agonies, too shaken by the great forces, rattled out of all my learning, made too puny to hold on to my understanding of the gods. I do not like to be struck, or flattened, or thrown out of my equilibrium without knowing the purpose behind it. The whys and wherefores of tempests at sea are the most uninterpretable. Storms are commonly employed by bad dramatists when they've run out of things to say and want to use some event which they don't have to explain except by saying: 'Oh, it's the gods.'

I cannot get away with such simple explanations. To guess is alien to my nature. I must know.

So I was grateful for the soft weather which we enjoyed. Day after day went by in tranquillity, not a cloud in the sky, our only visitors being dolphins and the birds passing high overhead as they flew back from Africa and their winter roosts. The only disturbance of our peace was the occasional stiffening of the cords and the swelling of the sail as the breeze picked up, or the cook's call at mealtimes, always a welcome sound as the food aboard the ship was excellent.

We anchored in the sea-roads of Sybaris after dark, the last of a large number of ships which would wait until dawn before entering harbour. As there was nothing to see I went back to my couch. As I lay there the most delightful scents were brought to me on the air. Getting up, I joined the master at the bow and asked him about the source of these perfumes.

'Be thankful that they're so sweet at the moment,' he said. 'Once you get inside the city they can be overpowering.'

'Do these perfumes come from great gardens, rose farms or orchards?' I asked. 'The smell is so strong.'

'No, no, it is just the Sybarites themselves. They like to shower themselves with scent,' the master explained. 'It is said that some swim in baths of fragrant oil and soak their hair in the essences of flowers.'

Then the dawn crept up behind us and shone its light over our shoulders towards Sybaris so I could see the source of the fragrances. The city stood within tall, protective walls, its roofs ascending to a great general height, with many edifices constructed on a colossal scale. She filled the eye, supreme over land, sea and heaven. Even the distant mountains which stood behind the city at the edge of a broad, deep plain were dwarfed by this verticality and the sheer size of the place. Buildings were crammed together so high into the air that they seemed to bulge beyond the walls like dough being squeezed in a baker's fist; temples spilled over temples, roofs and towers blended in enormous areas of earth-red and marble-white confection.

It was so vast and vigorous, so over-built and bold, that the thought of landing there filled me with unease.

Was even my soul, the soul of Kallias the Elean, foremost Iamidic diviner of his generation, strong enough to deal with such an earthbound force?

TWO

There was no-one waiting to receive me when our ship tied up alongside the south harbour wall. No music. No signs or emblems. No-one to guide me to my lodging. No-one to make me feel warm towards this towering, brash place with its ponderous, big-bellied merchants and fawning clerks, its swarming thousands dodging between the brightly painted chariots and waggons going to and from the port.

I had to stand by my baggage and guard it while I waited for the emissary to come back from the city hall, where I had sent him to ask why I had been so neglected. It took him all morning to do so.

I suppressed my impatience by asking a few passers-by who were not too busy to talk if they would give me the layout of their city. That was simple enough: an oblong, four gates, the circumference of the walls being fifty stadia. Three main roads out: to Kroton in the south; to the western coast and the colonies of Laus and Poseidonia (this, they said, was a wide highway called the Road to Prosperity); and the road north to Metapontion and Siris. These roads and others out of Sybaris were roofed over to a distance of twenty stadia to protect travellers from the sun and rain. My informants were very proud of the cost, which the city had borne, but I silenced their self-congratulation when I told them who I was, my rank, my status within my calling, and how badly I had been treated.

Eventually the emissary returned. I was incensed to discover that he was alone and had succeeded only in obtaining the address of the place where I was to stay: a hostel. This was a grave insult, and if there had been a ship leaving harbour which could have taken me back to the Peloponnese I would have taken it. But as it turned out, the hostel was quite acceptable and close to an old wooden temple of Hera which had been preserved in the middle of tall new buildings.

My apartment was extravagantly furnished, the origins of the pieces being as various and widespread as the trading world could offer. There were chairs and stools from Persia, cloths and candlesticks from Babylon, woollen carpets and wall-hangings from Egypt, and the Makedhonian couch was carved out of a single beech trunk. Every piece of stone and wood in wall and ceiling was painted indigo, yellow or black, and the floor mosaics were so real and lively that I spent the first few days creeping about for fear of damaging their delicacy. And the bedroom – it was not intended as a place of rest! Such hangings and voluptuous vases! Pots of sweet-smelling ointments were ranged on the windowsill so the slightest breeze brought me frankincense, spikenard and sandalwood. On the ceiling was a painting of Aphrodite spurning her lame husband, the smith-god Hephaestus (depicted as African black and wild-eyed), and offering herself in the frankest manner to the war-god Mars, who was completely scarlet, with shoulders as wide as his height. Not an easy scene to sleep under. Also, at the foot of the bed in an alcove, was a figure of Priapus, with a phallus long enough to go into his mouth.

In these early days I was discouraged from wandering about the city on my own.

It would not be true to say that I was a prisoner, but if I did venture into the street I was immediately joined by a civic employee who would whisk me off to a place of entertainment. These were usually comedy theatres or tavern shows, the kind of low-grade spectacle which can be found in any Greek city outside the religious festivals. But Sybaris did have one staged diversion peculiar to itself.

Schools of equitation were everywhere, both within and outside the city walls. When one looked at the large number of horses in the streets and the great herds on the plain, this was no surprise. There was also a marked disinclination on the part of Sybarites to walk, a rich man not thinking it strange to have his horse saddled in order to ride to the end of the street.

But these schools of equitation were not there simply to teach riding. That was only a small part of the curriculum. Their main educative function was to teach the horses of Sybaris to dance.

Attached to each school was an arena, and nightly shows were given to the music of the Sybarite bagpipes, a traditional instrument with two chanters and eight drones. There were a set number of tunes which each horse was taught to understand in terms of tempo and Terpsichorean style, and the performances were formal. Every member of the audience knew the music and the steps, and any deviation from them sparked off boos and whistles of derision.

As I had time to pass while waiting for the tyrant of Sybaris to return from his business in his dominions, I engaged one of these musicians to teach me how to play the instrument and a few of these dancing tunes.

As an admirer of the horse, that strong and noble animal, I had no difficulty in enjoying the dancing. There was much variety in this specialised art: regiments of the voluntary citizen cavalry giving displays, with several hundred riders at one time in the arena; solo performances by masters, duos, trios and so on.

On the rule of thumb that people should be left to get what pleasure they can out of this toilsome life, horse-dancing must come close to being the most innocuous and irreproachable of pastimes; but the bawdier amusements of the migrant workers and the poor of Sybaris were no more so to me. What can people do with their days and nights? They have their senses to play with and little else. The rich are no more inventive than the poor when it comes to wresting sensation from a sullen universe. The lengths that Sybarites will go to for amusement are notorious, but they go no further than those of Athens. How can they? There is no further to go.

When the civic employees dragged me from one inane entertainment to another, hoping to startle me by the depravity or originality which they displayed, I had to tell them that

I had seen it all before, except for the copulation with ponies. But even that was no real surprise from a horse-loving people who emulate the Olympians in their pleasure-taking. To me there seems to be no other model for us to use, and I have spoken openly on this topic at debates. What did puzzle me, however, was the assiduousness with which I was taken to view the low-life of the city. As a priest with that dignity, I had expected introductions to the better houses.

It was said that the Sybarites had a way of life that was too soft and easy. But such a colossus never arose out of idleness. Somewhere in the Sybarite character there was tenacity and energy, or had been ancestrally. If a man chooses to have his slaves iron out each of the rose petals in his pillow so he will not be disturbed by rustling, this need not stop him running a profitable business when he is up and on his feet. A wise man values his sleep as much as his waking life. What the jokes are really about is the lack of manly, fighting spirit in war, and a lacklustre showing in athletics. Sybaris, however, has twenty-five subject cities scattered about southern Italy. How are they policed, I asked myself, if she is so incapable of strong, physical action? And, as I have already mentioned, was it not this soft Sybaris that plotted to start a rival Olympic Games which would compete with those held in my own country? The venture failed because Sybaris lacked the true priests to conduct games properly, but the will to hold a great celebration of physical strength and skill was there. The Sybarites must admire the manly virtues, even though they do not prize them for their own use.

Telys, the tyrant of Sybaris, returned from his travels after I had waited seventeen days.

He entered the city in the middle of the night under a large moon set in a frame of benevolent stars, his cavalcade rattling over the stones. There were no trumpets or shouts as the retinue came down the Avenue of Herakles, and I watched from the balcony as horsemen and footsoldiers began to disperse through the streets.

Not long afterwards a slave brought me a message from

Telys. It had obviously been written while he was in progress, as the writing was shaky. It read:

> When you come to see me at noon today in my office, before entering into any discussion whatsoever I insist that you, who claim to be a hierophant of the Mysteries as well as a paid prognosticator, explain why you have failed to pay your respects to any shrine or temple within the walls of my city.

I sat in the moonlight with this discourteous missive in my hand, wondering about the nature of the man who had sent it. It was an admission that he had had me watched. Any member of the Iamidai, possessing the blessed, vision-inheriting blood of Iamos, the Elean ancestral prophet, would have been insulted. We are devout people, and we govern our religious practices well at all times and wherever we find ourselves. But Telys' message did not upset me. Rather, I warmed to this man and his priorities. Unlike many of the powerful men with whom I have had to deal, he was signalling to me that he took religion seriously and letting me know that I must not expect to be treated merely as a fortune-teller.

For this I was grateful.

So it was with a glad heart that I sat down and wrote this reply, which was sent by return, the swiftness of my response being intended to keep the thoughts of me which were active in his head in motion until noon when we would meet, and to give him some idea of my temper in advance:

> I give you greetings, and note that you did not see fit to send me any. As for temples and shrines, I know each one, even though I may never have set foot in any of them. Before we meet I should remind you: I am Kallias of the Clytiad family, a senior of the great prophetic people, the Iamidai, and a servant of the ubiquitous gods before all. I go where I am guided by the Eternal Ones. Otherwise, blame your officers; they took me where I went. Also you did not give me the reception which my

rank merits, and you have kept me waiting as if you were a nobleman.

When I arrived at the city hall for my meeting with Telys, I discovered that scaffolding had been erected during the night. Workmen were everywhere, long rolls of gold leaf over their shoulders. I took it for granted that they were sheathing the walls and columns with the stuff, that being a very Sybaritic thing to do, but when I looked closer I saw that they were actually peeling it off. Intrigued by this strange, contradictory circumstance, I stopped a workman who was passing with coils of gold leaf around his neck and a broad-bladed scraper in his hand, and asked him what was going on. He told me that Telys had ordered this operation. I asked for directions, and he took me under the scaffolding to a passage and left me at a bronze door which was being divested of gemstones by a man who was grumbling madly to himself.

'I put them in, so I take them out,' he said to me, 'but it's easier putting in than taking out, and so it should be, but where's the sense? I designed this door to last for a thousand years and break any thief's nails, but now it's too ornamental for his ideas.'

Interested in what he had to say, I encouraged him to go on, but he would not, inclining his head towards the door and what was on the other side.

'If he heard me complaining, I'd be for it,' he whispered. 'You'll have to introduce yourself. That's how he does things.'

I knocked and entered. The man in the room was sat at a polished table, his hands clasped tightly together near his chest. I waited for him to speak, but he did not. Instead he looked at his own image in the surface of the table and remained silent.

'Kallias of the Iamidai has come from Elis,' I said, bowing.

'So he has,' came the reply, which was sighed rather than said, in a voice that was purged of all interest.

'Did you receive my message?' I asked after a while.

He looked up for the first time, enabling me to study his face, one that did not discharge much of his essential spirit but rather guarded it. It was not composed of enlivened features, but had an odd fixity like a mask; that of a young man without the freshness and brightness. Instead it seemed to have age already built into it; a pitted paleness fused into his cheek and an obsidian blackness into his eye. His fair beard was reddish at the roots and trimmed close to his chin but left thick around his lips, where it was brushed into an upward smile. The inflexible expression which he wore was that of a man who always looks for what lies behind the reality which he meets.

'Speak to me when you feel inclined,' I sighed, imitating his tone deliberately as I sat down, uninvited, on a servant's stool by the door. 'I am used to being kept waiting in this city.'

Telys nodded, and I saw the movement of his red lips beneath his beard as he pursed them.

'I was warned that you are an insolent man,' he said, unclasping his hands which, once liberated, trembled slightly.

'Who told you that?' I asked.

'Those who have employed you in the past.'

'If you identify them I may have opinions upon their characters which will modify the reputation which they've given me,' I responded with some asperity. 'Were they complaining about my work? If so, I should be allowed to defend myself.'

'Your manner troubled them,' Telys replied, 'and I can already see that they may have had reason.'

'I've no doubt that you've been in touch with Epemenidos of Erithrai. That dispute was caused by his insistence in using the local descendant of the Herophile oracle, which has been long known to be defunct . . .'

'Never mind that now,' he admonished me. 'Whatever happened between you and Epemenidos is in the past. But what I would like to know is why they call you Kallias *the Sphinx*.'

I took umbrage at this, and it showed in my face.

'You don't like that name? Doesn't it mean that you take your time to get results and thrive on obscurities? I don't want you to behave like that here. We're in a hurry. This is an urgent matter.'

'The gods cannot be hurried,' I said as politely as I could, 'and I did not expect to come here and be asked to justify slanders that have been made against me.'

'Everyone has a good word to say for you, but also a few b-b-bad ones. Is that so surprising?' he said in a more emollient tone.

I did not make any answer, having picked up the stammer and knowing what it must mean to be a man of such power and yet remain at the mercy of a childish defect. Now his knuckles were as white as chalk.

'As you are known to be quick as well as insolent, Kallias,' he said slowly, pacing each syllable, 'you will have noticed that I have an occasional slight stutter. This only afflicts me when I'm very tired, as I am now. Whatever you do, don't take it as a sign of weakness.'

I stood up and bowed.

'Good! We've got that out of the way,' he declared briskly. 'Now, let's deal with this notion of yours that I'm not a nobleman. Who gave you that idea?'

He looked at me with such an absurd, boyish innocence that I could not help laughing, which was the right thing to do.

'Do I need to be of noble blood in order to have a working mind? Now, in your case it is different. You have inherited the blood of Iamos from your forefathers, blood that gives you the power of prophecy. That is worth something.'

Before I could open my mouth he had made another point.

'Sybarites have their pride,' he declared. 'Always remember that. We are not just men of money.'

He abruptly scratched his brow. High on his left cheek I saw three moles which fascinated me because they were in a perfect triangle: but as I looked at them I realised that they were cosmetic. Although painting the face is a common Sybarite affectation, and one I had noted already, the spots of Telys' cheekbone were too geometrical and not put there to beautify. When he caught my gaze he put a hand up and rubbed the spots away.

'Some foolishness?' I enquired.

He nodded, looking at the smudges on the tips of his fingers, then stared down again at his reflection in the table.

'I have not got as much control over myself today as I would wish,' he muttered. 'I have been dreading our meeting because you claim to have powers beyond those I can understand. They call Sybaris the superabundant state, but it has its drawb-b-b-backs, I assure you.'

Before I could say anything he got up and walked stiffly across to the bronze door. Although lightly built and carrying little flesh, his body movements were awkward, the result, I learnt later, of arthritis, a common affliction amongst Sybarites, due to the dampness of the coastal plain. As he opened the door, the craftsman who had been working on the other side was revealed with a polished ball of carnelian held in the jaws of his pliers.

'You're taking your time over that,' Telys said to him as we passed, 'and I heard every word that you said to my visitor.'

The man went pale and he loosed his grip on the pliers. The carnelian egg fell and rolled around on the floor.

'I've got very sharp ears,' Telys said to me with a sudden twinkle of mischief as we walked into the pandemonium of the entrance hall, which was now filled with spirals of gold which had been stripped from the walls, 'and I know that all men spy upon each other, more's the pity. Now, observe!' he commanded as we traversed the wide floor, gold wrapping itself round our ankles. 'Your informer was right. Things are having to change. I hope you'll think about what you see.'

'I always think about what I see,' I assured him with some irritation while trying to step out of a clinging cluster of gold leaf which I was dragging across the floor, 'and I would be a poor kind of diviner if I didn't.'

'One thing you're not is poor, Kallias!' he snorted, striding out into the open air.

'By whose standards?' I asked.

'By my standards.'

'By the standards of Sybaris?'

'Our resources are not bottomless. With your fee I could b-b-build twenty ships.'

'Then why didn't you?'

He shrugged and closed the matter.

When one lives close to peasants, as I have done most of my life when not travelling to do my work, one recognises their fiscal fears and defensiveness. Telys had just given me an insight into his ancestry, some Achaean farmer of yore.

'Perhaps I was not very adroit in sending such an innocent to negotiate with you, or perhaps I sent exactly the right man to get you here?' He paused, giving me a quizzical look and fingering his beard. 'I knew you'd walk all over him,' he said after a while, 'and that's why I sent you a n-n-nonentity. It's said that you like to get on top of people and enjoy the impression of being in charge.'

Before I could reply to this he had dived down a steep stairway into the basement of the building. He rattled down the steps so quickly that I nearly fell over trying to keep up with him.

'Where are we going?' I demanded, having to trot to keep up once we were on the level.

'To start work,' he replied, a gleam in his eye. 'We can't waste the time of an expensive man like you.'

He led me through several chambers full of clerks, and from thence down a corridor and up some stairs to emerge breathless and overheated behind a screen of ivory-inlaid wood, through which I could hear the murmur of a large assembly.

'Ready?' he said.

'For what?'

'Out there are the *azygous plutos* of Sybaris, the richest men of the richest city in the world,' he said, his voice so high it was almost falsetto. 'They worship what you worship. They worship gold.'

With that he thrust me beyond the screen and on to a platform.

There is no need to spell out the state of the air in the hall which was filled by the famous peacocks of Sybaris. The scent of the city had been strong when smelled from a ship in the sea-roads outside the harbour; now it was overwhelming, and my head swam. There were a thousand men with their boys and slaves packed into this one room. The slaves wafted their fans, but the air which was circulated was so heavy with perfume that it felt like liquid. I stood on the platform, supporting myself by leaning against the wooden screen while my senses cleared. The *azygous plutos* were lying on light, folding couches, their hats, sticks and shoulder-frames stacked beside them, their costumes glittering.

Telys called for silence. I saw hundreds of heads turn, bald heads, painted heads, heads sprouting stalks of silver. I could not take my eyes off one enormously fat man, who was so hot that he had brought a bath on wheels. While he listened to the proceedings his slaves continuously poured water over his head.

'At our last meeting I promised to find you the best guide to the future that I could,' Telys cried above the residue of the crowd's murmurings. 'You will all recall, I'm sure, our recent mission to the oracle at Delphi and the answer provided to our question: how long will our prosperity last? Not much help there.'

As he was speaking I noticed that he had not stuttered once, and that his stature seemed to have increased. With the *azygous plutos* looking up at him in all their gorgeous clutter, he seemed to be very confident. Certainly, there was no doubt who was in charge. But, I thought to myself, these are the richest men in the world. Why have they handed over their power to this odd young man?

Telys continued with his address:

'For the benefit of our guest, I will read out what the priestess at Delphi gave to our ambassadors. I know that Kallias is acquainted with this inspiring woman, he has her friendship, and I must assure him that no insult is intended; but what on earth were we meant to do with this?' Here he held up a wax tablet, waving it around his head before he began to read: 'All happy, thou Sybarite, all happy shalt thou remain in thy abundance for as long as thou honourest those who live eternally, but when it comes to pass that a mortal man is held in greater awe than a god, then shall war and civil strife come upon thee.'

He paused, the tablet held out towards me.

'The priestess at Delphi has not given us any help,' he declared with a note of sarcastic reproof in his voice. 'This is pure enigma. No *man* is held in greater awe than the gods in this city.'

I reverently took hold of the tablet, but Telys did not

immediately release it to me, pulling me across so he could speak into my ear.

'No *man*, eh?'

In no mood to play such games in front of an audience, I frowned and tugged at the tablet until he let go.

'Will you say something now?' Telys whispered. 'They've been looking forward to this for ages. Do mention money if you have a mind to.'

I began to speak. To explain the enigma of an oracle is not the best way to embark upon any political sea. I used the word 'hazy' and got no further. A tremendous bellow of laughter went up. This sound rocked me. I had not expected such an energetic response.

'Explain that you're serious,' Telys whispered quickly, 'you'll have to tell them that.'

I took my time about doing so, edging in my support of Delphi, then went on: 'To my knowledge, you have not asked me to come here to unravel old advice, given by someone else. What the priestess said then has its own time and meaning. Was it very recently?' I asked Telys. 'There has been a change. A new incumbent is in charge now.'

'Forget Delphi,' he said. 'Go on to your own powers.'

This was firmer ground for me. I recounted some of my more notable successes, and I could see that there were men in the audience who had heard of them.

Telys interrupted me after a while.

'Talk about how you're going to actually do the prophesying, the practical details,' he said in an undertone. 'They like to know the ins and outs.'

'I won't do that,' I replied quietly.

'You don't want to let slip any tricks of the trade? Quite right.'

Offended, I took my ear away from his lips. He chuckled to himself and made a few sounds of mock comfort, then gripped my forearm as he got to his feet and announced that it was time for union.

The *azygous plutos* stood up and started undressing.

'What is happening?' I whispered to Telys.

'It is a religious moment which I devised,' he replied.

When their clothes and headdresses had been removed by

their slaves, this not being accomplished without a lot of puffing and panting and showering of sweat, the audience stood naked.

'Write us a prayer to fit in here,' Telys said. By then the *azygous plutos* were dressed in black chitons and striped hose, which I had formerly only seen on archers in Asia Minor, though I was to learn that the merchants of Miletos, the sister-city of Sybaris in trade in Caria, clad themselves in similar garments.

'Now we can tell you everything,' Telys said softly once there was quiet in the place, the slaves having withdrawn, taking the couches, fans and costumes with them, leaving all the *azygous plutos* in ranks, wearing their identical garb. 'That ceremony is all that is left of the time when, in desperation, I had a try at religion for them myself. You will do better, obviously, being born to it.' He looked out over the *azygous plutos* with a wry, patronising air and smiled his double smile. 'You see, Kallias, these poor fools don't know where they're going,' he murmured, 'and they've left it all to me. My problem is that I don't know where they're g-g-going either.'

Then he made a curt gesture to the assembled men that they should sit on the floor, which they obediently did, and our business began.

It would be misleading if I described what took place in the city hall that hot afternoon as a discussion. It was not. Telys spoke for the entire time, allowing no interruptions or interference with his theme. If I could convey this by giving the gist of what he said, I would, but in fact he said nothing. It was all generalities, often couched in an odd slang which I did not understand. I got the impression of a cloudiness in his purpose, a lack of desire to make any proper point. True, he mentioned specific difficulties involving trade and finance, but these had no bearing on my function at all, and when Telys deferred to my presence in the hall, it was not to include me in what he was saying but to stress that I had come from the outside world, where Sybaris was little understood. As he went on and on, individuals in the steaming ranks of the *azygous plutos* succumbed to sleep in the heat, and I had to fight to keep awake.

That men of wealth should submit to this tedium, sitting cross-legged, moisture dripping from their chins, was astonishing. Half a day in the most uncomfortable heat listening to a catalogue of petty economic distresses and minor political upsets to do with water-supplies and street-trading licences! And what was I there for? A diviner? For no purpose I could fathom. Had I been brought to the meeting in order to be ignored? I was in the middle of the resentful feelings which this thought had created in me when Telys put his hand on my shoulder.

'Which brings me to this son of the Clytiad . . .' He paused and bent down to look at me enquiringly. 'Have I got that right?'

I nodded dumbly.

'. . . senior of the Iamidai? Possessor of the sacred visionary blood?'

I nodded again, inwardly annoyed at the flippancy of his tone.

'Bringer of rain, winner of wars, physician to plagues, arranger of marriages, seer of visions, foreteller of destinies. Why have I asked him here? What can he do about all these trifles, these gnat-bites? This is a man who deals with large issues. In his own words, the words which he used to our emissary – now resting in a remote mountain resort and not expected back for some years – I am an artist of the unknown. I say that he will need all his skills with us, because we do not even know ourselves. All we know, Kallias, O great prophet,' he said with a grave bow of his head, 'is that there is something wrong. Help us discover what it is. We have either a wound or a weakness or a void. Look at us!' He swept his arm round, taking in the exhausted audience, who were now struggling out of their torpor of heat and boredom. 'What future can be built out of this?'

The *azygous plutos* nodded their heads. I heard the pattering of their sweat on the tiled floor.

Telys then described the efforts of the Sybarites over the years to reawaken the heroic ideals of manly vigour.

'But you won't fight, will you?' he scolded the silent men. 'You don't have to. Whatever you want you can buy.'

His caustic tone did not seem to upset the *azygous plutos*. They sat and looked up at him with mute attention while their chitons turned into the deeper black of saturation.

'We even tried to steal the Olympic Games away from Elis, your home,' Telys continued, referring to the notorious plot which the Sybarites had hatched several years ago. It had been defeated because no-one in the Greek world would believe that there could be anything but a commercial reason behind it, 'but no-one would take us seriously. No-one runs in Sybaris, they said. No-one jumps or throws. In Sybaris they lie, if they can't lie they sit, if they can't sit they lean, if they can't lean they fall over.'

These insults seemed to draw the perspiring audience closer towards him, as if they wanted more. Telys turned to me and held up his hands.

'You see the state they're in? Nothing I can say will make them look into their hearts. They believe that by giving me the responsibility it will mean that they can forget about it. But I won't have that. This city is dying.'

I was surprised to note that this dramatic statement produced no response at all from the *azygous plutos*. They had the look of men who had heard it too often.

'We don't know where we're going, what we're doing, or why we're still here. The world is passing us by. Sybaris is stuck in a hundred-year-old honey-pot.'

This final remark was the only one that got a reaction. The sweating rich raised knowing, sad little grins and smiles, looking at each other in brotherly sympathy.

THREE

After the meeting with the *azygous plutos* in the city hall Telys gave me no time to recover, but took me straight to the city's south-western quarter, at a point where alleyways and narrow streets focussed on a series of stone steps where a secondhand clothes market was in progress, the garments on the stalls being of great richness and quality while the customers came from the poorer people.

'They are allowed to wear them in the privacy of their own homes,' Telys explained as he saw the question forming on my lips, 'and they look upon them as an investment. If a man wins the right to cross the Road of Prosperity into the northern quarters, out comes the clothes-chest and, within hours of entering his new house, he is acceptable to his neighbours.'

'But someone who aspires to such an improvement in status likes new things,' I commented as we hurried along, 'or so I believe.'

'That market is for clothes that have only been worn once,' Telys replied, 'and it is considered to be good luck for anyone to wear a garment that has been cast aside by an *azygous pluto* in this tradition.'

(The Sybarite term *azygous pluto* to describe a person of great wealth is quite precise in its way. It means one who is so rich that, by the time all is counted, there has been such accrual on that sum that the total is no longer any guide to his real worth.)

'You say that as though it offends you,' I said, skirting the stalls and their racks of glittering and gaudy vestments.

'It does.'

'Why?'

'There's something sycophantic about it. I'm thinking of having the market closed down. Sybaris has to mean something beyond its wealth.'

When dealing with men of power, one has first to identify their particular caprices. To an outsider these often appear as weaknesses, but to the owner of them they are strengths, part of himself. In general, the minds of rulers are more inconsistent than those of the people they rule, and the tyrant who has a free hand is the most inconsistent of all. The importance of a secondhand clothes market must not, therefore, be underestimated, and I was careful not to make this error.

'In that case, will you abolish the tradition of wearing clothes once and throwing them away?' I asked Telys, trying to find room beside him on the pavement. 'Would that change anything?'

'No. I'll insist that they're destroyed.'

'Ah, a development of the tradition,' I mused, looking slyly to see if he had appreciated my point. 'Will the *azygous plutos* go along with that?'

Telys laughed, showing broad, pink gums above his dainty teeth.

'What loss will it be to them?' he said. 'It is the servants and slaves who sell their clothes. Their masters and mistresses don't even bother to keep wardrobes. They throw the garments on the ground and take no further interest in them.'

'So you will be penalising the servants and the slaves?'

'Yes. That's what they deserve.'

For an established tyrant to find servility distasteful was an unusual attitude of mind, and not one I had encountered before.

'Servants and slaves in Sybaris are haughtier than those who employ them,' Telys explained over his shoulder. 'They are greedy, undisciplined and envious. This is transmitted down to the lowest of the low. Work it out, Kallias. Who gets admired for anything worthwhile?'

I stepped into the gutter in my anxiety to frame a reply, but he was already scurrying away from me, his robe flapping.

We arrived at a small square which had a crude stone

temple at its centre. It looked very ancient, the walls made of single flakes of limestone of great width and thickness, and it was roofed with salt-bleached timber. Telys beckoned me to step inside with him.

The place had bad drains, though it looked airy enough. There was a tripod with a lighted oil-lamp giving off a flame that was almost invisible in the light which streamed from the divisions between the pieces of the walls. On a square stone altar sat the figure of an obese, bald, old man carved out of black stone. It was an ugly idol, jowled and pig-eyed. The only delicate parts of the carving were the hands and feet, over which some trouble had been taken.

'Name this g-g-god,' Telys ordered me.

'He could be anyone,' I muttered, conscious of the worshippers listening and not wishing to guess wrongly.

'When I complained that you had not seen fit to pay your respects at any of our shrines and temples,' Telys continued, 'it was because I was disappointed that you had not done what I had expected, that is, rush off to the Temples of Apollo and Hera and ignore this one. Instead, you ignored them all. However, there is a case to be made.'

He paused and crouched beside the ill-looking figure, gazing into its repulsive face.

'This is the god Bes. I don't suppose you have ever heard of him,' he said.

I thought it wise to admit that I had never heard of Bes, but then there are hundreds of local deities in the world with whom I am not familiar, which is not to say that I have no influence with them through the higher pantheon. When I made this point, Telys sniffed rudely.

'That is a false argument,' he said, 'and the last one you will make, I hope. I did not hire you to supplicate the gods in any way – to be honest, I doubt whether they listen to you any more than they do anyone else.'

I shuddered, looking round the rough, old shrine. There was such a stink in the place, a greasiness from centuries of use and handling; the insides of the walls were marked with names scratched into the limestone. Bes' shrine reeked of a devotion which went back far beyond Homer's knowledge, to some pit of primordial, myth-generating slime.

‘This cult . . .’ I began to say, intending to question him about the advisability of allowing it to flourish if it drew people away from the Olympians, but he interrupted me.

‘It is not a cult. Every Sybarite comes here, from the highest to the lowest; they don’t venerate this lump of stone because it has powers, but because it has appetites they understand.’

His ever-smiling beard twitched, giving his features an awry expression. From his tone I could not judge how seriously I was meant to take all this.

‘In many cities the local superstitions have been rooted out,’ I said eventually, choosing my words with care. ‘Perhaps Bes belongs to another time.’

Telys shook his head and chucked the god under his many chins.

‘No, he is very much alive and well here,’ he averred, ‘and his worship will never be stamped out. Look.’ He took a few silver dinars from his purse and slipped them into the gaping navel of the god. I heard them rattle down a channel, then silence.

‘Where does the money go?’ I asked, my disapproval difficult to disguise.

‘I’ve no idea,’ Telys replied, ‘perhaps it drops into a bottomless hole. You’re the one who is supposed to know the ins and outs of the gods. Step back,’ he said suddenly, ‘and observe.’

A family entered the shrine. A man whom I presumed to be the father – he looked like an artisan of some kind – lined his children up beside Bes, then the wife held a tray of food close to the god’s head and the father spooned a dish of meat and gravy into its mouth. When that was all finished he stuffed pieces of bread down the idol’s throat with a curved rod, then poured wine after it from a tall, oddly-fashioned cup. Then husband and wife took either end of an embroidered napkin and wiped Bes’ mouth clean. Before leaving the shrine the man put coins into the god’s navel, and I was sure that I saw the gleam of gold.

At no time was a prayer said, or a head bowed or a knee bent.

When we stepped out of the shadows Telys was looking at

me with the expression of a child who has played a successful trick.

'What did you think of that?' he said, glee in his eyes.

I made no reply. Instead I questioned Telys about the curved rod, the cup and the embroidered napkin. All of these had been decorated with signs and symbols unknown to me.

'Every family has its own Bes utensils which have been passed down from generation to generation. That family was not rich. The spoon, the tray, the dish, they were simple enough, but money had been spent on the rod, the cup and the napkin, which are the most important.'

'Why?'

'No-one knows. Bes goes back a long way' he said, then told me to follow him. I trailed after as he left the shrine and went into an eating-house.

'Beef from our white oxen, c-c-cabbage to clean his palate before he drinks his wine, salt from our colonies . . . you get the idea?' he said as we walked back across the square with a tray carried by a waiter. 'I'd like you to feed the god. Just a token of respect.'

Because he knew that Bes meant nothing to me, this was little more than a dig in the ribs. Not showing any of the resentment which I felt, I did as he had asked but used the priestliness of my task as a means of raising with him the question of the next instalment of my fee.

Telys chuckled, wiping Bes' mouth and affectionately patting the idol on the top of its head.

'You see, Bes? He's yours already,' he said, tossing the napkin to the waiter. 'It doesn't take you long to win people over. You've got him thinking like a Sybarite.'

I supped with Telys that night.

At this stage in my acquaintance with Sybaris I was surprised at how biddable everyone was: even the great mass of the slaves and poor lacked that rowdy element which lurks in the centre of all dumb compliance. From experience, I had been looking to the rich for any signs of opposition or dissatisfaction, and I mentioned this to Telys once I had waited for him to get mellow, which he did with some relish after his hard day of public duties.

'Don't imagine that the rich are t-t-tractable because they like me,' he said with a laugh. 'It's simply because they've run out of ideas. They know that something is wrong, something down at the roots, but they're so infatuated with triviality and superficial f-f-fashions that they cannot penetrate that far. They sense the danger, but they can't identify it. Neither can I, yet. But when I find it I know that it will have to be cut out without delay. But who am I to criticise? Just one of them, the son of a son of a son who amassed a fortune. Take me as typical if it will help.'

His villa gave evidence of this. Opulence was everywhere, and it was clear that he was a keen voluptuary. Of all the girls and women I had seen I had not yet been able to distinguish which one was his wife, and he was free with all of them. This ran counter to my expectations of the fellow's character. I had readied myself for a little order and sanity in his home.

'I'm a Sybarite,' he said, reading my thoughts. 'Inside the problem, not outside. I do not pretend to be poor, which would be the worst kind of hypocrisy, nor do I praise poverty, which is the purest cruelty to the simple workman who labours for his comforts. I am, above all things, a citizen, and it is only as such that I can redeem our faults and assure our future.'

'And are you a genuinely religious man?' I asked.

'As much as any other.'

'To worship the gods through excess is probably hubristic,' I said, more as an idea than to chide him. 'Does too much ever charm?'

Telys pondered for a while, his hands running up and down the legs of an adolescent female acrobat who had arched herself over him. The girl had lost several of her teeth, probably in accidents arising from her tumbling, and false ones had been made for her out of ivory. When she laughed her whole mouth shivered. This seemed to amuse Telys, who snatched kisses from her.

'I could have lived my life in great comfort,' he said, holding up his hands and clapping as the girl leapt away and did a series of somersaults. 'It was never my ambition to become embroiled in city politics. Very often I regret allowing myself to be dragged into the hurly-burly of it all. But now it's too late. I've taken on the responsibility. But quite often I'd rather be shut of it.'

As gently as I could, I questioned him about his motives in engaging me. There was little in his character – which was not noble or simple – which suggested that he was a man of stern devotion to the gods. Instead I detected an ironic deviousness, an ability to skate over things while appearing to tackle them.

'What you are getting round to asking me,' he said, once I had finished, 'is why I decided to employ a diviner at all. You're right in your instincts, which are obviously very sharp. I'm not a religious man at heart. Perhaps I'm not deep enough for it.'

'Then why?'

'As a last resort.'

I asked him why I, personally, had been chosen.

'You were recommended.'

'By whom?'

'I promised not to say. However, I'll tell you that he is no friend of divination. It was only after he had failed to persuade me not to pursue the matter that I managed to extract your name from him: the b-b-best of a b-b-bad b-bunch, so he said.' He laughed, slapping me lightly by the hand as he beckoned over the acrobat, who had now finished her dance and was standing beside him, her chest heaving, sweat glistening on her forehead.

'Don't get bad-tempered with my honesty, Kallias,' he said, stroking the quivering girl's cheek. 'I know the old religion is under attack. The top thinkers have got their knives into it.'

'Who are these top thinkers?' I asked.

'Oh, I think you know.'

'Why don't you ask them to help you, if they're so good?'

'They don't have visions. All they do is knock things down. And they're not interested in our kind of problems. Can you imagine them bending their minds to the difficulties of people who have more than enough?'

'If you know that to be your ailment, surely the cure is to have less.'

'We can't find a way to do that without destroying the mechanism by which we have prospered so far,' Telys rejoined. 'That is why we have turned to you. If you can actually *see* the future, and it is bad, then that mechanism may start changing itself.'

'And if it's good?'

'When has religion foreseen a good future?' he cried. 'Priests have a favourite word: sacrifice. I know that's what we need, but you must give me the prophecy to b-b-bring it ab-b-bout.'

Telys' villa was in the foothills to the south of the city, across the Kratis, the river which flowed in parallel with the Sybaris for the last few stadia before entering the sea. The city was held between these two waters like a precious box in a pair of careful hands. From the terrace of the villa I could see the excellent choice that the original settlers had made, accepting the difficulties of building on soft alluvial soil and sand for the benefits of the defences provided by the lagoon on the eastern side, the two rivers on the northern and southern, and the mountains guarding the western, though at some distance. If a flank was exposed it was the latter, and the walls there, Telys assured me, were appropriately thicker, thicker even than the walls of the Temple of Poseidon, which were as wide as four men laid end to end. Size meant a great deal to the Sybarites, I had decided after my initial period of study; even their dress was designed to make them appear bigger. In this respect Telys was different; he seemed unimpressed by mere dimension. In his seraglio, for instance, there were only women of small stature, and he kept an aviary of the tiniest finches, of which he seemed very fond.

My second day at the villa was spent alone. Telys went into the city and I was left with this flock of spritely females, all of whom treated me with awe. Wherever I went in the gardens or fields, I was followed, but in respectful silence. My food was served by sweet, dignified, diminutive matrons wearing linen hoods, and there was no attempt at flirtation, for which I was grateful as I had a lot of thinking to do. This, I decided, was the reason Telys had left me to my own devices for a day: to give me time to get my breath back and put my impressions in order, and to untangle the various threads in the city's uncertain temperament.

In the late afternoon, when the first cool breezes were

beginning to come from the sea, a handsome, painted cart drawn by two black horses came along a track between two of the covered roads, traversing a field of ripened wheat. I watched it from the terrace, admiring the passage of the round-ribbed crimson awning through the dim gold of the crop. Because the traffic was invisible for several stadia outside the city walls, I did not know whether it had come from north or south, but I guessed that it was not originally a Sybarite conveyance, its style of construction being different from those I had seen in the city.

The cart came up the long, twisting track to the villa, the horses making the ascent without any rest. I did not go to see who the visitor was. An hour later, the cart left and retraced its path, now moving faster, the black horses trotting speedily along the track through the wheat.

When Telys arrived, he went to bathe and pressed me to join him. I had noticed that the man bathed very frequently, as did all Sybarites, too frequently for my taste, with too much finger-feathering massage, too much oiling and combing. However, it is not polite for any guest to be critical of his host's ablutionary habits, so I went along for my second bath of the day, having already been roped in for the early splash before Telys left for the city that morning. As I was tickled and rolled about by his tiny women I had to give him some idea of my progress. I was, I explained, disorientated by the city's mysterious sense of itself, the doom which it seemed to think inevitable, but for what sin? Wealth was not a sin. Hubris was a sin. To desecrate the sacred area of a temple was a sin. But I could not isolate the sin of Sybaris as it was perceived by either its citizens or the gods, and this was a great confusion to me.

Telys did not appear to be very interested in my perplexity, abandoning himself to the pleasures of the bath. I watched his women oil, scrape and scrub every part of his body, cleaning him as if he were a prized machine which must be kept in the best working order. His hair and beard were shampooed and finely trimmed, the barber snipping off the most minute lengths then taking the points of his scissors to the hairs in Telys' nostrils and ears.

'Any stirrings yet, Kallias?' he asked with a raised eyebrow. 'Any dreams during the night? Visions in the bath?'

Aware that I was deliberately being tempted into defensiveness, in which there were traps already set, I told Telys that I had spent time thinking.

'Good, good,' he said, 'though I didn't realise that divination is an intellectual thing. But I should have told you that we don't encourage work on festival days.'

'Which festival is this?'

'Something arbitrary;' he said with a wave of his hand, 'when it's too hot – and it has been stifling today – we declare a holiday at short notice. These festivals are dedicated to human weakness. In Sybaris that is a kind of god.'

His scoffing tone and manner were hurtful. I pushed aside the women who were picking over my skin like birds combing oxen for ticks, and plunged into the cold bath, swimming its length underwater before emerging and leaving the building.

My refusal to be an accomplice in the degradation of my calling stood me in good stead. By the time that we were called to supper Telys had become more respectful. We reclined on couches which had been placed on the terrace so we could dine in the lovely zephyr which was coming from the fragrant pine forests on the slopes of the mountains. He was elaborately courteous, gave me all his attention, and explained that he had not invited any other guests because he wanted me all to himself.

'At some time,' I replied cautiously, not wishing to alter his mood, 'I should become better acquainted with other minds which are as sensitive to the needs of Sybaris as your own. They might throw some light.'

'This is true,' he said, 'but few of my colleagues are able to express their misgivings as clearly as I can.'

'When you say "as you can", I am heartened,' I commented, using a particular smile, which can be charming should the receiver wish to take it that way, 'because I am, as yet, still a bit in the dark.'

This braced him up a little, and he darted sharp looks at me.

'Clarity is not the language of trade or war,' he stated calmly, 'and it is seldom a virtue of prophets.'

Four large male slaves entered from the gardens with an oblong wooden box with two sharp lugs carpentered on its long sides. Telys told the slaves to place the box on the terrace wall, below which was a steep drop into a vineyard.

'This gift arrived for me from Kroton today,' he explained offhandedly. 'They're always sending me presents, which is to be wondered at when they know we have everything. Sometimes I cannot understand why the gifts have been sent. The meaning is obscure, and therefore, tantalising. Last month I received a four-eared calf, which died within days. That was from Milo, the city's governor. You've heard of the great Milo, of course? That superb athlete and warrior, always at the peak of his strength and all that. So, a four-eared calf from a titan of brawn? What did that mean?'

'Could it have been purely a curiosity which he wished to share?' I suggested.

'You cover your tracks well, Kallias,' Telys sneered gently, beckoning the slaves to open the box. 'Why should people send each other unnatural objects?'

The front of the box came away under the iron levers wielded by the slaves. Inside it sat an exquisite black girl on a throne of purple cloth, her hands on her hips, the technical reason for the lugs built out of the sides of the box. She had a swathe of quince yellow linen around her waist and a coronet of sugared vine leaves, but what was beguiling was the shape of her breasts, two faultless cones topped by the black, tumescent nipples of Upper Egypt, and her bushy pubic hair, which had been carefully razored into a right-angled triangle.

'Pythagoras of Kroton sends his respectful admiration to Telys of Sybaris,' the girl said, in a faint voice, obviously exhausted by her long, hot internment, 'and may I have a drink of water?'

FOUR

I had a need for entertainment that night, and the arrival of Pythagoras' seductive geometry lesson did not offend me, except in its cruelty to the child, for she was scarcely more than that – but I was prevented from enjoying myself by my sudden fall into a cold gloom, which is a sure herald of my entry into an inner scene.

On these occasions I become taciturn and distant, turning away warmth and friendship to seek my own company. I have to prepare for what I know is coming.

This ominous feeling – familiar, but still feared – struck me down during the laughter which greeted the girl's message and her stiff descent to humble herself at Telys' feet. I sat very still, holding on to the back of my couch. I tried to disguise the powerful emotion which was savaging my heart. In this I succeeded for a while, but once the girl had been stroked and welcomed with a bowl of water Telys turned to me, wanting to talk about Pythagoras and his influence in Kroton. He immediately saw my distress but, of course, he could not guess at its cause, except wrongly.

'Is Pythagoras an enemy of yours?' he enquired. 'That would not surprise me, I must say. He is not orthodox in his opinions and, I suspect, thinks he knows more about the gods than the gods themselves. But you should be able to dispute with the man, at least.'

From within the chill heaviness of my feelings I agreed, advising Telys that I was known personally to Pythagoras, having been in company with the Long-Haired Samian in Elis, Egypt and other places.

'Now, if you will forgive me, I am tired and will go to bed.'

'Go to bed?' Telys echoed. 'I have a dozen people coming to join us in an hour or so. We must talk all night.'

The misery poured through me like poison. I could not pretend any further. Tears gathered in my eyes, and my blood thickened with anger.

'What's the matter?' he asked. 'Are you in pain?'

'I must leave you,' I declared, knowing that my tone was surly, but not being able to speak without it. 'We will talk tomorrow when I've rested.'

Telys tightened his lip, frowned, then waved me to go.

I strode down the passageway to my room, my heart beating hard. I knew that if he followed me and persisted in his remonstrations, I would unleash my tongue against him.

Upon entering my room I dismissed the slaves, closed the door behind them and bolted it, then climbed out of the window before they could come round to their accustomed positions as night sentinels. Once in the garden, I went down a path and through a gate into the vineyard, losing myself between the high plants. I did not stop walking until I had reached an oak tree at the foot of the slope. By this time I was in the power of the despondency, a strong physical state which locked my blood in my veins and sent a chill through my whole body, I climbed the tree and sat in a fork. Then, being convinced that I was far enough away from the villa, I let out my cry.

This sound is not one that I wish to share with anyone. I have always contrived to protect others from it, even enemies, as I cannot believe that it is my right to cast another soul into the same disgust with life. Over the years I have learnt that to be alone is the first requirement, but the second is as essential as the first: I cannot be in the open but must seek shelter, a tree, bushes, a cave, but never a house built by man. When the full force of this prostration has borne me into the depths, I know that I must prepare for the inner scene, but that may take hours – sometimes days – to appear. On this night, with my cry going over the plain of Sybaris, I clung to the rough trunk of the oak and prayed that it would come soon and liberate me from the killing, mortal misery which I was suffering.

It would be a misrepresentation of this feeling if I claimed that I had got used to it. Such acuteness of emotion breaks through all habit and foreknowledge, wrenching the mind and senses out of any past and into the agony of the present. My astonishment that I can bear the pain is always fresh.

It was dawn before the inner scene began. I had groaned and cried all night in the arms of the oak, a tree I had chosen because of its Heraklean nature, knowing it would sustain me, and I was shedding new tears – tears of gratitude – as the consuming sadness was lifted from me and my eyes began to prickle, my teeth to ache and my ears to ring, all prelusive manifestations. Birds began to hurl themselves in and out of the oak. I saw the earth begin to bulge. Three green jets of water burst out of the sea. Then I heard a voice calling up from the bottom of the tree, asking to know who I was and what I was doing.

It was the keeper of the vineyard on his morning rounds. He was not a slave, but a freeman who tended Telys' vines for a share of the produce. All this he managed to convey in his first barrage of questions, standing firm when I shouted at him to go away and leave me alone.

'I know your rank,' he called back, 'and I know that you are a prophet, also I know that you are a guest of the house and everyone is out looking for you. I think it's best if I stay here and keep an eye on you in case something happens.'

This time I could not reply as the inner scene swept into the landscape at terrible speed. As I hung on to the oak I had a last sight of the man below me. He had squatted down, his staff across his knees, and was watching me like someone looking up at the stars.

Then this last human sight had gone, thrust aside. The stench of torn earth, ripped up sea-beds, thousands upon thousands of breathing roses, smote me, each odour flowing separately like banners in a breeze. Then I vomited violently. As I drew breath from the convulsions there came the rich, sexual smell of women, the sea when it lies green and oily before a storm, and burning lime. Again and again I retched, my cheek pressed against the rough bark of the tree. Meanwhile all was darkness out in the plain of Sybaris. I could hear the great upheavals, the wrenching and buffeting, but it was all taking place in a reeking gloom, full of gusting wind which flung grains of sand against the leaves of my oak so the whole tree hissed.

In the roaring darkness below I heard harsh coughing, then a mire-encrusted arm waved, the veins under the skin as wide as a track across the countryside. I saw that the god was held face down in the black earth at the city's north side. His legs were free, and he kicked great furrows with his heels while his fists pounded at the fields and his torso shook and swayed over the fields. Beyond him the green jets of water still spouted over the harbour.

It was the god Herakles in his African form, freeing himself from the riverbed, I reasoned, as great handfuls of sand were flung into the air in his efforts to pull his face out of the ground. In the hissing of the grains of sand upon the leaves I heard affirmation. But there was no means of questioning the god through this mayhem. The sight of Herakles in his sweating, hairy nakedness struggling to wrest his head from the earth was an awesome one, full of meaning and portent, but no sign was being granted to me, no clue to an interpretation.

With a bellow the god tore his head out of the riverbed, tossing banks of earth and sheets of water into the sky, then sat like a baby, his great legs thrust out in front of him, and rubbed at his eyes. As he did so a white bird flew out from under his right eyelid and fluttered across towards me, a fish held in its claws. The bird seemed to be injured and flew in a haphazard fashion, dipping down close to the ground then struggling up higher. When it got over the tree the bird hovered for a long time, shaken by the blasts of the god's coughing and throat-clearing.

Then it dropped the fish into my lap and flew away.

The fish was covered with green slime and had its tail thrust into its own sharp-toothed mouth. As it wriggled in my lap it consumed itself, grunting and squeaking while it did so. When it had reached the point where the mouth was chewing through the back of the head, the fish sprang into the air and became a circle of flying light which streaked between the three green jets which rose out of the sea. They then reformed into a chair of twisted canes of sea-water. Herakles sat upon it, and the chair cleansed the black earth out of his hair, the dirt running down his chest and belly into his boiling groin.

Over the city the circle of light was still flashing, dancing east, dancing west, as though looking for somewhere to go. It descended to the god's second finger on his right hand, but it would not fit as a ring. It tumbled with the filthy water into his groin but emerged, shaking itself. Finally it fell to the ground and rolled into the city, getting smaller as it went.

The god yawned, put his hands behind his head and leant heavily back against the cane chair made from the spouts. It collapsed under his weight, and he fell backwards into the ocean.

Then he was gone, having slipped into the sea without a splash or a ripple. I waited, knowing from experience that this was unlikely to be all that I had to witness. The air cleared. The deep craters and trenches from which Herakles had ripped himself were healed over, and the river returned to its usual course.

It was all quiet in the vineyard, so much so that I could hear my heart beating in my ears.

I had learnt very little. Herakles had been stuck in the earth, freed himself and sat on a throne of water which had collapsed. A bird, a fish, but no lines of verse, nothing. I studied the city walls as they glowed in the early morning light, hoping to see another beginning, maybe the circle of light peeping over a rampart, or another bird. No further grant of vision was made.

I had seen the god Herakles in many forms over the years. That he favoured me was beyond doubt. I had seen this god weep and smile, I had seen him eat and drink and perform many bodily functions. I had stood beneath the cataract of his urine, beside the mountain of his dung, and seen the shooting of his seed. Always, he had spoken to me: not always in words that were immediately understandable, but there had been something to go on.

While I lowered myself to a bough nearer the ground and paused to collect my wits, I also recalled that I had never seen the god in difficulties before; he had always been at pleasure, or at ease, or pursuing some goal. This inner scene of mine had shown the god fighting to escape, fighting like the old, earth-bound Herakles before his death, the Herakles who was only half-divine, the Herakles of dreadful labours and torments.

I shinned down to the ground and stood in front of the keeper of the vineyard, who had remained in the same position, squatting with his staff across his knees. The man regarded me respectfully and touched his forehead.

'No harm has come to you,' he said, standing up. 'If it had, I would surely have got the blame.'

He preceded me at a gentle pace towards the villa, chattering about his concerns. I said little, hoping to deflect any natural curiosity, but there was no need for me to be so cautious. All the man wanted to talk about was the hunt which had been made for me over the estate during the night, and how the slaves set to guard my bedroom had been whipped for negligence.

When we arrived in the courtyard, Telys' head steward was giving orders to the assembled household servants and farm-workers before sending them out to renew the search. There was a shout as they saw me, but such was my hunger and thirst that I ignored the head steward's glad cries, pushing past him and through the excited crowd into the kitchen. Without waiting for the cook to prepare a meal, I ate what I could see, tearing off pieces of bread, eating raw vegetables and meat, then proceeded to the wine jars, where I drank several quarts from the neck, until I could swallow no more. The greater need gripped me as I sat holding on to my distended stomach, belching helplessly. Obedient to its Heraklean command, I turned to look for a woman to slake it, any woman. A female slave came into the courtyard carrying a basket of washing. She was in her middle years, heavy-limbed and slow. I called her over and had her on the floor, roaring like the god as I came. Then I slept.

I woke where I had fallen. A pillow had been put under my head and a woollen blanket thrown over me, to keep the cool of the wine storage room at bay. It was quiet, but I could hear whispers as people passed the heavy wooden door. I lay still for a while, my body aching emptily, my head full of ringing sounds. It had happened again, that onrush of voracious appetite which always came after one of my inner scenes, leaving me abased and exhausted.

Upon my entering the courtyard there was a general movement away, a retreat in awed nervousness. I mustered my dignity, stretching my limbs, which had stiffened on the stone floor, and glancing up at the sun to ascertain how long I had been asleep.

It was mid-afternoon, and the cicadas were in full song. After striding up and down the courtyard a few times I went to the bath to be cleansed, finding the profound silence of the attendants who looked after me an enjoyable balm. When the masseurs worked on my body their hands trembled so much that I felt the tremors through my flesh. These people were afraid to touch a man who had so recently been shaken by great powers.

It is my practice to commit the inner scenes to writing only when I have extracted their complete meaning. If I am unsure of what has been communicated, then I find that writing it down compounds the difficulty, giving the utterances and images a false authority as sense, before any has been made. I believe in the necessity of this precaution to such a degree that some of my most intense and portentous visions have remained unrecorded and now exist only as cloudy memories.

In the process of divination I refuse to be hurried. On past occasions, when it was obvious to those who had employed me that I had been in receipt of theophanic news, I have been pressed to reveal it to the point where I have been made incapable of interpreting my inner scene to any advantage. The whole business takes time, and I must be left to myself in order to get the best results.

That Telys was not going to be patient in this respect was obvious. If I was going to have a chance of extracting something useful from what I had seen in the oak tree, I would have to withdraw into a solitary place.

When I had finished my bath I went to my room. Every step I took was shadowed. Once I had shut the door I lay on the bed and waited for the evening, my head full of the preliminary catechism, which was not too hard, but I knew that the secondary and tertiary meanings would take at least two weeks.

Northwards of my house on the coast of Elis is a shallow valley screened by wild olives and shrub oak. In the wet months an underground stream feeds a pool beside which is a natural seat, a kind of rough throne in the rock. Here I sit for days sometimes, even through the coldest nights, watching my reflection and those of clouds, stars, the moon, passing birds, in the water's surface. From there I enter into many places in dream and supernal cogitation, cooling down urgent passions. Here is where I would choose to be to interpret inner scenes. No person on my estate is permitted to disturb me when I am by the pool. If I have been away for seven days, there is a standing rule that a man shall be sent to a nearby hill, from the summit of which the pool is visible. From there he checks to see if I need assistance.

To have that kind of relentless, inward genius for dwelling on the mysteries which wind through our human blood, is not a privilege to anyone but a diviner. And we are proud of this power of self-absorption of ours. Without it we would not have the channels through which theophanic manifestations can be conducted. What may appear to be obsession with self is only a means of keeping in contact with the efferent minds of the gods as they shower the universe with energy, life and death. Our patron is, of course, Narcissus, son of Cephisus, whose story is much misunderstood because the poets have distorted it. Narcissus is reputed to have fallen in love with his own reflection in a pool, thinking it to be a nymph – an unlikely error for any man who knows his own body – and to have pined to death because he could not possess the watery image. However, within our profession there is another account much older and more credible than this folklore, namely that Narcissus perceived the essence of the sacred form through his own reflection, which he fully recognised as his own, and realised that humanity was forever trapped between perfection and imperfection.

It was the knowledge that he could never attain his perfect self which drove Narcissus to die of grief by the poolside. It is said that he actually watched himself expire, the final light going out in his real human eye and the eye that watched him from the water at about the same time, except that the one in the pool lingered for a lightning flash longer.

I slept and was woken by a messenger from Telys.

The note said that because I had thought the Sybarites to be so biddable I should come and watch a riot in the poor quarters, which might change my mind for me.

My choice now was whether to ignore this ironic summons and vanish into the mountains, or to obey Telys' order, leaving it until later to explain how I must be allowed to go into seclusion in order to ponder on the meaning of my inner scene. For me to view an ordinary civic disturbance would not be conducive to careful, well-balanced divination, but the prospect of seeing the poor of Sybaris in argumentative mood attracted me. When I had talked to them at the riverside field of assembly only a couple of days ago, they had been quiet and well-behaved. What had inflamed these tractable people? When I put this question to the messenger, he told me that Telys had forbidden him to discuss the matter with me, or to pass on any information other than the summons.

As I left the villa on horseback I saw the keeper of the vineyard standing at the gate. He went down on one knee as I passed. The messenger was ahead of me.

Stopping my horse, I beckoned the vineyard man to come to my stirrup

'What is your name?' I asked him, looking down into his sunburnt face, which was wide and brown-eyed, much younger than I had remembered.

'Leogoras,' he replied.

'Have you spoken about what you saw?'

'I have.'

'Say nothing else. When I come back, I'll need to talk to you on an important matter.'

Leogoras nodded and looked along the track. I saw that the messenger had come back to find out why I was not following him. Without any further word I spurred my horse up to join him, offering the explanation that I had long been interested in the cultivation of vines.

*

Smoke rose from the city in several places, thin, twisting pillars which went straight up into the sky because the air was still that day. We galloped down the covered Road of Prosperity, passing the conveyances of many citizens who were removing themselves from the danger and heading into the foothills. They did not seem to be unduly worried; indeed, most of them were drunk and had with them musicians whom they shouted at to play louder and louder in order to drown the sounds of insurrection.

When we reached the western wall it was locked and manned by yellow-coated soldiers. These men were part of a voluntary company of rich youths who had fought with mercenaries and citizen armies in Sicily, sent there by their fathers to gain some of the better attributes of a free Greek. The messenger had an altercation with them, no single individual being in command, and the upshot was that we had to ride all round the walls to the northern gate, because Telys had now ordered that the western exit from the city be shut to stop the riot spilling into the farmlands, where fires might be started among the crops and herds. Upon arriving at the northern gate we encountered another band of disorganised youths, who tried to send us on to the gates at the port, but we were saved the journey by a mass of wealthy citizens coming up the Avenue of Olympia with drums, horns, whistles and flutes, all in absurd mood. When the gates were opened to let them out, we entered, pushing our way through these strangely defiant revellers.

There were no signs of a riot in this part of Sybaris. The streets were strangely empty as we trotted towards the city hall, past the great Temple of Poseidon and the law courts. Even the agora was deserted, but we could see the mass of people blocking access into the poor quarters and across the avenues which separated them from the rich. These were troops, we discovered; mercenaries who were kept in barracks to the north of the lagoon. I had not seen any evidence of their presence thus far in my time at Sybaris, which was part of the policy which Telys had employed to avoid the impression that, once in power, he had turned against those who had put him there – the poor.

Telys was not in the city hall. To discover this took the

messenger an age because the place was in chaos, full of crying women and children who had taken refuge there. After enquiring from a freshly wounded man, a weights and measures clerk of the city who had been hit in the face by a tile, we learnt that Telys had last been seen in the slums of the south-eastern quarter, where the riot had started. The clerk advised us not to venture into the area without an armed escort, but there was none available so I followed the messenger on foot across the Avenue of Aphrodite and into the street beside the city treasury, which was guarded by several ranks of bearded Scythians in black armour, men whose ferocious countenances would have stopped any riot which I might happen to lead.

The messenger questioned the Scythians and discovered that the riot had boiled over from the south-eastern quarter and into the south-western, a pitched battle having been fought with troops as the mob emerged into the wide Avenue of Aphrodite and attempted to march on the city hall. The troops had forced the rioters to go into the south-western quarter, separating the mob into two halves. The more militant and determined rioters had fought their way towards the Temple of Apollo across the south-western quarter, intending to converge on the central agora by that route.

I knew my duty, and informed the messenger that I must go to the Temple of Apollo by the most direct route, no matter what the risk. He was a brave man and did not question my decision, pausing only to recruit, by offering them money, two sturdy youths who were helping with firefighting. The four of us moved quickly into the Avenue of Dionysos which was jammed with carts bringing seawater into the blazing quarter we had just left, then headed up past the civic fountains, across the still-deserted agora and into the Avenue of Herakles.

By this time I was torn with doubts. Had the inner scene referred directly to this insurrection? From past experience I knew that any prognosis which I might be able to make from what I had seen would not affect the immediate future. The gods do not resort to the device of warning bells, because their concerns are with rhythms which define fates, not the emergencies of day-to-day life. Yet there were so many echoes already – the water, the columns of smoke, the violence – which fitted the inner scene's events (not helpfully, as yet, but, at least, in action), that I became apprehensive, thinking that this case could be different from all those which had gone before.

FIVE

The side of the Temple of Apollo which flanked the Avenue of Herakles was guarded by cavalry in the same yellow tunics as the boys on the western gate, only these horsemen wore breastplates of bronze and long green sashes. They were drawn up in line, but there was a huddle of them in the middle of the avenue where three dead horses had been dragged and several injured men lay propped up on the carcasses awaiting treatment. The messenger was known to the captain of these troops and he let us through the line, warning us that he did not know what was happening on the other side of the temple.

The calm inside the temple was eerie, made more so by the pigeons which flapped in the roof. There were no officers or sacristans at their posts, though the lamps were still lit. Not a single guard stood by the huge statue of the god. My rage against those who had deserted the shrine was evident, and the messenger had to take my arm to conduct me across the floor to the southern side.

When we appeared between the external pillars the sun was blinding, but I could hear voices. I saw a group of men standing in the middle of a seated crowd. Telys was there, keeping his distance from a wide, shallow market tray held by two yellow-clad soldiers. Fresh, red meat was heaped on the tray, still oozing blood.

From what Telys was saying to the crowd I was able to work out that these were the remains of a Sirisian fish merchant who had been torn to pieces by the mob. He had landed his catch that morning, bringing a strange fish to market which had never been seen in Sybaris before. The Sirisian had demanded a very high price for it, one that was so extortionate that the people had become enraged. Too many foreigners came to Sybaris imagining that they could charge what they liked and people would be wealthy enough to pay, it was said. The merchant had insulted their pride. I learnt that the ship belonging to the Sirisian had already been sailed out of harbour by the terrified crew.

The gist of Telys' speech to the mob was that they should be satisfied with their vengeance and not think to pursue the fishing vessel.

The tone which he used to them was so conciliatory that I was dumbfounded. Where was his authority? The tyrant of the city was virtually crawling. No wonder I had been given a false impression of the common people at our first encounter! They had no concern for rights and wrongs, only whims which were as flimsy and indulgent as their richer counterparts.

But I said nothing, feeling so strongly the impact of the parallels between visionary and real events that I was unnerved. The fish which had been brought to me; the throne of water. There were still details of interpretation which I had to work out, and that always took time, but the import of my inner scene was clear.

The gods wished me to assume power in some way. Whether in partnership with Telys or whether by deposing him was not yet clear, but I knew that the gods had put the fate of Sybaris into my hands.

My mood against the crowd which sprawled indecently over the temple precincts, its blood-lust slaked, laughing, sporting, congratulating each other, had been one of disgust, but now I felt appeased and elated.

When Telys saw me standing on the temple steps he beckoned me to join him but I refused, walking instead to the place on the steps where the great mess of blood showed the actual killing had taken place. In my state of high euphoria, speech was impossible, so I stood there and pointed at the stain.

Telys shrugged, picking up the severed head from the tray and pulling apologetic faces at it as he walked over to me.

'They're sorry,' he said to the head, then repeated it to me. 'Things just got out of hand.'

I turned my back on him, maintaining a front of anger and disapproval because I could not share my moment with him. I spotted the Bes design on the tray which had carried the head.

'Leave those pieces!' I shouted, as people began to edge towards streets which would give access to the Temple of Bes, the tray of flesh carried between them.

'Let the dog have his bone,' Telys murmured.

'No. There must be a proper burial for two reasons,' I replied. 'There will be enough trouble with Siris as it is, and the gods claim the victims of sacrilege as their children.'

Telys rubbed at his forehead.

'They've done this before,' he said. 'Nothing anyone says can stop them. And it's always in the markets.'

He bent down and put the severed head between his feet, smudging the stone steps with blood.

With an exclamation of horror I grabbed the hem of his mantle and ripped a piece off it, spinning him round.

He lurched back, arm raised.

'How dare you!' he snarled.

I carefully wrapped the head in the piece of cloth. I pointed at the blood on the steps.

'We are in the sacred precinct of the god Apollo's temple. You have desecrated it with the blood of an unlawful killing. Only blood from the proper temple sacrifices may be shed here.'

'Ah, but I must make a point, Kallias,' Telys replied, wrapping his torn mantle around his legs and glaring at me. 'You are wrong. This blood was not *shed* here. Blood is shed at the place where the injury is sustained, not where the corpse may be carried to. He was not killed in the precinct of the temple.'

'Do the gods distinguish between dead blood and live blood?'

'You tell me,' he replied harshly.

'An act of pollution has been committed,' I said, 'and these steps will have to be removed.'

Telys looked down. The limestone blocks which had been

smeared with blood were enormous benches of stone set into the earth.

'Later, perhaps,' he muttered.

'Now!' I commanded. 'Get them to start at once.'

'Kallias,' Telys said smoothly, 'don't make too much of this. These incidents flare up. We are sensitive about people taking our markets for granted. The Sirisian was wrong to insult us.'

'Do you have any respect for the god Apollo?' I demanded.

'Of course. We all do.'

'The temple has been shamed!' I thundered at him. 'First it is left defenceless by the cowards who are supposed to protect it, then you permit unlawful shedding of blood upon its fabric. This must be remedied immediately, or you will suffer the consequences.'

'Are you threatening me?' Telys whispered, his face close to mine so I could see the troubled gleam deep in his eye. 'Don't do that. Not in front of the p-p-people.'

Some amongst the crowd had heard what I had said. Now there was consternation. Women and children were thrust forward to plead with me to be merciful. Some went down on their knees, a few in mockery, but as the temper of the mob changed to contrition, they became serious. The word went amongst these foolish folk that the gods had been offended and reparations must be made immediately. Telys was pushed aside, and the men began to scrape out the earth between the steps prior to lifting them. I remained where I was, determined not to budge until the work was carried out. One by one the steps were lifted out. It was the work of less than an hour for so many.

When the last bloodstained limestone block was taken out it was the one I was standing upon, and I remained, allowing the crowd to carry me on their shoulders to where the other long benches of stone were stacked.

They asked me if their labour meant that they had been forgiven. I told them that it implied no such thing. All they had done was to show willingness to atone, and that could affect the future, if the god believed that they were sincere. But the sin of polluting Apollo's temple with innocent blood remained, and it would stand on the city's record until a way was found of expunging it.

The crowd was shocked by my words and there were some murmurings against me, but the majority were cowed and afraid. I told them to go back to their homes and behave reverently. As they moved away, casting doleful glances over their shoulders at me, Telys came down from the gaping hole in the temple steps from which he had watched my dealings. He offered me a hand to get down from the pile of stone.

'Very impressive,' he said, 'but you would never have got away with it if I hadn't ap-p-ppeased them first.'

I brushed this aside and demanded to know where the fish was.

'I don't know,' he replied.

I strode away from him, heading for the port.

He ran after me.

'We must talk, Kallias,' he bleated at my elbow.

I did not slacken my stride.

Once I had passed through the eastern gate and entered the fish market I questioned the first people I saw, a group of men who were trying to repair their stalls, which had been smashed up during the riot. They told me that the fish had been brought into the market in two halves, split down the middle, with the liver and roes still in place. When the original trouble started at the market-master's desk, the fish itself had not been attacked because everyone had been afraid of it. The market-master had acted quickly, assuring the outraged customers that the creature would not be offered for sale.

Several fishmongers had taken it out in a boat and dumped it into the sea beyond the entrance to the lagoon.

I immediately instructed the fishmongers to take me to the exact spot.

We did not have far to go. Our boat was in the channel at the lagoon entrance when the two halves of the monster fish were spotted floating in on the current, side by side. The fishmongers refused to go too close, now being in a state of religious terror, but they agreed to shadow the progress of the remains until they were beached on the sand dunes at the northern end. Telys had stayed with me and he had the courage to get out of the boat and wade the last part, helping to pull the great weight of the fish, each section as heavy as a calf, further up the shore.

The evening star had risen, and I did not have all the light which I needed to study the creature. With Telys' help I rolled one side over on to the other so that the fish could be looked at in its original shape. It had a massive, carbuncular head, full of knobs crammed together, a wide upcurving mouth lined with razor-sharp pointed teeth, no eyes, a long, slender, tapering body, and, from the declivities in the flesh left after their removal, the genitals of a man.

'Unless I am mistaken, this is what has upset people,' I told Telys, tracing the outline of the genitals with my finger.

He sat down on the sand and shook his head.

'It was the insulting price which started it,' he said in a fatigued, complaining tone. 'They're more excitable about that than the organs of any sea-m-m-monster.'

'This fish must be taken to the Temple of Poseidon and buried within the sacred area before sunset tomorrow,' I told him. 'It must be given a sarcophagus of the best marble, which I will design for you here and now. Send your builders down straight away.'

I quickly sketched the tomb of the fish in the sand. It was based on an upturned boat which, I thought, would be a symbol of apology for what had been a human mistake. As soon as I had finished drawing in the sand I let Telys look at what I had done, then called the fishmongers to come shorewards in their vessel. They could take Telys back into the city to make the necessary arrangements for the tomb to be built.

He obeyed. Not without reluctance, but he obeyed.

I went into the dunes until I could see no light and hear no cry. There I sat till the morning star, not happy, not sad, but knowing in my heart that I now had the city in my hand, should that be my desire.

I walked around the edge of the lagoon until I came to the place where the Sybaris river flows into the sea. I followed its northern bank up to the Metapontion road and the bridge into the city at the northern gate.

On the eastern side of the temple, between it and the offices of the civic law and defence departments, was a shining, hog-backed structure. Slaves with brooms were brushing away the last of the stone chips and mortar dust. It was an exact realisation of my drawing in the sand, even down to the kinks in the line which my trembling finger had made.

At noon the fish, now sheathed in copper, was carried into the sarcophagus. I performed a penitential ceremony of my own devising, a homage to the wonders of the ocean and Poseidon's power as brother to Zeus, Demeter, Hera and Hades, the lord of the Underworld, the dead and the rich. A lamb sacrifice was made, because I thought it wise to make it clear that the fish was not our sacrifice; because its nature was dualistic, being part man, part creature, the god might think that he was being mocked by having his own creation offered to him as an oblation, and this could be interpreted as insolence.

At the end of the funeral ceremony I slipped in a few words of comfort for the Sybarites who were there in their thousands, both rich and poor, all dressed in their finery, the rich fantastic and fervid with their morning wine, the poor gloomy and contrite, wearing their best clothes as a mark of outward regret for their savage and irreligious behaviour during the riot of the previous day. I used lines from one of my favourite poets, Sappho of Lesbos, a woman who venerated Elis, my homeland, and the prophetic genius of my people.

I did not make attribution to Sappho, as this would have brought criticism down on my head. The lines which I incorporated into my new liturgy for the burial of sea-monsters were as ambivalent in their meaning as its fish/man nature and the state in which it was entombed, in two halves. When the ritual is employed again, I doubt if the officiating Elean Clytiad (for I will only pass it on to members of my own family) will completely grasp the image I had in mind when the poetry came into my head. I was looking at the Sybarites in their finery: their riches seemed to salute the earth. They were dressed in the manner of happy gods, delivering their city into my care, full of blessings and gratitude. They stood obediently round the fish's tomb, their eyes raised to me, waiting respectfully for what I would say, submitting themselves to me as an agent of the gods on earth.

I had to begin with heavenly minded Sappho, of course.

'The Eternal Ones do not favour those who cannot enjoy life,' I sang over their heads, then, changing to an Egyptian love-poem which I had learnt from a brilliant Memphis beauty in my youth, 'wear flowers and be lucky,/ but my discretion is such/ that of the things which might come of it all/ I will not give a single hint.'

This was no obtuseness on my part. I had learnt those verses at a serious time when I was struggling to place human love in its proper philosophical setting. When I had been learning it none other than the great charlatan, the Long-Haired Samian, Pythagoras, had been in the great hall of the priests' brothel at my side.

I had been happy then. And I was happy now.

Telys stood beside me during the ceremony, determined to be associated with whatever could be taken as redemptive. He was there to forgive, and there to be forgiven. He it was who had appeased the mob, giving them a sacrificial victim, but he managed to suggest by his bearing and the way he looked at the crowd that his hand had been forced. By his firm alliance with me, the emergent strong man in the matter, he was able to imply that greater powers than he could control had been at work and that he had temporarily been blinded to the real issues. Now that I had sorted these out and reconciled the city with the gods, he could reassume his position as a responsible leader with me by his side, always ready to enlighten him when events became enigmatic.

I did not attempt to defeat this strategy. There was alive within me an excitement which had been created by the accord between what I had seen that night in the vineyard and actual events.

The wise course of action now was to conceal that I had had an inner scene at all and wait to see what happened next.

This was my intention, but Telys had already got wind of it. Leogoras, the keeper of the vineyard, had gone to Telys the next morning and told him that I was now his lord. He had asked to be released from his contract as a free man cultivating the vines for a fourth share, offering to forego his part of this year's harvest for a cash sum far below its value, so he could give it to his family while he followed me. When Telys had questioned Leogoras, the foolish man had taken him down to the oak tree and shown him marks on the bark where I had scored it as I hung on in my throes.

He had reported to Telys everything which he had heard me cry out. This included the words *fish* and *head*.

Once the funeral ceremony was over, Telys lost no time in taking me back to the villa and confronting me. When he demanded to have the details of my vision, I assured him that he would be told when the time was right.

'But can't you see?' he insisted. 'If it's generally known that you have the city's interests so close at heart and are able to work from within, then your use to me as an intermediary, an expert, a counsellor, is enormous. People are already saying our names in the same breath – Telys and Kallias – we go together in their minds.'

Telys had come to the fore in the political life of Sybaris in the most unusual way.

Jostling for power in the municipalities is customarily connected with wealth and status, often through war and various crises, and in this Sybaris was no different, but it was the manner in which he rose to eminence that was strange.

The city had been at peace for several years, its business life as secure as ever. The profitability of trade was almost mechanical, the markets certain, the prices going ever-upwards, the costs pegged at a low level. It had been this way for as long as anyone could remember: a relentless prosperity. Nothing seemed to threaten the city's economic strength.

What dissatisfaction there was came from the young. The sons of the merchant families had nothing to do once their education was complete. Tired of excess and dalliance, they went to Sicily to fight in the wars between the Carthaginians and the Greeks, but most soon returned, having discovered that they were of a different breed from the hard-bitten warriors of that harsh, rocky island.

The Tyrrhenian trade brought these youths into contact with a virile, warlike race which treated them with intense respect, needing their goodwill to continue the supply of olive oil, cloth, pottery and luxury goods. These fine folk, tough and alien as they were, put great value on friendship with a city famed for its effeminate, self-indulgent ways. Sybaris was praised in Rome, capital of Tyrrhenia, where the wines, garments and ornaments of Sybaris were greatly prized. The cruel put away their swords when they thought of Sybaris, knowing that to destroy the city would mean cutting off the supply of many things which make life sweeter.

But where is the pride in having a power such as this? Can a man boast about money without looking small? So the young rich looked to the poor of the city for something with honourable strength, some proof of a submerged potency. They went amongst the poor at night, often in disguise, and did their best to make friends. Many adopted simpler dress and spoke with less refinement. Some went through secret marriages with low-born girls. Meanwhile, the poor looked on and wondered, and a grievance grew in their hearts.

Telys, for all his faults, had a quick mind. He had been on the fringes of this movement amongst the young *azygous plutos*, but playing rather than committing himself to the spirit of it. One day he would mock their ingenuousness, the next he would be found in the poor quarters, his arms around carpenters and market-vendors, telling them what great fellows they were and buying them drinks. But he had an advantage over his fellows inasmuch as he understood the sour attitude which was prevalent amongst the poor. He realised that they did not wish to be patronised, only to possess what these spoilt youths had been given by their fortunate birth. Once he had perceived this he withdrew from the movement, knowing that it would produce nothing but dissension between fathers and sons and rich and poor.

He was right. Enmities arose. Brotherly love became debased and false. The wives from low-born families were increasingly put aside, and it was in this area of the conflict that the spark was struck which had ignited Telys' political career.

SIX

Hearsay is an unreliable source of history. In Sybaris this was made doubly so by a lazy intellectual life, which seldom stirred itself to record the past. The ceaseless and effortless creation of wealth over two centuries had slowed the spirit of enquiry down to a snail's pace. The attitude to past events was that they had happened and were therefore irredeemable. To understand history made as much sense as giving medical treatment to a dead man.

With this proviso in mind, and with no records in the city's archives, I drew up this account of Telys' rise to supreme power. It has faults, reeking of gossip as it does, but it is all that I could come up with.

At the time of the harvest of Olympiad 44,* in the month in which Anares, Orion and Hyades return to the night sky, the city had been ruled by an oligarchy of rich men. A tribunal which had no prominent leader was in charge of the government, and a council – seldom summoned – acted as legislators. Few new laws had been enacted over the last fifty years, because the Sybarites had discovered that too many prohibitions stifled trade, so they had kept the administration as free and loose as possible, trusting to common sense instead of a comprehensive codex.

This meant that crime was a popular sport in Sybaris, there being so much wealth on view. The rich moaned, but they preferred to have that inconvenience rather than accept onerous civic control of their activities. If keeping business free of

* 508 BC

restriction meant more theft, so be it. Those who complained against the city's lawlessness were the poor, for a thief habitually robs those around him for his day-to-day living expenses while attacking the rich once in a while to build up a fortune.

The daughter of a metalsmith – not a poor man, but an artisan whose workshop was outside the southern gate on the banks of the Krati (no noisy workshop was permitted within the city walls, as it might disturb the sleep of the merchants) – was secretly married to the eldest son of a family which traded in iron. His name was Hippoclos and hers was Deidameia.

The marriage took place in Poseidonia, the trading post which the Sybarites had built on the shores of the Tyrrhenian Sea. Hippoclos was forced to spend much of his time there, overseeing the import of iron from the island of Aethelia, which is one hundred stadia from the coast. This island possesses an abundance of iron ore, and the inhabitants smelt it into lumps about the size of a large sponge, and the smoke from their furnaces is so thick that the island is covered in darkness, so it is said.

Hippoclos kept his secret wife in Poseidonia for three years, and there were three children. His father was such a lazy man that he never made the journey along the Road to Prosperity over the mountains, nor did he ask any questions. As long as the business was being properly managed and the money kept rolling in, he was content to let his heir run his own life; also, he was such a libertine himself that the idea of marriage was not one which agitated his mind, his own wife having been put away many years before.

Then the father fell sick and called his son back to Sybaris to care for him. A younger brother was sent to handle the family's business in Poseidonia, and Hippoclos returned. The father realised that he had not long to live and pressed Hippoclos to get married so that a grandson could be born before the old man died. At this point Hippoclos decided that it would be easier to reveal Deidameia's identity to his father – who had, up until then, assumed her to be a concubine of some kind – and introduced the three children, all of whom were male and healthy. After his initial surprise, the old man was well pleased. The effort of chivvying his son to get married had been burdensome to him, and he was glad to get the matter out of the way so conveniently. He was in no way affronted by the fact that his daughter-in-law was from a family of lower rank and, indeed, said that he was proud of having the daughter of an ironworker in his house, that skill having contributed greatly to his own wealth.

Within weeks of Deidameia's acceptance into the family great thefts began to take place at the houses and villas owned by the old man: gold, silver, jewels, carpets, cloth, anything above common value. The old man, now on his last legs, maintained his customary Sybarite's coolness in the face of these losses. In his defiance of his illness, and in order to show that he was far above being concerned about such paltry matters as theft from his millions, he threw parties and banquets, inviting Deidameia's family so that he could demonstrate his approval of her.

Deidameia's parents were both dead by then, but she had nine brothers. None of them had followed the metalsmith's trade, but they appeared to be doing well in their respective callings. The old man, who was losing his mind towards the end, afflicted by weakness and debauchery, often enquired how these brothers made their livings, but their answers were confusing.

On the night of his father's death, Hippoclos was duty bound to remain with the body until the sunrise, as was the custom. His wife brought him food and drink with her own hands, left it on the windowsill, then disappeared. That night every article of value in the family's possession, from houses, villas, warehouses and stores in various locations over the city, was robbed; in each case a key had been used to enter the premises.

The enormity of the crime – stealing a man's birthright as his dead father's body was cooling from life – enraged everyone. It was soon deduced that Deidameia, acting in collusion with her brothers, was responsible. A manhunt began, and the trail of the thieves was followed northwards by land, but it was a false one, deliberately laid to throw pursuers off the scent. Deidameia and her brothers had loaded a ship with their plunder and had sailed into the night, never to be seen again.

A crime of this size requires punishment. It cannot be left to decay in the imagination. When a city, which is habitually indifferent to what views the greater world may have of it, becomes self-critical because its people feel foolish and blemished, their assertions on the nature of justice can become tangled and peculiar. Once Hippoclos had made his complaint to the city's prefecture and the matter became public knowledge, the poor decided that the fault lay with him for marrying secretly, without his father's knowledge, and bringing shame on them because he had not been able to accept Deidameia as a suitable bride for his rank; and the rich said openly that it was the innate dishonesty of lower orders which had made this massive act of robbery possible, for without the help and connivance of hundreds of people who must have moved the goods – the quantities were astonishing – the theft could never have taken place on that scale. It was therefore an act made by one class against another, a deliberate assault upon the rich by the poor.

As the culprits had sailed away into nowhere – reports later said that they had been seen in the city of Tartessus in the south of Hispania, but these were never confirmed – the oligarchy had only one person who could be taken to court to test these conflicting opinions. This became necessary as tempers rose and hostility between rich and poor manifested itself in sporadic violence and unrest, which often affected the running of the port.

The trial of Hippoclos on the charge of having his birthright stolen was brought by the city treasury. It argued that as he had, by filial disobedience, taken the thief to wife, he had rendered himself incapable of inheriting his father's fortune, on which taxes must be paid. This trumped-up charge was known to be as tenuous as it sounds, but it satisfied both sides: the poor believed that it had some substance, and the rich thought that it was so ridiculous that Hippoclos would be vindicated and his defence turned into a means of attack.

To prosecute the case, the city treasury brought a famous advocate from Athens, a silver-tongued fellow of aristocratic style called Antybios. He was a lover of the theatre, and there was much in this matter which appealed to him, as he never tired of saying. However, he was not always light-hearted, and one of his axioms which was delivered during the trial deserves respectful examination. He said: 'Theft takes place in the heart. I will give you a case: there are two men in the street. One is robbed at knife-point; the other is approached by a friend who says, "Lend me your money." The borrower does not pay the money back and avoids his friend for the rest of his life. Who is the greater criminal? The thief or the friend?' How this arose in the course of the proceedings I do not know but, I suspect, it had something to do with the nature of trust.

To oppose Antybios, Hippoclos engaged the services of a young lawyer who had recently returned from studying in Akragas, where his father had sent him after an unfortunate love affair with an older woman. He was a friend of the family, had no reputation, and had offered to defend the accused for no fee.

His name was Telys. And the older woman had been a slave.

It is worth noting here that the Sybarites treated their human chattels very generously and took the same care of them as they did the sources of their wealth. The expendable riches came and went, they were for enjoyment and leisure, but the fabric of their wealth, the material, the trade, the agreements and essential relationships, of these they took particular concern. A good slave was cherished, and cruel treatment was rare.

Yet all things had their place. Whereas it was perfectly acceptable for a young man to enjoy the beauty of a young slave, even to be enchanted by her for the period which is natural to such infatuations, it was not correct for him to waste his time on an older woman whose beauty had faded, and, least of all, to fall in love with her.

The woman in question had been Telys' nursery wet-nurse, a mere fifteen years old when she was used by the family in that capacity. From what I have learnt, she was of great beauty, and when Telys was twenty-five she was forty and still in full possession of her good looks. Also I am given to understand that the child which had brought her into milk so that Telys could be fed by her was sired by Telys' father, and was therefore his half-sibling in blood. All this is incidental to the story of the trial of Hippoclos, but it may help in the understanding of the frame of mind in which Telys approached the contest.

Antybios concentrated upon the deceit which Hippoclos had practised upon his father. The flouting of parental authority was not uncommon amongst the rich of Sybaris, but the ordinary folk maintained the time-accustomed discipline of obedience to the head of the household. Whenever Antybios harped upon this theme – and he was an orator much given to harping – the crowd would applaud long and loud and chant slogans. Telys, in his turn, could only attack the convention whereby the rich avoided interbreeding with the poor to such a degree that a young man had been driven to a subterfuge in order to live with the woman he wanted. He did not score heavily on this point, so I was given to understand, as the poor traditionally argued that the offensiveness of poverty was something which they felt themselves and had no wish to be wedded to.

This show-trial went on for weeks, and was so popular and well-attended by city- and country-dwellers alike that the harvest went ungathered. Nature then stepped in with an abundance of pests, a very early frost, high winds which scattered the argosies which had set out during a spell of unusually calm weather in the Aegean. But still the people remained glued to the case, both rich and poor following the details with passionate interest, arguing them over amongst themselves each night, listening to self-styled experts and lecturers who set up shop on the fringes of the trial, buying commentaries (some of which came into my possession, enabling me to reconstruct this story), and generally squeezing out of the proceedings as much support for their various positions as they could.

When the cold weather came and the Pleiades had gone down, not to be seen for another half-year, the trial was still in progress and the judges were too frightened to draw it to a close, knowing that a decision either way could break the city into two irreconcilable parties. Much of what had been argued appears specious to the outside eye. It was nothing to do with the charge, or the treachery of Deimadeia and her brothers, but everything to do with the tensions inherent in the unequal possession of wealth. No Athenian lawyer, no matter how brilliant he might be (and I give leave to doubt that he was), would be able to settle that one; the advantage always lay with Telys, by virtue of his birth as a free citizen of the city and as one who had fallen into an error of love himself.

The powerlessness of the court to decide this question eventually undermined the authority of the oligarchy, the tribunal and the council. Whether Hippoclos was innocent or guilty of the ludicrous charge sank into unimportance. What mattered was a face-saving judgement which would keep the city in one piece. The issue could not be forced either way, and neither side would contemplate surrender.

As the ears of wheat rotted on the stalk and the grapes shrivelled in the fist of the frost, Sybaris began to fall apart. It was only saved at the last moment by the suicide of Hippoclos and the speech which Telys made to the court, a speech which brought him, as smoothly and as naturally as a breeze brings a ship, to supreme power in the city. For an account of this remarkable peroration I have had access to Telys' original notes and also seventeen written records, all differing in style and detail, but essentially reporting the argument as the same. As Telys' oration took seven hours to deliver, I will not convey it in full but give only the salient features, hoping to illustrate the strength of his reasoning and his speedy exploitation of the sympathies which were aroused on both sides by the death of his client.

He arrived late at the law court that morning, having kept the crowd and the judges waiting as it was his turn to speak next. People spotted him coming down the Avenue of Herakles pulling a cart with the assistance of two other men; one was Metrodoros, a leader amongst the poor; the other was Saphnis, an eminent member of the tribunal and chief amongst the *azygous plutos*. The three of them were abreast, Telys between the shafts, Metrodoros on the right hand and Daphnis on the left. In the cart were several earthenware jars of the type which housewives in the poor quarters used for the storage of food.

When they had crossed the agora and drawn the cart to the

foot of the law-court steps, Telys called on the ushers to bring the judges out into the open. Antybios made a protest which detained them for some time, but the spectators shouted him down and he was compelled to withdraw. Once the judges had come out of the law-court building, Telys mounted the cart and stood amongst the jars; lifting one up he pointed to marks made with chalk on the side.

With brevity and directness he told the crowd that the vessel contained the heart of Hippoclos. It had been found at the Temple of Bes in the south-west quarter early that morning. The other jars contained limbs and members, which had been left at every temple in the city.

Telys had been woken from his bed before dawn by a message telling him to come to the Temple of Apollo to meet Hippoclos, but when he had arrived there were only two slaves, who submitted to him, confessing that their master had instructed them to kill him and dismember his body, distributing it throughout the temples. Upon hearing the news, Telys had been enraged by grief and had killed the slaves. They had been so saddened by their dreadful work, he added, that they had been glad to be rid of themselves.

The crowd went wild, the news of this martyrdom encouraging them to extremities of mourning. The customary coolness of the rich broke down into frantic anguish, the poor found themselves in the thrall of an immense satisfaction of which they were both ashamed and proud. Hippoclos loved us, they declared.

'Not only did he love you, but Sybaris also,' Telys declared during his long speech, 'it was for unity that he offered up his life.' Then he went on, drawing a thousand lessons and conclusions from it all.

If my information is correct, it was shortly after this moment that Antybios slipped away, going straight to the port to find a ship that would take him back to Athens. As an intelligent and wily man, he knew that the case was lost.

From the accounts in the city treasury which cover this period and mark the beginning of Telys' reign, the fees and expenses which had accrued to Antybios during the long trial were paid within three days of the funeral of Hippoclos taking place, were stamped with the virgin signet of the city's new leader, and were sent with his thanks.

I did not have this perspective upon the sacrilege which Telys had allowed when the fish-merchant had been killed on the steps of the Temple of Apollo; this recent history coming to hand much later. Deformations of truth had taken place in the public memory, and with such partisan misrepresentation that no balanced examination of Telys' actions had ever been made. His probity had been a side-issue; the emotion which had been stirred up by the trial of Hippoclos being so dangerous that people knew, in their deeper natures, that an outlet must be found rather than a solution. In providing an open opportunity for grief and contrition, Telys had chosen accurately, and he had risen on the fountain of it like a ball; but with me, he had an outside mind to deal with, uninfluenced, accustomed to struggling with great forces, not gullible or tied down by local history.

After all, my territory lay between god and man, not rich and poor, or Sybarite and Sybarite. However, when I learnt the history of Telys and his rise to supreme authority, I knew that he had called me in to straighten out a sword which he had twisted towards his own heart.

Anyone who has seen power working on the godless human mind will know what I mean. When there is no awareness of an omnipotent authority which sees and understands all, people who feel the thrill of taking the reins, and know how easy it is to get the horse of humanity to go where one wants, will get lost. There is nowhere for them to travel towards, no goal. Improve the drains, pave the roads, feed the hungry, provide every civic amenity there is, but without the gods there is no place for any soul to go, not even downwards. The pains of Hell are nothing compared to the nullity of the in-between, the limbo of disbelief, where all the worst crimes are committed by those whose imaginations are dead.

SEVEN

By the laws of Zeus the Hospitable, I was a guest under the protection of a man who now had cause to fear and hate me. Telys had clung to his authority by following my lead, but I knew his character by now and what I might expect. He had brought me to Sybaris for his own use and purposes, not for the city's good, because that good could not be perceived. Telys had decided that his power and the destiny of the city were interdependent: once I had demonstrated this in some way I would be pushed aside, probably without any life left; but only if I allowed this exploitation of my gifts.

In the afternoon of the day when the tomb of the fish was sealed, I met with the Council of Elders. Telys excused himself – which was a surprise – leaving me to discuss the reconciliation of the city with Apollo, whose temple had been polluted during the riot. That the men in the chamber with me were not sincerely religious was obvious from the start; what concerned them most was disobedience by the poor, the damage to property, the slur on the laws, and as I already knew, that Siris would cause problems, the dead man having been trading under the protection of Siris as a free citizen.

The Elders assured me that the situation was even worse than it appeared, because Siris had recently been wooed by the Krotonians in an attempt to control the access by coast road from south and north into Sybaris. The killing of a Sirisian citizen under sacrilegious circumstances would drive that city further into the arms of Kroton unless full reparations were made immediately. The Council already had information that when the fish-merchant's crew had fled the harbour they had sailed straight to Kroton, because that had been the direction of the prevailing wind and they had been afraid of pursuit by Sybarite ships.

'We should send two embassies,' said Saphnis, the tall old patriarch playing with the rings on his fingers, 'one to Kroton to speak to the Sirisian's shipmates and apologise; the other to Siris to explain what happened and to assure them that full payment will be made on all counts. We must not delay. I propose that Kallias here goes to Kroton because I hear that he knows Pythagoras, and I have no doubt that once this matter becomes an issue in Kroton, then Pythagoras will become involved, as he loves moral questions.'

I could not help smiling at the assumption that a man like Pythagoras would make the distress of a few foreign fishermen his concern, nor did I see the moral question as being at all tortuous. It was very straightforward – one should not kill merchants for charging high prices. That had been the original cause of the riot after all, and it was made more unacceptable and reprehensible because every commodity was expensive in Sybaris. I made the point to the Council that the whole issue was fundamentally a religious one, and would have to be argued on that basis.

'That brings me to my next proposal,' old Saphnis said, nodding his gleaming, frankincensed bald head. 'We should offer to build a temple in Siris. Let them choose which god it will be dedicated to . . . whichever one they're short of . . .' He yawned, the dark-blue rings under his hound's eyes stretching into ellipses. 'Perhaps Kallias should go on both embassies? He can put our case with the most authority. By his prompt action he has given us some arguments to play with . . . some excuses of a sort . . .'

Telys came into the chamber at this juncture, which was fortuitous as the councillors were starting to doze off, summoning slaves to bring more pillows and to be gentler with their giant fans.

I noticed that no vote was taken on the proposals which Saphnis had put forward, not even a show of hands or a sound of common assent. Saphnis was the obedient instrument of Telys to such a degree that everyone knew where the inspiration for the old man's ideas had come from and, as such, that they could not be opposed.

Telys was very friendly towards me, warm, smiling, solicitous, repeatedly enquiring about my state of mind and whether I had recovered from the shock of the dishonour which had been done to the gods. As we left the chamber he turned to me with a gleeful light in his eye.

'Any decent Greek would be appalled by what has happened here,' he said, 'but it is only an outward sign of what is happening to the city's nature. As a people we are becoming more and more faithless where the gods are concerned. You know yourself that we have, until the last ten years, been a pious people. You must have seen the temples which we have built at Olympia and Delphi in the past, great treasuries, overflowing with gifts, but now? It's not a serious thing in Sybaris any more.'

His hand was gripping my elbow, steering me down a passage to the rear of the city hall. I stopped, bracing myself in a doorway.

'Where are you taking me?' I asked, a chill of fear running down the back of my neck.

'Home,' he replied brightly, his thick eyebrows dancing up and down as if he were talking to a baby, 'so you can prepare for your journey.'

'To Kroton?'

'Yes; first to Kroton, then to Siris.'

'Have we got time? Surely this is an emergency. Wars have started over lesser issues,' I said, allowing myself to be taken from the doorway. 'I think someone else should go to Siris. After all, that's not going to be such a difficult matter, not when you're offering them a temple as compensation.'

Telys shook his head and opened a door into the street.

'No-one has your credibility in a situation like this,' he told me, setting off down an alley opposite, 'our priests come from families so rich they have lost all reputation as devout men. This is something which you will have to watch out for yourself if you continue charging such exorbitant fees. There is, in everyone, a strong feeling that those who serve the gods should not expect to receive all their rewards in this world.'

I did not rise to the bait, but began to prepare the reply

which I would give him when a later opportunity arose. Because I was engrossed in this process of storing up a consistent argument against his calumny, I did not observe how he was leading me away from where the transport to his villa might be waiting, but deeper into the south-western quarter, so recently the scene of the riot. By the time that I had woken up to this deviation he was in the hallway of a dark, stone-built house covered with flowerless creepers of a dark-leaved variety. When we reached the courtyard I saw that these plants had been trained over the top of it to make a kind of roof which had been reinforced with thatch. Beneath the roof was a stone-lined pit which went down to a considerable depth. At the bottom slumped a thin, ash-headed man, his head bowed to his knees, with each wrist manacled to the sides of a rack. He looked up and stared at us, his eyes dull.

'This is the culprit,' Telys said, kicking a small stone down into the pit. 'He has a grudge against the Sirisians. Some dispute about fishing-rights; lobsters are at the bottom of it, I believe. You're a wicked, bloodthirsty old rogue, aren't you?' he called down to the prisoner, kicking another stone. Then, turning to me with a fierce grin, he said: 'Amazing strength for a man of his years. He took the head off that fish-merchant with a little knife which he uses for shellfish. He was so quick about it that no-one saw it happen.'

'So how do you know he did it?' I asked sourly.

'He confessed.'

'Is that why you're going to torture him?'

'Ah,' Telys replied with mock-sadness, 'the old devil withdrew his confession, and now we will have to bring it back into his mind. As you can see, he's not strong, except for his powerful fingers, and he might not survive the interrogation.'

I walked away from the pit and sat on a mossy bench which stood in a corner, a great fatigue weakening my knees.

'Why are you behaving in this unsavoury manner?' I asked as he sat down beside me. 'I'm not a fool, nor am I a dishonest man.'

'You need to see things for yourself,' he replied, his teeth showing through his beard. 'This affects your embassies to Kroton and Siris. I want you to be able to tell them that the criminal who murdered the fish-merchant in the sacred precinct of the Temple of Apollo has been caught and will suffer the supreme penalty, if he lasts that long. This will impress them.'

'I know that this is the way things are done,' I replied heavily, my head laid back against the cold wall and the creepers which snaked over it, 'and I know that Sybaris is not the only city where such injustices are perpetrated, but why do you need me to be a part of it?'

Telys adjusted his posture, putting his elbow up on the armrest of the bench and propping up his chin like an actor who wants the audience to believe that he is thinking.

'Do you believe that the earth is hollow?' he asked eventually, inclining his head to look up at the sky. 'These thoughts must be constantly running through your mind. Another one, I suppose, is did the poets invent the gods so they would have something to write about? Now that's an idea that has often troubled me.'

'You are pretending to care about religion,' I said.

'No, I do care. What we are expected to believe in order to live and thrive is the most pressing question which faces us. As I have told you, we in Sybaris have a great sense of being in the wrong. We must do something about that; but it must be effective.'

His tone had changed, touching a chord of angry despair. He got to his feet and walked over to the edge of the pit to look down.

'What does he matter?' he said, 'And what would you matter if you were in his place? Would the gods rescue you? I'd wager everything I own that they wouldn't.'

'I have been in pits before now,' I said, 'and got out of them.'

'Talked your way out of them, I've no doubt,' Telys jeered. 'But the gods? Do they care? Eh?' he demanded. 'So much for your knowledge of the divine mind! In that moment – a casual moment, I would think it was – when the gods decided to pluck us from nowhere, from some void, what was behind it all? Something to play with? Something to f-f-fondle? Do you know what I think when I go into a temple? I look at the statue, I look at the altar, and I say in my mind, "There's no-one there."'

I refused to respond, keeping my eyes on the tangled creepers overhead.

'You down there!' he shouted, 'What do you think? Is Athene going to rescue you as if you were Odysseus? Or don't you count at all? I say that you don't, and I'm your fellow-man. Aren't you wondering why you were born? Come on, you must be concentrating on the whole question right now. What else is there for you to think about? What are you worth?'

There was no response. Telys got up and walked over to the edge, lifted his mantle and pissed down upon the condemned man. Outraged, I ran across and pushed him away, sending him stumbling to the wall. When I looked down into the pit I saw that the prisoner was still in the exact position as he had been when we had entered, head bowed. He had made no attempt to move himself out of the way.

Telys laughed.

'We must wrestle one day, Kallias,' he remarked warningly. 'They didn't tell me that you were a man of such strength. But you must keep your temper under control.'

'My vows rule my temper,' I said. 'A brave thing for someone in your position to do; humiliating the helpless. If you have cause to do such base acts, that is one thing; but to enjoy them is another; and to humiliate the soul of anyone is the right of the gods, not man.'

Telys nodded several times throughout my censure, then muttered, 'I know what you're up to, ambitious priest!' and leant right over the pit, pursing his lips to send down a gobbet of phlegm.

'You haven't said a word, have you, Herophantos? Speak to Kallias. Explain why I am like I am,' he called down derisively. 'Let's hear you.'

The prisoner glanced up and smiled, his eyes dead.

'Tell this monkey that it's the office he craves which makes me strange,' Telys called down, 'and how alone I am in my thoughts. Ask him why he should want to share such misery.'

I left the courtyard, unable to stand the display any longer. In my life I had seen many excesses of the depraved and vicious human mind, much of its activity aimed at the weak and fallen. It was such a common part of my travels that I had ceased to be trapped by pity because that rendered me powerless, crumbling my resolve as a champion of the fate which guides both gods and men. Herophantos was doomed, I could see that. What circumstances had put him in the pit, I did not know, but his demeanour was that of a man who has accepted his destiny. But for an outsider, a man who still enjoyed freedom and life, to mock him for his pain, was intolerable. Nothing makes me more angry than fools who sneer at those caught in the coils of fate. My remedy, the means by which I can pacify my rage, is a priestly one which falls within my power as mystagogue of Mysteries. I applied it to Telys with full force as he hurried after me through the house.

'When you are as near to death, and in another's hands, and knowing it to be your true fate, as that man is,' I called over my shoulder, 'remember those whom you have destroyed. The gods will give you an end which takes them into account, I promise you.'

After a visit to several addresses to pick up gifts which I would take to Kroton, we went to Telys' town house in the north-eastern quarter, behind the barracks for the mercenaries, the red-haired and blue-eyed Scythians whom I had seen guarding the treasury during the riot. In order to outstrip his neighbours, Telys had added three storeys to his the original building, but the result was not a happy marriage between old and new, the upper levels being overdecorated and too ornate for the simpler structure beneath. A series of twisting ladders ran up and down the exterior walls, developing into walkways and suspended terraces high above the ground, all wreathed in vines and trained fruit trees. Hundreds of bats were fluttering around the house as we entered, and when I was shown to my quarters I found Leogoras, the keeper of the vineyard, chasing bats out of the room with a stick. As I came in he stopped and knelt in front of me, two bats hanging on to the front of his woollen smock like black badges.

'What are you doing here?' I said in surprise, bending forward to pick the bats off, carefully putting them on the windowledge, from where they flew off.

Leogoras remained on his knees and did not reply, his open, healthy face showering me with adoring glances.

'Well?' I said, giving him a poke on the shoulder.

'I thought that you were talking to the bats,' he replied. 'I was waiting for them to answer.'

I left the matter of bats to one side, bringing to mind the information which Telys had given me about Leogoras' decision to abandon his livelihood and family in order to become my servant. I had little doubt that this was not the truth, and that the keeper of the vineyard was being insinuated into my service as a spy.

I sent him out of the room, giving the excuse that I wished to have some time to myself. When, an hour later, after I had taken a nap to settle my mind, I opened the door, there was Leogoras outside, his countryman's visage beaming.

'All will be well,' he said. 'To have a master who sleeps so soundly is a great advantage. What will be the first order that you will give me? Make it a solid one; for food or wine. That would be a good beginning for us both.'

While I had been half-asleep, going over recent events in my head, I had taken the decision to employ him. I did not believe in his honesty, or his admiration of me, but he was a manageable person, very amiable, and good-looking in his fresh, vital way. Also, he made me want to laugh. Whatever he said had a delightful edge to it, a strange sweetness which might be found in the spirit world rather than this one. This did not preclude my suspicions of treachery, charm being a quality unillumined by the virtues.

'A plate of white beans in vinegar, and some milk,' I said. 'An hour later, an apple cut into four parts with the core taken out. Then, when I knock on the door, a pair of eggs fried in olive oil with bread, and a hand's length of steamed blood-sausage in a cream parsley sauce on a separate plate, plus a large well-eared cup of Samian wine with a slight chill on it.'

Leogoras rubbed his hands approvingly, his head going from side to side as he went over the order in his mind.

'Are you sure about mixing vinegar and milk?' he asked, shifting awkwardly as if embarrassed to ask the question of a man who knew his own mind so well. 'It would sour my stomach, I'm sure.'

'Not if it's mule's milk,' I flashed, pushing him towards the door. 'Get on with it.'

Leogoras smiled broadly as he backed into the passage, his hands laid flat upon his wide chest.

'You must be careful about the jokes you make,' he advised me, 'Don't forget, I believe that you can do anything. If you say to a female mule, which never bears young, "go into milk", it will obey. For all I know, you have been wandering about the plain of Sybaris doing just that, and mule's milk is flowing out there. What am I to think?'

'With me you must remember one rule,' I warned him, seizing his ear between my thumb and forefinger, 'always use your common sense. If I say something, then take it as straightforwardly and exactly as you can. If I say milk, I mean cow's milk. If I say Samian wine, I mean wine from Samos and nowhere else.' Then I twisted his ear right round, bringing tears to his eyes. 'But if I say bring me goat's milk, don't bring me cow's milk. Is all that clear to you?'

Leogoras nodded frantically, and I released him. The look which he gave me was rueful, reminding me of my own children and their glances after a sore chastisement, but there was nothing darker. He went away rubbing his ear and muttering, but there was a spring in his step which I took to be his joy at getting his own way and becoming my man.

I received my food and drink properly and promptly, and he did not chatter or interrupt my pleasure in any way, waiting outside the door until I called for him. When he entered the room I told him about my impending journey to Kroton, and said that I wanted him to accompany me.

'I am going to speak to the leading men of Kroton,' I said, 'one of whom I already know: the man Pythagoras. It will not be in my interest to be anything but frugal and sparing in diet, apparel or entertainment of the senses while I am with him, as he sees all indulgence as signs of weakness, and I have no wish to give him that impression. So, with the moon waxing to the full, and knowing my own nature, I need to expend those energies and motives of desire which might trouble me in the immediate future, the gods sending them to me with great regularity.'

Leogoras assumed that I was making a demand upon his

body and indicated to me that it was at my disposal, but I explained to him that I did not require that of him.

'You're a handsome man,' I told him, 'and there are many good points in your favour, but I am used to females. What I want is a tall, stately Lydian woman, slightly mannish, rough hair, dark, shining skin, mature, large in the hips and wild-eyed, with a light boy attendant.'

Leogoras took a moment to note the details of my order.

'Do you want me to find one and bring her here, or do you want to go out and lie with her in a house elsewhere?' he asked finally, his question in keeping with my requirements regarding directness and exactitude.

'I want to go out,' I said, 'and I want to be carried home.'

I gave him an hour to locate the woman I needed. He returned in half that time, and we went out together. I noticed that we were not followed, which reinforced my opinion that Leogoras was now doing the work previously performed by agents of the city's prefecture in keeping me under surveillance. The brothel was not, as I expected it to be, in the poor quarters, but up near the tower on the corner made by the northern and north-western walls. From the window of the room where I wrestled with the big, strong Lydian (she was a handspan taller than me, and muscled like a boxer), I could see the moon on the Sybaris river, but there was not much Heraklean force in my votive desire. I knew that I had taken a precaution which was not necessary, but I have learnt to obey the small fantasies of mind which warn me how I might be tossed about by passions at the wrong moment. I have always known that it is not hardship for me to be ascetic and do without, but desire is like water. It builds up behind the dam, and the gods have a great aversion to obstacles which get in the way of the natural flow of life.

As I returned to Telys' house in a litter with Leogoras strolling along beside me, one of his hands resting delicately but possessively on the shaft, I could see that his curiosity had been aroused. The training of a good personal servant is a long business, and getting off on the right foot is important, so I made him wait. A close retainer must respect the essential singularity of his master, the essence of his privacy, even though he is privileged to see and hear everything, strength, weakness, good, evil, the whole man.

'You keep darting little looks at me,' I said to him as the litter-bearers crossed the Avenue of Olympia in the moonlight. 'Don't think I haven't noticed.'

Leogoras took his hand off the shaft and pushed back his thick, curly hair, then rubbed at his eyes.

'I have taken a vow,' he mumbled.

'What kind of vow?'

'Not to ask you any questions. How can a man with your powers be held responsible to an underling?'

'Tell me about this vow,' I taxed him, leaning sideways to grip his shoulder in a companionable way.

'I made several vows once I had severed my connection with the vineyard and my family,' Leogoras said as he tilted towards me.

'Who supervised the taking of them?'

He told me, this good, earnest fellow, that he had taken his vows at the oak tree where he had found me in the midst of my inner scene. As soon as I learnt this, I was overflowing with explanations which would satisfy his curiosity.

'I am devoted to Herakles,' I told him, putting my arm round his neck. 'That is the first thing that you should know about me if we are going to get along. Whatever I do, I have Herakles in mind. Without him, I am nothing. Without him, the world is nothing. There are moments when he seems, to me at least, to be the one god.'

I felt Leogoras shudder under my arm so I clasped him tighter, so tight in fact that the litter-bearers shouted out warnings that I was in danger of upsetting the vehicle.

'To have such a vigorous and mighty force active in my being means that I must let it out frequently or I will be torn apart,' I whispered. 'He appears to me in his strength, the strength enters me, I must let it loose in a manner which he understands.'

Leogoras stumbled as we went down some steps that had been made slippery by the sea-mist which had rolled in and dimmed the honey-coloured moon. I held on to him and could not resist pressing his big, tousled head to my cheek. In his hair I could smell the land, the faint redolence of manure.

'The boy told me that you exchanged clothes with the Lydian, and marched up and down the room talking in a high-pitched voice,' Leogoras whispered.

'Stop!' I called out to the litter-bearers. 'I want to get down. Pay them, Leogoras. We will walk from here.'

My mood was soaring by now; ripe, loving, full of humour and generosity. I had an itch to sport, to laugh in the streets. Back at the house I knew Telys would be waiting, probably with a pack of his cronies. I had ignored him deliberately, giving myself over to my god and my new man. I did not want to talk about politics, or guilt, or unknown wrongs. The wine was harvesting my thoughts, but not with a sickle; with a sweet tongue.

The litter-bearers trotted off into the mist, and I was left with Leogoras. The city around us was a pale, quiet beauty. In the night air I could smell the ocean and it reminded me of my home, so I sat down and wept. When I had finished and Leogoras had tenderly wiped my eyes, we sat side by side on the ground and I told him the story about Herakles killing his best friend in a fit of rage, and being condemned to be the slave of Queen Omphale of Lydia for three years.

'During this time, dear Leogoras,' I informed him, 'Herakles underwent a change. He dressed like a woman and took up effeminate ways, giving his male nature to the queen, who became masculine and played that part.'

'But why?' Leogoras asked in his innocence.

'It was a release for him,' I explained, touching his plump cheeks with my fingertip. 'He could be weak and forget the responsibilities of his tremendous strength. The story has always touched me deeply, and whenever I feel that I am on the edge of something which I do not quite understand, I take refuge in Omphale for a little while and emerge as refreshed and liberated as Herakles did, going on to greater conquests and feats of manhood.'

We did not return to the house but stayed out until dawn, moving around the city, entering any place which gave out sounds of music or revelry, never staying long but tasting the wine and the debauch, enjoying my fame and the welcomes I received wherever I went. As the night went on I became increasingly enamoured of Leogoras who called on the skills which he had practised in his vineyard days, keeping me upright and ready to flower, but not allowing me to blossom into nothingness.

When we got back, Telys was up and about. He took one look at me and turned away, his brow troubled rather than darkened by anger. While I gently ridiculed him for his concern, he told me that while I was out a robbery had taken place and my treasure-chest had been taken.

My knees gave way, and I had to lean against the wall with Leogoras holding me up. Inside the chest had been three and a third talents of gold, that being the second instalment of my fee, since paid up by Telys; plus twenty-five Persian darics and thirty-eight Cyzikene staters which I had brought along for general living expenses, wishing to keep the talents intact in order to take them back to Elis. In addition there had been a small hoard of white gold electrons which I had collected over the years, intending to use them as dowry payments for my daughters. I have special affection for these nice little coins and like to keep them with me. All told it was a great sum but, according to law, I had no claim on Telys because I had dismissed his slaves and sentinels, declaring (as I had done) that my security had become a private matter. Nonetheless I hastened to enter a claim against him in the courts that morning before I set off on my embassy to Kroton, stating that as a guest in his house it had to be my reasonable expectation that he would prevent theft, inasmuch as if it took place the implication would have to be made that he had engineered it, and that I had removed myself from his guardianship in order to be free to do my work, not to make others free to rob me.

As I boarded the penteconter which was to take me south to Kroton on that forenoon, a written decision on my claim was handed to me by a court messenger. It stated that as an alien I had no citizen's rights at all, only customary kindness which was generally made available to visitors of my rank if they were invited to the city on public business. However, should this kindness cease to be appropriate it could be withdrawn. Also, if I wished the thief to be apprehended, I would have to pay for the police work involved. To this end, half of the value recovered would be payable to the city treasury.

As the gangplank was being taken up prior to our departure, another messenger arrived from the prefecture to tell me that my money had been found and the miscreant, a certain notorious criminal named Herophantos, who had been in custody on a charge of sacrilegious murder, had escaped, committed the theft, and had then been killed while trying to avoid arrest. My money would be held pending a coroner's judgement.

While the penteconter was rowed out into the lagoon I kept my back to the city, not wanting to imagine that broken-spirited creature in the pit. He would not have had the strength to climb the stairs to my room.

At a single stroke Telys had put me in the wrong, denied me my rights, halved my wealth, expelled me from the city and made success in an impossible venture the condition of my return to claim the remaining half of my money, which he would release when he felt like it.

When we got out to sea and the oarsmen settled into their rhythm, I stood at the stern with Leogoras and made myself look at Sybaris. It was no longer beautiful to me, its deathly pale elevations rising from the plain like a threatening fungus.

EIGHT

There are two parts of my character which I keep forgetting to be wary of: first, my propensity for political meddling; and second, the closeness of my innermost, essential being to the surface. When these became mutinously restless after long periods of fallow spent amongst my family, farming my land, bringing up my children and all those activities which take place in a small compass, I must look out for trouble. I become over-excited and ambitious and stretch self-belief to ridiculous limits, pushing aside the knowledge of real life which my hard experience has taught me. Here I was, at the mercy of a clever strategist; a man who was not all good or all bad, but haunted by a sense of unknowingness. In this he was not alone. His people shared the dread, and his general lack of principle in dealing with it. Because of their weakness and ignorance in this matter of destiny I had assumed that my greater strength in that arena would give me paramountcy. All this error of mine had arisen within less than a quarter of a waxing moon, and I stood with the sea-breeze in my face, amazed at my own stupidity. Time after time I had made this self-same mistake. Time after time I had been compelled to redeem myself in the eyes of those who commissioned my services before winning them back to my side.

Now, here I was, outwitted but eminent in Sybaris; the envy of everyone of priestly aspirations in the place; a friend and enemy of the undisputed leader; but thrust on the outer point of an extremely dangerous mission which one of the city's senior diplomats should have undertaken. Behind all this frenetic jockeying and switching of fortunes was one point of illumination – my inner scene; a gift from my guardian deity, the impact of which I had wasted by being cryptic, and by trying to squeeze too much to my advantage out of the city's predicament. I felt ashamed at being caught out yet again, and a host of uncomfortable memories assailed me.

'Are you feeling seasick?' Leogoras asked me as I crouched by the gunwhale.

I shook my head and motioned him to sit further away. His very sturdiness and naivety challenged my confidence in myself. If Telys had outmanoeuvred me, what had I done to this poor simpleton? Before I had arrived in Sybaris he had had a sensible function – what could be more useful than a keeper of vineyards? – and a settled, congenial family life. All farmers are superstitious and their father-poet, Hesiod, has seen to it that they feel themselves to be the roots of human religion, seeing every shift of wind and lift of sap as emanating from the bowels of Zeus himself. But I am not a Hesiod man. If I had found a stranger sitting up a tree in my vineyard I would have chased him off the property with dogs, not given all away to follow him in his abstractions.

The wind grew cooler and Leogoras brought me a woollen cloak, squatting cheerfully down beside me, contriving to touch my hand with his warm palm.

'All will be well,' he whispered, winking. 'I feel it.'

The last thing that I needed at this moment was optimism of the brainless, agricultural sort, so I rebuked him.

'No-one will defeat you,' Leogoras said. 'There is not one of those who are gathered in Kroton who can humble you in argument.'

I looked at him questioningly. His response was to wag his big, square head, the breeze lifting his curls.

'I'd back you against every one of them, individually or together,' he said. 'What do they know? None of them can hold a candle to you.'

'Who are you talking about?'

'The thinkers gathered in Kroton.'

'Don't irritate me,' I warned him. 'Today is not a good time for playing games.'

'The crew tell me that there are a number of thinkers who

are with Pythagoras in Kroton. The heat of their arguments is said to be unbearable,' Leogoras continued blithely, 'and hundreds of people gather outside the house hoping to pick up a scrap of the conversation. If the thinkers go for a walk in the fields or along the shore, they are followed by hordes of admirers. It has got so bad that Pythagoras has had to ask for protection from their enthusiasm. You know how he hates to be idolised, considering it to be debasement of any man's dignity to worship anything but truth.'

I replied that I had not noticed this antipathy to praise in Pythagoras, then told Leogoras to discharge all the news that he had gathered about this momentous meeting. He recounted to me how the presence of Herakleitos the Obscure from Ephesus; Xenophanes of Kolophon, who had come down from Elea; Anaximenes of Miletos, and his famous fellow-countryman, Anaximander, whose hundredth birthday was the cause of all these philosophers being together in Kroton, had provided a big talking-point in every settlement on this part of the coast.

'It is rumoured that these philosophers have decided to agree on what exactly is the basic substance of life and the universe,' Leogoras added, 'and, as you might expect, there is a lot of public interest in that.'

My heart sank even further as I contemplated what lay ahead for me. I knew every one of these men. We had crossed swords in all the corners of the Greek world. To have to face them on such a mission as the one I had been sent on would be humiliating, and they would squeeze every drop of advantage out of it they could. Although they disagreed amongst themselves on many points, they were in accord in their antagonism to my profession, seeing divination as an inferior mode of thought when it comes to tackling the major questions which surround human existence. But though they were scornful privately, in public they had to be cautious when contradicting the opinions of a man such as myself. To be guilty of impiety could still mean the death sentence, so in our contests they had always been clever if we were out in the open, full of traps and subterfuges which they hoped I would fall into; whereas if we were at a drinking-party or in some quiet room with no-one listening, they would be much braver and attempt to destroy my arguments outright, insulting the gods and our religious traditions and beliefs.

And I would have to meet them as a supplicant, a hired tongue asking fishermen for forgiveness, stripped of the status of an intellectual equal, unable to share in the glory of their significant proceedings. And how they would rub my nose in it!

Telys had sent me into this den of lions deliberately, hoping to reduce me to total dependence upon his protection. Now I could add the shattering of my reputation as a philosopher to the other destructive blows which he had rained down upon me since I had saved him from the repercussions of the riot in Sybaris.

A cold wind began to blow from the north-west as the penteconter passed Cape Trianta, bringing a chill, buffeting blast from the high mountains. The sail was raised to supplement the work of the oars and our vessel was soon moving forward much quicker, its red ramming beak charging through the dark blue waves. At the outset of our voyage the master of the penteconter had estimated that we would arrive in Kroton too late to enter the harbour in daylight – the distance was just less than five hundred stadia, well within the oarsmen's reach for a day's rowing – but now, with the strong following wind, we would make up some time and be there earlier. This put heart into the oarsmen, who had no desire to sleep a night at their benches outside the harbour, no vessel being permitted to dock during the hours of darkness. We ploughed along at a fine pace, taking me closer and closer to my confrontation with each stroke of the great timber oars. Gulls followed us, shrieking; the pennant of Sybaris with its white ox turning to look over its shoulder, head up, rear quarters raised like a whore, phallus dangling to its knees, rippled and streamed at the masthead. I stared at it gloomily, belabouring my brain to abandon all thoughts of lost money, injustice and apprehension about the future. Before I presented myself at the house of Pythagoras – something which I could not duck out of without being accused of discourtesy and cowardice – I would have to prepare my arguments.

'Leogoras,' I said, 'you can be useful. I want to try some ideas out on you.'

His eyes brightened with enthusiasm, and he edged himself closer to me so the sound of the wind was lessened between us.

'Pretend that you are a simple Sirisian fisherman. Can you do that for me?' I asked him. 'An ordinary come-day, go-day working man.'

'It was only a matter of days ago that I was a simple vineyard keeper,' he replied, 'so it shouldn't be too difficult.'

'First, you're out in the gulf, fishing. Everything is as it should be . . .'

'Ah, no,' Leogoras said, holding up a finger. 'It wasn't like that. From what I heard there was a storm, a storm that was so small and localised that the fisherman could see the edges of it not ten arm's-lengths away.'

I frowned at this fresh information.

'Is a storm of that nature common around here?'

'It was, according to what I heard, as if the storm had been placed over the fishing-boat like a bowl over a piece of meat to keep the flies off,' Leogoras told me earnestly. 'Not one of the men on board had ever seen anything like it in all their time at sea.'

This news cheered me enormously.

'Do you know any more about this?'

Leogoras nodded, clutching my arm and holding on as the vessel lurched through the trough between two big, shining waves.

'The net was out, and they did not have time to bring it in before the storm descended on them, so I was told,' he said confidentially, his face against my shoulder. 'When the storm left them, which it did with amazing swiftness, flying off into the sky, they felt the fish in the net. Its strength was so great that it pulled the boat backwards for a long time before it tired and they could bring it on board.'

This was exactly the kind of thing that I needed to hear. Although fishermen are not famed for the quality of their minds, any fool should have been able to interpret what had happened. This had been a direct, forceful intervention by a god into human affairs.

'Hold on,' Leogoras said warningly, 'there's more. A gull flies over the boat and drops a mussel into it. The shell moves like a man's lips, and it says: "Kill the fish, cut it into two parts along a line from nose to tail, then put it up for sale in the fish-market at Sybaris at this price." Then the mussel stands on its end and scratches into the woodwork, "Twenty-five Persian darics. Thirty-eight Cyzikene staters. Seventy-nine white gold Lydian electrons."'

The hair stood up on the back of my neck.

No-one in Sybaris knew the exact amount of money which had been stolen from me.

'Do I talk in my sleep?' I demanded.

'How should I know? I don't sleep with you, or I haven't as yet,' Leogoras replied.

'You haven't listened at the door?'

'Why, you're trembling!' he said, holding my shoulders and looking into my eyes which were, I know, full of terror. 'What's the matter?'

He was the only person I could tell. Somehow I had forgotten my suspicions of him, and I remembered how he had been so patient, gentle and respectful when he had found me going into my inner scene up the oak. So I told him, the facts spilling out of me. As I spoke I saw his expression change to wonderment and he embraced me closely.

'The gods are speaking to you very clearly,' he whispered, shielding me from the gaze of the curious as our behaviour attracted the attention of members of the crew. 'What is it that they want of you?'

'I don't know,' I sighed, allowing myself to sink into his arms, 'but it won't be easy, whatever it is.'

'The gods wanted the riot to happen? Is that what you think?'

I nodded, smelling the earth still on him from his vineyard days.

'Which means that I was intended to go to Kroton,' I murmured, a strange joy beginning to flourish in my breast, 'and I am being sent to fight the case for the gods at the house of Pythagoras.'

*

We arrived off Kroton two hours before sunset. Two warships from the city had shadowed us from the point where the Aesarus river runs into the gulf not far north of the harbour, and as we prepared to enter they increased their speed and cut us off, signalling that we must wait and be boarded. When this was achieved I was called forward and taken on to one of the Krotonian vessels with Leogoras, and the penteconter was turned round and sent back northwards, the oarsmen complaining at the extra distance they would have to cover before a friendly harbour would take them in.

'This is a semi-hostile act,' I told Leogoras as the master of the warship took us below to a small, dark cabin in the stern, 'so we must be careful. Under normal conditions an ambassador from a neighbouring city would be allowed to enter harbour in his own ship with his flag flying. To be treated in this way means that the Krotonians are not prepared to grant me full rank, or give my mission any recognition. Everything is under the table, which is a bad sign.'

As we passed the tall, white pharos light at the narrow gully between the sandbanks which guard the port of Kroton, the master of the warship came down and informed us that we would be taken immediately to the Temple of Hermes, where the Sirisian fishermen had taken refuge, seeking the protection of the god. The city had allowed them to exercise this right of sanctuary once the story of the riot in Sybaris had been told to the council, and it was therefore religious sanctuary that had been granted and not political; no negotiation with the city's secular authorities was appropriate.

I asked him if this was the view of Pythagoras, and was told that Pythagoras had not been consulted, because the matter was too minor for his consideration. All that the city fathers expected of me was to talk to the Sirisian fishermen and then depart, having put the minds of these men to rest on the subject of their safety. Kroton had no interest in keeping a gang of foreigners in sanctuary for any longer than was necessary, and it expected Sybaris to foot the bill which the temple officers were presently paying to provide customary hospitality to the refugees.

I braced myself for the next stage, which was not long in coming. From behind a wooden screen at the rear of the cabin stepped a young man who announced that his name was Actaeos, son of Belocles, a disciple of Pythagoras.

'As an old friend of yours,' the youth said blandly, pushing a lock of long, loose yellow hair out of his eyes, 'my master Pythagoras recommends that you get this business at the Temple of Hermes over as soon as possible. Admit that Sybaris is in the wrong, give compensation and pay Kroton for an escort to conduct the Sirisian fishing-boat back home. This will be accepted by both the fishermen and the city fathers. Then request permission to visit Pythagoras for old time's sake. A few friends are with him, people you know, and he'd like you to stay for a few days.'

The youth paused, straightening the folds of his mantle along the line of his leg. 'That is my master's message,' he said, finally looking up, his blank, good-looking face pulled into a haughty grimace. 'Will you make any reply, or will you be happy just to accept?'

'Actaeos,' I said, 'it is not as straightforward as that, as Pythagoras knows. Tell him that I will deal with the problem at the Temple of Hermes in my own way and as best I can. It is a religious affair and therefore, with his views, it need not concern him. When I have completed my business there I will ask for permission from the city fathers to visit my old sparring-partner, and we will see how they react.'

As I made this answer, the vessel touched the wooden jetty at the southern end of the port. Actaeos looked up and smiled, his light eyes wide open like an unshuttered lantern.

'That's exactly what my master said you would say,' he chortled, 'almost to the letter. Isn't it astonishing how much that man knows?'

When the master descended to the cabin he saluted Actaeos and allowed him to go out ahead of us, deferring to him as if he were a prince, whereas I was bundled along the deck and across the gangplank like a criminal being unloaded into the hands of gaolers. There was no carriage waiting to take us to the Temple of Hermes, and we were made to walk the whole distance under escort.

This was a smaller, more compact settlement than Sybaris, the proportions of its public and religious buildings more modest and its streets narrower. I saw it as typical of the smaller cities which clung to the coastlines of Italy and Sicily, slightly provincial, rough at the edges, untutored in style perhaps, but the air! It was nectar. After Sybaris and its feverish sweetness and fragrance it was like a mouthful from a pure mountain stream, running with health and vitality. I breathed deeply, taking the cool air to the bottom of my lungs, glad to be off the sea, ready to do battle. Our escort was made up of young soldiers, sons of the city in short green jerkins, armed with polished clubs of twisted wood. Their bodies were magnificently muscled and lean, and they marched at such a pace that we had difficulty in keeping up with them. This was a tactic to discomfort us. My response was to encourage Leogoras not to show distress. He grumbled, muttering to himself as he trotted along under the weight of my baggage that it was all very well for me to disguise my fatigue, but he had burdens to bear. As I listened to him, while hurrying to stay at the heels of the superb, athletic youths, I realised that this was the first complaint I had heard him make. From then on I did not have any worries about his ability to switch from being free man to servant, this proof of a rapid adaptation to the ways of servitude having been made, but I hoped that he would not make too much of a habit out of grousing.

NINE

The head of the sacerdotal college attached to the Temple of Hermes was waiting for us at the bottom of the steps. I groaned inwardly as I recognised him: Phalanthos, a slippery-minded Achaean who claimed cousinhood with me. We had last met in Ephesos in the year when I was summoned to the court of Darius, the Persian king, and we had travelled part of the Royal road to Susa together. The last time I had seen him had been on the banks of the Tigris river when he had said goodbye to me before returning to Ephesos, being ill with fever.

'Ah, Sphinx, I suppose that you are surprised to see me alive,' he said with a ghastly grin which revealed his twisted teeth. 'Will you dine with me?'

'Will that mean talking business?' I replied, turning my cheek to be brushed by his fangs. 'Or will it be just old friends getting together?'

Phalanthos smiled widely, and I swore to myself that I must give him no further opportunities to be humoured by me, the display of teeth was so repulsive.

'I think that we are expected to deal with the current difficulty,' he replied. 'The members of the senior priesthood here are all from the important families, and Kroton-born. They feel that it would be better if you dealt with someone who is of the Iamidai, and an alien himself. They have no wish to be involved in this quarrel at all.'

I raised my hands in the air in a gesture of appeal, espying the faces which peered from behind the sanctuary wall.

'All I want is to talk to them,' I shouted. 'It is a simple matter, easily settled. They have nothing to fear from me.'

Phalanthos did not smile this time. Instead, his expression grew serious.

'Come to my house,' he said under his breath. 'There are developments which you should know about. I know that you don't like me, Kallias, and you never have, but you have no option but to trust me this time. We are of the same blood, remember that.'

I stepped back, flummoxed by his unaccustomed directness. Phalanthos had never been a straightforward man, having that oily cunning which many priests cultivate in themselves, under the mistaken impression that it is the best way of coping with the impossible demands which the faithful make upon them. My memory of him was of an equivocator, a cheat and a mind addicted to false argument.

'Liking belongs to its own time,' I muttered in my embarrassment. 'People change.'

'Don't be humble, it doesn't suit you,' Phalanthos said, linking arms with me. 'Tell your man to bring your bags. I don't live far away.'

The fitness of the inhabitants of Kroton was further demonstrated by the distance which Phalanthos, a wheezing, wine-sodden hypochondriac as I remembered him, made us cover to his home on the other side of the city. I commented upon the improvement in his health, and asked if it could be attributed to the invigorating air.

'Which comes first: the air or the ethic?' he said, hanging behind for a few steps in order to poke the sweating Leogoras in the back with his ceremonial staff and make him walk faster. 'Everyone in Kroton is devoted to the ideal of mental and physical excellence. If anyone wishes to live and work here, they must accept the rule of health. You can recall what a sorry creature I was, Kallias: always ill, always abusing my body, lazy, decadent, and all the foolishness which follows on from that. When I came to Kroton and asked for permission to stay, the authorities took one look at me and said that they did not encourage cripples to settle in their city, but if I was serious then they would look at me again in six months. Off I went into the mountains. I ran, I threw rocks about, I chopped wood, I lived off fruit and bread, I stopped drinking wine. I tell you, Kallias, you would have been astonished at the transformation.'

'But why did you want to live in Kroton so much?' I asked him. 'There are plenty of other places in Greater Greece, all the fine cities in Sicily and up the Tyrrhenian coast, Syracuse, Rhegion, Akragas, for instance.'

Phalanthos led us through an archway with a wooden gate. Once we were through it, there was a rose garden waist-high in blossoms. Phalanthos held the thorns aside with his staff as I followed him.

'I notice that you did not mention Sybaris,' he said, 'but that is another question, which we can come to later. Let me answer your question, Kallias.' He paused, his staff laid against a towering bank of white roses which glowed in the purpling air of the evening. 'I hope that you won't laugh when I tell you that I had come to a point in my life when I was full of self-disgust. I had been taught by several experiences that I was worthless; a charlatan, a dishonest poser, a parasite upon the credulous. Every aspect of my character appalled and nauseated me and, I must confess it to you as a fellow who follows the gods, I had thought seriously about ending it all. There was no comfort anywhere. Everything was fake, inside and out.'

I could not help putting out my hand to touch his, which was stiff holding the staff against the great swathe of roses. To hear him talk this way was very stirring.

'Yes, Kallias, you are not in company with the Phalanthos whom you once knew. Let no-one ever convince you that people cannot change their basic natures. I stand here as a living testimony to the fact that they can.'

He released the heavy crop of white roses, which swung back into Leogoras' face as he came up the path. While the poor man swore and fumed, fighting to get his hair out of the thorns, Phalanthros continued with the account of his metamorphosis.

'It began, this life-saving transformation of mine, when I went to the Olympic Games six summers ago, hoping to get some work at the festival, pulling a few family strings, you know the kind of thing,' he called over his shoulder in a gentle, self-deprecating tone. 'What a state I was in! To be in Elis, rubbing shoulders with the highest – I saw you there but avoided you, I was so ashamed – and have nothing to show for my twenty years in the priestly craft! Well, the urge towards death was very strong. I moped about, hanging around the temples, doing minor odd jobs for my keep, and every day I kept running into my reputation for shady behaviour. Then, when I was at my lowest, I went to the arena and saw this man. I tell you, he shone. Never in my miserable life had I seen such beauty and strength. He was a miracle of humanity, this fellow. He won everything that he contested, and I followed him around like a starving dog, because he was a vital force which I needed to keep me alive. This man, this paragon of goodness and power, was Milo of Kroton, the greatest athlete of our time. I can see that you had guessed his identity some time back.'

We had arrived at a house. Lights glowed in the porch, and I could see wooden pillars holding up a roof of thatch over a terrace which fronted the garden. Beneath the roof, which was whispering in the light land-breeze, sat a woman with folds of linen over her knee. Her head was bowed, and a thick tail of plaited golden hair hung down to her waist, swinging as she worked her needle in the candlelight. With women I sometimes suffer acute premonitions, not of danger (which would be useful), but of my response to them. Before she looked up, I knew the effect that her glance would have upon me.

'Stand up!' Phalanthos cried out jovially. 'We have a famous man come to visit us.'

The woman lowered her needle and stood up, a long piece of blue wool dangling to the ground from her fingers. The linen slipped from her lap, but she caught it before it fell to the earthen floor. Her deft speed in doing this was a delight to me, as it activated the bright nobility of her expression and shook her tall, well-made body.

'This is my adopted daughter, Isotima,' Phalanthos said. He had not lost all his old wiliness, and had immediately spotted the moment of my enchantment. 'Let me warn you. She is beautiful, as you can see, but she is not as other women are.'

Isotima raised her head, and her eyes looked straight into mine. They were slightly reddened by her needlework in the bad light, but their slanted brilliance was not dimmed. From the light which poured out of her through those dazzling eyes, I knew that if she was not as other women are, it must be to her advantage. There was no madness there, no injury of the mind. She was a mate of the highest quality for me.

'What is the matter with her?' I asked, refusing to drop my gaze. 'I cannot sense anything that could be wrong.'

Phalanthos laughed, and sat down on a bench as his slaves brought water and towels to wash the dust from our faces, hands and feet.

'She cannot chatter like other females,' he said. 'Something happened to the poor child which made her not want to speak ever again. We have tried every inducement to loosen her tongue, but without success. However, she remains as lovely as you find her, but silent.'

Sadness descended upon me as I looked at her. She smiled, then returned to her work, the long golden tail of hair twisting and shining as it swung in the light, accompanying her unspoken thoughts as she struggled with the knowledge that my eyes had not left her.

'When did this happen?' I asked. 'Was it something in infancy? A great shock, perhaps?'

'Not at all,' Phalanthos replied with a rueful shrug. 'She stopped talking only a month ago. Before that she was just like all other women, her voice never still, tinkling away.'

There were other concerns which had to come first. This was not the time to explain to Phalanthos that his adopted daughter, whom he obviously loved very much, had been touched by a particular fate which was now with her. Any continuation of our discussion about her was prevented by the arrival of a cart with a deputation of three of the Sirisian fishermen, who had decided to speak to me off the sacred ground of the temple. They were simple, doughty characters, subdued after their fright at Sybaris, but underneath their respectful attitude I could see that they were restless and pugnacious.

The leader was a bearded, hook-nosed man of Arab appearance, whose scowling face belied his nature. He was a born diplomat, and took a long time to get round to what he wanted to say. When he finally got to the point, I discovered that the Sirisians already knew that the price which the mussel had told them to charge for the sacred fish was exactly the sum which had been stolen from me in Sybaris. When I looked to Phalanthos to credit this news, he told me that a rider could travel along the coastal plain from Sybaris to Kroton faster than a ship, if he had fresh horses along the way. More than that he would not commit himself to, which I took to be a sign that his old, two-faced ways were returning.

'Do you know if anyone has arrived from Sybaris by road during the day?' I asked him bluntly. 'It's the only rational explanation.'

'Yes, the only rational explanation,' Phalanthos concurred, with a meaningful look. 'But there are events which are very much under scrutiny in this city at the moment; I think you know to what I'm referring. News can be dispatched by non-human means.'

I put it to the deputation that I could not guarantee their safety from the gods, just as I could not guarantee my own. I did not know the full details of their previous lives, what they deserved or did not deserve. If the gods were acting directly through me in matters which affected them, then, perhaps, they would be better off remaining close to me until this phase of their involvement had ceased, then I could look after them as best I could. If they did not find this attractive (and I had my own misgivings about it, because there were another fifteen of them waiting in the sactuary), then they could take a risk and sail back to Siris, calling in at Sybaris to pick up a payment in compensation of their losses and suffering, which the city treasury would give them upon delivery of my note to that effect.

'The choice,' I said, 'is yours.'

'Do you feel that the gods will send you a message again through us?' the leader of the deputation asked me.

'I don't know,' I told him, 'and I can't say that I yet understand the first one. But it has often happened in my life that a coincidence proves to be no more than that, and the gods have nothing to do with it.'

The Sirisian deputation looked doubtful, saying together

that an exact sum like twenty-five Persian darics, thirty-eight Cyzikene staters and seventy-nine white gold Lydian electrons was enough proof to them that I was an instrument of divine authority, even though I did not know the meaning behind it. If I could affect their lives from afar as I had done on the day that the sea-monster had been caught in their net, then I could do so again, so there was no advantage to them in being under my immediate influence, as it was no protection against anything.

There and then they had decided to accept the money and return home, asking only that I should pray for their safe passage and make sacrifices and libations on their behalf in the great Temple of Poseidon, who, they suspected, was the god involved. Up until this time and our meeting, the god Hermes had provided a guardianship which seemed to consist of doing as little as possible and sparse rations, and they would be glad to see the back of his temple and sail away.

Once the Sirisian fishermen had departed with my note to the city treasurer of Sybaris safe in their hands, Phalanthos led me to another part of the garden, where couches had been laid out. The kitchen was close by, and his slaves served us food by the light of a fire in an iron basket which hung from a bracket set into the outer garden wall. As I reclined there, recovering from the encounter with the Sirisians and feeling quite pleased with myself that it had been settled so quickly, I began to think about Isotima. The sweet, mild wine of Lagaria had been served to me, a drink of high repute amongst doctors, who praise its powers of revivification. I caught Phalanthos smiling at me as I drank it, and wondered if he had been such a good host that he had chosen a vintage for me which would promote desire. We ate cold fowl and oat biscuits, and I waited for her to appear, not wishing to be too forward. As his adopted daughter and ward, she did not require the same protection as a child of his own blood; besides, she was a woman of twenty-five years at least, and would know her own mind.

When his slaves brought in a roasted hare and a huge loaf of freshly baked bread filled with goat's cheese, obviously the main dish of the evening, I got up and looked towards the house, walking up and down with my cup of wine in my hand.

'Are you restless?' Phalanthros asked. 'Perhaps the voyage unsettled your stomach.'

I shook my head, sipping my wine to hide my face.

'There is no need for us to dine alone,' I said offhandedly. 'I'm not dangerous. Now that my business is completed I can relax. You haven't told me about your wife and family. Where are they?'

'My wife is away at the moment. Her sister is married to a farmer near Cape Lacinium to the south. She has taken our two sons with her so I can have a little peace,' he replied.

'These sons are yours?'

'Certainly they are,' he said with some surprise. 'Who else's would they be?'

'I'm sorry, Phalanthos, but it was only because of your relationship with Isotima that I was emboldened to ask the question. You have been so charitable as to take another man's child into your care that I thought you might have done the same with these boys as well.'

Phalanthos frowned and sat upright on his couch, putting aside the bronze plate which was in his hand.

'What are you talking about, Kallias?' he said, appearing to be puzzled.

Without hesitation I apologised, thinking that I had offended him by putting a slur on his virility, but he assured me that this was not the cause of his confusion.

'Who is this Isotima you refer to?' he said. 'You must be mixing me up with some other person. Your life is so busy, Kallias, that I expect you have forgotten where you are.'

I sat down on my couch, very shaken. For a moment I believed I was going mad.

'Leogoras!' I shouted. 'Come here!'

He came running out of the kitchen with cream on his mouth, and stood before me.

'When we arrived in this house, was there anyone here?' I demanded.

'Anyone?' he echoed me, stupidly. 'How d'you mean?'

'Answer the question!'

'There were people,' he said, his hand slowly going across his lips.

'What people?'

'Well, it's quite a big place. I saw people round the back and working in the garden.'

Phalanthos looked at me from under raised eyebrows.

'Come with me,' I ordered Leogoras, then added. 'Will you accompany us, Phalanthos, please? We must sort this out.'

'Of course,' he agreed, coming to my side and taking my arm. 'You work too hard.'

I led them over to the terrace with the thatched roof, where Isotima had been sitting when we arrived. When we got to the place I saw that it was filled with bales of straw. There was no room for anyone to stand, never mind sit.

'This straw has been put in here recently,' I declared.

'That's right,' Phalanthos said. 'It was put here only three days ago. I'm having the roof repaired when the thatcher gets here from another job, which should be tomorrow.'

'No, Phalanthos!' I shouted, suddenly enraged. 'It has been put here since I arrived. Your adopted daughter was sitting here!' I strode between the bales of straw, hurling them aside until I reached the place, 'And she was sewing!'

Phalanthos sat down on one of the bales and put his hands in the air in a gesture of resignation.

'If that is what you want me to say, then I'll say it. That's what happened. This woman, whoever she was, was sitting here, sewing, and her name was Isotima. Please don't let it trouble you. We'll finish supper, and you can have an early night.'

I grabbed Leogoras by the wrist and led him to the place where she had sat.

'Did you see her?' I demanded.

'Yes,' he replied immediately.

'What did she look like?'

'She was a woman,' Leogoras replied with conviction, 'and she was sewing. Yes, and she sewed well, from what I could see.'

Tears of vexation came to my eyes: seizing him by the ear, I gave it a twist.

'You've learnt that much from what you've heard, bone-head! What else did you notice about her?'

Leogoras winced, bending down to reduce the pain of my hold.

'It wouldn't be right to speak about it in front of her master.'

'Why not?' Phalanthos said. 'We're not talking about a real woman at all.'

I released Leogoras and went a little way into the darkness of the garden, trying to compose myself. When I returned I told Leogoras that if he had been a slave I would have had him tortured to tell the truth, it was so important to me.

'When we arrived here,' he told me, 'I was exhausted after that long walk from the Temple of Hermes with all the baggage. If you remember I just flopped down at the side of the house and got my breath back. But I will say this, I heard you talking, and I heard the master of this house's voice, and there was a third voice, which was a woman's.'

My outrage was so great that I lashed out and knocked him sprawling into the straw. He bounced back, his fists raised and his eyes aflame.

'Don't you ever do that to me again!' he cried. 'I don't mind you twisting my ear, because that's just one of your tricks, but I won't be knocked down by anyone.'

'She was dumb, you fool!' I seethed. 'That much I know for certain. And her hair was in a long plait which went down to her waist.'

'What colour was her hair?' Phalanthos asked.

'Corn-coloured.'

'There are no women with fair hair in this household,' he assured me, 'nor in the households of my neighbours. You have seen something, Kallias, which is not unusual with you. You are always seeing things.'

'Yes,' I said, holding my head, 'I am!'

Phalanthos took my arm and led me back through the garden as if I were an invalid. As we went along the path he comforted me, giving assurances that the episode would go no further.

'It would sound bad if the world at large knew that the great Kallias had lusted after one of his own visions,' he chuckled. 'You do desire this woman, I believe?'

I nodded, taking Leogoras' shoulder to lean on as the full enormity of my passion struck me.

'Once that happens, then a man has little hope left of remaining sane,' Phalanthos mused. 'Falling in love with flesh and blood is hard enough, but with an apparition! Well, you have my sympathy, I must say. Come and sit down.'

We had returned to the open area by the flaming basket. A large group of men in dappled fawnskin cloaks and ivy wreaths stood by the wall watching me arrive, the fennel wands in their hands switching backwards and forwards in time with my slow, faltering steps.

'If it's not my old friend, the Sphinx,' I heard a familiar voice say.

Then its owner smiled at me, and I saw that he was now even more magnificently handsome than I had remembered. Although he had twenty more summers in him than I had, he had greater youth, the silver youth of the eternal. Even his eyes were brighter, his mouth rosier, his face more noble and refined now, with the ageing skin drawn tighter over his skull. Many have written about the beauty of Pythagoras, surely one of the most fortunate of men ever to have been born into this world. To be given the highest attributes of both mind and body, and to have survived envy and the fury of rejected lovers so long – he was now at least sixty, by my calculation – was a remarkable achievement. Yet I could not help feeling, even in my weakness and confusion, that as I looked at this paragon in his sacred Bacchic dress, his long silvered hair falling from his ivy-bound brows like a magic curtain, behind which his tirelessly active eyes glittered, always darting, flickering from one thing to another, that I was looking at a gifted lunatic.

'Kallias,' he crooned wickedly, his hand outstretched, but still with the votive wand dangling from it in an insulting manner, 'we've caught up with you at last. Are you quite well? You appear to be a little unsteady on your feet.'

The other revellers laughed, crowding together behind their leader to watch the sport.

'I've had a shock,' I replied, straightening myself up, 'but now I see that you're here I'm getting over it.'

Pythagoras flicked the fennel wand so it lightly touched my cheek. I stepped back, affronted.

'Only a blessing,' he smirked, 'but, at least, it is a real touch and not an illusion, eh?'

The gang of cronies and admirers bellowed with drunken laughter as I shrank away, unable to keep up my composure any longer. I turned to look for Phalanthos, needing to curse him for his betrayal. After all, I had come as a guest to his house, and he had fed me to these wolves. But Phalanthos had gone, retreating into the darkness to escape my anger.

'Get me some wine!' I snapped at Leogoras as I sat down on a bench and forced myself to look my tormenters in the face. They were all thoroughly enjoying themselves at my expense, pointing and cavorting about, shouting out jeers, taunts and insults as Pythagoras stood, one hand on his hip, gazing at me in sardonic mockery.

'So, how are you going to shoot your seed into a phantasm, Kallias?' he said sardonically. 'I suppose you'll have to go into one of your famous trances.'

The laughter became deafening, then the crowd descended on me, flicking their fennel wands so I received scores of lightning stings, which had to be taken in good humour as none was more than a kiss. Leogoras stepped forward to defend me and drive them away, but I signalled to him that all was well now. I had my self-control back, and I would handle the matter.

'I see that you still like to drink,' Pythagoras mocked as I took the brimming cup from Leogoras, 'and you manage to keep a good-looking servant. Will you ever learn to deny yourself, Sphinx? Think what all that indulgence has done to your mind over the years.'

'A toast!' I cried out, raising my cup and getting to my feet. 'To the nymphs and the naiads, the Nereids, the oreads, the dryads and the hamadryads, in fact to all those sweet spirits who have mortal form and can make us love them.'

I had hoped that this gesture of masculine comradeship would dissolve their glee, but I had miscalculated. Pythagoras merely gave me a pitying look and stroked his long hair contemplatively.

'You sadden me, Kallias,' he murmured. 'Not to have

improved at all over all those years since we last met! To be still making it up as you go along, wriggling and squirming to get round the truth . . . what can I say? I suppose it shows that you have a persevering spirit, but that's about all.'

With that he turned his back upon me and drifted away, followed by the majority, who were sticking to him in case there was more fun in the offing. An old man was left behind, supported by a big black slave who held him under the armpits. I recognised Anaximander, the venerable pupil of Thales of Miletos.

'Don't take it too hard, Kallias,' Anaximander quavered. 'We've been at it for days, you know, nothing but talk and drink, talk and drink. I'm exhausted, I must say.' He tapped the slave on the arm. 'Put me down next to my friend over there,' he said. 'We're going to have a chat together.'

The slave obeyed, and Anaximander settled down beside me like an autumn leaf, steadying himself on my shoulder. His ivy wreath had slipped down over his eyes, and the fawnskin cloak hung on his shrunken form. A strong smell of excrement issued from the old philosopher, and he shrugged apologetically as he saw me wrinkle my nose.

'I can't take this kind of festivity any more, but I thought I'd make this one my last,' he wheezed. 'Every drop of wine goes through me these days. But forget the stench, Kallias. It has nothing to do with what we want to talk about, has it?'

It was an act of kindness that he performed for me by staying behind after the others had gone, helping me overcome my humiliation. We sat and talked, until he knew that I had got over my shame. I watched him skilfully guiding me from one subject to another, nothing too serious or for too long, and I appreciated the wise skills which come to the best of us with age.

TEN

More than fifty people had arrived with the philosophers: disciples, hangers-on, friends and gate-crashers, as well as an army of slaves and retainers. After I had finished my conversation with Anaximander I edged into the thick of the throng which followed Pythagoras. I strolled amongst the starlit fruit trees and rose bushes, getting myself closer to him.

Phalanthos' slaves gave up trying to serve this crowd with wine and brought out the full skins, then went to the walls of the house and garden to beat off the general public, which was trying to gain entry at every point. The noise was intense, more like a battleground, with shouts and screams. The debate continued throughout the night, veering from farce to tearful seriousness, descending into the most acidulous imprecations, erupting into fisticuffs and scuffling, but the purpose was maintained. Once they had had their fun with me and I had been flattened to their satisfaction (though I never surrendered to their underhand methods of argument), some form reappeared in the rolling discussion which had, so I was told, taken the crowd in and out of several houses that day.

I was able to have some time with Herakleitos, an arch-enemy in thought but a companion who had shared some good times with me in the past. He was not as drunk as the others, complaining that his bowels had been inflamed by something he had eaten. For a young man he was not in good trim, too lean and sallow, and his caustic melancholy was now inscribed upon his features. We sat behind a hedge of rosemary, sheltered from the worst of the antics which were being performed throughout Phalanthos' garden, and exchanged accusations of inconsistency, fatuity, and dullness of mind, but we were aware that it was amusing to be in each other's company again.

'I can no longer take you seriously, though,' he told me, his arms wrapped round his knees as the air grew colder around us. 'I came here so that I could be present when the gods were put to death.'

I shuddered, glad that there was no-one else within hearing distance.

'We are at a crossroads, Sphinx,' Herakleitos continued. 'If we do not reject the gods as they are presented to us now, the choice for thinking men is going to be terrible. No sane, intelligent person can look at the world around him and let it speak. According to you he must block up his ears, except when he listens to ridiculous stories. What can happen to science? I have discovered, as you know, that the essential element of reality is fire. Few argue with me about this. Fire is the living sign of the great flux of the universe, the energy created between opposing forces. Nothing is still. We must change to keep up with our own world, but you say no. In fact, you would burn me in the very fire I believe in in order to preserve the hegemony of your infantile tales. Something must give way,' he added morosely, his heel making dents in the black earth, 'or we will always live in an age of fear.'

'You're quite wrong, of course,' said a voice from the other side of the rosemary hedge. A large, pale face was thrust through the branches; and it sneezed several times as the flowers showered their pollen.

'My name is Hekateios, of Anaximenes' party from Miletos, and I am known to you, Herakleitos,' he announced, his long, stooped body forcing its way through the hedge, 'and you know that it is my opinion that air is the basic substance of the universe.'

'Go away,' Herakleitos said wearily. 'You're too drunk to talk.'

'I am not drunk, I am ecstatic,' Hekateios replied, settling down beside us. 'I've been looking for someone to listen. Yes, I say that even Herakleitos is air. Everything is air. And, I tell you, even the stars and planets are air, their luminosity produced by rarefaction. Look at them! All air!'

He lay back, his arms behind his head, stared at the night sky for a moment, then fell asleep.

'There are too many ideas,' Herakleitos said woefully, getting to his feet and looking around the garden. From every corner of it came the sound of argument, some soft and harmonious, some furious and aggressive, some good-humoured, interspersed with laughter, some harsh and frustrated, straining to win a point.

'There are as many alternatives to the gods as there are gods,' I said good-humouredly, 'but I don't offer that as a defence of my beliefs. As you know, my argument is simple. I have faith.'

He turned to me, giving a glance of burning resentment, and stumbled off. I followed him. Before I could catch up, Pythagoras appeared in company with a man who was wearing a golden mask over his eyes.

'I want you to meet Omil,' Pythagoras said.

My hand was seized in a powerful grip which crushed my finger-bones together, a pain which I was intended to suffer. As I stiffly withdrew my hand I saw that the half-naked body of the reveller was superbly muscled, the cords of his thick neck as beautiful as columns in the temple. Black, curly hair tumbled down on either side of the mask, joined to a full beard in which moved a wide mouth lined with frighteningly white teeth. As this man Omil spoke, his lips moved far to each side of his mouth, showing great chunks of his molars, and I could see the workings of his tongue.

'You are the only one here who is wearing a mask,' I said, nursing my hand to show him that I had taken some hurt. 'Why is that?'

'It is my wish to be unknown, but now I am past caring,' he replied in a firm, manly tone which contained no trace of drunkenness. 'How are things in Sybaris?'

I looked round for Pythagoras, but he had gone.

'There has been some trouble in the streets,' I replied, edging away.

'Which do you prefer? Sybaris or Kroton?' he asked me,

staying at my shoulder as I picked my way between the people and headed towards the house.

With a strong sense of forboding, I said: 'I have not seen Sybaris in the best light. Given more time I might find it congenial. Which do *you* prefer?'

For some reason, maybe the man's natural authority, I felt that my question, given as a copy of his own, was insolent.

In answer he tipped up his chin and pushed the golden mask up from his eyes, and I recognised the great athlete and leader of Kroton, Milo.

'You prefer Kroton,' I said, bowing.

I had seen this man's prowess at the Olympic Games in Elis two summers ago, and six summers ago. Of all the athletes Kroton had produced, and there were many at that time, and of the highest ability, he had been the best. To watch him in action gave the human form of the gods meaning for me. Nature could not produce another beauty to rival our physique in its perfection. But these were not my concerns as I stood by the wall of the house in his company. Great athlete he might be, god-like even, but what was he doing here?

He had read my mind, seeing my consternation at meeting him.

This made him chuckle and rub his enormous chest, then he took me in his arms and hugged me like a bear, kissing my cheeks, then my mouth, thrusting his tongue into it.

I struggled, falling backwards so he had to hold me up. From here he took me entirely in his grasp, lifting me from the ground, then carried me into the house.

In a room lit by several oil-lamps he threw me down on a bed and started tossing cushions at me. When he had tired of this game, he sat by my side and stroked my face.

'Now, Kallias, friend of the gods, one of the few true ones I fear, tell me this: can Kroton ever become like Sybaris?'

I was terrified of this fellow. His strength was ten times that of mine, and I knew that Pythagoras had delivered me to him.

'Speak up, man! this is important to me!'

'I cannot say . . .' I began.

'You will say!' Milo boomed ferociously, his great teeth bared, 'because it is all that matters. The future is Kroton or Sybaris. Kroton or Sybaris. That is how I see it. However long it takes, wherever the world wanders in its thoughts, that is going to be the choice. I want my city to be the model for everyone. How can I do that with the gods as they are? They encourage decadence and indiscipline, but what is my other option? Pythagoras? The squabbling of vain, conceited old men? We must reform the gods. That's the way forward.'

After giving me a chuck under the chin which made my teeth rattle, Milo left the room. I heard him singing at the top of his voice as he went down the passage and back into the garden.

No sooner had the sound gone than two ruffians rushed into the room with a woman carried between them. They threw her on the bed, grabbed my wrist and manacled us together, then rushed out again without a word. I lay side by side with the woman, my mind whirling as I tugged ineffectually at the manacle which shackled me to her. She did not speak or move. Sitting up, I looked down at her face. It was Isotima, and she had been strangled with her own long plait of hair, which was knotted round her neck. Around her waist was the long red piece of wool which she had been using to sew the linen when I first saw her. I pulled at it, finding that it ran right across the floor, through the door and into the passage. Then a man entered, a wooden mask over his face, leaves in his hair and wine spilt all down the front of his chiton. He was winding the red wool round his hand as he entered, humming a dolefully whimsical tune.

'Ah, Milo said that I'd find you here,' he said, sitting on the edge of the bed and pushing Isotima's legs aside, 'and here you are. Don't worry about this creature.' He patted her hip. 'A common criminal; an infanticide, I understand, who accepted a few extra days of life as payment for her moving performance. But, you get the point, I hope? We have all had enough of spurious religion. No matter what kind of opinions we all have here, and we differ on many points, we are in accord on that. So, no more lies, Kallias, no more inventing visions to suit your own p-p-purposes. You have to own up, or stay chained to this dead whore until she gets to be as rotten as you are.'

He took the wooden mask off his face, but I had already identified Telys by his voice.

'Own up to what?' I asked.

'That you are a d-d-deceiver.'

Telys stroked his hair into place behind his ears, a morbid expression invading his features.

'If you only knew how I've wanted to believe in you,' he sighed. 'It would have made my life so much easier. But I've decided that you're a fake. What am I going to do with you?' He paused for effect, then took the end of my nose between his finger and thumb and squeezed. 'I know,' he said with sudden loudness, as if making an announcement to the world at large, 'we'll put you on trial.'

ELEVEN

Before I could regain my composure there was a commotion outside the room, and all the philosophers came crowding in with Milo.

Telys greeted Milo, and they embraced.

'Enemies, you see, Kallias?' Telys said with a sly grin, 'But what does that mean today? For a new age one needs new friends. Now, I say, the trial will begin. I'll defend you. I'm good at that. But I strongly advise you to plead guilty; then, just for fun, we'll ask for leniency.'

As they crowded round the bed, the cups in their hands showering me with wine, Leogoras burst into the room. He had been searching for me in the garden, and was wielding a stick. When he had pushed his way through to the bedside and found me lying next to Isotima, he hesitated, his expression askew with embarrassment, and muttered: 'I'm sorry. I didn't realise that it was all sport in here.'

'This is no shameless act of indecency, Leogoras,' I told him with all the dignity that I could summon up. 'I am lying here like this against my will, but it may not be too serious. Put down your stick.'

He obeyed, sitting on the side of the bed and clutching my ankle as if he would stop me being hauled off.

'The charge is simple enough,' Pythagoras declared, putting on a magisterial air. 'Foisting a lie about gods upon mankind is a severe accusation to bring against anyone, Kallias. Be prepared to argue for your life. All of us here have clear minds. We will give you the benefit of the doubt, if you admit any.'

As the philosophers laughed and playfully prodded me in the ribs, Leogoras saw the manacles which connected me to Isotima. He also realised that she was dead. The poor man was so appalled that he cried out, clutching at my legs.

'You see how his acolyte worships him,' Pythagoras continued above Leogoras' sobs and yells. 'I take this to be proof positive of the deceit which Kallias practises upon the untutored mind. This fellow, his servant, has told half of Kroton already that Kallias speaks directly to Herakles himself, and is spoken to. Also, so we hear, Poseidon sends Kallias messages. There are frequent visions, conversations, intercourse of all sorts, including the most recent evidence we have: the discovery of Kallias in bed with one of the Fates.'

The laughter of the philosophers went on for a long time. Some laughed so much that they vomited. I could see old Anaximander shaking in the arms of two disciples, who were so convulsed that they nearly dropped him. Meanwhile Leogoras moaned and hung on to me, and I found that to be my only comfort.

'Citizens,' Telys said, standing on the bed beside the corpse of Isotima and putting one foot up on her neck, 'be reasonable, I beg you. Is it fair to blame this one man for all the dishonesty which goes under the name of religion? Did he create the gods? Did he invent the stories? Did he, personally, pollute the popular imagination? Surely you can see that he is only the instrument of an ancient untruth. If we can get him to confess that, then I think it is your duty to release him with a caution.'

A shout of disapproval greeted this suggestion, and I was pummelled vigorously.

'Behave!' Herakleitos said, pushing Telys aside and sitting on Isotima's chest. 'Give me your attention.' The crowd quietened down, watching his seared, inward-looking countenance for the first sign of a witticism, but they were to be disappointed. 'I am angered by all this. This man's religion offends me. Once it was my own. I come from a family of royal descent, for whatever that may be worth, high priests by blood-right. And it is as a son of that house that I speak now, not a clown, nor a drunkard, though I am drunk, which has only served to make me even more eloquent than I usually am.'

Laughter began, but he cut it short with a savage gesture.

'No! It is no cause for humour. I am in earnest. If we are to begin our great enquiry into the true state of the world, we must scorn the whole idea of Zeus and the ridiculous Olympians. Let us all agree that prayers and sacrifices to these monsters of superstition are meaningless. Religious people say that they purify themselves by blood on the altar. Pythagoras tells me that this wretched woman, sad demented creature that she was,' here he bounced up and down on the ribcage of Isotima, forcing the remaining breath out of her lungs in a most ghastly, harsh sound, 'sacrified her own baby for some priestly purpose approved by the Carthaginians and their god Baal. She knew that it was against our law, but she went ahead. So, let us not joke too much about the power of religion. We think hers is a cruel, heartless faith. She thought ours was a piece of play-acting. It is neither of those things. Religion is the greatest danger to the sanity of mankind. There are many bad and few good men. If we arm the bad ones with a working lie – and that is my definition of religion! – then we are handing the future over to the storyteller who needs no truth, only lies to glide along the weaker levels of the mind.'

The sincerity of Herakleitos silenced everyone, including himself: putting his face into his hands he sat still for a moment, then got off Isotima and pushed his way through to the wall, where he leant his brows against the stone.

'Bravely spoken,' Anaximander quavered, 'but who dares to say it out in the street?'

'Kallias could,' Pythagoras replied. 'He has the authority. There is no-one in the Greek world who has such a reputation for seeing the gods. If he admitted that he had been lying, well, it would not be such an uphill battle.'

'But you believe in the soul, Pythagoras,' I challenged him, raising my fettered hand. 'Isn't that what you've told me many times?'

'Yes, I do.'

'Then what is the soul for?'

'We need not know its function, only that it is there.'

'A faint-hearted reply, if I may say so,' I persisted. 'And please don't give me your hypothesis that the soul is some transferable energy of being hopping in and out of various animal forms, or I'll go even madder than I am at this moment. None of that makes sense. The gods have revealed themselves; that is what I say, and what Hesiod and Homer said, and those who went before. We did not ask them to show themselves. The gods appeared to us by an act of their wills, and nothing you say or do to me will make me admit to anything else.' I sat up and threw my head back, shaking the manacles so they jangled. 'So why don't you act like decent, intelligent men and free me, then we can carry on our discussion as equals?'

My courage at making such a statement while outnumbered, under attack and without any allies, was warmly applauded, but it was my advocate, Telys, who turned the mood against me.

'Sphinx wants to go free,' he declared, 'but I think my client has unfinished court business before this can be granted. It is my advice that before he leaves he must re-affirm his credentials as a priest and completely recover his status as a great mystagogue.'

He leant over me and pulled Isotima's chiton up.

'The defence and prosecution agreed no progress could be made in this case until the accused had given proof of his integrity. What better character reference could he provide than a live demonstration of his passion for a dead truth.'

Everyone in the room fell silent, unable to believe that I could be forced into such an act. Telys looked around, his fixed grin lifted even further.

'She's ready for him. You see how Sphinx can arouse lust, even after all signs of life have gone?'

The woman's vulva was full of the juices discharged after death.

'Once the prophet has impaled this myth, surely we must take him seriously?' he said, sniffing. 'But we can't keep her here for too long. She's not as fresh as she was.'

I was paralysed with horror, watching him play with her. How could such foul mortification be planned for me? While he rubbed at her like a farmer will a mare, I did not remember those other times when I had seen injury and hatred produce such acts of bestial abuse, reducing victims to animalhood. But why did these thinkers, these wise men, these governors and generals, want to do this to *me*, a priest of the Mysteries? How had I come to deserve such treatment?

'This poor woman was some mother's daughter,' I said lamely, pulling Isotima's chiton down. 'Think of that. Show some respect.'

'Oh, no,' Herakleitos said, 'You thrive on your desires, Sphinx, you always have. You justify the gods through them, and your own actions. I'm a fastidious man, but I think it's right that you should fuck one of your own visions in front of us.'

Too shocked to reply I did not resist when Telys, Milo, Herakleitos and Anaximenes held me down. At this point Leogoras flung himself across my body, yelling defiance. Milo seized him by the locks, lifted him in the air, held him up by one hand for a while, then handed him over to some of the disciples to be restrained.

'We are determined that you shall go through with this,' Telys said to me, exposing my genitals. 'So you might as well show some enthusiasm.'

I sobbed, unable to keep my strength in place. All was water and madness. The corpse's knees were bent and her thighs pushed as far apart as they would go, and I was lifted up and pressed, flesh to flesh against her. I cried out when the contact was made, but they could not get me into her. With boisterous shouts they rocked me back and forth to sea-shanties, poured wine on her belly, stuck their tongues in my ears, prodded me, cradled my balls in the palms of their hands, made the cries of cocks, but all to no avail. I was not to be raised to the point where I would desecrate my living body by plunging into the womb of the dead.

'Stop that,' I heard Pythagoras say, 'but hold him tight for me.'

I was kept where I was, on my knees between the opened thighs of Isotima. Pythagoras sat on the bed beside me.

'Remember Egypt,' he whispered in my ear, his long fingers curling around my flaccid member. It instantly responded to his touch, standing, head swollen, a clear jewel of fluid sparkling at its eye.

Pythagoras gave me an intimate glance as he laughed, then he signalled to those holding me to push forward while he guided the aroused phallus. I cried out as the coldness struck, and I heard Leogoras' frantic bellowing as I was rocked in and out.

Then I went as cold as Isotima. It was nothing. It would be done. Soon it would be over.

I lunged into cold flesh with a driving will of my own, knowing that I could break through this ultimate insult and emerge intact, leaving it in silence, absorbed. With a score of hands on my hips, back and shoulders I thrust madly away until I came, a thin fish-bone of feeling.

When it was over and they had left me alone, sinking into their own reflections, I turned away from Isotima, drained of everything and said: 'My curse upon any man who ever speaks of this again.'

No-one disputed the justice of what I had said. Instead, they looked at me with the dumb wonder of those who can only relate another's suffering to their own fears, and in this they were now weaker than I was.

'This m-m-man deserves our respect,' Telys said eventually. 'He has gone through the ordeal that we set for him and come out of it well. I, for one, will never allude to the incident again, and I'm sure that I speak for everyone. Kallias has power, let us not doubt that. He can advise us what the gods expect, if the gods exist. For my part, I say that this test was necessary. Now I know that he is no weakling, and a practical man, I can mostly trust his visions once he shares them with me, which should happen shortly. That is what I have come here for above all.'

My heart descended as I listened to his glib obtuseness. All the fun had gone out of the philosophers, the stimulation of my debasement draining from their over-exerted senses. They began to sit with their backs against the wall or the bed, and I sensed that my hope for a quick resolution of all their nonsense had gone. Telys had come to Kroton to nail me down, and he would not let me go without getting what he wanted.

'What does it matter?' Herakleitos grieved from a corner

where he was slumped like a beggar, pessimism scrawled all over his face. 'Let the priests have the world. It's not worth having anyway. Men are bad. The gods don't exist, but if they did, they'd be as bad as men because they would only be copies of men. If we are created, then it is only in order that we should die; and if men wish to live, it is only because they know that they shall die. To have children is to bring more destinies of death into being. We have seen enough today to convince us that there is no natural good in anyone. It is all force and fire, nothing else.'

The philosophers declined into a black, grieving moroseness in the wake of this declaration. Their misery seemed to cheer Herakleitos up and he got to his feet, showing some of his old aristocratic bearing.

'Let the prisoner go,' he said. 'We are caterwauling because we are not immortal.' Then he strode from the room.

'Come back, Herakleitos!' Milo shouted after him. 'Don't slide off. We need your opinion.'

'He obeys no-one,' Anaximenes commented from the foot of the bed, where he was resting his face against the curved instep of Isotima's foot, 'and he's right not to take any notice of politicians. You don't think properly, you see.' He hiccupped and seized one of the corpse's toes, waggling it. 'You don't know anything. All you're interested in is power over other people's daily lives. To do what?'

'Yes, to do what?' snarled Hekateios, thrusting his mottled face into Milo's. 'My master is quite right. You politicians pervert philosophy. You twist everything to your ends.'

'That's not quite what I said,' Anaximenes called out hastily, as he saw fury start to discolour Milo's cheek. 'What I implied was a disfiguration of knowledge . . .'

The remainder of his speech was curtailed as Hekateios flew across the room and crashed into the wall after a heavy blow from Milo's fist. Pythagoras attempted to intervene, but he was violently pushed away by Milo and forced to keep silent.

'Don't say a word,' he warned Pythagoras. 'What irritates me most about you philosophers is how you preach nothing but impractical notions, and then pour scorn on those of us who have to govern.'

'But don't I help you?' Pythagoras asked gently. 'Surely I'm of some use in Kroton? We work together, don't we?'

There was a strong murmur of agreement, which Milo raised an arm to quell: however, he did not concede the point but shrugged his massive shoulders and sank into a resentful silence, frowning heavily.

'I want to hear what Kallias has got to say on this question,' Telys said lightly, breaking the tension as best he could, but keeping the argument alive. 'I've ridden long and hard to hear him discuss this kind of subject amongst his peers. There must be valuable wisdom which a man of his experience and knowledge has to impart.'

The response of the people in the room to this carefully contrived taunt was subdued but intense. Their contempt for me was almost tangible, but they dared not pass comment before I replied, otherwise they would have dismantled the precarious perch on which the tyrant of Sybaris had deliberately set me.

It was the kind of moment when a man has to puff himself up, to gain his full height and dignity and deliver a coherent, witty answer. There I was, tied to a corpse on a bed, surrounded by leering revellers in wine-stained fawnskins and battered ivy wreaths. Already the dupe of a cruel practical joke, I was the only one who could defend the old ways and their mysteries. I had been deliberately hobbled so my authority and reputation could not run against them. From this position of total prostration, I was now supposed to come up with cogent arguments about the nature of good government!

'Well, Kallias?'

Telys leant over and ruffled my hair as if I had suddenly become a schoolboy and he a teacher. I shook my head indignantly and glared up at him.

'You ask me for answers when you do not even have the courage to admit the real questions,' I said. 'All this is merely a disguise for your own confusion.'

'Confusion?' Telys murmured, stroking my head as I strove to get it out of his reach. 'Oh, I'm not confused. I know what I want.'

'Then tell me!'

'One insight into the way ahead. Could you manage that?'

'You shall have it once you decide what you think is wrong,' I said, 'without that I can do nothing. To me Sybaris is much like anywhere else. All its problems are small. Unrest about ephemera! Nothing! Where are the wars, the plagues, the barren queens? You don't know your luck.'

I would have gone on, wresting the argument away from the sham disputations back to the real question which Telys had dodged yet again: what did *he* perceive as the malady of Sybaris? But just then Hekateios sat up, snorted blood out of his nose, saw Milo in front of him and staggered to his feet, fists raised. Before he had time to strike a blow Milo was on to him, battering him about the head, throwing him like a bag of feathers. No-one attempted to intervene to prevent Hekateios being killed. They simply stood and watched as Milo, the great athlete, smashed the poor, puny drunk around the room, finally hurling him into a corner where he lay gasping, then heaving blood from his lungs.

Milo sat on the edge of the bed and nursed his knuckles, cursing under his breath. His eyes were numb and newly dark with flashes of surface fire, like those of an enraged bull which can only express its rage within severe limitations but yearns to set fire to the universe. Into the aftermath of his madness I dropped the vigorous seed of another question which, in view of Milo's violence, they might care to contemplate.

'The lives of people are not that dissimilar when they are reduced to the lowest level,' I said, above the coughing and spitting which Hekateios was doing by the door as he tried to get it open. 'Does it matter whether a man is a politician or a philosopher or a priest or a farmer? Our basic situation is the same. The conditions of life are tragic. Happiness is the worst part of it, because happiness creates hope for more happiness. That will always be the main challenge of government: aspiration. And I say that religion controls it best. Does anyone agree?'

But Telys was not in the mood to be sent on a detour. When the philosophers started to make sounds in preparation for a new stage in the debate, Telys silenced them and stabbed a finger in my chest.

'You have seen a vision which has a bearing on the future

of my city,' he hissed, his sharp eyes boring into mine, 'and you hid it from me. You saw fit to tell this man, a vine-pruner!' (here he prodded Leogoras in the back) 'and a notorious gossip, now everyone knows about it. The lowest begger in Sybaris knew before I did. Now, I want to hear it from your lips in front of these men. Let them judge what it is and what it's worth.'

'This is not the place to do that,' I said. 'It would debase that which has been revealed to me.'

'Then let it be debased,' Telys retorted. 'Convince me that your vision is true, and I will commit the city to your care and retire to grow grapes.'

Hekateios rushed into the room with an axe upraised in his hand, heading straight for Milo, who was bending over his fist examining the damage he had done to it. With a scream of fury Hekateios lunged forward to strike at Milo's head, but Leogoras was too quick for him, grabbing his wrist in a dexterous hold and throwing him while holding on to the haft of the axe. As Hekateios fell, his voice at the highest pitch of frustration and spite, Leogoras used the axe in one swift motion, severing the hand of Isotima which was manacled to mine, then hurrying me to the door past the astonished philosophers.

Once we had pushed our way through the crowd around the door of the house, my bloodied manacle hidden in my sleeve, Leogoras took me to a quiet part of the garden.

'We must leave this place,' he urged me. 'These people are out of control. They will end up hurting you.'

'They have not frightened me, Leogoras,' I said. 'This is not the first time that I have been manhandled by my opponents in intellectual disputes. Get me a cup of wine, if you can find one. Something strong. And something to eat.'

Leogoras pleaded with me to take his advice before further trouble overtook us, but I was adamant. The clever trick which had been played on me had not made me angry; on the contrary, now I could see how these men, philosophers and politicians alike, desperately needed the gods to hold their minds together. Without those sacred bonds there would be madness and anarchy in our world. In their mortal weakness they had made a target of me in order that they would not have to mock the gods firsthand and take the ultimate risk of alienating the creative force which made them question life so much. But they had to move forward, these restless men, and the gods seemed to be in the way. This was their error, of course. To perceive the gods as a stumbling-block is always an excuse for misunderstanding our position in relation to them.

Leogoras returned with a wineskin and a piece of cold chicken wrapped in pastry. We had to pound the wineskin to get the wine out of the neck, but once it began to flow I found it rich and sweet. Leogoras suggested pouring some of it over my wrist to help us work the manacle off, and we tried this but without success. As I was eating the chicken a figure approached us, standing tall and white as a ghost in the darkness.

'Is that you, Kallias?' a voice said, a voice I knew.

'Who wants to know?' Leogoras demanded belligerently.

'Xenophanes?' I asked, lifting my hand.

The figure came forward and sank to the ground beside me.

'Here's my hand,' he said, fumbling with mine. 'Oh, what's this?' He had encountered the manacle.

After I had explained what had happened, Xenophanes was silent. Of all my adversaries over the recent years, he had always been the most pungent in argument as well as the most erratic. As a philosopher he did not suffer from the mystical obsessions and inconsistencies of Pythagoras or the misanthropic disdain of Herakleitos. However, as a campaigner against our religion he was the most resolute and unswerving. Many hated him, and he could not travel as freely as he should have been able to, often being forced to disguise himself as a musician.

'I declined the offer to participate in the stupid prank which was played upon you,' he said in his light, silvery voice. 'As a friend I wondered whether it was my duty to warn you about it, but then I thought, Kallias has the wits and strength to be able to cope with that little bit of nonsense. Have you recovered?'

I assured him that I had, and offered him the wineskin to toast our reunion.

I could hear him banging and crushing the wineskin to get something out of it. When he had finished he tossed it away.

'Empty, like the heads of these fools,' he said with a laugh. 'Pythagoras can't make up his mind whether he wants sense or some religion which he has made up for himself. The only reason that he brought us all together was to confirm his own bewilderment. The man wants power above all things, but he won't admit it.'

'And what about yourself, Xenophanes?' I asked him. 'Where are you now with your thoughts?'

'Where am I?' he chuckled lightly. 'Sitting in the dark.'

'We are all doing that tonight,' I countered, 'but seriously: have you anything to tell me? We have some time.'

Leogoras reminded me that he was definitely of the opinion we should move on, but I told him to be quiet.

'When we spoke last, had I reached the conclusion that there is one superior being?' Xenophanes said melodiously, a touch of satire in his sing-song, reminiscent of a liturgical chant.

'No, you had not,' I replied, 'though I did suspect that you were edging towards that.'

'Ah, you're so perceptive, Kallias. You know what I think before I think it myself. Did you foresee that I would say that this superior being is God, All and One, and nothing like the mob of hedonists and delinquents that you adore.'

I politely requested an account of his reasoning, which he gave me, acknowledging my patience by nudging me with his shoulder.

'I can't resist the temptation to poke fun at the ridiculousness of your ideas, Kallias. You're an intelligent man, but you're afraid to face up to truths which are unavoidable. You know as well as I do that we've grown out of that stale folklore which was passed on to us by the poets. It never had a proper philosophical base. What I now argue is that God is One, Omnipotent and Spherical.'

'Why spherical?'

'It is the supreme form, possessing an eternal dimension.'

'Only on one plane, and even that is not infinite except in that it has no end.'

'What else is infinity?'

'You can see all round a sphere,' I argued. 'Can you see all round this God of yours?'

'You can't see all round a sphere *at once*.'

'Can we go now?' Leogoras muttered from beneath a bush, where he had laid his head.

'Also, my God was not born,' Xenophanes continued, 'because the perfect cannot be born of the imperfect. My God is unconceived and eternal.'

'He's certainly unconceived by me.'

'Follow me closely, Kallias,' Xenophanes urged me, putting his head close to mine. 'There cannot be a number of gods, because that would necessarily imply that some were superior and others inferior, and the concept of an inferior god is not one which a sane man can accept.'

'An inferior god is only inferior to a superior god,' I rejoined. 'All that means is that he or she recognises a greater power which must be obeyed. What's inconsistent about that?'

'A God cannot be inferior to anything,' Xenophanes declared obstinately, 'that is the definition of God.'

'Your definition, perhaps, not mine.'

There was a pause in our discussion. We heard fresh waves of noises coming from the house.

'Are you still living at Elea?' I asked Xenophanes, sensing that we had gone as far as we could for the present.

'Yes,' he replied, 'I am, but I may move soon.'

'Is it a good place to think?'

'To be poor is easier. I'm glad that we were able to meet.' He stood up and brushed himself down. 'It sounds as though they're warming up to some new atrocity in there. This is only the old frenzy, you know that? Orpheus is not dead. Bacchus is not dead.'

'Nor are they spherical,' I said, 'which may be why they remain popular.'

Telys came to find me in the garden. He humbled himself, begged my forgiveness first, then my blessing, then all the others did the same, every one of them, even poor Hekateios, who had been granted some more time before his exile would take effect. Pythagoras, Milo, old Anaximander, Anaximenes, all the burning disciples, the youths with furious notions and ideals, knelt in the earth. Each one of them touched the iron of the manacle in a votive manner, full of respect, and when the metal was removed from my wrist by a slave with a hammer and chisel, the manacle was taken by us all to the Temple of Hephaestus the Softener, the blacksmith god whose furnace is the daytime sun. From there we went down to the shore and strolled arm in arm by the sea, a great company of men who were together in thought and reverence, some of us breaking away to bathe, others seeking the shade of the woods to sleep off the wine. I remained on my feet to the end, Leogoras by my side, knowing that I had behaved throughout in a manner which befitted my dignity and beliefs.

Before we parted, Milo held a short ceremony of farewell on the shore, and the outside world restored its grip upon us. The enmity of Kroton and Sybaris had not yet hardened into what it would later become. There had been much embracing and affection shown, but Milo the Athlete, the Clean-Living, the Pure and Healthy, had a final point to make. As Telys stood, isolated, alert, his sense returning from the Bacchic madness he had shared with us, Milo hung around his neck, the severed hand of Isotima the hand of Fate, and pushed him away.

TWELVE

We set out for Sybaris later that morning, a sombre and thoughtful part of Telys' retinue, thinking over all that had happened and trying to sort it out in our minds. I say *our* in this context, because Leogoras had, by his conduct, become a living part of myself, and I had taken him into my own awareness of life. If I had a pain, I shared it with him. If I had an idea, I put it to him. Any distrust which I might have had became inconsequential. Indeed, he could have been the spy whom I suspected (certainly he was a blabbermouth!), yet I could forgive all that had gone before. He was not my equal in any way, let that be understood, and he served me rather than I served him, but we were part of each other, with a dominance on my side. That is a union of sorts, one that Xenophanes should study if he wished to comprehend the various subtle relationships between superiority and inferiority.

Telys maintained his new attitude of careful amity, riding close to me, raising questions he had heard debated amongst the philosophers. When he told me that it was Pythagoras who had recommended me to him as the *best of a bad bunch* (something I should have guessed by now if my mind had not been in disarray), it angered me.

'The only thought and culture that we have in Sybaris is derived from elsewhere,' he explained, 'except horse-dancing. Other cities have someone, some poet or thinker, even a craftsman who's worth something. We have no-one. Everything in that line is second-rate. We borrow, we steal, we act as we do in trade, buy cheap, sell dear, and we glut ourselves on the wrong kind of quality. I thought you would strike sparks off us. You have seen things. Everyone knows that. So has Pythagoras, but now I am beginning to think he is an intellectual impostor. What he has seen is unworthy. It is not a revelation, like yours. It is a shiny mathematical sum. To my mind, Sybaris has been influenced by enough mathematical sums.'

There was a point here which I had to concede. Either a city had a creative way of looking at itself, or it did not. I put this to Telys, adding that it seemed to me that whether people came up with a worthwhile culture or not wasn't something that could be organised.

'That is a priest's answer,' he replied. 'You will if encouraged, now go on to say that if Apollo wished to hear new music played in Sybaris he would touch one of the citizens. But until then we must play other people's tunes.'

'The gods could be petitioned . . .' I began to say.

'Every artist goes through that rigmarole in his mind every day, petitioning for inspiration. If you'd kept your eyes open you would have seen them in the temples, asking the Muses for help. But nothing happens.'

'That doesn't mean it never will.'

Telys laughed and ruefully rubbed at the back of his neck.

'If you knew what I'd been through trying to get some sense of identity, some inner pride, into Sybaris, a pride that was nothing to do with its wealth,' he said, 'but every time it came back to money. I supported a group of playwrights and helped them to produce their work, giving them the best stages and actors we had. I thought that if I gave them enough time they would come up with something like the dramatists in Athens.'

'What went wrong?'

'First, they had no talent. It was all students' stuff, the flush of new knowledge on the adolescent mind, all that kind of thing. No new mysteries revealed, nothing that got inside the city, no pointers to the future. It was just hysteria, really.'

'Did people come to see these plays?'

'I made them. For a while I said that it was as important as attendance at the temples. At the end they used to sit there in silence, listening to these fools ranting on. And they'd applaud obediently, go home and forget about it.'

'You must have been disappointed.'

'So were the playwrights, when I sent them to one of our salt-producing colonies,' he retorted bitterly. 'I insisted that they should pay back all the money which had been invested in them. By my reckoning, they should be home in about twenty years.'

I could not help laughing, though his expression gave me little encouragement to do so.

'Do you accept that the whole experiment was a mistake?' I asked. 'Maybe these writers were fighting against impossible odds.'

'I gave them every opportunity,' Telys replied, glowering at me. 'What finally put the cap on it for me was when I commissioned all five of them to come up with a new form of drama which combined the best of horse-dancing and the theatre. The result proved that they were not only unable to adapt, but had learnt nothing, whereas we have both learnt a lesson, and it has convinced me that you are the man we need.'

I mentioned my money, and he brushed my concern aside.

'It is waiting for you in your house,' he said, a smile warming his face, 'guarded by the servants of your household.'

'My house? My household? What's all this?'

'You now have your own establishment. The city will pay living expenses, and you will have a free hand in all the temples. Now the air has been cleared, we can move ahead in an atmosphere of trust.'

I looked across at him, taken aback by the warmth and purpose in his voice.

'This was all a stage that we had to go through,' he said, one hand on his heart, 'now we are at the real beginning.'

The journey from Kroton to Sybaris along the coast road means crossing eight rivers. As we left Kroton it began to rain, lightly at first, then heavier. To the west, in the mountains, we could hear thunder. Within hours of the rain starting we could see the effect on the smaller water-courses, which quickly filled up. We hurried along, not taking shelter, our horses sliding about on the thin layer of mud that formed on the earth, which had been packed and baked by the summer.

When we reached the Aesurus river, it was already swollen and discoloured with flood water. Telys decided that it was still fordable, and sent two horsemen in to test the crossing. They had to turn back when their mounts began to lose their footings. We then began to follow the river upstream to find a crossing, but as we progressed, the storm in the mountains increased and the river rose before our eyes, now carrying trees and rubbish from the higher ground. It was early evening and already dark when we came upon a place where we could cross by a wooden bridge, which was on its last legs. One by one we led our horses over, then entered a deep wood to be out of the rain, which had redoubled in force.

We were now in the foothills of the mountains. The grey rocks glowed above us through the slanting rain, and it was treacherous underfoot. To ride our horses became impossible, so we led them between the pines, the branches scratching our faces and hands. Telys was ahead with the captain of his guard, following a trail of some kind, when there was a tremendous noise and lightning flashes not far away; shortly afterwards several large rocks crashed through the wood behind us, unnerving the slaves, servants and soldiers, who crowded together, making progress through the trees difficult. Telys returned and sorted them out into a single file again, promising that we would stop and make camp as soon as we found somewhere suitable. Everyone was drenched to the skin by now, and frightened of the storm's power as it continued to roll through the mountains. When the captain of the guard sent a message back that he had found a cave where we could shelter, everyone hurried along to get there as soon as possible.

It was a vast, pointed cavern which went deep into the rock, the floor covered with light green moss. At the back was a stream which spouted from a crevice, filling the cave with its sound. From what I could see, no-one had ever used the place for home or shelter before. There were no signs of habitation, no marks of fire, wood, bones, all those things.

Within a short time the slaves had gathered branches and built a big fire near the entrance. All our luggage was soaked and I had no dry clothes to change into, so I stood with the rest, steaming by the flames and watching the rain lash down into the wood. The thunder and lightning had ceased now, but the amount of water pouring out of the sky had not abated.

When I saw the first movements amongst the trees, I was not certain that they were real. Before I could be sure enough to raise the alarm, a slave who had been sent out to gather wood came running back into the cave, screaming and clutching an arrow stuck in the side of his neck.

Nothing happened for what seemed to be a long time. The rain slackened, a brighter light came into the sky, and our fire began to die down for lack of fuel. We had all been ordered to stay silent, which we did, except for the wounded slave who could not help whimpering in his pain. There were many movements between the pine trees now, flitting shapes, shrill, mocking cries, and the occasional arrow which flew into the cave and rattled on the sides.

The captain of the guard was of the opinion that our attackers were from the Durva, a clan of the Bruttian tribe which had never accepted the dominance of the Achaean Greeks since their first coming to this part of Italy to set up their cities. They had been in revolt for more than two hundred summers, and were hardened in their resistance to Greek rule of any kind. All citizens of Kroton or Sybaris who fell into their hands were killed as a matter of course.

There was a flight of arrows from the trees, some of which fell amongst the horses and panicked them. In the confusion I was knocked to the ground.

When I got back to my feet I saw a mass of half-naked tribesmen wearing fur and feathers, their upper bodies and faces painted white and blue, all standing out in the rain with their bare buttocks presented to us in the most insulting way.

The soldiers in our retinue instantly prepared to shoot arrows at these perfect targets, but Telys stopped them.

'They are only trying to provoke us so we can be counted,' he shouted. 'Let no-one speak but me. Keep very still.'

There were more than a hundred of the Durva, and we numbered less than thirty, only twelve of whom were armed. As the sun broke through the clouds and dazzled us with reflections in the rain, the tribesmen suddenly whirled round and charged us, hurling long ash-spears and stones from slings. Once these had passed over us, doing no damage except to the horses which we had tethered at the back of the cave, our soldiers fired an accurate volley of arrows into those of the Durva who were ahead of the rest, bringing several of them down, whereupon the remainder turned and fled, wailing and screaming. The captain of the guard immediately led his men out of the cave and captured the wounded tribesmen, dragging them swiftly back into the cave where they screamed and fought for a while, then lapsed into a sullen silence, their eyes closed as if in sleep, even though some of their injuries were severe.

The sun was clearing the sky of the last drifts of cloud. From our cave we could now see the ocean far away, and a great rainbow.

Telys crawled over to me.

'Can you use this manifestation of divine favour to persuade these people to leave us alone?' he said, pointing at the blazing arc of colours. 'Tell them that it is a sign that Zeus the Thunderer is displeased with them.'

'As diehards,' I replied, 'they probably believe that it is their rainbow, but I'll try.'

'You will? I'm amazed. You mean that we don't have to discuss the rights and wrongs of this?'

I gave him a look of contempt.

'This is an urgent matter. Do they speak Greek?'

'No. Anyone of the Durva who is caught speaking a language other than their own is put to death.'

'Will they exchange prisoners for our freedom?'

'The captain of the guard says that these men we have captured are willing themselves to death. Within a short time they will cease to be of any use to us. So, magician, you have ribbons in the sky and the most obstinate man in Italy.' He clutched at his ears, play-acting bewildered despair. 'You don't tell me that the storm was a punishment for my bad behaviour, my incompetence, my lack of proper human feeling; you don't talk about destiny? What must I think? A little wizardry would come in very useful right now. Do something! Look, the rainbow is fading. Get out there and make something up before it disappears.'

I refused, of course, not willing, even under that duress, to vulgarise my calling by an empty show of conjuration. Instead, as the rainbow melted out of the sky, I thought deeply about the kind gods who thronged the vantage-point of eternity to watch my life pass. I did not pray for our escape, that would have been ignoble, given the happiness I had sometimes known. If I was to die at the hands of the Durva and the false demons which they no doubt worshipped, then there was a significance in that. But I would ask nothing, leaving whichever god might have an interest in this confrontation to act.

The Durva came out of the trees again, lifting their skirts and presenting their bare buttocks to us once more.

Vapour was now rising from the grass as the sun's heat increased. Wild scents flowed from the forest. I saw birds of prey circling in the air, their thin screams as sharp as knives. Above us I heard the coughing of stags and the howling of wolves. Behind me the waterfall's music changed.

Out of the stream which spouted from the rock wriggled a mass of silver eels, which flashed over the floor of the cave, through the steaming grass and between the buttocks of the Durva warriors, shooting straight into their fundaments like well-aimed shafts. The Durva leapt erect, howling and screaming with fear, and fled. Before they could reach the forest, I saw the eels emerge from their mouths and fall to the ground, slithering back towards the cave.

I stepped forward to greet the eels as saviours, and in the hope of recognising a sign which the god might give me, to identify who had intervened so miraculously. The silver eels gathered at my feet in a great knot then disentangled themselves, forming three lines in the grass. When they were all in place, each slowly formed a letter, making words.

I read what was written. Once I had done this and committed the text to memory, the eels writhed in the grass again and made different letters and words. These I read, keeping the message in proper order. After the third configuration of the silver eels, they all wriggled away into the forest.

The awestruck soldiers, servants and slaves began to idolise me immediately, but I forbade it, advising Telys that we should be on our way and get clear of the place. He did as I recommended, but his questing eyes never left me, watching for signs of pride or the glimmer of residual magic, hoping to catch me out.

When he was about to kill the prisoners I counselled him against it, pointing out that if the god had meant those men to die, then action would have been taken to secure that end. They were left in the cave, by then in the last sleep before the death which they had willed upon themselves, two horses of ours which had been despatched because of their injuries lying beside them.

No-one asked me for the meaning of the writing which the silver eels had made upon the grass. Such was the reverence I received that a chair was made of branches, and I was carried shoulder-high once we were free of the woods. The motion of the human step below me was no comfort as I contemplated what I had been told at the cave, and I pitied those who carried me so cheerfully towards Sybaris.

That night we slept in a good stone house, the guests of a farmer, and the food and wine gave people courage to ask me to explain what had happened, even though they were still in a state of awe. Telys listened as I fended off the enquiries, nodding and smiling. From his attitude of dark, patient watchfulness I knew that he would approach me when the time was right and I would have to account for the mystery of the eels.

That night I slept in the farmer's bed, with Leogoras by my side. He could not sleep; wondering about the events of the day kept him awake, and the man was apprehensive about the eruptions of appetite which he had witnessed after my inner scene in his vineyard. I guessed that this was on his mind and soothed him, explaining that what had happened at the cave had been shared. Everyone had been privileged to see it, even the Durva. It had not been an inner scene of mine which had originated in my special powers, but a public demonstration of divine approval and support.

'That is what I do not understand,' Leogoras confided in me, his large wide-set eyes fixed on the ceiling, black waters mirroring every scrap of light in the room. 'We had just come from Kroton, where all that blasphemy about the gods had made my blood freeze. We were tainted and unclean, and Telys was one of the worst. Why did the gods save him? His conduct had been both dishonourable and irreligious.'

I took his hand and laid it on my breast.

'His destiny is not yet fulfilled,' I said, 'and I have had to change my views on what is blasphemous. To think without religion may be expected of us. Why should the gods be given the responsibility for everything we do? If they are limited by destiny, then they have many difficulties.'

'You are an impressive thinker,' he replied, turning on his side so I could not see his face, 'but I trust you. Now I will dream about those eels. There were so many of them! But you'll explain later.'

There was an unspoken agreement between us as we lay in the dark, that I would let Leogoras into what mysteries I could, and that it was up to me to calculate what he could understand. He was not born of the Iamidai. The sacred sounding-board of our family mind was not his, nor could I build it inside his head.

'Can impiety be useful?' he whispered, 'Even divinely inspired?'

I sat bolt upright, his question roaring into my half-sleep like a great wave from the sea.

'No!' I shouted, then: 'Yes!'

'Who is the god of eels?' Leogoras muttered, his doze unshattered by my reaction.

'Poseidon, of course.'

'Freshwater eels?'

I fell silent, racing through my calendar of emblems, favoured beasts and divine disguises, and not coming up with anything. The whole scripture failed to provide me with a clue about which deity was attached to either the concept or reality of eels. I had the divine message clearly in my memory, and I understood the sense of it, but Leogoras had unwittingly drawn my attention to the fact that I did not know who it was from.

'Leogoras,' I said, shifting over to take comfort from his warmth, 'it occurs to me that the gods can be overlaid, each one being partly the other. I have been thinking about what Xenophanes said to me at Phalanthos' house concerning the One God, and he may have a point. Our religion could be the scattered form of another, truer faith. Do you understand me?'

'I do, master,' he replied, 'but if we are the children of an age of scattered gods, what can bring us together? And,' he rolled over to face me, the tip of his nose touching mine, 'would that mean a better world?'

'Easier to deal with,' I whispered, 'but I won't see it in my day.'

Telys entered the room with an oil-lamp.

He asked me to forgive his intrusion, saying that he could not sleep, then came and lay beside me on the other side, the oil-lamp on his belly, its small flame rising and falling as he spoke. He was in a state of light-headed wakefulness, his mind refusing to calm down and let him rest. As soon as I had explained my last thought to him, relating it to the views of Xenophanes, I pursued the enquiry by bringing in Herakleitos and his notion of the constant flux of universal forces.

'If everything is affected by this flux, then the integration and disintegration and reintegration of any godhead becomes thinkable, doesn't it?' I suggested to him. 'The god which governs one moon, we'll say, is only a different version of the god which governed the previous one, or the one which will come after.'

Telys groaned, the flame on the oil lamp quivering as his stomach swelled.

'Don't speak to me of flux and uncertainty,' he said, 'not after what I saw today. That was living proof enough. All my doubts have gone. I sincerely believe in all the gods and goddesses, all the heroes, all the stories, all the poems and oracles, every article of it. To listen to you, the man who brought about this conversion in me, trying to undermine it is distressing; but then, today's occurrence was probably not all that unusual for a man like you.'

I avoided giving any answer to this half-stated question, not wishing to reduce the kudos which the defeat of the Durva had brought me, but I could not stop myself confessing to Telys that I was becoming confused.

'If I look at all these supernatural events they seem to cancel each other out,' I said, 'and I get a sense that I'm being teased in some way. When the gods are in that kind of mood they are very difficult to deal with. I must go over everything that's happened. All of these manifestations need to be carefully interpreted if they are to be of any use. If we act too hastily, without proper understanding, the delicate mechanism of these revelations can be destroyed. There is a precise meaning, which I must have time to find.'

'Is Sybaris doomed?' he asked me harshly, getting off the bed and pacing around the room with the little flame fluttering. 'Can you tell me that much?' An angry soreness throbbed in his voice. 'Did some god save us today only so he could destroy us for his own amusement later on?'

A suspicion had formed in my mind. I would have expected that Hermes was the kind of god to put together the elaborate display of power which had produced literacy amongst the eels. But Hermes is not a god who keeps quiet about his achievements. He tends to be conceited and boastful. It struck me as I watched Telys prowling around the room, that a god of some evil might have used our peril at the mountain cave to counterfeit goodness in order to produce a malignant result. I had been duped before.

'I must go to Enna,' I said, 'and enter the Underworld.'

Leogoras gave a horrified cry as he heard me say this, gripping my hand in fear.

I had carried a heavy burden since the episode of the eels. The message written by the slimy animals had been in the alphabet of Menos the Egyptian, letters more than a thousand years old, which had slowly changed to become ours but were now, in their original form, indecipherable except to the initiated. The decision to use Menos' alphabet was aimed directly at me. As a student at Memphis I had learnt all I could from the high priests, I had followed the eel-like twists and turns of these signs and their meanings, observing how notions bear their own lubrication on their backs once they enter the minds of men. The religion of those Egyptian priests was wholly that of the dead. I feared that the message I had received came from Tartarus, the infernal regions where the shades wander aimlessly, unwarmed by the holy sun. As I meditated upon these connections and apprehensions, I seemed to smell the gritty air of the builders' yards within the rising tombs of the Nile, where I had spent so many months, and I suddenly remembered the silver eels upon my plate in the seminary.

Telys put his face close to the tiny flame which was bobbing on the lamp's wick, very near to extinction.

'Are the signs very gloomy?' he asked. 'Be straight with me.'

He pursed his lips as if he were about to blow out the flame, then flickered his tongue like a reptile before drowning the light in a blob of his spittle.

'To go to Hell for Sybaris?' he said in a low voice as he opened the door.

'If that's where the truth is hidden, that's where I must look.'

'Have you been there before?' he said from the doorway.

'Only close, but never across the threshold.'

'And why do you suspect that Hades might be teasing you?'

'An intuition.'

'Could he be tempting you towards death?' Telys asked cunningly.

'There is no death,' I replied, 'unless life is present to experience it. How can there be non-being in such a universe as ours, where everything moves?'

He grunted and went out.

I was proud of my answers, even though I could not swear to them.

'I'd trust the eels,' Leogoras whimpered, his teeth chattering.

'You don't have to come,' I whispered in his ear.

'Oh, I do, I do,' he replied. 'To see if what you say is the truth. To my poor mind, to go to Hell, a man has to die.'

'Or conquer,' I said, putting my hands under his armpits and drawing him close, 'which is what I was endeavouring to talk about.'

We slept that way, my strange confidence clinging to the back of his fear, and I thought that our dreams interwined during the night, passing from horror to fearlessness, then from courage to quaking dread as the night-birds called and bears roared as they fed off autumn berries in the dark.

THIRTEEN

True to his word, Telys had provided me with a fine house in the wealthy north-western quarter near to the Temple of Hera, not far from the hostel where I had stayed after my first arrival; and therein he had installed Leogoras' wife and family, a move which I was glad of, as Leogoras was beginning to get in the way of my preparations for the descent into Hades' dark dominion, and was taking up too much of my time and attention. There were also seven good slaves, five of them female and all young, and a couple of Scythian bodyguards who lived in. Leogoras reverted to his role as head of his family, but he remained as my principal servant. I cannot pretend that he was glad to be rebuffed in this way, but I often assured him of my affection and trust. In my heart I hoped that the presence of his wife and children would dissuade him from accompanying me to Sicily when the time came. They were pleasant folk, full of good nature and high spirits, the best kind of country people, spontaneous in their celebrations, polite and thoughtful when it was needed. I became fond of his children; there were eleven of them, all lusty as lambs, and they lightened my dark contemplations during this strange time.

Telys left me alone, busying himself with the administration of his threatened state. He went to Siris himself to negotiate the gift of the temple in compensation for the death of the fish-merchant during the riot, and he returned successful. I must say that the conjunction of peace and domestic harmony with the anticipation of my dreadful pilgrimage was an odd one, but everything was allayed by the fame which I now enjoyed in the city.

A solitude was created for me. I became calmer, sweeter in temperament, and was able to devote myself to a study of both the Herakleian inner scene and its attendant manifestations on the Sirisian fishing-boat and the happenings at the cave.

I could not write out the full text of the message which had appeared in the grass in case it was stolen and taken to Telys by one of his spies in my household. But within the communication I discerned a rough poetic form, so I broke up the lines and made it into a rhythmical hymn, one that I could chant daily in order to keep the words fresh in my memory:

The face looks on thee
        through the mask,
turn not away
        to hide your endowments.
It is hopeless.
        Watch the gecko lizard
button-like in finding
        the eye-hole.
Its thread of silver slime
        is written for descending
a silver road.
Fly to the altar to lick ashes
        rather than blood,
on the counter-earth there are
        those who believe
that (here the text was illegible)
        grasshoppers,
        the blind pig,
        hot stones
        keep the hands
        warm.

It is not unusual for the gods to choose a seemingly inappropriate time to send forth a prophecy. They prefer not to be seen hitting the nail right on the head, but to creep round the side of an issue and slip their wisdom into the pocket of someone, as it were. I had no difficulty in recognising a sinister warning for Sybaris in what the eels had scribed for me, but the full import of the prediction was unclear. This was not an uncommon fault with oracular statements, but they were always induced by petitions and gifts, and the priestesses and priests were often mischievious or half-deaf when it came to passing on what the gods had said.

This writing which had been laid at my feet was a direct revelation of a divine mind, of that I had no doubt, but I would have preferred it if Sybaris had been mentioned by name, otherwise there was a chance that the god had sent the message to me because it was for my personal attention and referred to my private affairs. A connection that alarmed me was the one between the price put upon the Sirisian fish and the exact value of my treasure. This felt like a sardonic comment upon my wealth, a suggestion that I was guilty of avarice. Never, in my inner scenes over the years, had this question been raised, nor had my function as a channel for information, hints, clues or signs.

Now that I had received a rap over the knuckles, if that is what it was, I had to decide whether it was my fate or that of my client which was being prognosticated.

My reasoning, from the first, had been that as the miracle had articulated vague misgivings about wealth, then it was untrustworthy on two counts: one, that the Olympian gods have never cared one way or the other about how wealth was gained or by whom, provided that sacrilege or disrespect to them was not involved. They look upon prosperity as a legitimate gift, quite separate from ethics or just rewards on the human plane. If they wish to enrichen an immoral man they will do so, and not consider it to be any more than a temporary favour granted before they find the right moment to destroy him. The favour must be seen as part of the pattern in that man's fate, and that is all.

Why should the happy gods have strong opinions about money? It would make no sense. The powers which do brood about it are attendant upon Hades, the brother of Zeus, and he has a long-standing interest in the wealth of the world. He watches the rise and fall of trade, the value of currency, the needs and wants of people with money to spend. All the gold and silver and precious stones of the earth are his. The true worth of everything which mankind prizes most is governed by those metals and gems. Our commerce is a reflection of those valuables which he tosses from hand to hand while he listens to the thunder of our waggons overhead bearing produce, and the bump of our ships as they strike against the port walls. Whoever my little hymn was sung to, myself and my conscience, or Sybaris and its luxury, I knew where its meaning would be found: at the court of the great god of the Underworld.

In the event, it was to be many months before I went to Sicily. The weather closed in, bringing storms on the sea and in the mountains as the city prepared for its winter and I for mine. Few ships used the harbour, early snow blocked the Road to Prosperity at the high passes, and the Sybarites looked inwards, seeking their traditional pleasures behind closed doors rather than open banquets and festivals. With a touch of irony, Telys had provided me with a bursar to control my accounts while I was living at the city's expense: it was Herophantos, the condemned thief who was reported to have been killed while avoiding arrest for stealing my treasures. I had never believed this tale, even when it was brought to me by a court messenger, but I took offence at the nakedness of this show of Telys' power. To resurrect a dead man is the work of the gods. Those who pretend to have that trick up their sleeve are guilty of aspiring impudence. Although I knew that it was supposed to be taken as a joke, and I was glad to see the poor fellow alive after my last acquaintance with him in the pit, I complained to Telys about the appointment.

He came to see me on his way home one night, and explained that Herophantos had been the city treasurer under the previous administration. He was a very capable man with arithmetic but had no common sense, which had got him into trouble when he objected to the removal of several colleagues who had been accused of corruption. Now, having seen the error of his ways, he was glad to serve the city again in a minor capacity.

'Who knows?' Telys said. 'He might work himself back up to the top again.'

'Does he think that he's working for me, or working for you?' I asked. 'That would be useful to know.'

'He is part of a team, as we are. Did I tell you that some farmers who live close to the mountains followed our trail back to the Grotto of the Sacred Eels and found the Durva warriors, untouched by any wild beast or fowl, sitting astride the dead horses that we left behind?'

I replied that I did not remember him telling me this news.

'I've been very busy since we got back. Trade has slowed right down, you know. At least fifty days earlier than usual. Business is flat. Anyway, as I was saying, there were the Durva, feathers as perky as ever, riding the horses of Sybaris, all turned into stone. What d'you make out of that?'

I confessed that I would have to add it to my stock of unexplained phenomena for a while, but added a word of optimism, saying that the implication was a good one at first reading.

'The implication?'

'Yes, I think it might refer to an improvement in relations between Sybaris and the Durva, but I need time to work it out properly.'

Several days later I learnt from Leogoras that Telys had sent a deputation of eldest sons from the wealthiest families of the *azygous plutos* to find the tribal headquarters of the Durva to offer them a treaty of friendship.

The deputation did not return until the day of the solstice.

I was, by then, much more settled, having been left in peace to plan my journey and mull over the recent period when so much had happened. By now I was embracing many new friends, the priests and acolytes of Sybaris, people whom I had not consorted with in the early days after my arrival, because of their impious indolence and inability to perform any kind of sacerdotal service. However, a few months of hard work and instruction had purified them, bringing them back to the altars of Sybaris charged with a new sense of duty. Their loyalty was, I must admit, primarily to me. If my standing had not been so high, it would have been impossible to reclaim them from their idleness and dissipation.

The solstice is equally shared by the gods of light and the

gods of darkness, and I had set the ceremonial fires to be lit in every temple at the moment when the sun went down behind the mountains. As it happened, it was one of those dim, dove-grey days, and we had to guess when the sun had disappeared. I was officiating at the old wooden Temple of Hera, which had become a favourite haunt of mine, and I was surrounded by priests and altar-boys, when there was a commotion somewhere near the western gate at the end of the Avenue of Herakles. It was so loud that everyone ran to see what was the matter, but I remained behind with my party, following the liturgical procedures which I had laid down.

There was a speech prepared in my head, telling the citizens about my intention to go to Enna and enter Hell on their behalf, and I was determined to do it, come what may. Telys had, for once, kept his promise and not told anyone that I was going to the Underworld to save the city; but for that he had an obvious political motive. Once the people knew that I, a stranger, would take such risks for them, his tyranny would become precarious. The one unstoppable force in politics is sacrifice, as it is in religion. The old heroes did not understand this too well, but the measure of how the world has changed since the Fall of Troy can be taken against this dictum of mine.

The uproar had been caused by the return of the deputation. They were so emaciated that they could not sit their horses properly, and had been tied on with ropes. Every one of the young men had been castrated by the Durva.

Telys brought them to the Temple of Hera and stood with the crowd as I chanted my litany of petitionary prayers, hymns and libations to the god Hades, brother of Hera and therefore a deity who might share her temple, there not being one already dedicated to his worship in Sybaris.

It was only later that Telys confessed that he had accidentally left something out when he had told me about the discovery of the petrified Durva on their Sybarite mounts in the Grotto of the Sacred Eels.

Upon being touched by the farmers who had found them, they had crumbled to dust.

*

In spite of his dishonesty and deviousness, Telys and I grew closer together during the cold months. The tempo of daytime life had slowed right down, icy winds blew from the ocean and the mountains, snow often filled the streets, and people stayed in their houses. Sybaris, being what it was, used wine and sexual games as a means of warmth and entertainment. There were feasts, dinners, banquets, these celebrations occurring with everyday regularity amongst the rich, the torches of Eros and Bacchus being sent from house to house, each one trying to outdo the other in lavishness, spectacle and expense. This relentless pursuit of pleasure was, in fact, more of a flight from boredom, for this was a common malady in Sybaris, and a murderous one often attested to by suicides. The funerals of these wealthy unfortunates were always well attended, and I did hear of cases where the actual act of self-murder had taken place during a bout of festive drunkenness. One dinner which I attended had a band of Tyrrhenian businessmen as guests, and they had brought their rough northern manners with them, teaching the Sybarites the most outlandish nonchalance while at sex. It was the custom in their country, so they claimed, that a man and woman or a man and boy could have intercourse anywhere in the house or garden, and at any time. The acts of copulation or sodomy were so familiar that no-one ever bothered to take any notice, and it was a point of style amongst all the people, high and low, that no person should be curious about what was being done.

Once this was explained to the Sybarites they had, of course, to try it out, and this was pursued with all the zest imaginable, but the sight was reminiscent of children fighting in a playground. I had soon had enough of this foolishness and went my way, saddened by the waste. Such celebrations of desire need the gods to bless them. They should not be made in imitation of strangers. However, I later discovered that what the Tyrrhenians had said was true, even at funerals. No-one ever knows the name of his father up there, nor do people bother to knock when they go into rooms.

These days of feasting and entertainment took place in a time when my fame had risen to its highest peak. I was wanted by every host. I was deluged with invitations and I responded by accepting as many as I could. Most of them were from the well-born, but I saw to it that I was seen amongst the poor whenever they had the temerity to ask.

After a while this popularity of mine had an effect upon Telys. I began to hear things which he had said about me; that I had extraordinary powers of mind which would make men see what I wanted them to; that I took so long to come up with my prophecies that one might as well wait for the future to happen, because by the time I had spoken all would have been revealed anyway. These, and many other cuts and jibes, were passed on to me by well-wishers.

In return I sent answers by means of the same grapevine of gossip. To defend myself from the worst aspects of my new fame as a true instrument of the gods I had, in fact, been determinedly hard in turning sick people away from my door, telling them that I was not a physician, nor had the gods ever used me as such. When one of the *azygous plutos* offered me half of his fortune to cure him of a falling sickness, I knew that my refusal, and the manner of it would reach Telys' ears. I told the invalid that no amount of money could make me what I was not, nor could the same take away what I was. This seemed to clear the air for a while and Telys' suspicions abated, but I remained aware that he was forever vigilant, watching to see if I ever reawakened my ambitions to rival him.

And with my fortieth winter on earth came, yet again, love. As ever dangerous and dancing, promising all, giving all, then dying. Over the years I had come to know my readiness for this flourish when it comes to the cold time. Someone will appear in my sight, a flame will be lit, often against my will for the sadness it will inevitably bring, but I must go along with what happens.

There were ten or twelve false starts by the time the first snows appeared on the mountains, loosenings of the dormant blood as it awakened. In my anxiety to be in my stride, subduing the painful melancholies and ecstasies into manageable modes, I imagined myself in love to get it over with. Sluggishness and inconsistency in my affections convinced me each time that I had misread my heart, so these affairs were short-lived. Maybe it was my fear of the great force which always came once I had been plunged into these adorations of humankind that made me compromise, but once Luderma had appeared in my life I threw away all weak-heartedness and entered the communion of delight and suffering which is mortal love, god-like but doomed.

She was from Rome, a niece of King Tarquinius Superbus' first cousin, widow of a noble priest-magistrate of Veii, who had owned lands in Tyrrhenia near the mouth of the Tiber. After her husband's death Luderma had quarrelled with her eldest son, heir to the estate, who had driven her out. Defenceless, she had joined Rome's Tyrrhenian community, which looked upon the king's cousin as its leader. While living there she had become interested in antiques, seeking Greek, Minoan, Egyptian and Assyrian artefacts through Sybarite merchants, also doing some business in supplying the market with Tyrrehenian ware.

Luderma was about my age, her beauty of that fleshy, rose-haunted kind that a grown woman carries so well in the wake of children. When she came to my house to ask me to sponsor a youth for a post in the temple, I honestly took her for a woman ten years younger, such were her unspoilt looks. Her last child had been born eleven years before and, since then, although she had had several lovers, no further children had come to her womb. She was a flushed, jumpy creature when I met her, her Greek so bad that I could hardly bear to hear it spoken, but her brightness and cleverness were obvious, shining in her eyes. When she stood on the steps of my house, about to leave, her arm around the shoulders of the dim, ignorant youth, who had failed to impress me at all, she pleaded with me to make an exception in the boy's case because he had no other prospects of a career.

'If in doubt, make him a priest? Is that the idea?' I said scathingly. String-pulling was endemic in Sybaris, practised by high and low. I knew that the awkward youth at Luderma's side was the fourth son of a wealthy family and the despair of his father. No-one could educate or train the boy, because he was virtually an imbecile.

'He is able to carve the meat,' Luderma said in her vile Greek.

When I taxed her to explain further, I discovered that she was asking if an apprenticeship as a reader of animal entrails and organs might be a possibility.

She could not have made a more provocative suggestion. If there is a branch of divination which I hold in contempt, it is the interpretation of auguries from offal. What wisdom can be wrung out of a bleeding liver? It is with embarrassment that I recall my father's attempts to teach me the basic rules of this butcher's rigmarole. I had no difficulty in comprehending that the killing stroke of the priest at the altar is an illumination, a flash of creative fire between the human and divine, nor that blood is the headiest drink of the gods, but no self-respecting priest should be expected to root around in the bowels of dead offerings to find truths which have not already leapt out at the first liberating cut.

This aversion of mine has caused trouble in many courts and households, but I will not shift my ground. In order to avoid arousing too much hostility amongst my colleagues, including, I have to say, priests of the Iamidai itself, I refer to the reading of entrails as a lower branch of our learning, and recommend that recourse to it should be infrequent.

So, my rejection of Luderma's friend's son was not withdrawn. I had no intention of admitting an idiot on the grounds that he had been taught, at some time, how to dismember a chicken. I put this to her in those terms, allowing my indignation to show through, and she began to leave, with the sobbing youth held to her side. As is my custom, I insisted upon giving them both a Heraklean blessing as they left my house, but I had to run down the steps to do it as Luderma was upset and hurrying away as fast as she could.

From the moment my clenched fist pressed against her forehead our tragedy began, culminating in her suicide about a hundred days later.

In the process of our affair she was called back to Rome by her uncle, but she refused to go, thereby losing her house and income, which was confiscated by him as her protector. I was accused of consorting with the agent of King Tarquinius Superbus, an untrustworthy monarch as far as Sybaris was concerned, but this mattered nothing to me. All I thought about was Luderma. She came to live with me, and for days we saw no-one, locked up in our rooms, often forgetting to eat or sleep as we followed the harrowing path of Aphrodite's hunger. We became shells, spectres, blind and deaf to the city outside, our happiness as taut as a lyre-string, all thought of Hades held at arm's length.

But life in Sybaris went on as I and my lovely matron spent ourselves. Kallias, professor, priest and politician, sometimes walked the streets and carried out his business. Luderma even continued to trade with her contacts, collecting bits and pieces which she kept in the bedroom, clustered beneath the smiling Priapus. We went on with an existence which shimmered above the tumult in our hearts, but which had little or no reference to it. We were mechanical in our routines, but not in the way we consumed each other. That became more and more devastating, until I saw how it must end and begged her to leave me before it was too late. I confessed that there had been girls, women and youths who had suffered before her, emerging haggard and heart-torn from my winter. But she would not listen, my Luderma. Her life was over anyway, she said, this treadmill of lovemaking had done that, and love's end would be the beginning of death. So, let one run into the other! Why break up the natural sequence of events?

When her final sickness came, it flowered with the crocuses. She got ready to go to the Grottoes of the Nymphs on the Lusias River, where a cure was to be had. By then her large, excited eyes were ringed with purple, and her nose was sharpened by wasting. All the liveliness had gone, used up by my ceaseless worship of her body and spirit. She died on the Road to Prosperity, throwing herself under the wheels of her own waggon, though some said that she fell to her death because she was too weak to stay in her seat.

Upon receiving the news of her death from Leogoras, I sent him to buy me a certain breed of pig which I had seen in the swine-market, a pig marked with a saddle of brown. Leogoras did as I ordered, and returned with the beast in a cart. When I took the mule out of the shafts and began to pull the vehicle through the streets of the city down to the dunes, a crowd followed me, urchins and dogs leaping at my heels. It was grief's burden which I hauled through Sybaris, and my prayers were private, not priestly, as the old cart rattled down over the stones, the pig squealing as if it had already got wind of its fate.

Every diviner favours one beast above another. In the temples of Sybaris, the white ox of the plain is the most valued as an altar sacrifice, and the *azygous plutos* go to great lengths to obtain the best, with the widest span of horns. Goats are not popular in the city, possibly because the fertile land is wasted on them, and not many are kept except in the mountains. Sheep are everyman's standby, and all temples stink of them, but I am a pig man. The offering of a saddled pig for the corn-goddess to ride is at the crux of the Greater Eleusian Mysteries, and Zeus himself was suckled by a sow in the Cretan cave and kept alive. It is the highest gift which can be offered to Herakles and to Aphrodite because it is all edible, down to its tail, and the blood mades the sausage which was the prize when Odysseus beat Arnaeus.

I took the cart down to the sand at the edge of the lagoon and pulled it as far as I could into the sea. Luderma's voice began to speak as the waves thrashed around the axle. As I seized the pig by the ears and dragged it to the front of the cart, its eyes expanded, its snout contracted, and I saw my love looking up at me without fear. Then my knife freed her, and she sang in the severed throat.

Leogoras took the dying pig from me as I sank to my knees in the surf, all the strength leaving my limbs. I held on to the shaft of the cart and wept and wept, ducking my head into the sea to join salt with salt in the love-goddess' pig-pink foam.

It was cold, that ocean. When Leogoras led me out of it and made me run back through the silent crowd, across the dunes, through the city, it was to prevent my blood turning to ice. When we got back to the house he put me to bed with a quart of heated wine in my stomach and camphor under my pillow.

When I awoke the next morning, I saw that the thoughtful fellow had turned Priapus to face the wall.

He must have had an intuition that this was a merciful precaution to take; for the man had never endured a winter with me before or witnessed the ferocious self-disgust which the death of love engenders in me. Oh, for my seat by the pool at home in Elis and the understanding of my servants! What I would have given to be there, now that Luderma had been destroyed! The void which I now entered ached more because I was away from those familiar, dependable surroundings, and the phallic wrong was harder to right as I pondered on the course of Luderma's destiny, slain by my weapon, my edge and my ever-raised arm, with no child to redeem us.

The madness lasted half of a moon, and it would take too long to make an inventory of my strange deeds. When an action is not accountable to any reason but those which are hidden behind screens in the mind, it is pointless to seek a pattern in them. The mind keeps its shadows and its secrets, allowing the play of light upon what the gods will, for the mind is the inbuilt envoy of the divine power. We only see what we are meant to.

FOURTEEN

Since my visit to Kroton I had been turning some ideas over in my mind, some of them philosophical, but the one which appealed to me most was to do with education. The college which Phalanthos had founded at the Temple of Hermes in Kroton had struck me, at the time, as a vain and empty thing for him to do: he knew nothing, so how had he set himself up to teach it? Had no-one ever checked on his standing amongst his coevals? That Phalanthos should have become a senior priest was an indication of the decline into which our vocation was slipping. However, if this was to be remedied, then education would have to be the means.

I began my college without any formal announcement, putting all the members of the priesthood, high and low, male and female, into classes for instruction. If we were to win the battle against the doubters and the destroyers of religion, amongst whom I numbered Pythagoras, Herakleitos, Anaximander, Anaximenes, Xenophanes and all their crew, we would have to be prepared. As it was their practice to show a reverence to the gods in public and stab them in the back in private, my only way of bringing them into the arena for a genuine contest would be to organise our sacred rites, laws, mysteries and working methods into a formal discipline called Theology, which would rank equally with other academic studies at the Luderma College.

When I started these classes in a small room at the back of the old wooden Temple at Hera, they were not very well attended. The reason for this was that I had set a timetable which began at dawn, and all Sybarites like to lie in bed until the sun is well up into the sky. In fact it was the proud boast of the *azygous plutos* that they never saw the sun rise or go down: they were in bed for the first and on their couches in the final stages of their vinous afternoon naps for the second. Nonetheless, after a few days, word-of-mouth spread by temple workers about the quality of my teaching brought increasing numbers of youngsters to these dawn classes. Inside a short time we were crowded out with students, and I had to find larger premises.

My fees for the instruction were minimal and well within the capacity to pay of the pupils, who were mostly from the wealthier class of citizens, holders of traditional positions in the temples, which went with their birth and station. Thanks to this arbitrary selection procedure, the standard of intellect which I had to deal with was depressingly low. Over half of my college's students were of this sort, a drain on my time and energy and a looming embarrassment: I knew that if I ever put one of them into a debate with a disciple of Pythagoras or Herakleitos, they would be torn to pieces. So I began to get rid of them, quietly and subtly culling my herd of students until I was down to a body of bright, sharp, ambitious youngsters, who were like those who followed Pythagoras so devotedly.

In order to achieve this pruning down of the priesthood in Sybaris, I had to enlist the help of Telys, who controlled all the temple appointments. I was surprised when he asked me very few questions about the college and what I was doing, but I later found out that amongst the students whom I regarded as the pick of the crop were a few loose mouths, if not actual spies, and they had kept Telys informed, by chatter as much as direct espionage. When I approached him with a list of people whom I wanted to discard as temple employees, he simply looked down it, shook his head, asked what possible other use could anyone have for such oafs, and left it at that. Not long afterwards, the first of them went; a fiery young man with the brain of a cabbage, very well connected. He was sent to minister to the spiritual needs of a community of slaves and half-free workers in a small colony of Sybaris which had been built close to tunny-breeding grounds north of Rhegion, and was being constantly threatened by attack from Himera.

Others followed, sent on various missions or returned to their families, the girls married off once their sacerdotal chastity had been revoked, if it wasn't already a scandalous joke, which, in most cases, it was.

The replacements for these rejects were carefully chosen. Telys insisted that they had to be from the families which had always supplied the temples with fresh blood, but I pointed out to him that the blood was no longer fresh from that source; there were young Sybarites of low birth who were more suitable, I argued.

This caused a major disagreement between us, a disagreement which threatened to become a rift. The families of the *azygous plutos* had put their futures into Telys' hands. In spite of being weak, self-indulgent and uninspired as a political group, a condition which Telys attributed to an exhaustion of ideas, they were strong when it came to conserving what was theirs. Withdrawal from the sphere of the mind did not mean that they had pulled up their roots altogether; in many respects this intellectual insensibility of theirs was a sham, a deliberate measure which they had taken to enable them to sink those roots even deeper into the rich soil of Sybaris. If they professed to be too indifferent to thought to think, then no-one could expect them to enter any argument about the rightness or wrongness of their vast wealth. They had accepted Telys as tyrant, not because he would make them use their own minds about the future, but because he had promised to find other means of solving the problem; hence my engagement.

In the depths of the winter there was a kind of peace in the city. Many mistook it for a new harmony between the haves and the have-nots, or a sign from the powers-that-be in the spirit world that everything had been sorted out. But it was neither of those anodynes. The pain of Sybaris was merely sleeping, ungoaded for a while.

It was the activities of my college which brought the city out of its thick-headed slumber long before any sign of spring. It was the moon of Lenaion, hardly thirty days beyong the solstice, when the chill winds were still howling out of the mountains, that Xenophanes came with his seven-stringed lyre down from Elea, having walked all the way down the snow-bound Road of Prosperity, to challenge me to do two things: first, openly to debate the existence of the One God against that of the plural gods of the Pantheon; and second, to take him with me to Hell when I went, because it was sure to be warmer there.

Xenophanes made his journey to Sybaris in a spirit which it was difficult not to admire. He had been in trouble since his return from Kroton and Anaximander's birthday bacchanals, and had ended up at loggerheads with all the other members of the Eleatic school over his concept of the One Unknown God, as he now called it (he would not allow a gender to be applied to this deity).

He had taken great pains to come to see me, and from the look of him he had been having a thin time of it in Elea that winter. None of the other philosophers in the city would give him house-room, he told me, and this was all due to the unpopularity of his One Unknown God Theory, compounded by his auxiliary Indeterminate Sex of God Theory, which had proved to be equally unacceptable. I had no hesitation in taking him into my own household as my guest, thinking that I would enjoy his company and silver voice, and it was not too long before he had insinuated himself into the college, 'to provoke discussion and act as a catalyst', as he put it.

By this time I had formulated great sections of my Theology, gathering the legends and stories which had been passed down to us by Homer, Hesiod and customary sources. Much of it had been written out by temple scribes. When Xenophanes had rested and recovered some of his strength (he was much frailer than he had been, his lovely bell of a voice now cracked and wheezy), it was inevitable that he should become interested in these documents and what they contained. To be sure, I felt apprehensive of allowing him to read them. Other people, poets amongst them, had brought criticism and punishment down on their heads by tampering with the poems, but my defence was that I had only extrapolated the creed of our religion out of the treasury of those sacred texts. Not one word had been altered. With my interest in Herakles always to the fore, I had produced a gospel of his actions (he was a man of few words, therefore I had little to go on as to what his opinions were), and it was this little book which Xenophanes came upon one evening when we were together at a late supper.

I had been teaching a special class of advanced students, using the life of Herakles as an illustration of the relationship between god and man. Herakles was born of the union between a god, Zeus, and a human being, Alcmena, the wife of Amphitryion of Tiryns, lord of the Argolid people. The intention of Zeus in mating with Alcmena while taking on the physical shape of her husband was to provide the Argolid with a leader of great strength. This, I told my students, demonstrated the flexibility which existed between the two states of being, but only if one of the progenitors were divine. I knew of no case which had been proved to my satisfaction where a man had become a god solely by his own efforts, no matter how heroic he might have been. Either the godhead was implanted at birth, as in the case of Herakles, or it was entirely absent. One could not earn divinity by good behaviour.

None of my students had endeavoured to contradict this argument. They had accepted what I said without question. But when Xenophanes picked my book off the couch where I had left it and dipped in to the text, he immediately started to tackle me on some details, which eventually led us to consider this assertion of mine.

'My interest,' he said, 'is not to prove that Herakles was either mortal or immortal. To be honest, I don't think it is important, because the whole story is obviously a throwback to a time when people just didn't have enough to do with their minds; but what I need to find out from you, professor, is how this belief of yours in the Herakles fantasy affects your view of power.'

My reply was immediate and incisive.

'All power emanates from the gods.'

'The strength of Herakles, his brutality, let's call it, is human. It's an extension of athleticism; Milo of Kroton is a disciple of Herakles more than you are. You're not particularly strong, are you? Perhaps you'd like to be? Is that why you're so devoted to this cult of the bone-headed half-god? Because you're a frustrated strongman?'

I countered these jibes with dignity, trying to steer the conversation back to a more stringent discussion of my theological statement that no man can become a god, but Xenophanes refused to stick to the point.

'If you had been able to throw the discus further than anyone else, would you ever have become a diviner? Have you ever fought in a battle? I doubt it. All your courage is tucked in behind a pile of mouldering fallacies.' He beckoned the slave to fill his libation-dish, and poured the wine into the palm of his cupped hand. 'To me! To the enquiring mind!' he shouted, then lapped it up. 'To the One Unknown God!' He paused, listening as if he had spoken the phrase again. 'Ah, I'd better change that to "The Unknown One God", in case it gives the impression that there may be two.'

I was saddened by his abuse of my hospitality, and this must have showed in some kind of sorrowful grimace.

'Have I upset you, Kallias?' he said. 'I did it intentionally. Someone has to start undermining this enormous structure of fatuous lies you are erecting.'

'We should talk about something else,' I said coldly. 'You're being more offensive than usual.'

'Indeed, I am an offensive man,' Xenophanes replied, then his head fell forward on to his chin, and he began to snore. He was not fully recovered from his recent exhaustion, his debilitated body failing to cope with the food and wine after such a long and arduous journey. As I looked at him, I felt a twinge of fear that he would not live long. He must have had a sixth sense that I was watching him, because he opened one flickering green eyes and said:

'As for this business of going to the Underworld to find out whether the gods are playing tricks on you, we're all dying to see how you get on. Don't you realise that the gods have been pulling the wool over your eyes all your life?'

'Go to sleep, Xenophanes,' I said gently. 'You don't understand at all.'

'I do!' he squawked suddenly, struggling to his feet. 'I understand only too well.' He staggered over to the window and breathed the icy air deeply into his lungs. 'Home of the Sybarites! Full of temples. All the best work, the best stone! And they don't believe a word of what they claim to! Not a scrap. It's all habit.' He turned from the window, burning himself on the brazier and hopping around the room, nursing his hand. 'You're the high priest of habit,' he shrilled. 'And I say that you've never seen or heard or touched a god in your life! All you've done is to personify fear.'

I could not remain in the room with him a moment longer after this insult. Drunk or sober, alive or half-dead, it was too much to take from him. When he saw me going towards the door, he ran across and barred my way.

'Don't leave me alone,' he whimpered.

'Why should I stay here and listen to your ridicule?' I said hotly. 'I don't have to endure this kind of treatment from a guest in my own house.'

'No, no,' he murmured, meandering away and sitting down on his couch again, 'it's not your house. You don't have to go to the halls of Hades, my dear man, you're in them already. This is the Underworld. What true life is there here?' With a wild shout he leapt to his feet and kicked over the brazier, scattering red coals over the wooden floor. Some flew to the fringe of linen curtains which I had hung on either side of the libation altar, and set fire to them. I shouted for the slaves to come and extinguish the flames, and started to pick the glowing charcoal off the scorched floorboards with a pair of serving-tongs. Meanwhile, Xenophanes was throwing coals out of the window and shrieking imprecations at the city, his behaviour leaving me in no doubt that his destructive philosophy had finally driven him insane.

Xenophanes did not die.

In a strange way, which I can now account for, having become that much sadder and wiser, we grew closer together after his outburst. Reason was not his strong point, nor did balance and calculation play any large part in the activities of his mind. He was certainly brave, if unstable; and I cherish the courage of the outsider, having been one all my life, made so by my preference for the spiritual life above the material.

I persuaded Telys and the Council of Elders to give refuge to an extremist philosopher. But Xenophanes was not well. Years of privation had taken their toll. I saw to it that he was cared for, and he seemed to be happy more often than not.

One of the features of his philosophical development at this time was a move away from the concept of the Spherical God, which ceased to interest him, and into the notion of the Infinite Earth. I can see him now, standing shakily on widespread feet, his wine-cup in his hand, (reciting one of his peculiar elegies). I remember one of these poems had a moment which always made his face light up. As his skin became more and more transparent as death drew near, the man seemed to glow from within, and I'll swear that I saw his delicate, wayward soul trembling within his eyes as he sang:

The world has no end, so be glad
for your child, and glad of a hole
in the always hospitable earth.

FIFTEEN

At this time, when the sun was bringing the longer day out of the winter night, I had news from home: my wife had died in childbirth.

When I had left for Sybaris she had been two months gone in her time, but it was her fourteenth pregnancy and there had been no reason to imagine that she would not have an easy delivery. My steward, who had sent the letter, mentioned that my wife had been anxious about whether I had remembered to make the necessary oblations and appeals on her behalf to Zeus, but on her death-bed she had been satisfied that I had because the child, a son, had survived, and she had been convinced that her own demise was a marker for the destiny of our family perhaps, but nothing more.

I had, of recent years, not been very fond of my wife, sensing a deepening disobedience in her, but the memory of this did not assuage my guilt when I recalled that I had not given her a thought since coming to Sybaris. In fact I had forgotten about the forthcoming birth altogether. This was most unlike me. In my travels I have always kept my family in mind, putting them in my prayers, sending them gifts and messages, but Sybaris had pushed them all right out of my thoughts. What was this power that the city had? To succeed where Athens, Corinth, Smyrna, Thebes, Susa had failed? Such forgetfulness deserved a stronger cause than the tormented and confused city I was living in, its stature so mean and meagre when I compared it to the great civic luminaries of the east, in all their energy and artistic splendour. What had made me so blind and deaf to my own past? Was it the money? The challenge? Did I care all that much whether this lucrative giant stayed alive? Each question was impossible to answer with any of my old honesty. I was enmeshed. Through gaps in the Sybarite net I could see what I had been, but I could not squeeze through to rejoin myself.

The death of my wife, though I did not mourn her too much, put my new self into perspective, and I was not wholly delighted with what I saw. Somehow the strange stickiness of Sybarite opulence had trapped me, keeping me a prisoner in the web of their riches, where I squirmed and struggled, dreaming up new schemes of escape, negotiating with the Telys spider for a greater share of my own captivity, or plotting to oust him and take his place. But I had seen great abundance before, the riches of Midas and Croesus had not evaporated from the earth. Any man who has seen the court of the Persian King has laid eyes on all that the world has to offer. Yet none of those golden cities was troubled in the way that I knew Sybaris to be; troubled in soul, but unable to be open about the force which twisted their eyes inward. It was Cleobulus who wrote on the wall of the shrine of Apollo's oracle at Delphi, 'Moderation is best', enabling us to deduce therefore that 'Excess is worst', but if that is confined with Chilon of Sparta's 'Know thyself', which was written alongside, then one gets into deep water.

The Sybarites knew their greed, and their greed was themselves. There was nothing in what they had encountered in religion or philosophy to turn them against this instinctual craving (not that they had given either force a proper chance), so they were like a madman who acknowledges his lunacy, allows it to subvert his nature, then clings to it as his only salvation from reality.

During seven days of ritual mourning for my wife, when I went into the sand dunes each day and wandered up and down, thinking the best thoughts which I could about her, I worked hard to dispel my haziness about the attraction which Sybaris had for me, trying to give myself some direction.

On my last afternoon in the dunes I came across a young bush of broom, already in tight golden blossom, and realised that spring was near. I knew that my journey to Enna could not be put off for much longer.

With the aid of a cadre of my most able students at the college I had done a full decipherment of my inner scene, and was ready to present it to Telys, when I learnt that he had been consulting Pythagoras throughout the winter and now had plans to remodel Sybaris' constitution to create a state based on Pythagoras' Monadic Flow System and Milo's manic pursuit of physical fitness. So, armed with my exposition and feeling betrayed, I went down to his office in the city hall and confronted him, tossing my closely written notes on to the table.

'What's this?' he asked. 'Your resignation?'

'No, it's what you hired me for,' I replied bitterly. 'You don't have to wade through it all. Just skip through to the conclusion and recommendations.'

'When we've paid so much and waited so long?' he sneered. 'I'll pore over every word, I can assure you. This must be the most expensive piece of long-term divination ever commissioned. Won't you sit down while I read it?'

I sat in a corner while he studied the document, his tufted eyebrows raising and lowering. Now and again, he sighed or cleared his throat as if he were about to speak, but did not. While he studied my findings I rehearsed what I was going to say to him about his underhand methods.

When he had finished reading, he turned the pages over and put them face down on the table.

'Thank you,' he said, 'that's all very clear.'

'You understand that Herakles, in one metaphysical dimension, is the city, which is weakening itself by drinking at the river of its own name, which makes any man timid, so we're led to believe, which is, essentially, a comment upon your timidity about the future: also he represents superhuman confidence,' I said, talking too quickly because I was nervous of the impending clash between us, 'which could be yours.'

'Yes, yes, I got all that. We have got to believe in ourselves, is what you're saying. That's very useful when you know that something is fundamentally wrong. What's that? Six and two-thirds talents of gold's worth? Am I getting value for money?'

I flushed at this jibe, but kept my temper.

Suddenly Telys laughed, his unpleasantness evanescent as a raindrop in a fire.

'How dare I complain? A man who will face the greatest test of all for people who are not even his own kin deserves better. When do you plan to begin your journey to the Underworld?'

I hesitated, not wanting to give too precise a date.

'You are still going, I assume?' Telys asked. 'Do say if you've changed your mind. The people will need to be told. I don't want them accusing you of making empty promises.'

I mentioned the day when Arcturus would completely leave the ocean as my provisional starting time, which seemed to please him. But when I mentioned the route of my journey he began to frown and scratch his head.

'What d-d-d'you mean?' he stuttered with a sly grin. 'It's all straightforward, isn't it? You must die. In fact I've ordered the public executioner to stand by for when you need him. What you might do, when you have time, is to decide what method you'd like him to use.'

I should have laughed, but I could not: instead, I felt pity for his ignorance. The man was so earth-bound that he could not understand how a true servant of the gods could cross into their domains without death: Odysseus had done it, and Herakles. Orpheus had opened the way to the Underworld by simply playing his lyre.

'Oh?' he said when I told him this. 'You should have spoken before. I'm afraid that the people may want some kind of blood-sacrifice, followed by a return from the dead. They will be disappointed.'

I left his office, not having raised the question of Pythagoras at all, and returned to my house.

Three days later, having put all my affairs in order and prepared myself for the journey, I left Sybaris by the western gate, consigning my college to the care of our senior lecturer in Astrology and Bird-Flight, and my reputation to the hazard of a triumphal return.

We left a land where anemones and polyanthus were beginning to show in the fields, and headed west into a territory which had not yet awakened from winter. Before leaving the plain of Sybaris I buried my treasure in a grove of Aleppo pine, having told Herophantos that the chest he would be guarding until my return was empty. This did not unduly disturb him. With the ups and downs of his life, he said, it made as much sense to stand sentinel over nothing as something.

I had bought a covered waggon from a corn merchant, a light vehicle with two solid-looking horses to pull it. The two of us could lie down in it side by side, using our baggage as headrests. I took five of the slaves, two of them young men who had plenty of strength, and they all shared two mules for riding. It was a larger company than I had intended, but I was feeling vulnerable.

In my letter to Telys I had been very clear that I was not running away, stressing my need to approach the Underworld obliquely rather than head-on.

As we reached the first gradients on the Road to Prosperity and began to climb up from the plain, we encountered two Jews, a man and his wife, who were on foot. They had been living in Sybaris for several years, members of a small community of their race which had settled in the south-eastern quarter as weavers. Originally they had been in Babylon during the long captivity of the Jews, but when this had come to an end seventeen summers ago, these Jews had decided not to return to their own country but, instead, had set out to find a new life elsewhere. Ravek and his wife were quite old, and they were carrying a loom in pieces on their backs, so we took the heavy wooden sections on the cart and they helped to push as the horses pulled up the increasingly steep slope. As I walked alongside them I asked a few questions in case they might be agents of Telys, or robbers with accomplices hidden ahead in the forest.

'Why are you leaving Sybaris?' I enquired.

'It is too much like Babylon,' Ravek replied curtly.

'Was it that you didn't prosper?'

'No, we prospered, but we sold all we had and gave it to our children. To us, Sybaris is not congenial. Our children like it, so I said to them, 'You stay, your mother and I will go somewhere else and set up the loom,' and here we are, on our way.'

I asked him to be more specific, and found him cagey.

'I feel uneasy there,' he told me grudgingly, his head bent, 'perhaps it's too big, like Babylon was, or too much is going on in the streets.'

'Has anyone ever interfered with the practice of your religion?' I asked him, knowing that the Jews are fanatical devil-worshippers.

'We don't have a religion,' Ravek muttered, spitting, 'so it has never caused us any trouble.'

I could not let this pass. I knew from my contacts with Jews in Phrygia, Lydia and Caria, that they venerated a jealous demon, who inflicted great suffering on them. For this they adored him, admiring every whim and caprice that the demon indulged to their disadvantage. The demon's name, as far as I remembered, was Yahweh, and there were a host of sub-demons, Adam, Moses and Abraham being some of them, I could recall. In terms of theology, which is what now interested me, Yahweh was not the demon who controlled the universe, but concentrated his power upon the Jews. But as a tribal deity he was a maker of great mischief. As I spoke to Ravek I decided that he was shielding Yahweh from me, refusing to encourage even a scrap of understanding.

'Don't be afraid,' I said, putting a hand to the cart, 'I'm only curious.'

'You are also the high priest of Sybaris,' Ravek whined, 'so the less I say the better.'

It was dark before we could make very much progress up the pass. There was a hostel by the roadside, but it was still shut for the winter. We made camp in the yard at the back out of the wind and sat around a fire. Ravek and his wife kept apart, but the heat eventually drew them towards the flames.

'What is your destination?' I asked him.

'We don't know. Wherever we find ourselves when we can go no further,' he replied, his long, sharp face gleaming in the firelight. 'It doesn't matter.'

The intensity of his sadness communicated itself to us all, and we waited for him to continue, but he lowered his head and pulled the cowl of his long robe over his face. As we sat there, listening to the sounds of the high places in the night and looking at the stars which were sown across the sky, I saw the cloth near where I knew his mouth must be, moving. He was praying, I decided.

'To call me the high priest of Sybaris is inaccurate,' I said, leaning across and pulling the cowl away. 'I am a diviner. In your religion do diviners play a part? For instance, did anyone foretell the end of your captivity in Babylon?'

Ravek stared at me with dark eyes which were set deep on either side of his beaky nose.

'I told you, we have no religion,' he barked.

'You were praying.'

'I was cursing my luck.'

I left him alone. During the night it got so cold that I ordered the slaves to break into the hostel so we could shelter from the freezing rain which had started to fall. When we moved inside I found Ravek and his wife already curled up in a corner, and I was angry that they had found a way in without telling us. When I went across to remonstrate with him I saw, by the light of my torch, that they had eaten a meal while separated from the rest of us, and now lay together with a long bundle wrapped in red and yellow cloth between them, fast asleep.

When I stirred him with my toe he did not wake. Too tired and cold to maintain my resentment, I let them sleep on.

At first light a squad of Scythian mercenary horsemen arrived at the hostel and arrested me.

I was taken to Telys' villa, which was only thirty stadia away, and Leogoras was left behind with the slaves and the Jews. I travelled on horseback, sharing the mount of the officer, who refused to give me any explanation.

I found Telys waiting for me with Pythagoras and Milo. I was offered breakfast, which I refused, then use of the baths, which I also refused, saying that I wished to get our business over and resume my journey.

'All in good time, all in good time,' Telys said resolutely. 'I won't delay you long, but you left Sybaris in such a hurry that I wasn't able to invite you to this meeting, and I think it's important.'

'Couldn't you have told the officer that this was not an arrest, but an invitation?' I challenged him.

'Scythians don't know the difference. Be at your ease, Kallias. By noon you can be on your way. In fact, I'll send slaves and horses to help your people get the waggon up the pass while we're talking.'

'I'd rather that they just waited for me,' I replied. 'If you start moving them around, I might never find them again.'

Pythagoras had decided to put on a good-natured front for my benefit. He tutted in disapproval at the ugly mixture of menace and frustration which had infused every word Telys had said to me.

'Give Sphinx a chance,' he said. 'You can't expect him to shift his attention from his great religious pilgrimage and think about our proposals without some difficulty. He's had no warning, he's not prepared.'

'Not prepared for what, Pythagoras?' I demanded caustically. 'With Telys here, disloyalty is a habit of mind. I've got used to it.'

'It is not disloyalty,' Pythagoras said. 'Be patient. He is only considering ideas, one against the other. Can one be loyal to ideas? They come and go.'

Milo guffawed and stretched out his enormous thighs. They had been rubbed with oil, and gleamed like a pair of dolphins. I looked at them with appalled fascination.

'Were you really setting out to go to the Infernal Regions?' he tittered, rubbing his thighs in the most disgusting manner. 'Come on, Kallias, admit that you were running away from the axe.'

When I denied this, he laughed out loud, slapping his thighs so they shook.

'If you want to go to Enna, then the shortest way is to sail across to Naxos which is to the south. Why are you going west?'

'I will make my own itinerary,' I retorted, 'but you'd do well to remember that the Chalkidians in Naxos are not particularly friendly to people from Sybaris, nor, before you mention it, are the ones in Katane, further down the eastern coast of Sicily. I have studied the entire island for a safe place to land and have a chance of reaching Enna, which is right in the middle of Sicily. The only stretch of coastline where I can make the attempt is near Himera in the north, which is best approached from a port to our west.'

'Himera is a very violent city,' Milo said, tightening his

knees so muscles bulged at the joints, 'there is always trouble in Himera.'

'But amongst themselves;' I pointed out, 'Himerans don't hate us. They trade with the Tyrrhenians, who have good relations with our city, and the Tyrrhenian navy rules the ocean north of Sicily.'

'It pleases me to hear you call it *our* city, Kallias,' Telys chuckled, his hand on my shoulder, 'and be assured that while you are away your treasure will be guarded in its new home. But for safekeeping, I think you should let me have it dug up and returned to old Herophantos. You can leave it where it is if you want to and see what happens when the snow melts in the mountains, but I wouldn't advise it.'

Not annoyed that he knew so much in this case, I said that I would probably have it moved, then I turned to Pythagoras, who was laying out a pattern of pebbles on a table.

'What's this? Are we going to play jacks?' I asked. 'Is that what I've been brought here for?'

A pebble rolled off the table. Telys picked it up and placed it back in position.

'Before you go, it is only fair that I tell you what is going to happen while you're away,' he said. 'Sybaris is going to adopt Pythagoras' Monadic Flow Theory, and Milo has agreed to help us establish a Health and Fitness Council, based upon the one that is so successful in Kroton. I should explain that this is not intended to exclude or cancel your efforts, but supplement them. I still want you to go to the Underworld for us.'

While the sun rose I was forced to listen while Pythagoras outlined his crazed hypotheses that all truth stems from Number, and Number One is the root of all existence.

At one point I interrupted him to say that his theory had the appeal of an abacus, but little else. He puffed himself up, played with his hair, and proceeded to do many tricks with his pebbles, demonstrating how his sacred numbers could be arranged to show mysterious alliances with the Infinite. I tersely suggested that his God, the great Monad, the Number One, was nothing more than a glorified sum.

At this Milo became incensed, his square-jawed meaty features shuddering with exasperation. When he strode across and confronted me, his mighty arms flexing and tightening, I was certain that the man was going to attack me. With the memory of the beating he had given Hekateios at the house of Phalanthos resurgent in my mind, I hastened to justify my doubts, but Milo leant down and thrust his black beard into my face.

'Don't talk to my friend Pythagoras like that again. It upsets me,' he growled. 'I love his mind, you see, and whatever comes out of it. In Kroton we respect the body, that's a simple matter, flesh is very straightforward, isn't it? But the magic of the mind? For that we need a genius, and Kroton has the best.'

I nodded, and assured Milo that I had always held Pythagoras in the highest esteem.

'Do you believe everything he says?' Milo demanded.

I stared down the hanging front of Milo's chiton. His pectoral muscles were clenched, and ridges of tendon ran out in star patterns to the points of his shoulders. The man's chest was a battleground of forces.

'Much as I'd like to agree on every point, there are issues on which we think differently,' I said with all the courage that I could find.

'Do you believe that he can fly?'

'No, I don't.'

Milo knotted his hands together and cracked his finger-bones to show his displeasure.

'You must know about the javelin which Arbaris, the high priest of the Hyperboreans, gave to him. All he has to do is sit on it, and he can go anywhere,' he declared, smacking the outside of my leg so my knees collided painfully. 'Don't be foolish.'

'Have you got it with you?' I asked Pythagoras, who was watching Milo's interrogation of me with a supercilious smile.

Pythagoras shook his head, and told me that he had left the javelin at home.

'And he can write on the moon, put bears into trances just by looking at them, and remember three previous incarnations. Tell him who you've been during your other lives,' Milo persisted.

'Oh, let's not go into that now. Kallias has heard all this before, and he is not a sympathiser.'

'We've been considering a union between Kroton and Sybaris,' Milo told me in a friendlier mood. 'How does that strike you?'

I looked at Telys, who raised one eyebrow. I took this to be an encouragement to speak my mind, misled again by that ever-present smile.

'Sybaris must be a thousand times wealthier than Kroton,' I said. 'One must therefore ask, is Kroton a thousand times healthier, fitter and better governed than Sybaris, if this union is to be founded on the principle of a fair exchange?'

Telys frowned, got to his feet and took me to one side.

'That wasn't the right thing to say,' he whispered.

'Isn't it the truth?'

'Sybaris is rotting from within,' Telys muttered, leading me further away and out of earshot of Milo and Pythagoras, who were keeping still, listening as hard as they could. 'What are riches worth if they choke the p-p-possessor?'

'But these are shadows, fanciful doubts,' I said. 'Who understands the basis of your fears, Telys? How can you give away the sovereignty of your city because of a malady that may be solely within yourself? All these two want is the money. Once in power, they'll get rid of you.'

'We are heading for disaster,' Telys hissed, 'I know it. You have been no help in getting to the root of the problem.'

'Perhaps there isn't one?'

'Well, according to you, there is now,' he said in exasperation, inclining his head towards the men from Kroton.

Before leaving, I penned a note to Telys, entrusting it to his steward. It was a dangerous thing to do, but an upsurge of anger against Milo and Pythagoras made me imprudent. There is something about ambitious, cocky confidence tricksters which enrages me, especially those who debase their intelligence and inspiration merely to achieve wealth. Amongst these I number Pythagoras as being in the first rank, and Milo somewhere near the bottom, as the man has the brain of an ox. Here is what I wrote to the tyrant of Sybaris, urging him to keep his autonomy:

'If you can accept that I am a man in two parts – my self as diviner and my existence in the commonsense world, these being necessarily separated; and if, for the sake of argument, we agree that, for the moment, it appears as though I have failed, or am, at least, tardy in providing you with insights into the city's future; then perhaps you will heed what I say in commonsense, imagining myelf to be now, in some degree, a citizen of Sybaris. From this standpoint I feel entitled to ask you several questions, but haste prevents me from expressing them all, so I will stick to a few. Do you honestly believe your anxiety about what fate awaits the city is shared in any general way? Do you think that to impose your irrational nightmares upon your people is good practice? To join Sybaris with Kroton will mean that the philosophy of Pythagoras will be given power in a place where it would not naturally have thrived. The comparative poverty of Kroton has been a fertile field for Pythagoras and his cult. I leave you with these hasty thoughts, and exhort you to keep the city free until I return. At the risk of repeating myself, I use this last opportunity to remind you: it's the money they want, and if Kroton is such an universally successful place, why hasn't it done as well in trade as it has in athletics?'

SIXTEEN

On my way back to the hostel on the pass I saw an impressive sight. The first spring convoy out of Sybaris was now well along the Road to Prosperity, emerging from the covered way to the sound of drums. The big transport horses which pulled the waggons had not been excluded from dancing lessons, and they stepped ponderously from side to side, swaying in rhythm as they hauled their loads up the gradient. I watched them for some time, enchanted by the nobility of the spectacle. Sybaris does have something of its own, I decided as I moved on, when a cartload of goods can be moved with such pride.

After a while I heard the drums slow as the leading waggon encountered the first steep slope. Musicians ran up from further back along the convoy and marched beside the horses, urging them on. For the basic hauling step of the long journeys the Sybarite bagpipe was not employed, but only flutes, cymbals and drums. However, each of these great draught animals had been schooled to the bagpipe, and there was a festival devoted to Bes which took place at the end of each successful journey, where these huge horses would perform with the most astonishing lightness of foot.

However, these thoughts were not in my mind as I was hurrying back to the hostel. I knew that if I did not get back soon we would be stuck behind the convoy as it went up the pass and forced to travel at its slow pace for the whole ascent, the road not being wide enough to permit any overtaking of the wide-axled waggons.

When I sighted the hostel I was glad to find that Leogoras

had worked this out for himself, and already had our waggon out on the road ready to move. I shouted and waved, indicating that he should get going, as the heavy drums were beating nearer and nearer. By the time I caught up with our waggon, it was climbing steadily. On my way past the hostel, I noticed the Jew standing on an outcrop of rock, looking down at the convoy, and I could swear that the man was weeping. When he joined us later on, I found the opportunity to talk about the length of the line of waggons which we could now see clearly, but with its tail still under the covered way.

'A stirring sight,' I said to him as he plodded along, head down, with a hand on the rear of our waggon in a token of help to our horses, 'but we mustn't let them catch up with us.'

Ravek made no answer, but spat on the road.

'Has all the snow gone from the top of the pass, I wonder?' I added chattily. 'If not, we'll be making a way through for them. But the waggon-masters would never have set out if they hadn't made sure that the road was open, don't you think?'

Ravek grunted that this was probably so. Leogoras halted our horses for a breather and I stepped to the side of the road, touching shoulders with the Jew.

'Before setting out, everyone in that convoy submitted their fates into the hands of Mercury,' I reflected aloud, 'a god who is a byword for speed, but also inconstancy. He sends men in all directions at his will, not theirs. Are you sad at leaving Sybaris when you see the might of the place?'

Ravek wrinkled his nose.

'From what I know, Mercury is also the god of scholars like yourself. Where does he lead you? Do you always trust his signposts?' he said sullenly.

Chastened by this, and feeling compassion for the fellow, I left him alone and went to join Leogoras at the horses' heads.

In our much lighter conveyance we managed to keep well ahead of the convoy, moving up through swathes of spring flowers and across ice-cold streams towards the snows. Other waggons had been ahead of us, and there was a way across the drifts at the top of the pass. These ruts were not old, their surfaces frozen but free from fresh snow.

'Tyrrhenian waggons made these,' Leogoras said, 'they're not as wide from wheel to wheel as ours. There were two of them, by the look of it.'

A new country opened to our eyes in the west, full of forests and high peaks. We could see the road zigzagging down, disappearing into woodland, straightening out over broad pastures. It was a long way before we would catch sight of Laus, the colony of Sybaris on the coast. Before we started to descend I walked back and took a last look towards Sybaris, but cloud had come down, obscuring the plain. I was above the level of the mist, and I could hear the convoy coming up, but could not see it. Now the sounds were the cracks of whips, the creaking of wood and leather, the rumble of wheels and the rhythmless crashing of hundreds of hooves, all music gone.

When I returned to our waggon I saw that the Jews had gone on ahead, walking down the slope at a faster pace than we would be able to maintain, the pieces of their loom on their backs.

'Did he say anything before he left?' I asked Leogoras.

'No, he just waved.'

'Nothing about meeting up later on? They're running a big risk by going on alone. Those forests go on for ever.'

'I think he's in a hurry,' Leogoras suggested. 'Besides, I don't think he likes company. I saw you talking to him. Did you say something to put him off?'

The slaves hauled on the brake-levers as the waggon began to gather downward momentum, shoving at the horses, which were scrabbling for footholds on the stony surface.

'All I discussed with him was . . . How shall I put it? The subtle and unreliable character of Mercury? Not knowing where to go.'

'He knows where he's going,' Legoras said, pointing with his whip at the two dots, which were now far down the western slope of the pass, 'and I'm glad I don't have to go with him.'

*

That night we camped in the middle of a pasture, well off the road, Above us the mist had come down, and all was silent. We worked out that the convoy must have stopped at the head of the pass to camp, not wishing to risk the descent in cloud. I imagined that great mass of waggons axle-deep in the snowfield, and felt glad to be where I was, in a sheltered hollow beside a small stream, with a fire burning.

Halfway through the night I was wakened by Leogoras, who took me outside the waggon to look up the pass. Far above us I could see lights and hear the squealing of brakes.

'The convoy is coming down by torchlight,' Leogoras said, 'we'll have to get moving if we want to stay ahead.'

There was a part of me which wanted to let them pass and take the consequences of a slow journey to Laus, but I saw the sense in keeping ahead. We stirred the slaves awake and got the waggon back on the road. By the time we got moving, we could hear the shouts of the army of torchbearers who were leading the convoy down.

'It must have been too cold for them up there,' Leogoras said with a grin as he sent two of our slaves ahead with brands from the fire. 'As you know, master, a Sybarite doesn't like to be uncomfortable for too long, if he can help it.'

At the end of our second day on the Road to Prosperity, having made good time through the forests, we came upon the Tyrrhenian waggons, which Leogoras had guessed were somewhere ahead of us. They were parked under tall firs, their bright colours standing out in the gloom. I sent Leogoras across to find out how these travellers would feel about sharing a camp for the night.

'They're carrying corpses back to Tyrrhenia,' he told me when he returned. 'Just our luck. It could have been an interesting evening.'

'So they didn't want us to join them?'

'They were all for it, but I'm not.'

I walked over and tapped on the painted tailboard of the waggon which Leogoras had approached. An old man with cropped silver hair and a cleft chin poked his head out and beckoned me to enter. Inside the waggon there were three other men, two of them youths dressed in military gear. They were reclining alongside a pair of coffins, one large and heavily ornamented, the other slender and neatly decorated with figures of children, birds, fish and flowers.

After I had greeted them and accepted a cup of wine from a jug on the larger coffin, I asked where they were headed.

'First to Veii with the lady, then on to Populonia with the old man,' the silver-haired leader told me. 'A ship is waiting for us at Laus, and we'll sail up the coast.'

The only place where I could find a seat in the waggon was on top of the smaller coffin. I hesitated, a feeling of dread flooding through my legs and making my knees knock.

'Don't be afraid to sit on your old love, priest,' the leader said jovially, 'she can't bite you in the backside now.'

I was the only one who could have laughed, the other three Tyrrhenians not having sufficient Greek to understand the joke; but I did not.

Since the death of Luderma, I had not involved myself in her affairs. She was not of my religion, and I knew that there were strict rules to be observed about funeral arrangements and the settlement of her estate.

'We had to keep her and the iron merchant in Sybaris until the pass was open,' the leader explained, giving me a sympathetic pat on the knee. 'Don't worry. The lady is well embalmed and wrapped up good and tight, not as you remember her. My name is Thefarie, by the way. Will you have food with us? Your man didn't seem too keen.'

He chuckled and translated his wisecrack to the others, and they laughed obediently. Either his language required far more words to express a notion than Greek, or he added something, because it took much longer and they responded twice.

'We are not allowed to eat meat on these journeys,' Thefarie explained. 'I was saying to these men that if you don't want to have a meal with us, perhaps you will ask us to have one with you. We can bend the laws a little when accepting hospitality.'

I took this opportunity to release myself from these mournful surroundings, clambering out of the waggon as quickly as I could and inviting the Tyrrhenians to come over as soon as they wished. It was some time before they did so, and I had taken wine to quell my melancholy at encountering my dead love again under such circumstances.

It was not a morbid evening that we spent, however. There was an accord between the natures of Thefarie and Leogoras which made sadness impossible. Thefarie was a most irreverent man, but there was a sincere wholesomeness in what he said which made it pointless to take offence.

'A Tyrrhenian has to be taken home after death. It doesn't matter where they've wandered, in what state of being they've got themselves in, they have to be shovelled up and carted back to the old family home,' he told us.

'Is that so the spirit can be at rest?' I asked.

'Oh, no. We don't believe that the spirit is attached in any way to the corpse. What they have to go back for is the feast. It's the duty of every Tyrrhenian to give a final banquet. Huge sums are spent on it. Often an estate will be bled dry to make a proper show.'

I cringed, turning away from my food, the obvious question unspoken on my lips.

'Yes, Kallias, she'll have to sit there and preside. Her son, the present lord, will be there, and all her other children and relatives,' Thefarie assured me cheerfully, 'and anyone who matters in Veii.'

'There was no love lost between Luderma and her son,' I said.

'That's all forgotten now,' Thefarie declared. 'Forgiveness of old wrongs is immediate. As soon as the eldest son heard that his mother was dead in Sybaris, he would have started to build a magnificent tomb big enough to hold all these guests.'

'You have this feast *in* the tomb?' I asked, incredulous.

'For several days. When it's all over it's sealed up with the crumbs on the floor and the wine-stains on the wall.'

While I shook my head slowly from side to side in wonderment at the imagined scene, Leogoras changed the subject, asking Thefarie if he had seen the Jews.

'Yes, they passed us going at a great rate,' he replied, grease running down the cleft of his chin. 'We called out to them, but they ignored us. They looked like people who had urgent business ahead.'

When the Tyrrhenians had left and the camp had settled

down to sleep, I lifted the side of the canvas near my bed and looked across to the waggon where Luderma lay, remembering all that had passed between us.

Next morning we were up early. I said farewell to the Tyrrhenians and my dead love, not unhappy to learn that they could not travel with us. Under customary law they had to limit their speed to twenty-eight times that of a lengthening shadow.

In Laus we found a ship that was sailing for Poseidonia that evening. It was a small vessel that was not waiting for the Sybaris spring convoy like the rest of the ships in the harbour, but was carrying a special cargo. Because it was not a Tyrrhenian ship but originated in some town to the far north, I did not suspect that it was waiting for the very cargo which I had been haste to leave behind that morning. I had already paid for our passage and was settled in by the time Thefarie and his funeral waggons arrived on the quay.

I cancelled our passage. Thefarie proved himself to be a true friend, interceding on my behalf and saving me the penalty of lost money.

'When I explained the circumstances,' he told me as we unloaded our baggage, 'they were full of sympathy. They also knew that if they didn't act reasonably we wouldn't use them again. After all, ferrying corpses for us is good business all the year round.'

A day later we set sail in a Tyrrhenian ship bound for the iron islands, carrying a cargo of dyestuffs and cloth, due to call in at Poseidonia with letters and gifts from home for the Sybarite colonists there.

Ours was a swift ship, which was why it was entrusted with the first personal messages of the families of Sybaris to their kin after the winter. We left a full day after the funeral ship, but we sighted her before sunset. Only one sail was hoisted in the south-west wind. It was bright red and cut in the shape of a hawk, not the most efficient design for gathering the force of a breeze.

'They'll have a rule for it,' Leogoras mused. 'You're a gambling man, master. You take a guess and I'll take a guess. The winner gets a silver drachma.'

'I don't have to guess, Leogoras, so I won't take your money unfairly,' I said. 'I'm beginning to understand the Tyrrhenian mind. That ship is sailing at the speed at which a hawk hovers.'

'Then it's motionless!' Leogoras protested, 'and I can see it's not.'

'No, hovering is a form of motion. As the hawk's eye moves in search of its prey, it shifts a little. The speed of death is at the centre of a hawk's hover.'

Leogoras was silent. We passed the funeral ship on the starboard side. As it slipped behind us into the darkness he turned to me and said that I had probably interpreted the rule rightly, but if he had offered me the bet in the early days it would have been a form of disrespect.

'You have allowed me to become too familiar,' he said, 'and it has reduced my complete faith in your powers. This is nothing to do with my belief in you, only the wearing down which comes with being close to any man. From now on you must treat me harder and keep me at a distance, otherwise, when we submit ourselves to the ordeal of the Underworld you will not be able to provide the leadership I need.'

There was so much sense in this that I could not argue. But as I stared out over the darkening sea and the ship became isolated on the open waters far from land, it caused a loneliness in me.

SEVENTEEN

When we arrived at the port of Poseidonia we found it blockaded by over thirty Tyrrhenian warships. A dispute was in progress over an item of business affecting the price of best quality tin. From what I could glean from the master of our ship, the Sybarites had started importing high-grade tin from the Casseterides, islands beyond the Straits of Herakles to the far west of the Mediterranean, in an attempt to force the Tyrrhenians to lower their prices. Telys himself had visited the colony to negotiate with the tin-masters the previous year, and an agreement had been reached, but the Tyrrhenians had changed their minds.

As we were not permitted to land, our ship was anchored close to the cordon of vessels in the blockade. Before long I noticed activity in the harbour area and many small boats coming out. They were manned by Sybarites who had identified our ship, and they were on their way to plead with the commander of the Tyrrhenian fleet to allow them to receive their letters and presents from home. These negotiations took most of the day, and there was a great deal of milling about by the small boats, then our ship was signalled to come alongside the Tyrrhenian flagship, and the parcels and sacks were taken out. While the transfer was taking place our ship was boarded by a party of Tyrrhenians, including the commander himself; a magnificent young man in the prime of life, with a mass of gleaming curls, brilliant eyes and the reddest mouth imaginable. It sounds as though I am describing a Greek, but this was not the impression he gave, in spite of his vibrant handsomeness. His skin was soft and brown, and there was something about the set of his eyes which reminded me of Egypt.

This man spoke to the master of our ship, who pointed me out. As the Tyrrhenian party strode along the deck Leogoras rooted in our baggage for his sword, ready to protect me against all odds, but I stayed his hand.

'My respects to you,' the commander said through an interpreter, a willowy old man who leant on a staff. 'It seems that we have been brought Kallias, a man we know plenty about.'

The Tyrrhenian naval officers laughed, their eyes glittering with enjoyment. I was obviously the butt of a witticism of some kind.

I looked at the commander. He was short and compact, and exuded life and authority. There was a freedom in his movements, an untrammelled quality which I recognised. Without further hesitation, I prostrated myself.

'There is no need for an interpreter,' I said, 'I have been taught enough of your language to hold a simple conversation.'

'Ah, my mother taught you something, then!' the commander rejoinded. 'A great woman, you will agree.'

There was nothing in this man's face to remind me of Luderma. The fruitful beauty of his presence induced no reminiscence, but then, I thought, all my recent memories of her had been in death. This splendid male was her child. And he had probably been the one who had driven her from his home. From this realisation my mind raced on, calculating that I was probably going to be the victim of some filial vengeance ordained by customary law.

'Your mother's body is coming on another ship,' I told him. 'I encountered a good man called Thefaries, who had been charged with conducting it home.'

'Yes, Thefaries is known to me.' The commander thrust out both his hands. Around both wrists were bangles of ivory, which clashed together. 'My name is Scamano. I have come to thank you.'

I allowed him to take my hands, knowing that they were cold and clammy. The contrary nature of the Tyrrhenians was legendary. The scandal of Luderma's fate had been known all over Sybaris, and her household had been outraged by her death. I had received much criticism for the way I had behaved.

'When I threw her out of my father's house after his death, she was a mere shell,' Scamano said, putting an arm around my shoulder. 'She would not take a lover. She sat in her quarters, pining. If I had not kicked her out and forced her to go to Rome, she would have died within half a year. Now, we have business to talk about. Come aboard my ship.'

Unable to take in everything that he was saying, I allowed myself to be led past Leogoras, who was wild with apprehension, but too wise to challenge Scamano, once he had seen me prostrate myself before him.

'I'll be all right,' I whispered, 'but come for me if I'm still on the flagship by the time it's dark.'

Scamano took me to his cabin, a small room made of sweet-smelling woods. When we had sat down and wine had been put before us, he informed me that his mother had left a will. It had been brought to him by a Jew, who had carried the document on behalf of the Sybarite lawyer. I realised that this messenger must have been the embittered Ravek.

'We have an arrangement with Sybaris that our civil laws, wherever possible, will apply,' Scamano explained. There are small taxes to pay on my mother's estate, but the bulk of it is going to be yours. What do you want me to do with it?'

So, Luderma, who had given me all of herself and died for it, had also given all her wealth to my other passion. It was an accurately aimed shot, and my self-esteem shrivelled.

I asked Scamano to divide the sum due to me into three equal parts: one to be my contribution to the building of her tomb, if Tyrrhenian custom would allow it; the second to be paid into my college funds; and the third to pay for my passage to Himera.

This latter payment was a good way for me to raise the question with him of how I could find a ship to take me to Sicily. With Poseidonia blockaded and no traffic going in and out, I could be stuck there for months.

My ruse worked. Pleased by my contribution to the cost of his mother's tomb – an enormous expense in Tyrrhenia – Scamano swore that he would see me across to Sicily somehow, even if it meant taking his whole fleet there on manoeuvres to cow the Greek cities of the northern coast.

'This blockade will be lifted in a few days,' he assured me. 'The merchants are close to agreement, so I'm told. If you can be patient, Kallias, I will send you over with an escort. I would come myself but, as you know, I have family business sailing up from Laus, and she should be here by tomorrow.'

And that is how we got to Sicily. Four Tyrrhenian war-galleys made the crossing in three days and put me and Leogoras ashore at night, then sailed off west to menace the shipping lanes. I had arranged with Scamano to sell our five slaves at the market in Poseidonia, and for the money to be added to the sum despatched to Sybaris for the college, an account which was accessible to me when I needed funds in the future.

We set out from the shore, heading by starlight towards the south-east, where Enna lay deep in the mountains.

Away from the coastal plain, Sicily is a hard country; dry, stony and severe. Once we were a day's march from the sea, I approached a farmstead and bought a young mule to carry our baggage. We stayed with the people there that night, rough folk whose blood had been that of Ionian Greeks from Zankle subjugated later on by Dorian exiles from Syracuse. They had fled from famine to famine; now, all brightness gone, they had found land on which merely to subsist. Their lord was the tyrant of Himera, whom they had never seen. When I revealed my profession to them, they were pleased and refused payment for our stay, asking instead for my help with a field which they had made out of a nearby hillside, stone by jagged stone. I petitioned Demeter, the goddess closest to all who till the land, and one much in my mind as I approached the dominions of Hades. But by the look of the wispy shoots coming up in the parched earth of the field, it would take more than prayers to make anything flourish in that arid place.

Leogoras had been seasick during the crossing from Poseidonia. Once on land he appeared to recover, but by the time we had obtained the mule and pressed on into the mountains, it was obvious that he was seriously ill. The earth kept moving, he claimed, and he could not hold anything down for long. I allowed him to ride the mule and walked by his side, his hand on my shoulder, but he could not hold his seat in the saddle when we began to climb the trail which would take us into the high mountains.

I decided that we should stop so he could regain his health. We found a grassy place beside a stream and camped there under some pines for three days until his fever died down. I used this time to prepare myself for the ordeal ahead, knowing that Enna was near. With the text of the eels fixed in my mind, I chanted it hundreds of times while I sat beside the stream or cooked food for the sick Leogoras, or wandered in the scrub with the mule as it fed. I had done the right thing with this enigma. At no time in my career had I ever claimed to understand a sign which confused me. The life of a city was at stake, one that was rapidly taking hold of my heart. For I was no longer the man who had sailed from Elis, but the man who had arrived in Sybaris.

We moved on, taking it slowly while Leogoras got his limbs working again. I was not navigating from any map, or with any sure knowledge of direction, but only from a pull which Enna was exerting upon me. For a priest of the Iamidai, a diviner of such blood as mine, steeped in the Great Eleusian Mysteries and loyal unto death to Demeter and her daughter, Proserpina, who was carried from the fields of Elis by Hades to Hell, there is no need of signposts on the way to Enna. I could feel it drawing me across the mountains, and soon we were there.

From the broken crest of a hill we looked down into a valley which I knew must hold the entrance to the Infernal Regions. I spotted a small, stone-built house and some farm-buildings. Beside a grove of oak trees was a small lake, and the whole floor of the valley was full of swine.

'Is this it?' Leogoras asked, plainly disappointed.

I nodded, my spirit tightening as I saw a human figure walking around the lake with a fishing rod and a dog at his heels. As we began to descend the track, I realised that Leogoras' question had an intimacy that I had not heard from him since we had discussed the hawk sail on the way to Poseidonia.

'You've become familiar again,' I said. 'Did you mean to be?'

He nodded and held the mule's rope close to its mouth.

'If it had looked like Hell, then I'd have kept my distance,' he told me, 'but this could be anywhere.'

When we were close to the house I saw the man laying fish out on a platform of sticks to dry. He had built a kind of windmill over the platform, with rags tied to the vanes to scare birds away. A gusty breeze was in the valley, making the windmill turn, and the man had to keep ducking to avoid getting a blow on the head. Long before we were within calling distance I heard him laughing, a high, whinnying sound.

'Sphinx! At last!' he called out through a thick white beard which was tucked into his girdle. 'I've been waiting for you.'

Since hearing the man's laughter I had been holding back a suspicion that was now confirmed. In spite of his unkempt appearance, I recognised my brother.

The last time I had seen him had been at the ceremony in Elis, when he had been cast out of the Iamidai for malpractice and exiled. Later on we had been told that he had become a reformed character and had been given a custodian's job at a shrine somewhere. To have a twin who was such an embarrassment had never been helpful to me in my work; but to have him appear at a time like this was a great nuisance.

'How did you know I was coming, Geron?' I enquired, accepting his embrace, which was redolent of pig ordure and smoked fish.

'The tyrant of Sybaris sent a pigeon to the tyrant of Naxos. The tyrant of Naxos sent a pigeon to the tyrant of Katane. The tyrant of Katane sent a pigeon to the tyrant of here, who is me!'

Pleased with his joke, my brother capered about, hugging and kissing me, then pulled me by the hand.

'Come into my palace, Kallias!' he cried. 'You see how well I've done for myself.'

With even more of this disagreeable chatter Geron led me into his house. If it was not prepossessing from the outside, it was worse inside. He had a rough table, a stool, a low bed made of branches and a large cupboard with a lock. As his food was stored in jars and boxes all around the kitchen, I could not guess at the function of the piece of furniture. It did not occur to me that it would be full of clothes, which turned out to be the case when I asked Geron to satisfy my curiosity.

'My ceremonial vestments, my dear brother. I have all sorts of hats and copes and cloaks, every colour you can imagine. And they're worth a fortune, I can assure you. Try to touch one.'

I put my hand out towards the garments hanging in the cupboard, and Geron's dog immediately snarled and bristled. It was a small, nondescript creature, but it managed to puff itself up to double its size, and its teeth were blue and broken, and looked as if they would give a poisonous bite.

'Down, down! Don't you recognise the great mystagogue, Kallias? King of visions! Most favoured son of Iamos!' Geron said.

'So many clothes, and all different,' I marvelled gently, wanting to ease him out of this rivalrous attitude. 'Do other people come here?'

'No, but all the tyrants in Italy and Sicily have boasted at one time or another that they're brave enough to face Hades in a good cause. It's a gesture, of course. They have these robes made and kept here – each city has its own, and the one for Sybaris is, as you might expect, the most gorgeous – but they're never used. My salary is linked to the number of visits . . . well, you can work it out for yourself.' He paused, stroking the dog's ruff, which was still half-raised as it glared malignantly at me. 'So I had to take up pig-farming. I had a few animals which it was my responsibility to keep ready for sacrifices, and they gave me a start. Now I've got eight hundred and seventy-four. The drawback is that I can't eat pork.'

Leogoras burst out laughing. I had noticed that he had warmed to my brother as soon as they had met, listening to his chatter with more interest than it merited.

'Sybaris' ceremonial robes are in good condition,' Geron said, grabbing a couple of sleeves and pulling them slightly forward so I could see the golden fabric. 'There's one for you and one for me. When we've had a bit of time together, I'll show them to you and we can try them on. You're not in a hurry, are you?'

I lay in the cool while Geron took Leogoras down to the lake to show him how to catch fish with a pickled pig's tail. My thoughts were mainly about my sons, none of whom had shown any interest in following the life of a diviner. Instead they wished to farm, or fight, or become orators, lawyers, anything but be like their father. The only follower I had ever had on the male side of the family was Geron, who, after a disastrous career as a courtier, had followed in my footsteps, only to be cast out for claiming false visions. He had been discovered with a collection of wax tablets on which he had scribed variants for any number of inner scenes. Many of these had been stolen from the genuine manifestations which I had witnessed and unwisely told him about.

Meanwhile my sons, with this example in front of them, lost much of their respect for my work. They are modern thinkers now, not prone to take the gods too much to heart.

I slept with this sadness about me and woke when Geron returned, bursting into the house with Leogoras laughing on his arm. They had caught no fish, they told me, but the sunset had been marvellous, and now it was time to drink.

'I want to go now,' I said, looking meaningfully at the cupboard.

'Now?' Geron said recoiling. 'Oh, brother mine, don't be so hasty. Go tomorrow. Go the next day. Let me have some time with you and this fine man you've brought along.'

'No, I'm ready to go now. It is your duty to help me, not be an impediment. Where is the entrance to the Underworld?'

'Go in the daylight. Take a last look at the sun,' Geron pleaded. 'Go drunk; I would. Do you have to do this, Kallias? Pretend to go. Make it up. Say you went. I tell you, I'm not sure that this entrance is working any more. No-one has used it since I've been here, except a few hedgehogs I've dropped down.'

'Be quiet, Geron,' I reproached him. 'Remember for once in your life that you are of the sacred blood. I have never broken my word to a client. I have never cheated or lied. If I have failed, then I have always admitted it, but never have I failed because I wanted to.'

Geron sat down on his stool, his white hair sticking up all round his head. He had looked so happy coming in, like the boy I remembered.

'There's nothing there, Kallias,' he whispered. 'We'll have to go through this whole ceremony, which will take at least five hours, and at the end of it . . . there's nothing.'

'How do you know? This is the first time you've had someone who has been serious about going down, isn't it?'

So, it was decided. As a slim moon rose above the crest of the broken hill behind the house we began our preparations to make our descent into Hell, the order of the ceremony laid out on the table in front of us.

EIGHTEEN

The authorship of the ceremony was ancient and anonymous, twelve seals of the Iamidai appearing along the left-hand margins, each from one of the controlling families which had been in authority in the year of the seventeenth Olympiad in Elis. There were aspects of both the Greater and Lesser Eleusian Mysteries in the ritual detail; the use of the mirror, the comb and the lyre's plucking-bone were there, and references to the ploughing and opening of earth which Demeter annually commands. There was no mention of the sea, sturgeons, scallops, periwinkles or Aphrodite in this prescribed procedure for a ceremony far from the ocean, as one might expect, nor were Dionysos and his raving queen, Thyore, included, even in those parts of the text which touched upon death and resurrection. At the heart of these ordinances was the potent figure of the ravished wife of Hades, Proserpina. It was into an identification, a spirit-singularity with her that I would be impressed by the forces released within the rite.

'There is no mention of sacrifice here,' I noted.

'Look at the end,' Geron said, 'it's a matter of choice. The subject can propitiate whatever god he pleases, but he is forbidden to use any animal other than swine. That's a separate ceremony, which can be done by attendants during the actual time of the descent. If you want to offer a pig, or two pigs, to Herakles – you're still a Herakles man, I suppose? – then I can do that for you by proxy.'

I thought about this for a while. My brother was not the kind of man to whom I would entrust my welfare unless I was around to supervise.

'My credit with Herakles is strong enough as it is,' I said, not wishing to hurt his feelings. 'Let us concentrate on getting the ceremony right. It doesn't lay down the place where it should be performed. Is that an oversight, or is there a temple of sanctuary which we haven't seen?'

'It's done in the open, down by the side of the lake,' Geron explained. 'Shall we dress up now?'

Vestments were not referred to in the text of the ceremony, and I saw no need to encumber myself with the heavy robes which Sybaris had sent. After all, it was not as a representative of the city that I was acting, but as a priest having sacred knowledge which urgently needed clarification. I told my brother that I would enter the dominions of the lord Hades in my own clothes.

'Do you mind if I dress up in mine, then?' Geron asked. 'Otherwise the thing will never get worn.'

I assented, not caring what he wore. The essential matter was to have the ceremony performed correctly.

'If there isn't a temple or a sanctuary, then I assume that there's a cave or a hole in the ground that we use,' I said, going to the door. 'There must be an actual entrance of some kind.'

Geron took his robes out of the cupboard and locked it, then joined us outside, shutting his dog inside.

'Follow me,' he said.

Leogoras had a bag in his hand. I asked him what was in it, and he showed me. There was a change of clothes, a knife, a length of oiled rope, a lump of cheese, two apples and a towel.

'Where d'you think you're going, Leogoras?' I said with a touch of scorn, 'to see your grandmother?'

'I thought these few things might be useful,' he replied.

'Leave them behind,' I ordered him. 'We will live as the conditions permit.'

Leogoras returned with his bag and obediently put it inside the door of the house. The dog barked and tried to get out, but Leogoras closed the door behind him and trotted along the path to catch up with Geron and myself.

When we reached the edge of the lake, Geron led us round its shore of black stones to a clump of trees. There was an oak, a beech, an ash, a fir, an olive, and a cypress. Beneath the cypress was a tall, oval rock standing upright on its flatter end. It had two round holes in the narrower part. Geron put his robes over the branches of the olive tree and began to change.

When Geron had donned his magnificent robes he stood by my side, and we carefully went through the ceremony, often referring to the text. When it was over I handed him the comb, mirror and plucking-bone, and crouched down to wash my hands in the lake.

'No, you mustn't do that,' Geron said hastily.

'Why not?'

'You must only touch the water at the proper time. Come with me.'

We followed him a little further on. A spur of rock stuck out over the water. Geron walked to the edge of it and pointed down. Below, the water was at first blue and clear, then indigo, then black.

'The procedure is as follows,' he said. 'We bring the oval rock over. You put your hands through the two holes and I seal them together on the other side with some clay from beneath the er . . . cypress? I think it's the cypress . . .'

'Please be sure, Geron,' I urged him. 'Is it the cypress or not?'

He went back to where we had performed the ceremony, poked about under the trees, then returned.

'Sorry, it's the oak,' he told me with an apologetic grin. 'There's a very small spring which feeds the lake which comes through this green clay.' He showed me a handful; wet, sticky stuff, the colour of jade.

'Then what?' Leogoras asked tremulously.

'Hold on, don't rush me,' Geron replied, rolling the clay into a length between his hands. 'We have to wait until the clay dries . . . that will take a while. And we mustn't forget that there are two of you, so you'll have to face each other with the stone between and both get your hands through the holes . . . ah, I mustn't forget the rope.' He went and pulled out an end of white, woven rope, from beneath a bush. 'This is to get the rock back, you understand.'

'Yes, yes.' Leogoras quavered, his eyes on the deep water

below the spur of rock. 'And us? Do we come back up the rope?'

'I think you've worked it out already, Leogoras,' my brother said. 'It's very simple really.'

'Into the lake?' Leogoras yelled suddenly. 'We'll drown!'

Geron shook his head and held Leogoras by the wrist.

'Why, man, you're trembling all over. Hear me out. This clay which I bind your hands with will only hold you for as long as it takes to get to the entrance. Then it melts away in the water, as one can imagine. After that you are free to go through. But without the rock, you see, you would never get down that deep.'

'And you guarantee that we won't drown?'

I told my brother not to answer Leogoras' craven question, adding that I accepted, on both Leogoras' part and my own, that there could be no guarantees of any sort.

'All is chance,' I declared.

'But I'm not a priest,' Leogoras insisted. 'The chances aren't the same for me. Has this worked for other people?'

Geron admitted that no mortal had attempted the descent from Enna until now. The last occasion when access via the lake had been used was, to Geron's knowledge, the time when Hades himself had abducted Proserpina from the fields of sacred Elis, carried her over the sea to Sicily, then plunged into the lake. Upon being further interrogated by Leogoras, Geron owned up that there was no proof that Hades had used the rock, or whether the lake had existed at that time.

'So whose idea was it?' Leogoras persisted.

Geron was silent, shifting uneasily. The rock had been in place when he had arrived at Enna several years ago, he said. The previous custodian had disappeared, leaving no background information about his duties. Geron had had to piece it all together himself.

'You mean that you had to ask around for advice?' Leogoras asked him, his eyes narrowing. 'Who did you consult?'

Geron gave him a long list of names. They were priests and officers from the Sicilian and Italian Greek cities, some of whom I had heard of, and I knew one or two of them personally.

'And who did you ask at Sybaris? As if I didn't know?'

Leogoras demanded sharply. 'And Kroton? It was Pythagoras, wasn't it?'

Geron looked at the ground, raising his sleeve to half cover his face. Leogoras' temper had got the better of him now, and his honest, ruddy face was livid. When Geron saw Leogoras picking stones off the shore to hurl at him, my brother ran off, his heavy mantle flapping like the wings of a golden bat, with Leogoras in pursuit.

The mirror which we had used in the ceremony had fallen out of Geron's pocket as he fled. I picked it up and looked at myself, then returned to the edge of the lake and gazed at my reflection in the water. It was the same moment of locus and focus that I always sought in Elis at my pool when life became too strong. There was nothing below me that I feared more than myself. I went over and lifted the stone, dragging it across to the spur of rock. The green clay I left aside, not wanting to test my courage that far. To wait for it to dry in the sun would take a few hours, and by then Leogoras would have persuaded me that the whole thing was a murderous conspiracy.

Leogoras was still chasing Geron around the shore of the lake and throwing stones at him when I put my hands through the holes in the oval rock, said a final prayer to Hades to ask forgiveness for modifying the rite by not using the clay to bond my hands, giving as my excuse a shortage of time; looked at my image in the lake – a man, pale with fear, but intensely contained within the sacrament – embraced the oval rock as if it were the earth-goddess herself, then toppled myself into the centre of that reflection, my hands gripped together.

The water was warm when I entered it, but as the weight of the oval rock carried me swiftly down into the darkness it became icy cold. Above me I could see the beauty of daylight shivering over the disturbance I had made, then it settled into a dim blue haze. As the pressure built up in my lungs I tightened my hands together, plunging down into total blackness, my faith hardening into a pure jewel of terror, my last look upwards catching the white rope as it snaked down behind me like the birth-cord of a baby slipping from the womb.

When I took my eyes away from the upper world, determined to face bravely all dangers on this journey of mine, I hugged the oval rock hard and prayed for succour.

A voice in my ear said: 'Breathe!'

To do so was death. The voice came again, exhorting me to breathe.

'Who is this?' I asked.

The oval rock shuddered and said: 'Thales.'

My lungs were hurting. The real world had gone. No thinker, divine or secular, would deny Thales, the father of all philosophy, trust. He proposed that everything was made of water.

I opened my mouth and water rushed in.

It struck my lungs and filled them. There was an instant of horror as my being recoiled from the weight and cold of the dense fluid, but I did not suffocate. With caution I breathed out again, and noted that my mind was still alive. As I did so, the darkness cleared and the oval rock settled on to a field by a grey sea.

The rock remained upright, embedded in the soft soil. With great awe and respect I stood beside it, in case it should speak again. It remained silent, a wind from the sea whistling through the two holes where my arms had been.

Now air was air, light and transparent, but it retained the lake's chill upon it. I was afraid to leave the side of the oval rock. It had been my saviour and, to me, it was Thales still, a man whom I had never met except through the workings of his mind, but who had been sent to guide me to this place.

All was silent and motionless. Then something moved, and I saw that what had appeared to be a heap of stone was, in fact, alive. At first I thought that it must be a sheep or a goat from the flocks of Hades, which had been put there for me to make an entrance sacrifice, but the form of an aged, white-haired, man emerged, sitting with his back to me and facing out to sea.

As I walked towards him the ground began to smoke and the wind blew harder, howling through the holes in the oval rock to make a mournful sound. The soil crumbled beneath my feet, releasing blue, thickening gases. I had seen these strange lights before, when attending thanksgiving services on great battlefields, the generals and kings standing with their feet wreathed in the corruption of the slain hosts below.

By the time I reached the seated man the stench of death was everywhere. I tapped him on the shoulder and he turned his head, looking up at me from behind the kind of mask that actors wear for comic roles.

'Which way to the court of the lord Hades?' I asked.

The old man took off the mask.

'Be gone, Sphinx,' he croaked, 'While you have time.'

He was so dried up and wasted, so beaten down, that I did not recognise myself until I heard the voice, which still had some force in it. But my mind worked on, trying to find an alternative explanation for this phantom who seemed to be a form of myself.

'Father?' I said. 'Is that you?'

My father had been a bigger man than I, and it was only in certain parts of our temperament that we were similar. In looks I more resembled my mother. To have accused myself of being my own father seemed to anger the old man. He reached up and plucked my sleeve.

'Before you go grey, hasten towards the truth,' he gasped, then his eyes fell out and rolled down to the sea. I chased after but failed to catch them before they tumbled into the grey waves crying: 'Look for us again in Miletos!'

When I turned round I saw that the old man had gone. Where he had been sitting was a heap of dust, which was already being blown away in long plumes by the wind.

I walked back towards the oval rock, which was still where it had landed. The ground under my feet was solid now; the smoke, gas and stench had gone. Some grass had grown, and there were a few little blue flowers. My heart was heavy, however, and I wept at the burden which I now carried. To have seen myself in that state! So worn-out, so sick and feeble, all pride beaten out of me!

When I heard the bee, it was the sweetest sound that had ever come to my ears. The creature was perched on the lip of one of the blue flowers, gathering pollen. There was no other sign of life in this sad place.

I knelt down and kissed the earth beside it, glad that there was honey even in Hell, then watched it fly off on a zigzag course towards the sea.

When I got to my feet the wind picked up and the oval rock called out its summons; walking over to it, I thrust my hands through the holes and clutched them together on the other side, now in a hurry to be taken far away from this place of desolation. The oval rock shuddered and the air thickened. Against my cheek the stone surface vibrated as the rock began to descend through cold water again. I heard laughter close to my ear, and saw the hideous visage of Bes. Then I was drawn through his navel by a powerful suction.

When I looked out from his belly I saw that I was in a chamber cut from rock. There were torches everywhere and a great feast was in progress, the people crammed together. On a golden chair sat a woman with a bunch of red flowers between her bared breasts and a young tree in a pot between her knees. Although her face was covered with paint and her hair combed up around her head in imitation of the rays of the rising sun, I recognised Luderma.

I was at her death-feast.

Beside her lay her son, Scamano, his hand propping up his chin as he watched the antics of those present. From the state of the chamber and the guests it looked as though the feast had been going on for a long time. Some slept, some reeled about, others drank, ate, sang and caressed.

To be here was a stage on my journey to Hell. I was inside the god of Sybaris, looking out on a scene of death-in-life and life-in-death. Was it here that I should put the questions I had come to ask, or would I be granted an audience with Hades later on? There was something in the air of this chamber, something to do with its badly played music and incoherent speech, that made me yearn for sense.

I recited out loud the hymn which I had made out of the miraculous writing from the Grotto of the Sacred Eels.

The celebrants quietened. Everyone turned to look at me. Scamano sat up, one hand on his mother's thigh.

'What's that song?' he asked.

This was no answer. I was prepared for Hades to adopt any form in which to communicate with me, but he would never use such tones of innocence. Scamano was himself, and this a reality which I had reached from Enna. It was not the place where my questions would be answered, but a means of purging my guilt. Once that was done, I would be ready to face a god.

Bes gave a great belch and vomited me up. As I ran towards the entrance of the chamber, I saw him fill a cup and raise it towards me in a scornful manner.

No-one was following me. I paused, crouched in a corner, watching the torchlight on my love's face as the feast recommenced, Bes now as ruddy and real as any merchant at his pleasures. Luderma not so, however. The embalmers had given her the pallor and dignity of a statue.

I crawled out of the chamber. The oval stone stood blocking the entrance, starlight visible through the holes. I did not want to put my arms through, but would rather have gone out into the night. There was some space to one side of the stone and I tried to squeeze through, but it shifted across to block me off. When I attempted the same thing on the other side, it moved again.

Defeated, I turned and looked back towards the chamber, hearing the sounds of the feast. I could not go back in there, no matter what happened. With resignation I put my arms through the holes and embraced the stone. It immediately began to descend again.

My strong faith had been with me at the lakeside at Enna. When I had taken my life in my hands and submitted to the ordeal, it had been with the confidence that I was leaving one reality in order to arrive at another. Thales had aided me, but only to confront my decayed self on that desolate coast in some blighted future. Now I had been shuttled back to a real happening by the demon Bes (for that is all I held him to be), to atone for my weakness in love. Driven backwards and forwards, battered by conscience and fear, my grip on my beliefs was being deliberately loosened, or so it seemed to me as I plunged downwards through the icy darkness.

At the moment when I saw the circle of light below, the oval rock began to squirm violently, and I felt strong arms pinioning me.

'Let go!' a voice said, then I felt a thick, wiry mass of hair pressed against my lips and I had my head out of water, bright daylight blinding me. I was pulled on to a bank by a man with a long, iron-grey beard who flung me down.

I sat up, now knowing whose voice I had recognised; it was my old body-slave, Frakdurma, whom I had left behind on my estate when I had sailed from Elis; and I found that we were both beside the Narcissus Pool.

I could not speak but lay on my side, the grass touching my cheek as if to reassure me that I was now in a safe place.

'If I'd let you drown, which is what you want, I know, they'd have me beheaded for neglect,' Frakdurma growled as he wrung out his beard. 'You know as well as I do that it's against the law for any one of the sacred Iamidai blood to pollute themselves by committing suicide. Forget Sybaris, can't you!' he shouted shakily. 'Sybaris has gone, but we're still here.'

He pulled me to my feet and took me by the shoulders, staring into my eyes.

'No more of this, Sphinx, no more! I've been with you since you were a boy. Listen to me now! You did not bring Sybaris down. It was her fate to be destroyed. Think of all the other prophecies which you've made, and when they've come true, did you blame yourself? No. Then why such guilt over this one? Cities rise, cities fall. It has always been so.'

I was incapable of answering him. Suddenly he made a strange, womanly sound in his throat and started to carry me down the track towards the house.

'I cannot think very well,' I managed to say.

'Then keep quiet,' Frakdurma muttered.

'You keep mentioning Sybaris as if it were no more.'

'Best not to talk, master. Put that place out of your mind. Nothing will bring Sybaris back, or your poor brother Geron.'

There was a wooden seat under some plum trees which were in flower. I told Frakdurma to let me sit there for a while.

In my wet clothes, I shivered in the cool breeze which was blowing from the invisible sea. I was in Elis and in the future; that much the logic of what I was living through had told me. But I was still in the cold waters of the lake at Enna, travelling through my nightmares again, which had been as real as the wooden seat below me and the flowering plum above.

'Frakdurma,' I said as he squeezed water out of his leather waistcoat, 'how did you happen to be up at the pool?'

'I was told to watch you. We've been taking it in turns to keep an eye open,' he replied gruffly. 'I've spent a lot of time sitting up there, with no-one but partridges to talk to.'

'What did you see today?'

He looked at me askance, briskly rubbing the dampness off his gnarled hands.

'What d'you think I saw?'

'Describe it to me.'

He took a deep breath and gave me an impatient glance.

'Well, master, you know as well as I do, but I'm bound to obey. You went up there at daybreak. You sat in your place, staring into the pool like you've done for weeks . . .' He paused and lowered his eyes, then resumed: 'Day in day out, you've been sitting there, wasting away in your mind. Not like the old days, when you were thinking things out, but withering.'

This time he had to stop. His hands crept under his waistcoat and crossed to his ribs, holding himself.

'I've tried all sorts to stay awake, to keep my attention on you, but human nature being what it is, sometimes my eye wandered off after some item,' he said, his head bowed. 'Then I heard the splash, and you were gone. It was what we've all feared.' He was mumbling now, his shoulders drooping as if he anticipated the lash of punishment. 'No interest in life, in your family and friends, your work . . . none of that old spirit of yours . . . everyone said that it was only a matter of time before you did it. I never believed that, master. Not Kallias, I said, not him. He's been through it all before. He's seen the worst, been in the thick of things so long that one city won't bring him down. Don't you all remember, I said, how this man has lived? What he's seen in his head! Oh, master! Speak for me!' Frakdurma fell to his knees and implored me to save him from being beaten for neglecting his duties.

'No-one will know,' I assured him, beckoning him to get up. 'But you must swear not to tell anyone what happened. Let it be between us.'

When he had settled down and stemmed his tears of

gratitude, I asked him, as casually as I could, how long it had been since I had returned to Elis.

'Oh . . .' he squinted and thought for a while. 'From moon to moon, three times.'

'Have I got better since then?'

'I would have said so until today. As you know, master, you're a difficult man in the cold, quite unpredictable. But when I remember the state that you were in when you got back from Kroton, well . . .'

'From Kroton?'

My heart sank. What had I been doing in Kroton? It was a question I knew not to ask at this moment.

'The laugh was that the amount of money you brought back with you weighed more than yourself. That's one to be remembered. My, you were thin. You were like a man made of straw.'

Piece by piece I extracted from him the circumstances of my return from Italy. He was a garrulous old man and very attached to me, so he rattled on freely. I had been locked in a numbed despair, malevolent to myself, refusing to eat or stir from my bed. The story of what had happened at Sybaris had not been brought by me. News of the catastrophe that had gone ahead, arriving before I did. When I had come home with my treasure I had not spoken to anyone about the city's destruction, or my part in it, but lapsed into morbidity.

'Are you feeling happier now?' Frakdurma asked, looking towards the house. 'They'll be calling us to dinner before long.'

The confusion in my mind was clearing. As Frakdurma had run over these events for me I had begun to realise what had happened: I had been given the vision through which to make the prophecy. It was terrible, this vision; worse than death in many ways, but godly. Between the time that I had first embraced the oval rock at Enna and emerged at my pool in Elis, the world had been transformed. Another dimension of myself had lived through that time, but the holding self, the diviner, the believer, had actually been given more than he had asked for.

'Don't mention Sybaris again unless I ask you to,' I told Frakdurma.

'I'm not surprised you don't want to be reminded,' he replied. 'I won't bring the subject up, I assure you, master. There're plenty of other things to talk about. Though the fate of Sybaris is a great tale.'

Under those virgin-white trees in Elis that spring day my wisdom suddenly flowered. I saw that the gods – whichever one had presided in this case, I would never know – had given me a gift of insight that was as vast as the constellations, crammed with stars of time; not by being shown the future, but by being taken *to* the future. Everything that would happen, had happened. All I must do was record it, return to Sybaris and complete my task. Above my head some early bees were probing the plum-flowers for nectar. My search for a way to return through time to Sybaris would have to be as exploratory as theirs, trying every opening, going by instinct. But before I approached that problem I would have to discover the full details of what had happened. To do that, I would need to find witnesses closer to the events than old Frakdurma and the *great tale* he knew. Perhaps I had told it to him? But in this I was not a reliable informant as, from what he had said, my part in the tragedy was not an honourable one, and this I soon confirmed.

The full story of what had happened to Sybaris and my part in it I learnt from writings which I found in my own room, laid out in my own hand. They were notes and diaries I had kept.

From reading them, I saw that I had behaved shamefully.

At the bottom of the same cedarwood chest where I had found my account of the fate of Sybaris were twenty-five Persian darics, thirty-eight Cyzikene staters, seventy-nine white gold Lydian electrons, six and two-thirds talents of gold, and a packet which bore the seal of Kroton, which contained another three and a third talents.

All this I sent to the Temple of Zeus at Olympia as a gift, notifying the arch-priest of my withdrawal from the cult of Herakles and my future exclusive dedication to Demeter, our mother. The money I gave without specifying any special employment for it, except by requesting that it should be used in the service of his powers where they seemed to be most merciful. On the same day that I despatched this treasure, I shaved my head, swore never to eat meat or drink wine again, and told all my children, women, relatives, servants and slaves that from henceforth they were released from any duty to hold me in affection or respect.

Seven days later I left my home in Elis and crossed to Zykanthous. The only luggage which I carried was the sweat of my brow under the sun, and I fasted for the three days it took before a merchant vessel from Didyma bound for Syracuse gave me a passage back to Sicily, where I knew that I must begin to look for a way to re-enter the moment when I had plunged into the lake at Enna.

There are many sides to Hell, and it is a land of many corners, but the ultimate Hell lies in knowing the future.

NINETEEN

When the vessel docked at the peninsula harbour of Syracuse in the south-eastern corner of Sicily, I was recognised by refugees from the fallen city of Sybaris, who were waiting for ships to carry them to new lands. These unfortunates set up a howl of rage and disgust at the sight of me, and I was forced to run away. It was not long before the civic authorities tracked me down, however, having set up a hue and cry that the Sphinx was in Syracuse. I was arrested and brought before a magistrate to see if I qualified as a guest-friend or welcome visitor, or whether I constituted a threat to the state. When the magistrate heard who I was he was astonished that I ventured so near to the scene of my crimes.

'We have no regrets about what happened to Sybaris, but your behaviour has become a legend of infamy,' he said. 'I cannot believe that any citizen of ours in his right mind would have invited you here.'

I told him that I had come without invitation, at my own risk, adding: 'All I ask, your honour, is that I should be permitted to cross the territory of Syracuse on my way to Enna. I will not even stay the night or eat a meal here.'

'Sphinx, why are you going to Enna?' the magistrate demanded.

'I wish to make a petition to the god Hades on behalf of the victims of pestilence in Elis,' I told him, lying out of necessity. 'I now work for the sick and needy, having forsworn my old life. As you can see by my condition, your honour, I am a man who has little interest in himself. This is so true that should you decide to make an end of me, or throw me into prison or sell me as a slave, I will happily submit. But it will not help the sick, and Demeter, our mother, pointed me out in the sanctuary at Olympia as the priest who should make this journey.'

The magistrate withdrew to his chamber to consider the matter. When he returned I was told that I would be conducted to the western border of the territory of Syracuse and allowed to cross, but I must not, under any circumstances whatsoever, return.

'We don't want you here at all,' he said severely, 'not after what you did to the Sybarites. But for Demeter's sake you can go.'

A squad of young cavalry soldiers from the port barracks took me that very night. I rode mounted up behind the officer, a stout youth whose waist was so thick that I could hardly get my arms around him. They rode hard, not stopping once on the way, and I was dropped off in an open space beside a stream which was the border.

'Cross over the stream,' the officer instructed me, 'then you must walk until I can't see you. I've been ordered to patrol for three days to see that you don't come back, so don't try it. If you do, then I have orders to kill you. Understand?'

I told him that the situation was clear to me, then crossed the stream by some stepping-stones and walked straight ahead into the night.

When I had got well away from the stream I found a sheltered place under some bushes and tried to sleep, but it was impossible. The air was full of small noises. Owls flew by like ghosts, and I was sure that I heard the soft tread of foxes. When some large animal began crashing about not far away, I broke from my cover and began walking north-west again, guided by the stars. I had expected to be exhausted by now, but my body created fresh energy somehow. By dawn I was in the foothills, skirting all human settlements and flocks of sheep, as I had no wish to come into contact with anyone until I reached Enna.

There was plenty of water in the streams, and I found cress in a rock basin, and there was wild silphion growing in the marshy ground. It was not a feast, but it kept me going until I came across a clutch of six rock-dove's eggs and ate them raw.

That night I slept soundly, lodged in a cleft with branches pulled around me and a stick in my hand. I had no company in these higher places, no whistles or patterings, but in the morning I woke up with a start as a pharoah's hen, that foulest of birds, descended on the branches, thinking I was carrion. I leapt to my feet and drove it off with my stick, but it refused to fly away, surveying me from a nearby tree with malignant disappointment.

Now I was in the mountains. Before noon clouds came from the north, cooling the air and bringing rain. I walked on, less sure of foot over the slippery limestone.

When the cloud came down and I was forced to breathe the mist, I tasted sulphur. Later on in the day I saw in the north-east a wide pillar of smoke, and knew that it must be Etna, the volcano, beneath which is one of Hephaestus' forges, the lame and cuckolded smith-god, husband of hot Aphrodite; and also the smithy where the Cyclops fettles his weaponry. It is in the Etna forge that Hephaestus is said to have constructed the team of golden, mechanical women who help him in his work, fetching and carrying and holding his metal with pliers: these machines also share the god's bed at night, so that he can forget the treachery of his wife. Some argue that this is exactly the kind of story that does religion harm, pointing out that if Hephaestus is truly a god then he would satisfy his need for women in the usual way wherever and whenever he wanted to; but my case is that Hephaestus, having experienced the ecstasy of love with Aphrodite, could never accept a lesser delight. The mechanical women he made were an admission of despair, also a godly impatience with second-best; both of which bring the smith-god closer to us. I believe that as he lay in his bed with those cold, golden toys, he was presenting an ageless criticism against his father, Zeus; that the transient nature of love in the universe leads to artificiality. As this applies in the human sphere to precisely the same degree, it is a unique point of coincidence between the gods and mankind.

To have this long-debated thesis of mine running through

my mind as I came to the top of a narrow pass and, once again, looked down into the vale of Enna, was a strengthening mercy. Some certainty, some confidence in myself, had returned. At least I could think again, having spent so many days since my reappearance in Elis in a fog of unquestioning guilt.

I was at the opposite end of the valley from where I had first approached it. The house was further away and difficult to make out, because a heap of stone was in the way, a heap that was higher than the roof. Only one end of the building was visible. I noticed that the pigs had gone.

Dark grey under the clouded sky, the lake now had a different shape. Then I noticed that the stony shore had disappeared and the water ran up to the grass. The level of the lake had risen.

It was a cold day, but no smoke came from the house. With a heavy heart I trudged down the track and headed across the valley floor. When I reached the heap of what I had taken to be stones, I discovered that it was a great pile of pig skeletons, hundreds of them stacked one on top of the other. The house itself was empty, the furniture left as I remembered it. The cupboard was locked, so I broke it open. Thousands of moths poured out and filled the room. All that was left on the hanging rack was fragments and threads of cloth, the remains of the vestments that had been kept there.

I searched every corner for messages or clues to what had happened, but came up empty-handed. There was nothing to indicate that Leogoras was alive. Who would help me to return to that hour when I had plunged into the lake? There was no-one else to identify the time with me. Once again it would be left to the gods. I knew of no ceremony for reversing the power of Kronos, the god who had generated this hour, and the one that I must re-enter. Now that I knew the fate of the city in detail, it was my sacred responsibility to warn the Sybarites. How they would change that fate before it became a destiny was another matter. Whether or not I would offer my services for another contract, once the prophecy had been made, would require some hard thought. It was in my interest not to shame the Iamdai or be cursed as a betrayer, but my powers were limited to prognostication and petition. There is no diviner who can promise to undo what he has foreseen.

I left the house and went to the lake. The woven rope was tied to the trunk of the oak; following it, I was forced to paddle in the shallows of the lake where it had covered the grass. When the water darkened and I knew that I had reached the edge of the depths down which I had plunged, I picked up the rope and began to pull.

At first I thought that I was immediately moving the rock. The rope came in quickly, then it tightened and I could not shift it. After a few moments of struggle I had to rest, and the rope slid back through my fingers. When I resumed, there was the same tension and no movement, but I dug my heels into the grass beneath the water and hauled with all my strength, gaining a couple of arm's-lengths on the rope.

As I did so I heard pigs squealing; looking across to the house, I saw one right at the top of the pile of skeletons. It tumbled down the side, then ran off. With my next effort, in which I gained another full stretch of my hand, another pig materialised on the summit of the pile and clattered down. I realised that by pulling the oval rock up from the depths I was resurrecting these animals. With each pull of the rope I was drawing time back, as well as the oval rock.

I paused in order to offer my thanks to Kronos, believing that he must have heard my unspoken prayer, then put all my effort into hauling at the rope, laughing and singing with joy as I brought the entire pile of pigs back into the living world and dragged the valley into its winter past, through snow and hail, sun and windy days, flowers growing back into themselves, then into the autumn and summer before, when they had been in blossom. There was such tempest in the vale of Enna! And I was its master, god-like for the first time in my life, transforming the earth with my strength.

When the last pig leapt to its feet I saw that an altar had been beneath the pile. My arms and legs were aching now; tying the rope's slack to the oak so the oval rock – which had not yet appeared above the surface – would not go back down, I went over and examined the altar. It had not been there at the time of my descent, and it was of very rough construction, thrown together in a hurry. As I stood by it there were shades, grey slips of thought or presence which I could feel around me, and a feeling of panic which emanated from some being. Unable to make sense of it all, I returned to the lake and began hauling on the rope again, sharing my attention between the surface of the lake, where I could expect the oval rock to appear, and the altar.

As I edged the increasing weight out of the depths, three figures began to take shape at the altar, taking it down stone by stone. Two of these figures did the work of undoing the structure, the other stood by with folded arms, pacing nervously back and forth.

From his golden robes I recognised Geron, my twin brother, and knew that the other figures were Leogoras and myself.

But I could not halt in my work of raising the oval rock. It was now at its heaviest, the crown of it resting on the spur from which I had descended. Fraction by fraction I edged it up, until the arm-holes became visible, and it approached a point of balance. Once I had got it beyond that, it would fall on to its side.

The rope was cutting into my hands. Now I could hear Leogoras shouting at Geron as he pursued him around the lake shore, the last sight of him I had had before going into the lake a winter, autumn and summer before. Then the oval rock was up, evenly poised. I gave one last long pull, and it crashed on to its side on what was now dry land.

Leogoras kept running after Geron right round the circumference of the lake, returning to the place where I stood with my hands thrust through the holes in the oval rock, ready to descend.

'Don't!' Leogoras cried, waving at me.

I stood facing my breathless brother who was now half-strangled in Leogoras' fierce grip, those three seasons of flourishing summer, fruitful autumn and dead winter obliterated as my time of decision came again.

'If you go into the lake, then you're just giving them what they want,' Leogoras gasped. 'The ceremony was all made up by this scoundrel. I've a good mind to kill him here and now.

To betray your own kin! Have you no shame?' He shook Geron violently.

'I was forced to do it,' Geron whined. 'Pythagoras can destroy me if he chooses. What choice did I have?'

With a strange reluctance I let the oval rock fall and walked away, not able to look at my brother any more.

'What hold had Pythagoras got over you?' I asked, once my revulsion had abated a little.

'If I tell you, then you'll have the same hold,' Geron complained. 'It's nothing, really. Something I did a long time ago, when I was interested in his ideas about the transmigration of souls, some innocent experiments.'

'If they were so innocent, why daren't you tell your own brother – a man a thousand times your better – about them?' Leogoras demanded.

'Were you a disciple of Pythagoras?' I asked.

'I suppose I was, for a while,' Geron said with a whimper. 'To be honest with you, Kallias, I think I was in love with him. When that man pays you attention, it makes you feel as though you can do anything, but he's vicious at heart.'

'Unlike you,' Leogoras sneered, shaking him again.

I told Leogoras to release his hold on my brother, and led the way back along the shore toward the house, walking side by side with Geron to let him understand that I did not condemn his weakness. Geron had always been a bending reed.

'We will get you back to Elis, I think, Geron. That's the best place for you if you're afraid of Pythagoras. Keep out of the western Greek cities and states for a few years,' I said to him with as much kindness as I could summon up. 'Don't pit yourself against his strength, which is immense, or think that you can outwit him.'

'I know, I know.' Geron gabbled, anxious to encourage sympathy. 'Look at his hatred of you as well. It's fanatical. All because he thought that he could get you under his thumb. Not my brother, I told him. He's no-one's stooge. But Pythagoras is determined to have Sybaris. He'll let nothing stand in his way, that man. Do you know why, my dear brother? Because he's got this ridiculous idea worked out in his head about the way the universe works, and he's determined to be in control.'

'If that's true, Geron, why is Sybaris so important to him?' I asked.

'To pay for it all! Pythagoras intends to extend his empire from Kroton to Sybaris, then, with the treasure he'll command, he'll undermine the states and cities of Greece, then Egypt and Persia, the whole world.'

'And what about Milo? Where does he stand?'

'He worships Pythagoras. I've been told that they're lovers,' Geron explained, raising his hands. 'At his age! Milo just does as he's told. When they're alone together, Milo behaves like a little boy.'

'How do you know that, Geron?' I asked.

'Friends in Pythagoras' household,' Geron mumbled, eyes averted. 'People I respected, once.'

My brother had always had a weakness which allowed men of authority and charm to enslave his soul. When these masterful figures were finished with Geron, they inevitably cast him out. I suspected that his relationship with Pythagoras was of this nature.

We reached the house. I sat my brother down close to the windmill, which was throwing a strange, flowing shadow over the smoked fish.

'I have to know the whole truth,' I said. 'The failure of my purpose in coming to Enna has left me with nothing at all. I had something to go on, an inner scene, a direct manifestation, writing, but I couldn't trust them. Now I can trust them even less, because I'm certain what's going to happen in Sybaris.'

'How?' Leogoras demanded.

'Let's say that I just know *in my bones*.'

Neither Leogoras or my brother would have been able to understand what had happened to me during my attempted descent into the dominion of Hades. The deviation of time which I would have had to explain to them would have left their minds reeling: time as a road which divides on either side of a moment and then rejoins it at a point further on.

Geron reluctantly provided me with a full account of his involvement with Pythagoras. He had actually been in Kroton when I had visited the city to negotiate with the Sirisian fishermen, and had been present at the house of Phalanthos when I had been so dishonourably treated by Milo and Pythagoras. He had kept out of the way, unable to help me (or so he said) because Pythagoras had been watching him closely.

'The man is depraved,' Geron said in further explanation of his predicament at that time. 'It gave him pleasure to see me suffer because of my brotherly love for you.'

It transpired further on in my brother's story that when Pythagoras had learnt that I intended to enter Hell, he had sent my brother to Sicily with two other disciples from Kroton. There was already a votary of Hades in residence when they arrived, a very old woman who had been a seamstress in Akragas and had been sent to look after the civic costumes at Enna in the days when the notion of the great Greek city-states having the gall to beard the lord of the Underworld in his own kingdom was current. The two disciples of Pythagoras had suffocated the old woman in her own shawl and exposed her cadaver on the mountain for birds to devour. One of the disciples had then returned to Kroton, and the other had remained to keep an eye on Geron, instructing him how I should be entrapped in the false ritual and destroyed. This disciple had then sickened and died, leaving Geron alone to deal with me when I arrived.

Somehow my brother had to atone for his stupidity and weakness, and he knew it. Leogoras was seething with rage against him, pacing up and down outside the house, flicking the ends of the windmill with the point of his sword. If I had told him to cut my brother's head off there and then, he would have done it.

'In view of my failure to draw a response from the gods on this visit to Enna,' I said, 'I have to fall back on more tried and trusted methods. We will build an altar and make sacrifice.'

'Ah,' Geron said, relief in his eyes as Leogoras flicked the windmill round again, 'that sounds like a good idea.'

'We will not petition the gods,' I went on, 'we will importune them. We will deluge them with blood.'

My brother trembled, believing that the blood I had mentioned might be his. While I built the altar, assisted by

Leogoras, I let Geron stew in his fear, then told him to go and catch the first pig.

With a cry of gladness he ran off, and soon returned, dragging a beast by the back trotters. I ran through a brief form of the Heraklean rite then cut the pig's throat with Leogoras' sword, offering the life.

'Now, Geron,' I said to my brother, who had thought that he had been reprieved, 'I want you to sacrifice all the swine in the valley.'

He stared at me, sweat already beading his brow from the first chase.

'What, every one?' he croaked.

'Every one. You know the ceremony, all you have to do is catch them and kill them one by one. Under the circumstances, that's not too much for me to ask of you, is it?'

I fixed him with a solemn gaze in which I communicated both my disgust with his disloyalty and my willingness to forgive, should he take on this Heraklean task, one that the hero could have done as his thirteenth Labour after the bringing out of the three-headed dog Cerebus from the Infernal Regions, it was of such magnitude.

It took Geron four days to complete his task. His only help came from his one-headed dog, shepherding the swine from one end of the valley to the other as the pile of slaughtered pigs rose on the altar. I used this time to prepare myself for the return to Sybaris: working out how it could be possible that certain knowledge of the future which had been confirmed when it was past could be altered to save Sybaris.

TWENTY

We left Enna by the northern route, heading back towards Himera and the coast. My brother was given the mule to ride, as he was far too exhausted to walk. Also, for the first time that I could remember, his fatigue stopped his tongue and we could progress through the countryside without too much chatter.

Upon reaching the farmstead where I had bought the mule on our way down from the coast when originally travelling towards Enna, I was greeted as a saviour by the poor peasants. They took us up to see the field which I had petitioned Demeter to make fertile, and I was gratified to see how well the plants were doing. When they asked me to perform the same ceremony again, I advised against it, explaining that any god will become less responsive if persistently petitioned on a case where help has been granted. They accepted this guidance from me in good spirit, but when I offered to sell the mule back to them they were unable to buy it, having spent the money. Instead, they offered to give me one of their daughters in exchange. She was brought from the pastures where she had been tending goats and presented to me. I could see long, wide-set green eyes watching me over a half-veil.

'Her name is Nonios,' the mother said, 'and she has been on the earth for twenty-four summers.'

'Nonios?' I replied. 'Why have you called your daughter after one of Hades' mares?'

The woman shook her head sorrowfully and stroked the girl's cheek, then took the half-veil away. As she did so, the girl closed her eyes.

I saw that Nonios had a harelip; a repulsive disfigurement.

'She was kicked in the mouth by one of Hades' stallions,' the mother explained, covering the girl's face again. 'She was out playing when the god came by in his chariot. Take her, lord Kallias. She is a good girl, and the deformity is the only one that she has. Her body is perfect otherwise, and her nature is as sweet as honey.'

I looked at the girl. She was fair-breasted, and when she moved it was with a graceful ease. Beneath her rags she was long-limbed and well favoured: her hair was coppery red and long, tied back like the tail of a horse. She was a little gaunt after the mountain hardships she had lived through, but her eyes, skin and teeth were strong and clear.

'I'll take her,' I agreed, 'but I must know that she is willing to come, and that she is courageous.'

Nonios' willingness became obvious when she knelt on the ground and kissed my hand, submitting life and body to me. As for her courage, the entire family clamoured to tell me stories of her bravery against wolves, bears, serpents and thieves, and her accuracy with the sling.

'Nonios can knock the eye out of a hawk,' the mother said, 'but when I told you that she was my daughter I was not owning up to the whole truth, for which I hope you will forgive me. Nonios was brought to me by my first husband, who was a sailor. He brought her back as a child from some place to the west, an island, as part of his wages. But I have taken care of her as if she were of my own blood, and brought her up decently and religiously, I promise you.'

As we shared out the mule's burden between Leogoras and Nonios, (Geron insisted that it would take him all his time to walk, never mind carry a load), I had to stop the girl taking far too much of the weight, she was so desperate to please. When I chided her for being over-eager, she gave me an horrendous smile.

'I am a strong woman, lord,' she assured me. 'Don't worry about me. Make me work. That's what I like.'

We moved on that day. Nonios said farewell to the only family she could remember. At first I thought that she must be hard-hearted, because she was dry-eyed and formal, anxious to get away. But as we got beyond the farm and she lost sight of them all, I was glad to see that she shed a tear.

I had no choice but to go to Himera, in spite of the dangers. Nonios was useful to me when we reached the outskirts. She knew the town, and could enter it without fear of being treated as a stranger, having often been seen in the market. I sent her in to scout, telling her to go to the harbour to find out the destination of the ships. Meanwhile I remained with Geron and Leogoras in the scrubland which lay to the south of the town, waiting for her return.

She came back within half a day. There were seven ships in the port, she told me, two from Akragas, one from Syracuse, and the rest were home vessels. Of these, two were not going anywhere, one was bound for Zankle in three days, and the last was going to the Aeolian Islands that evening.

'That's our only chance,' I said. 'From the Aeolian Islands we can cross to Laus with a bit of luck. What size of vessel is it?'

'Smaller than the others,' Nonios answered, 'and the man who owns it is cruel.'

'How d'you know he's cruel?' Leogoras asked her.

'I have had dealings with him in the past.'

My expression must have shown the doubt and curiosity which had crossed my mind. Nonios raised her head higher.

'I have had to earn money in any way I could,' she said. 'What we grew for market was often too inferior to sell. How could I go back to them empty-handed?'

We were silent, chastened by her honesty. Then I felt angry at the thought of this Himeran sailor and his cruelty to her. What had he done? Had he mocked her ugliness? The protectiveness which rose up inside me had surprising force.

'He likes me, though,' Nonios added, reading my mind. 'I can make him agreeable.'

'No!' I said fiercely. 'I won't have that.'

'It's simple enough,' she laughed, giving a little shrug. 'I've done it before.'

'First, we will offer him money for the passage. If he asks any questions and looks as though he might inform the authorities that we're in Himera without invitation, then we'll find another way of making him take us,' I told her. 'A woman can get a promise out of a man like that which might last a day, but not a voyage across the sea.'

We entered Himera just before nightfall. Nonios knew a small gate in the walls which was seldom supervised. Once we were within the walls, I told her to guide us down to the harbour. The vessel she pointed out was a weatherbeaten cargo ship, very broad-hulled, and was being loaded with large bales of animal hair. I sent Leogoras aboard to contact the master and ask him to come to the side. When Leogoras returned, he was smiling.

'All done and settled,' he announced, pleased with himself. 'He was too busy to see you, so I organised it myself. "Four passages to the Aeolians?" he said. "Consider it arranged. It's not a luxury craft but I can make you comfortable."'

'Did he ask any questions?' I enquired. 'This sounds very slapdash on his part.'

'He said that it isn't his business who we are or what is the purpose of our journey. He's happy to take our money.'

The master came out of the hold. He was a short, stout man with a pointed beard and mean, light eyes which flickered everywhere like a sunbeam. When he caught sight of Nonios he stopped and grinned, fingering the golden curls which fluttered on either side of his bald head.

'You're not leaving us are you, flower?' he said sardonically. 'What will the menfolk of Himera do? Do you know what she's like?' He addressed this question to me, taking it that I was the senior member of the party.

'Are you a religious man at all?' I demanded vehemently, knowing that I must control my anger.

'Of course,' he replied with a lewd grin. 'I say my prayers when I remember.'

I beckoned him to come closer, and held him by the sleeve. My mind was unfolding a device as fine as woven cloth.

'This female is sanctified,' I whispered.

'Oh, yes?' the man chuckled.

'I have come here from the oracle of Aphrodite at Paphos, commanded by the elders of the sanctuary to seek out the new priestess. She always comes from Sicily, and she always bears this sacred mark.' I touched Nonios' harelip with my finger.

'Any man who aids the temple at Paphos in bringing her to her duties will be blessed with good fortune in love; conversely, any man who impedes her progress in any way will be struck down by disease of the sexual organs, culminating in impotence. This has been attested as true on every occasion when a new priestess has been sought.'

'Do the authorities know who you are?' he asked, his head cocked to one side. 'They'd be very proud to know that one of their street-women had become a priestess.'

'The tyrant of Himera is fully aware of our presence here,' I replied haughtily, 'but he is sworn to secrecy, because the new priestess must first be recognised in Paphos.'

This man – Xandros was the blackguard's name – was unwilling to yield his disbelief. He kept looking at Nonios and grinning, but my demeanour had him half-convinced. When I showed him the money and offered half at the outset of the voyage, he accepted it. Before I handed it over, I extracted a promise from him that no-one would be told that we were aboard.

'You have my word,' he said.

'This is a serious matter,' I insisted. 'To protect the interests of the sanctuary at Paphos, I must have an oath from you.'

He refused, protesting that he was not used to having to swear oaths to take passengers, but I finally won my point. Then, having done all I could to secure our safety, I made him take us aboard there and then to await the ship's departure.

To pass the time before we sailed, I sent Leogoras out for hot food, seeing that the galley on the ship was primitive and we could not expect much in the way of quality from there. Upon his return we sat together and ate, and Leogoras chose this as the moment to raise the question of my diet. He had noticed that since the episode at Enna when I had (as far as he could see, that is) decided to abandon my intention of gaining entrance to the dominion of Hades, I had not eaten meat or drunk wine. It was no pleasure for me to deceive the good man, but I had to do so, using the excuse that I had imposed these penitential restrictions upon myself because I had failed in my mission.

'So how long do you mean to go on with this mortification?' Geron asked. 'You've always enjoyed your food, and as for wine, well, you love it.'

'When it feels right to return completely to my old self,' I replied, relating this utterance to the cryptic knowledge that I had of events which lay ahead, 'and I have carried out my part of my contract with the city of Sybaris to the last letter, I'll celebrate.'

Geron raised his eyebrows. 'You're intending to go back, then?'

I confirmed that I was.

'Don't,' Geron advised. 'What do you owe a man like Telys? Nothing at all. Let him sort it out himself. If he had been straight with you from the beginning, it would be a different matter, but he's just used you as a smokescreen. He's never had any faith in divination. Pythagoras will have assumed that you're dead by now, and put his plan to possess Sybaris on to its final footing. He's had Telys as his mind-slave for ages.'

I was not yet ready to accept such wisdom from Geron, not after his behaviour at Enna. Forgive him I might have done, but I had not forgotten. Counsel about how I should conduct myself in an affair of this kind came ill from one who was so weak-hearted.

'It sounds as if you have already decided that Pythagoras has won,' I said calmly. 'What do you suggest we do, in that case?'

'We could just turn our backs on the whole thing and go somewhere else,' Geron suggested. 'I wouldn't mind going somewhere new.'

Leogoras had been resuming his instinctive friendship with my brother until this point. Now he curtly reminded him that it was my honour that was at stake, and therefore my future.

'Who would take my master seriously again if he let Sybaris down?' he said wrathfully. 'And what about my wife and children?'

Geron fell silent, staring down at his food. I looked at Nonios, who was sitting a little way off but listening intently. She had a hard gleam in her eye as she chewed a roasted lamb's knuckle through her divided lip. Then she sat up straighter, laughing with joy.

'They're casting off!' she cried, standing up to see better. 'Oh how I bless this hour.'

It was still spring, the season by which I usually measure the end of love's journey. With the death of Luderma still painful in memory (though not in conscience, as she had taken her choices and I had been forced into mine), and the nightmare of her funeral feast during the shuttling of the oval stone through time, I was convinced that my interest in Nonios was paternal at the most. Her fearsome face put me off any thought of intimacy, or so I thought. Her admirable qualities seemed to be the cause of my warm feelings towards her, but as the voyage along the north coast of Sicily began and we sailed into the night, I became aware that my blood was no longer in its old rhythm. The quiescence which the end of winter habitually brought to me had not arrived. This most unfortunate of women, a daughter of poverty and humiliation, had aroused me beyond sympathy or fellow-feeling. This was disturbing in many ways, mostly inasmuch as it proved how much I had changed since Enna.

Nonios was a straightforward woman. She understood that, as my property, I could take what I wanted from her. However, she saw that I had a tenderness towards her, and this she found difficult both to comprehend and manage. It made her reticent and over-respectful, attitudes which I do not encourage in slaves or servants.

It was a cold night with a northerly wind. Our quarters were nothing more than a space between bales of evil-smelling animal hair. Leogoras and my brother had already fallen asleep, curled up beside each other like two children. I could not keep my eyes closed, my mind too active for slumber. So much had happened to me that I did not fully understand. There had to be questions which hung over the experience at Enna. Had it been a dream? Had I simply gone there, found my brother acting as an agent of Pythagoras, turned round in defeat and headed back to Sybaris? This was the rational answer.

Nonios was lying to one side of me, her body held away as

if she was afraid to touch my person. As I stared into the night, still wrestling with my task to bring it under control in my mind, she got up and climbed to the bulwark of the ship. I thought that she had gone to urinate, but a few moments later I heard voices raised at the stern of the ship.

When she returned, I asked her if Xandros was being troublesome.

'Not any more,' she said, putting her head down to sleep.

'What did he say to you?'

'Oh, the kind of thing that he used to come up with; names, just names. They don't mean anything,' she said dully, her voice hardly audible above the battering of the waves on the ship's hull. 'He was a cruel man.'

I could not be sure that she had said *was*, but as I had already noticed that she had a leather sling wound tightly around one hand, I took the precaution of going to look for Xandros. The helmsman was sitting by the rudder, and I asked if he had seen him.

'He went forward after he'd had words with Nonios,' he told me. 'They had a disagreement, it seems.'

'Did she go with him?' I asked.

'No, she just waved at him, then went straight back where she'd come from.'

'Do you know Nonios yourself?'

The helmsman grinned, his teeth white in the night. 'Well, we all know Nonios in Himera,' he said.

I went back and sat next to Nonios, my back against the bales. When the sun rose I did an inspection of the ship, examining it from bow to stern.

There was no sign of Xandros.

The helmsman was Xandros' cousin, and owned a third share in the ship. When it was ascertained that the ship's master had disappeared during the night, this man, Rios, took over. He did not appear to have any suspicion that his cousin's death was anything more than an accident, nor did he appear to be too disconsolate about it.

As our voyage continued, I found that my urge towards Nonios fluctuated; mounting in the vigorous sea-breezes during the day, abating in an instant at night when I saw the sling wrapped around her fist. On the afternoon of our second day at sea I saw a huge white bird keeping pace with the ship. I invited Nonios to show us her skill by killing it in flight.

'If you command me to kill it, then I must,' she replied, feeling in a leather pouch for a stone, 'but I would rather not.'

'I want to see how accurate you are with that weapon,' I told her, 'that's all.'

She thumbed the pebble from her pouch into the wide part of the sling and drew back her arm, all in one smooth motion. When she released the pebble, it struck the bird's wing-tip, making it fall sideways towards the sea. Before it hit the water she slung a second pebble and knocked the other wing-tip, straightening the bird up so it settled on the sea properly balanced on its breast.

'Why did you leave it so long to punish Xandros?' I asked her. 'You could have destroyed him when you liked.'

'We needed the money he gave me in the past,' she told me, her wide-apart green eyes meeting mine without flinching. 'For the things he made me do I asked a good price, but once I came under your protection there was no need to put up with his insults any more.'

'What kind of things?' I demanded, unable to stifle the jealousy which surged up in me. 'Tell me.'

'He liked to use my face.'

Sickened by what I had learnt, I looked over the side and left her alone, my disgust for the perversions of mankind quelling all feelings of jealousy.

TWENTY-ONE

When we entered the main port of the Aeolian Islands, the town was in ruins, smoke still rising from the broken buildings. The Tyrrhenians had made a punitive raid a short time before. There were wrecks in the harbour itself which made navigation difficult, so Rios arranged for his cargo to be unloaded on to small boats and ferried ashore. He had been told that the Tyrrhenians were still in the area, raiding the smaller islands and likely to return.

We went ashore in the last boat of cargo. As we climbed on to the jetty, Rios' ship was already heading for the harbour entrance, sail bellying out. He had no oars to speed him if the wind changed, and it was blowing from a north-western quarter now, not the best direction to drive his ship along the westerly course.

There was nothing but misery in the settlement. No-one took any notice of our arrival. A continuous funeral was taking place on a hill overlooking the port, the dead laid out on the grass as though sleeping in the sun. The Tyrrhenians had been selective, I noted: they were all men of military age.

We found lodging for the night in the house of a widow. She had been fortunate. Her five sons were all away on a voyage to Rhegion when the Tyrrhenians had struck, but two of her daughters had been taken.

That evening the Tyrrhenians came again. There was no resistance from the people of the town. The warriors and sailors were in a gentler state of mind, and did no further harm than to drink themselves stupid and lark about amongst the ruins they had made. We kept to our quarters, but I sent Leogoras into the roof to keep a look-out for the officers of the Tyrrhenian fleet, hoping that Luderma's son, Scamano, would be amongst them. The vessel we had sailed in from Poseidonia was not amongst those now crowded into the harbour, nor did I recognise any of them from the fleet which had maintained the blockade, but I had hopes that my luck had turned.

Before nightfall a second part of the punitive expedition came into harbour, and Leogoras called from the roof that Scamano's flagship was amongst them.

Scamano was not aboard the flagship, having gone home to Veii for his mother's entombment, but his deputy remembered me and offered his help. He was older than Scamano, well-travelled but retaining a certain innocent charm. He had an artificial eye made from a polished brown soapstone, which he had chosen because the colour approximated to the colour of his good eye. As the artificial eye was completely brown and the good eye was only brown at the centre, this gave him an odd lopsided look. To add to this impression, he always held his head to one side when talking, and it was the side with the soapstone eye, as if the weight of it was pulling him down. The Tyrrhenian sailors called him Old Stonehead, but it was an undeserved epithet. Bucchero was an open, good-natured man, although not much of an admiral, according to the officers who served under him. If he could be lenient to free man or galley-slave, he would do so. He loved to drink, and he liked to have straightforward orders to obey. What he did not have was resourcefulness when faced with unforseen events. It was this weakness that we were to see too much of within one day of quitting the Aeolian Islands on our voyage north to Laus, where Bucchero had agreed to take us.

The Tyrrhenian fleet of seventeen warships was under oars, making slow progress against the wind, when a navy of strange vessels bore down on them. These enemy ships were painted white and carried only one bank of oars, each bow fitted with three pointed rams. They flew no flags and blew no trumpets. When the leading Tyrrhenian vessel was rammed, it was impaled on the long metal spikes and pushed backwards in the water, an astonishing feat of strength by the rowers of the white ships, who kept themselves hidden behind shields. The cry went up in the Tyrrhenian fleet that these strange vessels were manned by ghosts, and panic began. Bucchero was drunk, still celebrating his triumphs in the Aeolian Islands, and he had no idea how to bring morale back into his navy. He staggered about at the bow of his flagship screaming into the wind, his junior officers grim-faced by his side as they saw the destruction being done by the attackers. With his galleys scattering on every side, Bucchero gave the order for the flagship to turn and run with the wind. We escaped in this way, then spent four days scouring the seas for the rest of the fleet so it could be reassembled. When this was achieved, we were within sight of land in the east. Upon counting his ships, Bucchero discovered that he had lost only two in the engagement. It was said amongst the Tyrrhenian warriors that the enemy had treated them with contempt, ploughing through their famous navy as if it had been merely an obstacle on the way towards a fighting a worthier foe. This was a great insult to their manhood and the name of Tyrrhenia. In such a case, it was customary for the commanding officer to suffer death. There was a meeting of the senior officers on the flagship at which this sentence was passed, and Bucchero was told to prepare himself.

The priest of the fleet had been one of the casualties. Most of the officers had religious authority, having sacerdotal as well as magisterial duties as landowners at home, but they were unwilling to preside over the execution of Bucchero. Eventually I was asked if I would assist, but I declined, reminding the officers that my religion was not the same as theirs. They unanimously agreed that this need not be an impediment, as all gods were gods and shared the same natures. Bucchero himself affirmed this, saying that whatever I came up with as an appropriate rite for his demise would be acceptable to him.

We were anchored in shallow water no more than ten stadia from the shore. The coastline was low and green with few trees. I proposed to the officers that they should commit Bucchero's life into my hands and allow him to be landed with my company, then forgotten about. This, I argued, is a form of death for a nobleman. He will lose his status and reputation. His honour will disappear.

Bucchero refused to accept my offer, as I had expected he would. I must admit that I had had an ulterior motive, namely that I was anxious to get ashore and begin the overland journey to Sybaris without any further delays.

The time for Bucchero's execution was set for sunrise the following day. During the night I was wakened and found the ship very close to the shore. I was told to conduct my people down into the water, which was no more than waist-high, and our baggage was lowered to us. Then a party of Tyrrhenians cranked Bucchero down. He was bound and gagged, hanging from a small crane in the stern. When he was released into our arms, Leogoras, my brother Geron, Nonios and I carried him to dry land.

I was aware, even as we were carrying him, that Bucchero had sunk into a deep shame which rended him virtually inanimate. When we undid his bonds he lay on the sand and said nothing, seemingly incapable of movement. We had no option but to carry him again. This he allowed, but he would not help us in any way, or speak. It was as if we were carrying a dead man.

Behind the shore there were low sand dunes. Beyond that we could see little, though the earth smelt of marsh. We waited a few hours until dawn, when we were able to see what lay inland. It was an impassable swamp, so we were forced to go south along the shore, dragging Bucchero on a litter which Leogoras made from driftwood.

Leogoras and Nonios had been strong and uncomplaining through all this, accepting their discomforts and burdens, being guided by my decisions. But my brother was less so.

'If you'd kept quiet and let the Tyrrhenians do the proper thing according to their laws, this would never have happened,' he grumbled as I ordered him to relieve Nonios from pulling one shaft of the litter. 'We would have been taken to Laus and not ended up wandering about in this wilderness. Where are we? I've got no idea. There's no sign of life anywhere.'

I told him that I thought that we were a good distance to the south of Laus.

'Then why aren't we going northwards?' Geron demanded. 'If we keep going in this direction, what can we expect? D'you know this country?'

'No, I don't, but there is another route to Sybaris across the mountains. I think that we were put ashore nearer to that one than the Road to Prosperity out of Laus.'

We now had the mountains in view far over to the east. When we had got beyond the limits of the marsh, it was my intention to go inland and travel through the foothills in search of this route which I had heard talk of: it had been lightly used during the past few years, because it was too close to the territories claimed by Kroton and Rhegion and therefore a possible source of friction. I did not pass this information on to my brother, as it would have provided him with more fuel for his grievances.

'You *think*?' he said, scowling at me as we wound our way through a mass of stinking seaweed. 'What happens if you're wrong?'

'Then we'll have to find our own way.'

Geron laughed hollowly, now up to his ankles in ooze.

'And you'll expect us to carry this wretch on our backs, I assume?' he snorted. 'Can't you persuade him to stop this performance?'

Such hypocrisy! I thought. All your life, Geron, you've been dependent on others; now you can't spare this fallen man any pity.

We had walked from sunrise to noon, and still the swamp was with us on our left side, flat, green and evil-smelling. The Tyrrhenians had given us some provisions, and it was time to rest. There was a solitary flat-topped pine on the edge of the dunes, which provided some shade while we refreshed ourselves. Bucchero refused to take anything and lay with his eyes closed, scarcely breathing. Within a short time of settling under the pine and eating and drinking we all became drowsy. I noticed Geron fall asleep, then Leogoras, then Nonios; then, in spite of myself, I succumbed, tired out by the night's adventures and the long march we had done.

Nonios awoke me some time later. The sun was much

lower in the sky, and the wind had changed. She told me that Bucchero had gone, pointing to footprints in the sand which went straight into the sea. We went down to the edge of the water where the Tyrrhenian's tracks left off, and looked out. The surface was ruffled, but anyone swimming would have been visible.

'He could not live with himself,' I said. 'My brother was right to criticise me for meddling.'

Nonios sat down in the sea and opened her legs towards the horizon. At first I thought that the woman was washing herself, but then she called. A dot appeared on the sea's surface far out. We both saw it. Nonios curled her lip in what passed for her smile, and pointed.

'You're sure that my story about Aphrodite wanting you to serve her in Paphos is untrue?' I said as the dot came nearer. 'This is your doing. How long have you had this power?'

'Since meeting you, lord,' she replied. 'I dreamt that this man was not ready for death. I dreamt a life for him while I was asleep under the tree.'

'What kind of dream?' I asked.

'A carnal one.'

My heart suffered a pang as I heard this. Nonios knew that she had caused me anguish, and crouched trembling at my knee. I edged her away.

'The dream was without feeling,' she said.

Still hurt but slightly appeased, I patted her head.

'Are you able to have visions?'

'I am.'

I put my hand on the nape of her neck. As Bucchero swam closer, I slipped it to her shoulder then down on to her breast. She was warm and full, shivering like the new-born.

To some in this wilderness of the world comes a mate. I had struggled to find that lover amongst women of high breeding or beauty or possessions, or youths of such exquisite form that they transcended the base needs of a man's nature. My pride had kept me blind to Nonios, but now that she had shown that we were within the same gift I felt love's strength. She could see as I could see, and suffer. A terrible spite rose up in me as I stared at her disfigured face. Why did my fated love have to look like this?

I hit her across that hideous, divided lip, knocking her into the sea. She rose out of the water and remained on her knees as I beat her again and again, calling out that I submitted to this harsh fate, not in wisdom and understanding, but under the compulsion of love.

When Bucchero left the sea he approached us with smiles, greeting us as though we were long-lost friends. No excuse was offered, nor an explanation. He had gone for a swim like any man would do who wished to be cleansed.

When we returned to the pine we found Leogoras and Geron still asleep. My brother had always been a difficult person to wake, so I used this knowledge to teach him a lesson. I woke Leogoras, and between the four of us we picked Geron up and carefully put him on the litter, setting out again on our journey along the shore, with him lying on his back snoring as we went along. When he did emerge from sleep he did so with a loud shout of terror, looking wildly about him. We did not pause in our progress, only laughed at him a while, but I was glad to see that Bucchero had recovered enough fighting spirit to turn and give Geron a long, scornful look to remind him of the ungenerous remarks he had made.

We did not abandon the litter, but now used it as a carrier for our baggage. Each of us took turn to scout the edge of the swamp for firm ground which might give us a means to cross, but this eluded us. By evening we were still tramping down the shore, but some way ahead I could see that the land started to rise close to the coast, and we pressed on, hoping to get clear of the swamp by nightfall.

This we succeeded in doing, arriving at a series of grassy knolls which bordered the sea. There was no sand here, only rock and turf, with several tall beech trees bending their smooth boughs low over the water. There was no shortage of wood, but I told Leogoras to keep our fire small in order not to attract attention, for wherever the beech grows people tend to dwell, drawn to its stately shelter. Behind the knolls was deep forest, which Leogoras and Bucchero scouted together before we ate our meal. They found a spring at the foot of the knolls, and some edible plants to supplement our rations.

After we had eaten, Bucchero announced that he had

decided he must have a new name, and asked our advice on which one he should choose. Everyone except my brother immediately understood why the man was doing this.

'What are you trying to achieve?' Geron asked him in a waspish tone. 'Changing your name won't wipe out the past. You look like a Tyrrhenian. Everyone will know you're a Tyrrhenian, with that bronze skin of yours and those quarter-moon eyes.'

Bucchero ran his hand over his balding head and sighed.

'Has Geron always been your name?' he asked.

'Always!'

'Perhaps you should have changed it to improve yourself.'

Leogoras guffawed as my brother's face fell. Now that Geron was silenced, we began a discussion of a new name for our companion. It was no easy choice, because he wished to free himself from his ties with his people (as Geron had suspected), but had no wish to identify with any other country in particular.

'All names have an origin,' I observed, 'but the names of the gods must come from a time before mankind.'

Bucchero would not agree. He made the point that the names of the gods were different in each human language, which meant that mankind must have baptised them. Also, he had no desire to use a god's name at a time when he was feeling so fallible.

Nonios made a suggestion that silenced us all with its rightness. Without any hint of mockery she put it to the Tyrrhenian that he should split his name in half and take one of them, or, if he so wished, use both halves, but never together.

Bucchero bowed his head.

'There are children who have my name back in Tyrrhenia,' he mused sadly, 'and they can keep the wholeness of it, but I must take your wise advice, woman. I am Chero from this day on, though I will keep Buc in reserve for a time when I might need it.'

He then went into the darkness of the forest, saying that we should all remember that it was one man who was departing from the firelight and another who would re-enter it.

'Also, when I return, I will be in full possession of my new name, having thought my way into it. It would help me if you could call me Chero from now on.'

For a while we heard him wandering around in the forest, groaning and crying like a wounded beast. Once he had fallen silent we could not help but wonder whether he had taken his own life, unable to shed his dishonoured past; but he rejoined us before we settled down to sleep. He said nothing, lying close to the fire, his face covered by his hands. Out of respect for his anguish and the toils of his change, we left him alone.

TWENTY-TWO

It had been in my mind since Nonios drew the Tyrrhenian to her womb out of the sea that I should lie with her. This was in her mind also, and we had spent the remainder of the day aware of this mutual thought. However, once it was night we could not shut out the exile's pain, hearing him crash around in the forest, waiting for his return. We sat on the edge of the firelight, our flesh-senses ensnared by another's tribulation. Geron did not stay awake once Bucchero had gone, and Leogoras lay down with his back to us, though I knew that he was not asleep. Our desire was in a strange suspense, hovering in the dark like a blind hawk that cannot see its prey or stop itself hunting.

When Chero came back, I saw Leogoras glance at him before turning his face from the fire to sleep. I led Nonios further away, searching for privacy amongst the beech trees. We found a natural bed between two big, exposed roots and lay down together. It was too cold to be naked.

She began to fondle me in a skilful way that I immediately recognised. I told her to stop; that I wanted her to forget everything she had done around the port of Himera.

'What shall I do, then?' she asked me.

'Nothing,' I told her.

I gave her pleasure in every fashion I could; every delight which I could conjure; every part of her warm, salt sweetness coming under my tongue. When she attempted to respond, aroused to caress me, I refused to allow it. This was the only way to get the whore out of her, to purify her. Any pollution would flow through me, a vessel made by the gods to cleanse sacred places. As time went by and her pleasure mounted, she began to understand what I was doing and submitted to an even greater depth.

When it became impossible for me to keep my moment back, she clasped me into her with a ferocity that shook us both, growling into my ear. In the sleep that followed, I am certain that being so blended within each other, we must have had the same dream. Whatever it was, this dream, it did not linger into the morning. Neither of us could remember its shape or its story, though we could both recall its power.

We returned to the place where we had left the others, and found no-one there. The baggage had also gone. I could not believe that Leogoras had betrayed me, nor could I think of any good reason why Chero should decamp. After scrutinising the earth around the dead fire, Nonios said that there were footprints which did not belong to any of us; but we could not follow any tracks away from our camp because the ground was covered with dead beech leaves.

We searched the area of the knolls on all sides until we came to the south. The beech trees stood very close together here, forming a screen of low boughs already thickly in leaf. When we stood on the edge of a low cliff and parted the screen, we looked down on a narrow-necked bay with a wide beach. Drawn up on it were the white galleys which had swept the Tyrrhenian fleet aside so easily.

The men of this fleet were assembled in a crowd on the sand; tall, pale fellows with light hair. They seemed to be employed in some sport or exercise, because their ranks swayed backwards and forwards and runners broke from the mass and were chased up and down the beach. At the bottom of the cliff sentinels had been posted, and I was able to examine them more closely. They were fine, athletic men, lean and strong in the leg and shoulder, their garments made of grey wool, their principal weapon a long-handled axe with a small head. The most unusual feature of their dress was a long plait of hair which hung over the right shoulder, its end stuck in a small bronze pot worn in a harness. As I watched, one of the sentinels took the end of the plait out of the pot and sucked it for a while, then put it back into the pot.

Meanwhile the game continued. Men went back and forth

to the ships, some swam as they lost interest in the sport; it was a scene of recreation. Nowhere could I see Leogoras or Chero or my brother. Then I spotted an odd man out; someone whose stance was quite different to the towering, long-limbed vigour of these pale warriors. Even from the distance I was at, I could tell that he was a Greek: his gestures, his signals of knowing, the motions of his head.

My fear was that Leogoras, Chero and my brother were already dead. There was something about the style of these fair-headed warriors which spoke of speed, simplicity and lack of mercy. If they had wanted to take life as well as possessions, then nothing would have stopped them.

We searched beneath the beeches and found no evidence of struggle, no bloodstains or marks of any kind. To get closer to the beach where the warriors were congregated was a dangerous proposition, but the forest ran close to the edge of the sand, and I guessed that if there was a leader he would be established close to the point where the spring emerged and ran across the beach into the sea.

We crossed the knolls and entered the forest, making our way around the back of the beach. The stream from the spring wound in and out of the trees, and came out on the southern side of the bay. There were tall rocks at this point which made a natural enclave, and I could see activity around the entrance. Occasionally the game surged to these rocks and a great shout would go up, then the crowd would retreat in a high humour, laughing and shouting.

We got as close as we could without taking the risk of being seen. While we crouched in the undergrowth I saw the Greek coming along the beach, talking to a few of the warriors who had broken off from the game. As he approached the entrance between the rocks I recognised Phalanthos, the man who had helped to make such a fool of me at his house in Kroton.

The warriors finished their game as Phalanthos disappeared between the rocks. They sat on the sand, many of them making use of their plaits and bronze pots in the curious practice which I had noted.

I could not mistake my brother's scream.

I had heard it on and off all my childhood, and its note went right through me. Without further thought I broke out of the cover and ran towards the rocks. Before I could get close I was brought down by several of the warriors, their hard heads and limbs crashing into me. They snarled and shouted in their odd, mooing language, slapping my face and kicking my shins; then, picking me up, they rushed me over the sand and between the rocks.

My brother was lying on the sand, apparently unharmed. He was blubbering out information to Phalanthos, who was interpreting what he was saying to a white-haired chieftain. When Phalanthos saw me he paused and grinned, his ugly blue-streaked teeth revealed, then he raised a warning finger.

'Not as serious as it seems, Sphinx,' he said. 'No harm done so far. Bear with me. Let me deal with this.'

My brother stopped his account of our doings – he had got to the clash with the warriors at sea, but had not yet mentioned Bucchero, as was – and looked up at me.

'I can't stand pain,' he mumbled. 'They were starting to beat what they want to hear out of me.'

Phalanthos introduced me to the chieftain, who was not so old, in spite of the colour of his hair. The man's white-lashed, blinking eyes settled on me. As he began to speak he poked a long finger in my chest. His voice was full of slow, round sounds, almost plaintive in their alien music. Phalanthos interpreted what he said for me step by step: he, the lord Man-High Leaper, had no need to fight cowards, or the brothers of cowards, or the friends of cowards. He had come a long way at the request of his friend Phalanthos, who would show him the enemy. Was I an enemy?

Phalanthos leered at me as he translated.

'Well, are you?' he said

I could see Leogoras and Chero being held at the other side of the camp between the rocks.

'I am not,' I replied firmly. 'I am a traveller.'

Phalanthos translated for me. Man-High Leaper asked where I was travelling to: when Phalanthos translated this, he added that I should not mention Sybaris in my reply.

'Say that you are going to Kroton,' Phalanthos advised. 'Then he won't be confused.'

I followed his advice. As soon as Man-High Leaper understood what I had said, he shrugged as if to convey that all was well.

'I have told him that you are known to me,' Phalanthos oozed, 'and I ask you to remember that. You will come to Kroton with us, as that is where we are headed.'

Man-High Leaper waved us to leave him alone, taking his plait out of his pot, which was of chased gold. Before he put it into his mouth I saw a brown, sticky ointment on the end. It was evidently a comforter of some kind, as his expression relaxed once he had sucked for a while. I chose this moment to ask Phalanthos to tell the chieftain that I had a woman in my company, and needed his guarantee that she would not be ill-treated.

This he gave, but on the condition that he, Man-High Leaper, could have her if he wanted. This was the custom amongst the people of the Drume River when safety was given to strange women. Although he was a long way from home and on his way to a war against a very rich city (here he eyed Phalanthos in a challenging way, as if daring him to retract some promise), he felt that his traditions must be carried with him.

I could not argue, nor did I argue with my pride. My hope was that he would find Nonios too ugly. When I went into the forest and called out to her that she should join us – she had stayed behind when I had responded to my brother's cry – she appeared on top of the rocks above the chieftain's camp and I saw, to my horror, that she had a stone in her sling.

Within the time that it took me to shout a warning not to attack, she had broken the skulls of three warriors. The speed of her hand was faster than my voice could travel.

When it registered with her that I had commanded that she hold back, she stood on the rock and slowly wound the sling round her hand.

Once he had seen that I had control of the woman, Man-High Leaper was happy to leave her where she was. He went over and examined the dead men, all youths, fingering the holes made in their heads by the stones from Nonios' sling. Phalanthos was by my side, full of consternation and cursing me under his breath. When the chieftain called him over, he blanched with fear and gave me an accusing stare.

'He'll want compensation,' Phalanthos muttered, 'and lives, I shouldn't wonder.'

While Man-High Leaper talked to Phalanthos beside the fallen Drume warriors, I calmed Nonios as best I could, advising her to sit quietly and wait for my orders. She was so strong and quick that I feared she would escape somehow, leaving me behind. But my doubts about her loyalty were groundless. She obeyed me, sitting cross-legged on the rock and watching what was going on below her with an air of detachment.

Phalanthos called me over.

'Man-High Leaper is amazed at the accuracy of this woman of yours,' he said, his eyes passing signals that I should be especially intelligent while dealing with this situation. 'His worry is that he cannot tell the mothers of these youths that their sons were slain by a woman. That would be too shameful for them to bear. Instead, he is demanding the life of your servant. The families of the dead will be told that he was a great fighter who overcame these boys in battle, and was then slain himself. In addition, you can supply compensation in coin or treasure.'

I thought for a while. Leogoras had been within earshot, and I could not look him in the eye.

'Ask Man-High Leaper if he respects the gods of other people,' I said to Phalanthos.

The answer came back that he did.

'Tell him that this woman is a servant of the goddess Aphrodite.'

Phalanthos frowned and looked at his feet.

'Tell him!' I insisted. 'What do you stand to lose? If you don't help me, I'll tell her to sling more stones, and one of them will be for you.'

Phalanthos translated. Man-High Leaper replied that he had never heard of Aphrodite.

'Tell him that she is the goddess of desire.'

Man-High Leaper raised his eyebrows. His answer was that the Drume people had a male god to do this. Before I could continue with my efforts to protect Nonios, (I was groping towards a means of arousing a superstitious fear in the chieftain which might temper his demand for Leogoras' life),

Man-High Leaper picked up a long-handled axe and swung it on to his shoulder.

I thought that he had decided to ignore my efforts to deter him from his revenge and was preparing to kill Leogoras on the spot, but all he did was to clear a way through his warriors and pace out a hundred steps along the beach, then stick the axe in the sand side-on to the rock where Nonios waited.

Then he stepped back and waved to Nonios. She looked down at me to ask whether she should accept the challenge.

I nodded.

It was all one motion. The sling dropped to its full length in one hand. As it did so, the other hand came across and fed a stone into the pouch, and she swung. Unlike many slingers I had seen on the battlefield, she did not whirl it around her head, but only brought her arm back then forward, delivering the missile with a snap of her wrist.

The stone rang against the blade, shattering into fragments and knocking the axe over.

The Drume warriors let out their breath in wonder, then began shouting excitedly, raising their arms towards Nonios.

'Tell him to put the axe's edge towards me,' she cried, 'but they must stand well back.'

Phalanthos heard what she had said and translated for Man-High Leaper, who laughed with delight. He picked the axe up and stuck it back in the sand with the blade's edge pointing directly at Nonios.

She did not sling until the Drume warriors had been moved right back, explaining that she could not swear to the direction that the missile would take once it had struck the axe's edge.

Man-High Leaper pushed his men back, but lingered too near the axe himself. When he would not move – the man was showing off his superior eyesight, perhaps – Nonios slung her stone. It struck the edge of the blade and whirred past the chieftain's head. If it had hit him he would have died instantly.

The Drume warriors clapped and leapt in the air at this astonishing display of skill. When Man-High Leaper returned to us, he was pulling at his long upper lip and frowning. He told Phalanthos that it would be a pity to spoil such a story. When the fleet returned home, the tribe would be pleased to hear the details of this encounter. It would sound well in the history of this campaign, Man-High Leaper's last before he retired to breed sheep. Therefore he would like to know more about the goddess.

I began to tell him about Aphrodite, but before Phalanthos could finish translating the chieftain had marched over to the rock on which Nonios was standing and was pointing up at her, mooing excitedly.

'He says that she is the goddess herself, and not a servant at all,' Phalanthos explained. 'That is what he believes.'

I was not prepared to argue the point, if the chieftain's error would save us from retribution at the hands of the Drume. Without hesitation I gave all the attributes of Aphrodite to Nonios, adding that every stone she had slung was the testicle of a man who had shown her disrespect. Upon this, and other mysteries of the love-goddess' cult, I elaborated until I could see that Man-High Leaper was content to forget all about revenge and compensation.

All this had taken place with the morning sun behind Nonios on the rock. The Drume had been able to recognise that she was female from her outline and the way that she moved, but they had not been able to see her face.

When I coaxed her down and presented her to Man-High Leaper, he stared in disbelief, demanding to know why the love-goddess was such an eyesore. In my protectiveness I disputed this, saying that he should imagine her without the hare-lip, but he could not see it. I went on to say that the malformation was a kyphotic sign of her divinity. When she was seen from the other side, her celestial nature, her lips were the most beautiful thing about her.

All this went over his head, and he said that he would not include it in the story because it was too complicated. As far as he was concerned, she would be a beautiful goddess who had killed his men with the balls of lovers whom she had eaten. Back home they would understand that. Meanwhile I should keep the woman under control and watch that she did not use her sling again unless she were asked.

Man-High Leaper's fleet had called in at the bay to find fresh water and take some leg-exercise after a long row across from the furthest point of the north-western Mediterranean, where the Drume homeland was. Phalanthos had been sent there by Milo to recruit the warriors and their ships: a mercenary force known for their hard, driving valour and rapacity. I did not give Phalanthos the opportunity to lie about the target, this *very rich city* which had so concerned the chieftain. I knew that it was Sybaris. Nonetheless, unable to resist the temptation to deceive me yet again, Phalanthos laboured at convincing me that Kroton had employed these Drume River pirates to defend itself against attack from the Greek cities in Sicily. I did not bother to query this naively elaborate untruth, but concentrated my questions on recent news, conscious of how far events must have moved on since I left Sybaris to go to Enna.

Shortly after I had left, so Phalanthos told me, Telys had expelled all the *azygous plutos* from the city and confiscated most of their wealth and goods. This action had been approved by the people's democratic vote, and had been accepted as the only defence against an unknowable but threatened future. When I pressed Phalanthos to explain the thinking behind this decision, he was quick to assure me that Telys and the citizens had come up with the idea amongst themselves. They had not been influenced in any way, but sheer desperation, and my failure to divine the future, had brought about this radical move.

The *azygous plutos* had been driven out into the mountains and left to fend for themselves. They had wandered around, totally helpless, a prey for malignants and marauders, and had been saved by a party of traders from Kroton, who had led them to the city where Milo had given them refuge.

By now the five of us were aboard Man-High Leaper's ship, and heading southwards, keeping in sight of the coast.

'What does Pythagoras think of all this?' I asked Phalanthos.

'No-one knows. He has been working on something else.'

'Numbers again?' I asked, unable to keep the sardonic edge out of my voice.

'Probably, though he has been giving a lot of thought to the theory of *The Three Vehicles of the Soul* lately, and developing his ideas on the ultimate theo-political structure of Kroton's future.'

'So Kroton is clear about what is to come?'

Phalanthos smirked, refusing to be drawn.

'You should be glad that Pythagoras has such respect for religion,' he said. 'The other philosophers have become impatient with it.'

Now that my brother was back within the influence of Pythagoras, he lost no time in getting close to his creature, Phalanthos. By the time that we arrived in Kroton three days later, Geron was sufficiently in favour with Phalanthos to leave the vessel arm-in-arm with him, while we remained behind under guard.

The Drume fleet had beached in a shallow cove just to the south-west of Kroton. Man-High Leaper's men had been instructed to remain close to the ships and not to wander into the surrounding countryside, in case they got embroiled with the natives. It was while we waited for some message from Milo that I was able to try out the effect of the ointment with which the northern warriors consoled themselves so frequently. One of their number had become infatuated with Leogoras, liking his luscious, open looks and black, curly hair, so unlike his own. Whenever there was an opportunity, this man approached Leogoras to touch him. He was a very tall fellow, dangerously silent and intent. After his initial nervousness at this attention, Leogoras learnt how to sit still and allow himself to be stroked, which was all the taciturn Drume seemed to want.

My mind was not on the risk that I was taking when I quickly stuck my finger into the warrior's bronze pot as he sat beside me, leaning back and feasting his eyes on his beloved, poor Leogoras. Sybaris was in my thoughts more than the impulsive curiosity that prompted me, and it was the feeling of helplessness which my contemplation had produced that made me act this way. Also, upon later self-examination, I have to confess that the news about the banishment of the city's richest men had made me believe that it was because of my failure to divine a coherent pattern in Sybaris' future that Telys had taken this extreme step, thereby alienating the city from its most important men. What else was Sybaris but its wealth? Once that was gone in its natural form – the men who had made it – the actual value could only degenerate because it would no longer be able to reproduce itself.

So I took my refuge in the Drume's little pot, swallowing the sticky ointment. It had hardly any taste except a prickle of heat on the tongue. Nothing happened for some time. I continued to sit next to the warrior, while he admired Leogoras and caressed him.

The warrior's ointment, on which he was so dependent, had an unusual effect. I could understand how useful it was to him. Everything was reduced to an essence of particular being. All the mazes and adornments of mind faded away from every object as it was perused. A bird lost all meaning beyond its function of flight. Things and objects seemed to radiate their most graspable attribute, and the relationships which they had with other things and objects fell away. Vision was narrowed but not intensified. My eyes had, instead, the skill of removing layers of light, and my ears of quietening the resonances of sounds. In the depth of the experience which the ointment had thrust upon me, I realised that the gods had gone from my comprehension. Their names meant nothing to me. What did matter was my particular presence, that particular stone, this particular perception of existence as physical magic.

The narcotic was very powerful. It did not affect time's pace as many do, but made each instant as solid as a stab with a stick. How the Drume warriors lived with this sensation I do not know, nor why they venerated the effect. Whereas it had temporarily obliterated my awareness of the divine it had, perhaps, become the only guide to the spirit which they had. This would go some way to explaining their toughness and single-mindedness in war.

Upon my full return to my senses, my first sight was Leogoras, now peevish and fatigued by the doting Drume. Fortunately the warrior was soon called away and I was left with my servant, his excellence shining out of him for me. Always I had admired his farmer's healthy beauty, his high colour, bright eyes and frank countenance, but now I sought past those surfaces to the man I loved with my true heart, needing to reassure myself that he was still there behind his mask of material flesh, the essential Leogoras, and no *thing*.

All of this I wanted to say to him, and I began to speak, but when he turned his exhausted eyes upon me I desisted. He had had enough compliments for that day.

When I had been completely cleansed of the Drume's *iggfor ren* (the ointment's name in their language, meaning *plunder lick*), I had to be grateful that I had been spared the sight of Nonios while under its influence. Mercifully, she had gone off with Chero to teach him how to sling. When she came with her gaping lip and sat next to me, I was glad that the drug's fixity of vision had gone. Nonios was respectful towards my strange mood, believing that I was in the throes of a small prophecy, but she had bad news: I was summoned to the house of Pythagoras, and my brother Geron had reassumed his loyalty and allegiance to Kroton, denouncing me as an enemy of the city.

TWENTY-THREE

We were conducted to Kroton by a force of lightly armed infantry, young men who marched at a fast pace with us boxed in between them, carrying our own baggage. It was a deliberate ploy, designed to bring us to our knees; but we bore up well, taking the jibes and sneers of the youths in good part. These soldiers were models of Milo, wonderfully fit and impressive in their new equipment and uniforms. An urgency was in these boys, quivering in their slow minds, a hunger for conflict. It was bursting out of them, rolling through all their crude jokes and unkindnesses as we stumbled along, most of which they employed on my woman's looks. But Nonios was a match for them. Her days at the port of Himera served her well here, and she marched along with her head held high, fending off their cruelties with laughter.

On our way to the western gate of the city we passed field after field of men training for war; cavalry, infantry, siege-engineers and their teams. The race track and stadium were full of soldiers performing athletic feats, competing with each other in the full weight of their accoutrements. Bands played in the shade of trees, chariots were being greased and painted on the roadside. It was a scene of industry and purpose, portentous of a bloody future, the full horror of which I knew.

Once inside the city walls, I was separated from the others. I was taken to a cavalry barracks and locked in an empty stable, full of dung. More humiliation, I thought as I sat on the manger, listening to the stamping and banging of the horses next door; this is being done to me on the orders of Pythagoras. What is he saying? What must I interpret from this treatment?

Grief pushed these considerations away. I had seen Nonios, Chero and Leogoras swallowed up by Kroton, a city all too ready for bloodshed. In times of war the Greek mind becomes cold and practical. All sympathy is concentrated on the welfare of the home soldier, not his adversary, real or imagined. From experience I knew that by now all strangers within Kroton would have been rounded up and either expelled or incarcerated. Suspicion of disloyalty or lack of enthusiasm for the city's policy would have been enough to see honest citizens condemned to death. It was always the way once the government had aimed its arrow at its target.

But I had been hasty in these suppositions. On our way in from the coast I had tried to extract from the boys in our escort the cause of the hostilities which were in the offing. They had not answered me directly, but laughed and shouted 'Who knows?' 'You'll see!', nor would they identify the enemy whom they were so eager to fight.

I was brought some fruit and water by a middle-aged captain, a man with a harassed and uncomfortable look in his eye. Before he handed me the cup and fruit he sent a slave in to rake out the worst of the dung, and allowed me out into the courtyard while this was being done.

I thanked him. His expression discouraged any close questioning, but I ventured an enquiry about my bed, should I be made to sleep the night in the stable.

The captain told me that this was most unlikely.

'We need the stall for a horse,' he added, his voice low and, so I thought, tinged with shame. 'It is no place for a priest.'

'When am I to be taken to Pythagoras?' I asked.

'This stall is where his war-horse is stabled,' the captain replied, eyes averted. 'When he returns from manoeuvres he will look after you.'

He left, closing the door behind him and bolting it. I sat on the manger and sipped at the water, wondering at the workings of the Long-Haired Samian's mind. To stable me like his horse? With his horse? What was he implying by this? That I was serve him, to be his to bridle, to spur?

Night came, and I was still locked in the stall. The captain did not reappear, so I made the best couch I could out of the manger, which was too short for me, but gave some relief from standing and sitting. I must have fallen asleep in my misery, because I woke to a tremendous din as hundreds of horses came into the courtyard, and I could hear men calling to each other as the animals were put into the stalls. After some time, when my expectancy had subsided, I began to drowse, but with my ears pricked for any sound at the door. The rest of the building was quiet by then, broken only by the noises of horses settling. Nonios came into my mind in a half-dream, the hooves of the black stallion flailing over her as the King of Hell's chariot raced across the hillside of her home.

Such reverence arose in me that I got down from the manger and knelt, using it as an altar upon which I could imagine all that my soul needed. It had been many days since I had remembered to pray or give praise. Now, here I was, the smell of dung heavy in the air, the tired beasts of the creation tethered all around me, the recipient of a prophetic experience which no man had ever been granted before on earth; yet I found it hard to reach out for the gods with either gratitude or respect. Any prudent man would know that this was wrong, a fault in myself, a poison of doubt, and I knew it too. So I doubled my effort to pray, I twisted my spirit like a man squeezes the last drop out of a wineskin.

Still I could not find the path to the gods.

It was blocked by darkness, dung, suffering faces, marching men, but most of all, by the divine sin of destruction, a city's ruins thrown across the way.

Sybaris had lost me my heart-faith, though my head-faith persisted. In the toils of this realisation I fell asleep where I knelt at the manger, my mind now as empty as the captain's cup.

That was how Pythagoras found me when he led his horse in at dawn. He said nothing as I got stiffly to my feet, pushing me aside as he chose to do a slave's work, wiping the foaming sweat from his mount. I stood aside, listening to the incoherent squeaks and mutterings he was making as he rubbed the horse down. When he had finished, he came over to me with the stinking rag and wiped it over my face.

'So, how was Hell?' he said.

I did not reply, but wiped my lips clean of the foul horse-sweat.

'Your brother tells me that you didn't go. Is that true?'

I remained silent, head down.

'The Sphinx a coward? Who'd have thought it? Well, Telys is very disappointed in you. We all are!' He threw the rag into a corner and laughed, sour contempt in his voice. 'You've caused a lot of trouble in Sybaris because you wouldn't get your feet wet.'

'I had no reason to trust that ceremony.'

'What? With your own brother in charge of it? Your own blood? One of the true priesthood, Iamidai to the bone? Who better to administer a sacred process? But Telys had a feeling that you'd fail,' he went on. I saw the sharpness of his eyes, and knew that I must not treat him as if he were mad. No matter how he behaved, Pythagoras never acted spontaneously; everything had a purpose.

'He is not a religious man,' I replied. 'Nor are you.'

He looked at me for a long time, leaning against the wall with the sunlight falling on him from the open door. His beauty was still superb, even with my awareness of his evil. The years had not taken the sheen from his skin, and the lines which were drawn there were an embellishment, a decorative touch on something already perfect.

'It's over for you, Kallias,' he said. 'Your time has dribbled to its natural end. You're a slave to the past, I'm afraid. But I may still have some use for you.'

His first remarks had filled me with dread, sounding like a notification of my impending death; but what he had said latterly gave me guilty relief. What I needed was time, but I did not wish to seem craven in gaining it.

'What use can an old, backward-looking failure be to anyone?' I spoke with forced humour, hoping to placate him into further concessions. 'As you grow older, Pythagoras, a new youth seems to invest your enterprises. I can't remember you being a military man in the old days. In fact, if I remember rightly, you held soldiering in contempt.'

He thrust out his lower lip, obviously holding back his amusement at my self-deprecation.

'To make great changes, one has to use all the tools that are available. I have taught myself a few things since we were in Egypt together.'

This silenced me for a while. We had both studied under the same occult masters in Memphis, but he had been far ahead of me in the ability to absorb and understand sciences, laws and learning not contained within our Greek religion. He had favoured the Egyptians because their knowledge and beliefs were not cluttered by the work of poets. This absence had had the opposite effect upon me; I came to trust Egyptian learning less.

'Do you want to live?' Pythagoras asked candidly, moving towards the door. 'I have no further time to waste on someone who has proved to be an obstacle, but there are still some shreds of respect afforded to you. I might forgive.'

'For surviving? From what I can see, you have made use of me all along the way.'

'Only because I had to,' he said with a wry smile. 'That is a good way for you to look at it, of course: since you've been nothing but an implement, though a blunt one, why not stay that way? Telys is a young fool. He is lost already. What I need is help to get this over quickly, and with as little loss to Kroton as I can.'

'My retainers . . .' I began to say.

'Have them,' he replied impatiently. 'Just make up your mind. I have work for you *now*. If you want to do it, then you must decide before I walk out of that door.'

I could not say the words that would bring me down to the lowest pitch of self-esteem, so I nodded. He merely grunted, stepped out of the door then slammed it behind him, leaving me in the stable with his reeking horse.

I was released a short time afterwards and taken to a stadium on the northern outskirts of Kroton, where the *azygous plutos* from Sybaris were living in a temporary camp. Telys had allowed them to bring a large amount of baggage, and this was piled around the place, bales of cloth, chests, furniture, all strange and outlandish in this austere setting. There were over a thousand men living in tents, guarded by Kroton soldiers. The families of the *azygous plutos* had been forced to remain behind in Sybaris as hostages to the good behaviour of the exiled menfolk.

Pythagoras was at the stadium with Milo, meeting with leaders among the *azygous plutos*, when the cavalry detachment brought me through the gate. I was conducted to a tent of silver and green fabric which had walls of crated possessions, and there I found men from Sybaris whom I knew, old Saphnis, Telys' biddable councillor, to the fore.

I was greeted with enthusiasm and affection, or as much as these exiles could muster. They looked drained and bewildered, fish out of water. Milo swaggered amongst them radiating furious health and confidence, pinching their softened muscles, berating them for their spineless degeneracy.

'See where indulgence has got you?' he boomed. 'What value has all that mouth-work and balls-play got now? Where are all your past gluttonies? Why, if I set all thousand of you on ten of my children, they'd beat you to death with cabbage-stalks. Get fit, all of you. Exercise! How many have done the routine?'

The *azygous plutos* groaned and shielded their faces from his critical gaze.

'You must set an example,' Milo bellowed, poking Saphnis in the chest and taking a fold of his cheek between finger and thumb. 'You can't expect us to do all your fighting for you.'

'But it need not come to fighting,' Saphnis quavered, his eyes watering. 'We would like to negotiate with Telys. This has all been a mistake on his part. He's hot-headed, anxious to make changes, and we should have helped him. This action which he has taken has brought us to our senses, at least. All we want is to go home and help with his reforms.'

'Never mind all that,' Milo said roughly, 'I want all of you out on the running track. No excuses. If you can't be left to discipline yourselves, then I'll have to do it for you.'

Saphnis looked across at Pythagoras, his eyes pleading, but he got no help. Milo herded the leaders of the *azygous plutos* out of the tent and bellowed at the others, who were lying around waiting for the outcome of the meeting, to assemble in the open space where the foot-races are run. Once this was achieved he mounted the first bench of the stone auditorium and bawled out instructions for exercises; running on the spot, touching toes, press-ups, leaping in the air. The stadium was filled with the groans and curses of the Sybarites as they obeyed, some of them falling out to the side, clutching their chests and complaining of pains.

'Milo is going to kill them,' I whispered to Pythagoras. 'Is that what you want?'

'No,' he said with a sly smile, 'but he must be allowed to get them into a shape that he understands. If you think about it, Telys is the one who wants them dead.'

Milo was now running up and down the race track, urging the broken ranks of the *azygous plutos* to follow his example. Many of them had already fallen over and were lying on the grass, spewing and retching, and these he hurdled with whoops of mockery.

'What are you going to do with them?' I asked Pythagoras. 'No matter how Milo tries, he'll never make them into warriors. These men are merchants. They fight with different weapons.'

'We will do everything we can to improve them,' Pythagoras replied, 'everything that fits in with the working ethic of Kroton. Once they are as fit and strong as they should be, then we intend to ask Telys to relent and take them back. What do you think about that for a plan?'

One of the *azygous plutos* had gone blue in the face and was having a spasm on the race track. Milo galloped along, picked the stricken man up and hurled him bodily out of the way as he led the disconsolate, gasping remainder forward again. Within a few moments the man shook from head to toe, stiffened, twitched and lay still.

'Do I take it that the expulsion of the *azygous plutos* was Telys' idea alone?' I asked, as Milo began a series of immense bounds into the air, landing on his hands and springing forward off them. 'It was never part of his thinking while I was with him. It seems to have come from nowhere.'

'You must remember, Kallias,' Pythagoras murmured, saying under his breath, 'What a superb brute that man is,' as Milo somersaulted past, 'that you are seen by Telys as a man of religion, a priest, a seer. He would never discuss a *political* strategy with you. You have no expertise in that area.'

'Would he with you?'

'He knows that I am an expert on most things,' came the reply as he strayed away from me, climbing the tiered banks of stone to the top of the stadium.

That night I stayed at the stadium, sharing Saphnis' tent. He was incapable of thought, poor man, being shocked by the battering it had received during Milo's exercise session. He confided in me that his heart and lungs were out of rhythm, his bladder was over-active and strange pains kept lancing through his head.

'Can't you talk to Pythagoras for us?' he begged. 'This attempt to make healthy specimens out of us is a farce. Whatever faults Telys has, he has never physically afflicted us. This is worse than torture. If it goes on, we'll all be dead before we can get home.'

I was pleased that Saphnis should consider me an ally, though I found it hard to espy his reasoning.

'Pythagoras doesn't listen to me,' I told him. 'I'm as much a prisoner as you are.'

'We're not prisoners,' Saphnis answered. 'We have been given refuge. Not asylum, you note, only refuge. There has been an error in the way we are perceived in Sybaris. The blame for confusion, for lack of progress, call it what you like, has been assigned to us out of carelessness. Telys has been no more than a victim of his youth; and his legal mind looking for culprits, scapegoats.'

At this juncture Leogoras, Nonios and Chero arrived, having been allowed to walk from inside the city walls unescorted. They had been through several of the tents looking for me, and Leogoras had met many people he had recognised.

We embraced each other, glad to be reunited, but our meeting was sombre.

'They tell me that there are seven men who are ill tonight,' Leogoras told me. 'Their bodies can't stand the shaking which Milo's antics give them. They think that Milo is doing it as a sort of joke, trying to tell them something.'

I had worked out by now what it was that lay behind the regimentation of the *azygous plutos*. It was certainly not a preparation for warfare – these thousand dazed, half-crippled fellows would be of no use in combat – and there was no altruism in Milo or Pythagoras, so it must be a means of putting pressure on the exiles to go back to Sybaris, or to demonstrate their desire to do so in such a way that Telys would have to take notice. The inference I could draw from this was that Pythagoras needed to use the *azygous plutos* as part of his stratagem to start a war against Sybaris without Kroton appearing to be the aggressor.

Two of the *azygous plutos* expired during the night. Morning found me on the edge of a pit which slaves had dug outside the stadium wall to bury the Sybarite corpses. They were laid out in their richest apparel, their grave-goods in their hands and between their legs, but as the slaves started to shovel the earth over them and I raised my voice to the distant gods – oh how distant they seemed now! – it occurred to me that, in the pity of their predicament, the victims of their own weakness which had been caused by their overbearing wealth – these dead men would have been better buried naked, flesh to earth, bone to rock, in a final reassumption of their shared human peril within this world.

It was during these obsequies and the meditations which they encouraged, that I finally broke through in my understanding of what had happened at Enna. Pythagoras had undoubtedly plotted to end my life, that was clear, but it was equally clear that the gods had used the elaborate mechanism of his conspiracy to provide me with the prophetic knowledge I had needed.

This being the case – the gods using Pythagoras in his wickedness in my cause – might it not mean that the gods were indicating an ambiguity in Sybaris' destiny?

What they had truly intended to convey could be a reverse: that the *potential* destroyer of the city would fall, or could fall if the right actions were taken. Then the future I had encountered would merely be the opposite, like the other side of a coin. What people would be, or could be, talking about in the future might be the destruction of Kroton, Milo and Pythagoras instead.

I had started out taking great comfort from these thoughts, but as they deepened and I remembered the solidity of my arrival in Elis, the *history* which had been established there of Sybaris' destruction, I became less confident.

My best course was to continue working to make destiny swerve to one side, I decided, and leave the punishment of Pythagoras to those who could outwit him: the gods.

TWENTY-FOUR

It was now that time of the year when Atlas' six daughters appear in the night sky. Like Merope, the seventh, who hides herself away in shame for her union with a mortal man, I kept my knowledge of the fate of Sybaris to myself, determined that I would at least have the honour of completing my contract with Telys. Only him would I tell.

Each day Pythagoras returned to the stadium with Milo to supervise the physical improvement of the *azygous plutos*. As the exiles were put through their paces in boxing, throwing, leaping and lifting weights, Pythagoras often sought me out, claiming to enjoy the company of my *cult*, an ironic comment on my fate which had dwindled down to the loyalty of Leogoras, the friendship of Chero, and the love of Nonios.

He was most interested in Nonios, seeing that she was of low birth and so ugly. From our days in Egypt together, he knew that I was very affected by female beauty – we had sometimes clashed over the same woman, the victory always being his – and it intrigued him to find me in adoration of such a travesty. Whatever he said about her was polite, his enquiries always pertinent to my state of mind rather than her influence over me. Whenever Nonios came up in the conversation, Pythagoras seemed to lose his tongue's scathing edge. After a while I realised that he was, in a most mysterious way, jealous; not of my possession of her, but of my courage in loving such a woman.

On the day that Milo received a demand from Telys that all the *azygous plutos* should be returned to Sybaris to stand trial for corruption, sedition, blashphemy (an odd inclusion in the charges, I thought), I was sitting in Saphnis' tent with Pythagoras and my brother (now forced back into my company). We were discussing the irrationality of Telys' behaviour; throwing the rich out of Sybaris, then demanding that they come back to suffer punishment, thereby dealing out double punishment, when Pythagoras smoothly turned to Nonios and asked her opinion.

'Here is a man whom you have never met,' he said, leaning forward in a warm, interested manner, as though he thought her worthy of his closest attention. 'From your experience, what would you say about this tyrant in Sybaris?'

Nonios looked at me over Pythagoras' shoulder. He had put himself between her and myself, his long, scented hair hanging down to touch her thigh.

'My master tells me that Telys is young,' she replied. 'Why did these rich men give him so much power so easily?'

'Ah, I see that Kallias talks to you,' Pythagoras said, moving away a little. 'What else has he told you about Telys?'

'That he is often cruel because he is bewildered,' Nonios replied.

Pythagoras nodded, his eyes flickering an amused glance across at me; then he pointed at Chero and said:

'What does he think should be done with Sybaris?'

Chero stepped back, shaking his head.

'I am no-one,' he said.

'Your mind doesn't work? You can't see and hear? You haven't even got a hypothesis?' Pythagoras derided him. 'You're a Tyrrhenian, aren't you? I'd know that look anywhere.'

'I was, once,' Chero admitted.

'Another exile? You must feel at home here with these cast-offs. Don't worry. Your past doesn't matter to me. As far as I'm concerned you're Kallias' man, Kallias' cult-man. All I want to know is what a Tyrrhenian thinks we should do about a city that has grown so rich on the backs of his people.'

I could see that the servile condition which Pythagoras had assigned to him had jolted Chero back into his abandoned status as a nobleman. His neck was suffused by an angry redness, and his good eye flashed.

'Why should you do anything?' he demanded.

'A sensible reply,' Pythagoras rejoined amicably. 'Why should Kroton go to any trouble at all?'

My brother had insinuated himself closer to Chero, and imitated Pythagoras by putting an arm round his shoulder.

'You know a thing or two,' he said ingratiatingly. 'A man who has commanded the Tyrrhenian fleet can't be a complete fool.'

The shock that Geron's admission of his role as an informer produced was so great that I cried out: 'Is there any depravity which you will not stoop to? Have you no pride that will make you protect your friends?'

Pythagoras laughed and stroked me under the chin as if I were a child in these matters.

'Your brother has helped you, Kallias, not put you in danger. To be plain, if he had not given me the composition of your tiny, residual cult, your tattered scrap of your old dignity, I might have either ignored you or put you out of the way. But this small body of thought here intrigues me. It has so many facets. This woman, for instance. Marvellous! A whore you've transformed and now idolise.' He reached out and squeezed Nonios' breast. 'What knowledge she has of men; from common sailors to the most famous, though dishonoured, diviner of his day! And a disgraced admiral from an incomprehensible country! With a rock in his head!' Here he laughed outright, then kissed my Leogoras on both cheeks. 'And this beautiful, vital peasant you have as your bodyguard? A keeper of vineyards, no less. A devotee. More than that, Kallias, a Sybarite. Put all these with your twin brother, Kallias, and I have the perfect embassy to sent to Telys to open negotiations *on the future*.'

The emphasis which he put upon his final phrase stilled my whirling thoughts as I tried to keep pace with his teasing. There was no means by which Pythagoras could know what I knew about the fate of Sybaris. That terrible gift had been granted to me only, but his expression spoke otherwise. Surely the gods had not shared it with him!

'You are mocking me,' I said, agitated by this awful thought.

'Not at all. Telys is expecting you back from Enna. Just because he has taken action against the *azygous plutos* in your absence, it doesn't mean that he has released you from your contract. The man still wants his money's worth.'

I could not argue against this without appearing to be less honourable than I was, even in that time of shame. I did, however, have a point to make.

'If Telys is expecting me to continue to work, then how can I explain that I am returning to Sybaris on another mission; as a representative of Kroton to negotiate this complicated matter of the *azygous plutos*?'

'You will go to Sybaris with thirty men of standing from Kroton. Some of our sage councillors; wise, seasoned citizens in whom we place great trust,' Pythagoras replied. 'They will form the official deputation. You will be in company with them, or so Telys will be told, by mere coincidence. In that way Kroton will get the credit for saving you from danger, giving you hospitality and sending you back to Sybaris in one piece. And what would be more natural than that you should have *divined* the true intentions of our thirty ambassadors while on the journey with them? Telys will come straight to you, to discover the brief which I have given them.'

I was awestruck by the man's audacity. The suppleness and flexibility of his mind had always been a source of pleasure to me, even when I loathed what it produced in the way of ideas. Now it was turned to diplomacy. There was, I knew, more to come, more and worse.

'You will have to tell Telys that you have personally seen the preparations of the exiles for war,' Pythagoras added, the opaque lids of his eyes demurely lowered. 'Also you must mention the Drume fleet, the training of our regiments. These are things which you have seen with your own eyes.'

There was an uproar in the stadium. Pythagoras went out to see what had happened, and I followed. *The azygous plutos* were gathered around two of their number, who were wrestling. Up until this day Milo had not been able to awaken an aggressive spirit in the exiles. They would run or jump or throw (as long as it wasn't *at* anyone), but they had found it impossible to engage in sports where combat was at the root of the game.

Milo was running round and round the tussling men, his voice raised in delight, clapping his hands over his head.

'They're doing it!' he shouted to Pythagoras. 'They've got the idea at last.'

Up until the final moment before our ship was due to sail, Pythagoras led me to believe that he would let my people accompany me on the embassy to Sybaris with the thirty old men from Kroton. But, as the gangplank was about to be taken away, two officers came on board and took Nonios off, informing me that Milo had ordered her to be kept in the Temple of Hera until my return. Although I was bitterly distressed by this cold move to keep me obedient, the thirty ambassadors were pleased, because to have a woman on board was unlucky, and in Kroton any female child born with such a deformity as Nonios would have been smothered at birth. So, she was not only an omen of misfortune, my love, but a life that should never have been lived.

It was a rough voyage, many of the old men falling sick. With their slaves and servants they were a load too heavy for the vessel, so we moved slowly and with difficulty in the strong east wind. For three days we were tossed about, short of sleep, miserable and all getting in each other's way. The ambassadors became increasingly irritable, complaining, arguing amongst themselves.

We were kept anchored in the lagoon for two days while our request to meet Telys was considered. My presence on the ship was made known to him, but no quick response came. When we were permitted to land, I was herded along with all the rest.

Those two days of waiting in the harbour were an agony. The city seemed to be even more spacious than when I had left it, having grown by some means. The weather cleared up, and the strong winds were replaced by the lightest, sweetest zephyrs. They were scented still as I remembered them, but now more fragrant and exquisite. There was such repose about the place, such limpid calm, that my knowledge of its fate lay in my mind like a putrescence.

Then I recalled how the city had bustled down at the port; the movement of folk and vehicles, the cargoes, the goods and traffic back and forth. Ours was the only foreign ship in the harbour. It was as if it were the dead of winter when the ice stiffened the city's commerce; but now it was summer.

Sybaris was at a standstill.

When we disembarked I was told that I could go straight to my house, which I promptly did, glad to be separated from the old men of Kroton, who were working themselves up to the highest pitch of disagreeability. When I reached the house with Geron, Leogoras and Chero, it was under guard by Scythians, but they were expecting me and we were let through without incident. Herophantos was on the doorstep to greet us. As he bowed, I heard him whisper a warning that Telys was waiting for me inside.

Nothing had changed since I had left. I was surprised at the strength of the feeling I had of coming home. It was piercingly poignant, a lance in my heart. I had noticed that Herophantos looked drawn and reserved when he welcomed me, and his voice had carried a tense warning like an out-of-tune instrument, but it did not prepare me for the sight of Telys when he entered the hall.

The man had shrunk. His eyes had sunk into his skull, and his skin was pale and tightened around his cheekbones. The smile was still there in his upcurving beard, but it was askew, giving him a odd, demented look.

'You t-t-took your t-t-time,' he stammered.

He gave me a moment to settle my entourage into the house, following me around, mentioning that my money had been kept safe for me, that Herophantos had been active on my behalf, even the garden had been properly cared for; all said in a tense, attentive tone.

'Which one is your brother?' he asked as I ushered everyone into the main living chamber.

Startled, I introduced Geron to him. Telys examined his face closely, and pronounced that there was a resemblance.

'Though your lives have left different marks,' he added. 'His features are less severe. 'Now,' he said, 'we must spend some time in p-p-private.'

My impression that Telys had been hollowed out by his recent troubles was a false one. Once he had me alone, a different character emerged.

'Before we start,' he said flatly, 'I have no need of the details of your wanderings. I have been kept up-to-date. I know about your involvement with Kroton, the exiles, all that. None of it concerns me. All I want from you, Kallias, is the reason why you did not go to Hell as you had promised you would. Everything hinges on that.'

Boxed in by his pre-existing intelligence, I was forced to rearrange my thoughts. How could I explain it to him in terms that he would understand?

'We had the writing from the Grotto of the Sacred Eels,' he said acridly, 'we had your vision of Herakles. In other words, we had something to go on. But you were so cautious, Kallias. You wouldn't commit yourself to an interpretation until you were sure. Now, so I hear, you refused to make the descent according to the proper rite of entrance which is laid down at Enna. You behaved like a coward. Why?'

I noted that he had not stuttered once during the delivery of this imputation. Anger flowed out of him in an unwavering line, one that I knew would be difficult to deflect with the story which I had to tell. He had as much information as he needed to condemn in me my absence, but he had not done so. This was the straw which I grasped at as I asked him for time to give my account of what had happened on the lakeside at Enna.

'Let me tell it without interruption,' I asked him, 'for what you must understand is that I have been to a kind of Hell. When I have finished my story, then I will try to answer all your questions.'

Telys kept silent as I slowly took him through the stages of my descent from Enna, first with Thales, then to meet myself. I recounted the course of my journey with Bes, which raised Telys' eyebrows, then my appearance at Luderma's death-feast. Telys remained attentive right through to the Narcissus pool in Elis. When he saw that I wished to press on and not enter into any kind of metaphysical exegesis of what had happened thus far, he shrugged and beckoned to me that I should continue. There was his smile beneath the surface smile to deal with by then, a doubting, pessimistic grimace which played also in his eyes, which were fixed on mine.

There was still much to tell when I paused, exhausted by

the effort of putting it all into words. He opened his mouth to speak, but I held up my hand.

'Let me go through to the end,' I requested. 'It will be better that way. As I do so, I ask that you bear this in mind: could anyone ever have invented this experience? What I have told you up until now is marvellous enough, but what comes later will make you wonder to an ever greater degree.'

Telys sat back and hooked his hands under his knees like a child listening to a tale at bedtime. I could see that he had mistaken my exhortation to believe what I had said so far as a snare which would make his acceptance of lies of greater magnitude impossible to withhold.

'All this happened,' I swore. 'Stay with me.'

'I'm saying nothing until I have heard the whole story,' Telys replied. 'That is what you asked me to do.'

Now I saw him as one small, oppressed man in a room. From there his city multiplied, room upon room, house upon house, full of men, women, children, history, hopes. It was a time to be full of truth, but as I approached the moment when I had to reveal that I had arrived in Elis in a future time when the fate of Sybaris was known because it had already taken place, my tongue failed me.

'Go on, go on,' he urged.

'I cannot,' I confessed. 'If you have had difficulty in believing what has gone before, how can you swallow what it has led up to? You will suspect me of telling you this in order to take the heart out of your body, which you will read as some treachery of mine to help your enemies.'

'What enemies? The *azygous plutos*? They're nothing. As you know, my only enemy is ignorance. All I want is what I paid for: your d-d-divination!'

I told him the future of Sybaris.

'Total destruction?' he asked once I had finished. 'Nothing left at all?'

'Levelled to the ground,' I told him bluntly.

'Are you certain that this constitutes your prophecy?'

I told him, regretfully, that I was.

'Now, while I absorb this – and it does have the advantage of simplicity over the previous rag-bag of half-perceived notions and cock-eyed manifestations that you came up with

– you can entertain me by describing just exactly how you got back into this time, if that's not too tall an order,' he said meanly, getting up and walking about the room.

He lapsed into a haunted mood as I told him about my voyage to Syracuse and the adventures which led up to my return to Enna. When I described the mountain of pig carcasses on the altar he laughed out loud, then louder as I recounted how I had pulled the oval rock up from the lake and met my brother and Leogoras again at the moment when I had left them.

'Kallias,' he said when it was all over and I sat down, exhausted, 'you're one on your own. I'll have to give serious thought to the question whether I should release the final part of your contract fee. I think you may be mad.'

But the humour left him. There was a chill gleam in his tired eyes, and his hands were shaking. I knew that I had described something that had struck a chord in his own fears.

TWENTY-FIVE

Herophantos told me that since the exile of the *azygous plutos*, all work in the city had stopped. The process of disentangling ownership, tracking down the myriad interconnections of investment monies, sorting out the whole complex web of who ran the economic system of Sybaris, had been the occupation of all. Every urchin in the street knew something. The city hall had been bombarded with information and denunciations. Up until this day of my return, Herophantos assured me, not a single item of wealth had been reapportioned. There had been some rioting and looting, but that had been suppressed, the mass of the population throwing its weight behind Telys because it was believed than any panic measures to obtain the wealth of the *azygous plutos* would result in waste. *Plenty for all*, had been the cry, and still was.

'This is how Telys holds the citizens in check,' Herophantos said as his account neared its end. 'Their expectations are so great that they are willing to give him time. But they will run out of patience. The more intelligent ones amongst them know that it is not the objects of wealth that they should take over, but the means of making wealth. They talk in the taverns very knowledgeably about the Monadic Flow Theory.'

This last morsel of news sent a chill down my neck.

Telys returned at this point. He was accompanied by two heavily muscled black Africans. My brother Geron was in their grip, his arms bound.

'I've no time to waste,' Telys stated. 'Get out, Herophantos. If you hear noises, ignore them.'

Herophantos had no choice except to obey. As soon as he had left the room Geron began to gabble incoherently, tears pouring down his cheeks as he tried to get to his knees to beg Telys for mercy. The Africans hauled him upright again, their faces unmoved.

'Why are you maltreating my brother?' I asked as calmly as I could. 'Has he wronged you in some way?'

'No, he has helped me so far,' Telys replied, sitting down by the window. 'Are you aware that your own brother, your own blood, swears that you never made the descent at Enna; that you stood by the lake, saw what you had to do, then, like the coward that you are, you turned away. He knows nothing about Thales, you meeting yourself, death-feasts, appearing in Elis, Syracuse, all that.'

'That's so,' I replied. 'I have never told him.'

'Your own brother? He was there, beside you. He would have seen something, surely!'

'What Geron has told you is his version of the truth, and it is the only one that he has.'

Telys laughed and rubbed his knees.

'And your man, my former keeper of vineyards? What's his name?'

'Leogoras will give you the same account as my brother.'

Telys pondered for a while, staring at me now and then, shaking his head, shuffling his feet back and forth on the floor.

'So, Kallias,' he said eventually, 'what you're s-s-saying is that it was a trick of your m-m-mind.'

'No,' I answered him. 'It was a gift of time and place from the gods.'

'No, no,' Telys murmured, wagging his head. 'I'm not having that. It was a trick which you p-p-played up-p-pon yourself to cover your cowardice. Admit it.'

I denied this.

At a word from Telys the Africans threw my brother on the floor, seized his hands and feet and prepared to pull his limbs out of joint.

'If you own up to this deceit of yours,' Telys said sharply, 'I will permit you to leave Sybaris and go home with what you have. I cannot, however, undertake to pay you the third part of your fee. That would be ridiculous.'

'For my brother's sake, I would gladly accept this,' I replied, 'and if there is to be any compulsion, then let it be applied to me; but the truth belongs to the gods in this case. It is a sacred trust. I am on oath, as a priest of the Iamidai to never deny what the Eternal Ones have shown me to be true.'

Telys nodded to the Africans. With a twisting of wrists they dislocated Geron's arms and legs from their sockets and left him screaming on the floor.

No-one could be heard above the noise. I signalled to Telys that I wished to speak again. He gestured to the Africans, and they took hold of my brother's ankles and wrists and snapped his limbs back into their proper places.

'First, a word on my brother,' I said once Geron had quietened down. 'He is not a strong-minded man. My pity for him is great, but his suffering cannot change what I must maintain as the truth.'

'He would betray you ten times a day,' Telys sneered, 'so your lack of love for him doesn't surprise me. But, his pain is useless if it doesn't influence you. Take him away.'

I went down on my knees and begged for Geron's life.

'We'll see,' Telys said. 'Let's proceed with our business. I'm now in the position where I have to take you seriously. I have the feeling that if I put any kind of pressure on you, there would be no shift from this madness of yours.'

'I cannot disclaim a revelation. It would be the end of me.'

'Not for anyone? The lady with the harelip?'

My heart turned in my breast.

'She would never want me to.'

Telys sighed, stroking the woven fibres of his mantle. I could see that he had released his grip on a hope that he had been nurturing.

'If you have been in the future and you were told that Sybaris had been destroyed, what can be done about it?' he said, with his illusory smile more pronounced than ever. 'If that is what will happen, then that is what will happen.'

'I have thought about this a great deal,' I told him. 'Although this has been my clearest and most unequivocal act of divination, it may be that it only refers to my world; to my city, the city of my wealth, my personal Sybaris. To that end, I gave all my treasures to the Temple of Zeus at Olympia. When I survive, it will be as a poor man. That was all I could think of to do.'

Telys snorted and got to his feet.

'I've done with all this,' he declared. 'It was a stupid thing I did when I brought you here. You're an old fool, Kallias, a meddler in superstition. From now on I go with the new thinking.'

'You could change the city's name,' I suggested. 'Why don't you find a village, fill it with condemned prisoners, call it Sybaris, destroy it . . ?'

He gave me a contemptuous, pitying look.

'And that event would rock the entire Greek world, as you have described? That would make the citizens of Miletos go into mourning for the collapse of their trade? That would make the Tyrrhenians weep in the streets? All this you heard, Kallias. What does interest me is whether you'll be alive to see it, even though you heard it.'

Then he was gone, leaving me standing in a puddle of urine which my poor brother had involuntarily released during his agony.

That evening, when Leogoras returned from showing Chero all his old haunts, he told me that a curfew which would last for three days had been imposed. Also the gates of Sybaris had been shut to all traffic for this period. The reason given was that the accountants and investigators who were analysing the assets of the *azygous plutos* needed to have everything in an inactive state so they could more rapidly come to their conclusions.

I asked Leogoras for any other gossip he had picked up during his travels.

'You couldn't call it gossip,' he replied, 'more like dreams. Everyone is talking about the new system and the big share-out which is coming. They're all looking ahead, putting forward ideas about the new government, what they're going to do with their money, all up in the clouds.'

Chero told me that he had met some Tyrrhenians who had been preparing to return home. It was their view that normal business had collapsed in Sybaris, and it would be some time before it resumed. While they waited for this upheaval in trade to settle down and for Sybaris to find a new stability, they would investigate the possibilities of increasing trade with other cities in Italy and Sicily. They had been full of regrets about the disruption, but had been able to understand how the *azygous plutos* had affronted the citizens by flaunting their riches so ostentatiously over the years.

'Nevertheless,' Chero went on, 'the Tyrrehenians have always said that wealth has a natural limit at which men choke. Why, they ask, did the *azygous plutos* not choke like other men? Now it has had to be done for them.'

When the first morning out of curfew dawned, Herophantos went out with Leogoras to scour the markets for food, there already being shortages in the city, which the curfew would not have improved. They returned with plentiful supplies of meat, fruit and vegetables, the farmers having discovered that they were excluded from the proposed share-out of wealth by being resident outside the walls (this was one of the early regulations of the new officials responsible for economic planning), and they had resumed, albeit resentfully, their traditional livelihoods. While in the markets Leogoras had been told that the thirty ambassadors from Kroton had been taken to an abandoned village up in the mountains, dressed in cast-off clothing from the *azygous plutos*, stuffed with food, drenched with wine, entertained with music and shows, then burnt alive. The village had then been destroyed, not one stone being left to stand upon another.

At either end of the single street which this village possessed had been posted signs saying 'Sybaris'.

At the local shrine of the god Bes, my twin brother had been given a slow death, disembowelled and left to fight off the crows with his own entrails, cursing my name and all my ideas.

After these atrocities, I knew that Sybaris was a lost cause.

I knew that my brother had died vicariously for me; with his destruction, Telys had signalled that everything between us was over and I must go. He was now desperate so I could not trust him to treat me like a ghost for long. I warned Leogoras and Chero to be ready to leave at a moment's notice. Twice we made the attempt, but each time we were turned back; once at the port where I had arranged a passage to Metapontion, and once at the gate to the Road to Prosperity. On each occasion we were escorted back to the house and told that it was too dangerous to travel.

Some days after the last time that we were turned back I was granted yet another sign.

Since being parted from Nonios in Kroton, my lust had lain quiet, but I woke one morning with an erection at an absolute right angle to my body.

I called in Leogoras and showed it to him. He suggested that he should go out to find a Lydian whore or whatever might satisfy me, but I told him that there was no desire. Leogoras had a farmer's mind. Noting my reluctance to involve an outsider, and assuming this to be out of loyalty to Nonios, he offered to give me relief himself if it would help.

'No, Leogoras, though I appreciate your good nature in suggesting it,' I said to him. 'I'm convinced that I must look upon it as an *afflatus*.'

There was only one lamp in the room. I told Leogoras to extinguish it, then showed him the erection again.

The head glowed in the dark.

'And it doesn't hurt?' Leogoras asked. 'It looks sore.'

'Not at all,' I replied. 'There is just this phosphorescence.'

The physical being of a diviner is sometimes used by the gods to manifest a communication. We are employable in all our flesh and organs. In the past I had been afflicted by earache, alterations in my heartbeat and copious sweating, all of which, at their separate moments, had proved to be messages from the gods.

'What can it mean?' Leogoras wondered, once I had shared my supposition with him.

I told Leogoras to get me a litter so I could go out, the erection making it difficult for me to walk.

Leogoras accompanied me. We went down the Avenue of Dionysos to the Poseidon Gate, to get the benefit of the sea breezes. As we entered the harbour area, Leogoras stopped the litter and pointed.

The pharos at the entrance to the lagoon was always kept alight, night and day. It was one of the familiar sights of Sybaris, the tall lighthouse's fire sending its warning to shipping which approached the sandbanks around the harbour entrance.

As soon as I saw the pharos, my erection went down.

With a reprisal anticipated from Kroton any day for the massacre of the thirty ambassadors I knew immediately what the *afflatus* meant. I went straight to Telys and told him that he could expect an attack from the sea soon. When he questioned me on the source of my intelligence, I invented a premonitory dream.

The attack came the following night. The Drume fleet was sighted around sunset fifty stadia to the south, and the warning was brought to Sybaris. I felt it my duty to go to Telys and tell him that I had knowledge of the fighting strength of these invaders, and that Sybaris would be assailed by men who fought like demons and had no fear of death.

Telys' preparations to defend the harbour were designed by his mercenary general, Drynios, a man whom he had recruited from Metapontion where he had been living in retirement. The old soldier was an expert in naval warfare and laid a trap for the Drume which, in execution, deserves to rank with the highest feats of arms.

The Drume approached the entrance to the harbour at the dead of night. From the light on the pharos they saw only a few ships awaiting the morning in the sea-roads, and a deserted lagoon. With the harbour open before them, the Drume rowed in.

They were given time to spread themselves out. When the last Drume ship was in, three of the vessels waiting outside the harbour were quickly rowed over, chained together across the entrance and fired. Simultaneously, great cables which had been sunk on to the bed of the lagoon were raised, and tubs of liquid fire sent down them on pulleys to crash into the invaders. Drynios had prepared hundreds of these lethal weapons, and the cables across the harbour were so numerous that every time the Drume managed to hack through one of them another took its place.

Before long the Drume warriors were abandoning their ships and leaping into the water. They swam to the harbour walls with their weapons, ready to fight, only to be met by ranks of men armed with very long pikes, who speared them.

Behind came the whole of Sybaris, crowding at the pikemen's backs to see the slaughter. In the light of the burning vessels, it was an awesome sight. The shrieks of the crowd were demonic. It occured to me as I watched that it was a scene which one might have encountered in the Infernal Regions instead of here on earth; but then, I remembered, such imaginations are probably erroneous. Whatever horrors we can bring to mind mankind can perform in this life, it seems, without resorting to the lands of the dead.

Sickened by the spectacle, I went home. I tasted in my mouth the flavour of the strange *iggfor ren* which the Drume had carried in their pots, and hoped that this final super-reality of theirs had not been too enhanced.

When I got back to the house, it was deserted. All the slaves, Herophantos, the wife and children of Leogoras, and even Leogoras himself, were down at the harbour watching the slaughter.

Unable to bear the thought of being on my own after all I had witnessed, I went to the temple of Hera. The old wooden building smelt of summers long past, and the smoke from the harbour had not reached this part of the city. Upon entering I looked for someone to be with; anyone, a nightwatchman, an altar-boy, but the temple was empty. All the priests and acolytes were down at the harbour as well.

In the gloom of the cella, there was one tripod flame still burning. The others had been neglected and gone out. I went over to add more oil and relight the others. As I did so I heard a whirring up in the darkness behind the statue of the goddess, and took it for pigeons.

I fed the burning lamp with oil, then carried a flame to the others after I had filled their reservoirs. This all took some time, during which I heard the whirring again.

Once the third tripod flame was lit, I turned to go. Two of the lamps were put out, one after the other, and I heard stones skittering across the stone floor.

'Lie down,' came a woman's voice from the statue.

I knew it was Nonios. Her identity had blended with a goddess once, on the coast when Chero had walked into the sea, and it could happen again with Hera. The stones were hers, and the accuracy, but Nonios never whirled her sling.

But it was her.

She emerged from behind the statue and stood over me, her sling turning in her hand – to dry it, as she told me later, after her long swim when she had jumped overboard from Man-High Leaper's ship.

We lay together and wept while Hera watched.

Nonios later told me how she had come to be aboard when the Drume fleet sailed from Kroton. The chieftain, knowing that she was a hostage, had requested that she be allowed to come along to kill the keepers of the pharos fire with her sling, his plan being to send a small boat ahead in the guise of a local fishing vessel to put out the light so he could make his attack in darkness. Once the fleet had reached a point to the south, where Nonios could see the city, she had managed to slip overboard and swim to the shore. By the time that she had reached the southern gate, the attack had been made. Not knowing where I lived, and often having heard me speak of the old wooden temple of Hera she had gone there to ask my whereabouts. When I had entered she had not recognised me because I had been wearing a few items of protective armour, which I had put on in case the battle with the Drume had not gone as planned.

When I asked whether Milo or Pythagoras had known that she was with the Drume, and upon being told that they had given the actual authority, I realised that she could not be seen in Sybaris. I could not run the risk of Telys discovering that the woman who had entered my heart was within his reach.

Pythagoras was now in the unique position of making war against a city he effectively controlled by means of the domination which his ideas had over its leader.

The day after the destruction of the Drume, Kroton's army marched up the coast road from the south, its fleet keeping pace close to shore. Milo and Pythagoras had anticipated a quick victory. Instead, they found the gates of Sybaris shut against them and the city ready to withstand a siege.

Telys' preparations included a morale-boosting decree that every citizen would be issued with a number. This number would be entered on a register of entitlement to the aggregated wealth of the city, now an accounted figure which could be divided into ascertainable sums of ownership. This number would be sacred, and considered to be an integral part of the soul of each person. Upon the demise of each number, that number would be added to the number of the children, in the same way as the blood of the parents runs in the offspring's veins. No number would ever be destroyed. In the case of criminals, the number would be put under restraint but not expunged. Every number was an investment in the total number, and that total number was One in the first place and the number of the finite units of wealth within the city in the second. The last bit of good news which this proclamation gave was that the numbers given to a city of a hundred thousand citizens, that being the population, clearly tended towards the Infinite, which meant that the future of all citizens and the city itself also inclined towards the Infinite. And the Infinite has no end.

I walked through cheering crowds. Many of the people already had their numbers, and they chanted them aloud. Some had painted them on their foreheads. Their rejoicing made my head ache with sorrow.

Pythagoras faced Pythagoras: Pythagoras inside, Pythagoras outside. Across the walls of the doomed city the armies of Kroton and Sybaris challenged each other to a contest which turned on one man's concept of life. This war, as I perceived it, was an internecine affair, a world fighting itself, a clash within the confines of the physical world, hard flesh against hard coin, the perfect body against the perfect economy, but all would be fought out in the Pythagorean mind, with true religion banished from the battlefield.

Although rejected by Telys and scorned by Pythagoras and Milo, I was not ousted by any means. Religion was the sphere they had neglected, because it was beyond their comprehension. The attempt of Pythagoras to replace it by number, that which controlled the physical world which he was dividing into its separate forces, was an obvious failure. People could accept the validity of number in daily life, but never in the heavens.

That was still my province. When the war between Kroton and Sybaris was over, the gods would remain and the power of number be withdrawn into the lost ledger and the faded page.

In this I had my part to play; knowing the wide-ranging power and universality of Pythagoras' intellect, I had little doubt that once he had resolved the contest between the athletic and plutocratic to his satisfaction, he would turn his attention to the one territory left free from his misanthropy where the human mind could find solace and asylum: Olympus, and he would want it for his own.

TWENTY-SIX

Five days after the beginning of the siege, Telys ordered the re-opening of the Luderma College as an institution of the new learning, and appointed me as principal. I was marched in at spear-point and placed in my ceremonial chair by force. All the students from the previous regime were rounded up and brought back to the building under guard. For the first day of instruction – in which virtually nothing was taught, because I had no teachers, nor the new curriculum – the college was an armed camp, with the terrified students huddled together and staring at the wall under the supervision of soldiers.

When Milo's army had come up the coast, his fleet had not been able to blockade the harbour, being too weak, which is why he had needed the Drume. Telys had moved quickly once he knew Kroton was advancing, emptying the plain of livestock, bringing it into the city. Milo had immediately cut off access to the three land gates, leaving Sybaris only sea supplies, but such a vast metropolis had space to store immense amounts of food, and in the time between the amphibious attack by the ill-fated Drume and the arrival of the main army Telys' officers were able to fill the city to the point of bursting. There were so many horses in the agora that I saw people walking over their backs to get from one side to the other.

The paralysis which had held the city was cured by the arrival of the enemy. Everyone was allocated a task, and Telys' ability to organise and govern flourished once the emergency took hold. Whereas he had been confused and disordered during peacetime, the war seemed to bring his mind to bear upon the immediate future rather than that of the long term, with beneficial effect.

Chero and Leogoras were sent to a warehouse in the port, which had been hastily adapted to be a manufactory of incendiary liquids, mixtures of pitch, sulphur, charcoal, incense and tow, which could be flung down from the walls or fired at the enemy in tubs by sprung engines. They returned home each night stinking of the ingredients; but that could be washed off, unlike the pollution which I was being made to teach at the college.

The new learning was all Pythagoras. When the curriculum arrived from Telys, it was accompanied by a rambling letter that urged me to do my best to disseminate the ideas put forward in the texts, which were delivered at the same time. He wrote that there was no-one better to run an *Orphic school* than a man who was a graduate of Hell, and made reference to my *Proserpina of the Divided Mouth*. Then came the mystical nonsense with which Pythagoras had clouded his inhuman science and idolatry of number.

It was hot, and the students were fearful. Each time stones from the ballistas of the enemy crashed on to the building – the college was close to the western gate, and received the brunt of missiles passing over the walls – the students would tremble and lose concentration, making it necessary for me to go back over the matter I had been teaching. This I had to do because there was an observer from the city hall posted at my side, an ignorant artisan who had once worked in dyed leather; he was a member of the committee which Telys had appointed to supervise both education and religious practice during the emergency.

Milo, had taken up residence in Telys' villa. The citizens of Sybaris saw him running in to supervise the siege each morning with his staff-officers, leading them through the empty fields at great speed, with his baton of command in his hand. There was no sign of Pythagoras, however. Not that he needed a presence other than the one which he maintained in Telys' head.

The siege soon settled down to a rhythm of its own. Sybaris had been well sited by its founders. Flanked on one side by the sea, on two others by the Kratis and Sybaris rivers, only the western wall could be effectively attacked other than by siege engines, and that wall had been built with three times the thickness of the others, and its foundations dug to a depth which made mining beneath these defences a formidable task. But Milo seemed to be in no hurry to get the war over. He spread his army of 20,000 men out over the plain and held games every day. These were watched by the Sybarites, who could not help but marvel at the prowess of the athletes. All the throwing events were channelled in such a way that the missiles cames towards the city, and the long jump was altered to take place across the river, the contestants often falling in, to the delight of the Sybarites. These failures had propaganda made out of them, however, as the jumpers then swam at terrific speed up and down the river crying out challenges.

So it went on, this festive siege.

Few were killed except by errant stones from the ballistas. Milo sported on the plain in the beautiful summer weather. We sweated in the confines of a city stinking with animal excrement, but it was tolerable. As the days went by I began to see just how intelligent Pythagoras was being in his strategy, giving the city time to warp irrevocably its own spirit, deprived of any sane history, any connection with a prosperous past. Each day that Telys remained in power meant a further deterioration, another step away from salvation.

I was, in these opinions, a lone voice. The only hope that Sybaris might have would be aid from another city, but they all hated her so much that this was not likely. Only the Tyrrhenians or the men of Miletos might feel that it was in their interests to act as deliverer, in order to preserve the profitable commerce which they had enjoyed.

Arbitrariness was a feature of Telys' rule, and one which the Sybarites seemed to find acceptable because it was underpinned by the new obsession with number. In the fixity of the concept that all life is governed by the authority of the Monad god, the One, which multiplies into every personal number, the citizens found sufficient security to enable them to endure the tyrant's whims. The old religion was not abolished or even persecuted, I have to say, but there was no need for Telys to take drastic action to suppress it. The people simply stayed away from the temples, and religious observations were shifted to the playing of mathematical games in the home and the construction of *The Holy Tetractys* in the agora outside the city hall.

Some days into the siege, I was forced to stand beside Telys with a band of flute-players, bagpipers and drummers, and explain to the assembled people the meaning of the triangle of posts which had been erected overnight, a structure which took up a great deal of room in an already crowded area. The arrangement of the posts was as follows:

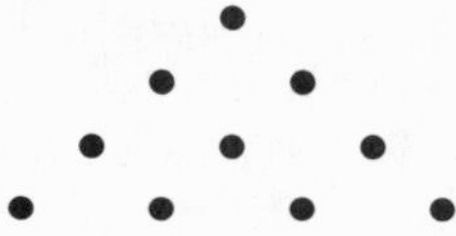

This represented the triangular number 10, one that is sacred to the benighted sect to this day. *The Holy Tetractys* is composed of the number 1 at each point of the triangle, increasing to 2 and 3 and 4 as each line progresses inwards, showing that the sum of any number of the series of natural numbers beginning with 1 is a triangular number, and that the sum of any number of the series of odd numbers beginning with 1 is similarly seen to be a square (which, mercifully, was not constructed due to lack of space, though it does not need illustration as it emanates from the same reasoning).

Needless to say there was a period of mystification amongst the Sybarites as they studied *The Holy Tetractys* and some began tethering their horses to the posts, but Telys persisted until there was complete understanding and respect for its symbolic authority.

At the same ceremony which established *The Holy Tetractys* as the centre of the new religion, Telys had himself declared *The Third Gnomon*: *The First Gnomon* being God; *The Second Gnomon* being Pythagoras himself; and *The Third Gnomon's* position falling to Telys. The gnomon numbers are the odd ones which begin with 1. When each of them is added to the sum of the preceding odd numbers, they make a square number into the next larger square, and this, of course, is a sacred metaphor relating to the hierarchy of divine power which stems from the Monad.

*

The Third Gnomon, for so I had to call him now, visited the college frequently during the siege. He seldom spoke to me, but often sat at the back of the lecture hall and listened. Even in his conceit, and after the terrible death which he had given my brother, I could not help but pity his situation or curse my own ineptitude.

I decided to make one final attempt to prise Telys away from Pythagoras' influence. What I had to abandon in my mind was the argument that ran: Pythagoras controls Kroton and Kroton is the enemy of Sybaris, therefore Pythagoras is the enemy of Sybaris as well. Telys had entered into a peculiar state of philosophical insanity, whereby he could not see the logic in this. What I had to do was convince him that the actual thinking of Pythagoras was wrong.

When he was at the college one day I invited him into my private quarters, asking him to leave his Scythian bodyguards outside so we could talk openly. This he refused to do, claiming that their Greek was so bad that it made no difference, but I knew that it was fear that I might prove treacherous which made him insist on their presence.

Without more ado I set out to demolish the position that Pythagoras occupied on the gods, demonstrating that his One Monad God was a notion and not a being, a number which could not relate to human life. In fact, I said, this god he imagines is no more than a representative of his own cold nature; without feeling, without mercy. To have enslaved two cities to the idea that the entire family of the Olympian gods could be replaced by mathematics was an achievement, I admitted, and not one which reflected glory on the priesthood, but it was only because people had a great need for order and harmony that they had succumbed. Both of these qualities were common amongst the Eternal Ones, I told him, but people have always seen the gods as Homer and Hesiod saw them, their more entertaining and sensational attributes being emphasised, rather than their quieter virtues.

Telys stopped me impatiently. 'You greatly misjudge Pythagoras,' he declared. 'I don't know what went on between you in the old days, but you must not refuse the man the credit of his genius.'

All that was left to me was to plead that an apology should

be made to Kroton for the murder of the thirty old ambassadors, as the only diplomatic move which might bring about the lifting of the siege. Before I had begun to speak my piece on this subject I was full of foreboding, knowing that Telys would turn my own words against me. It was my revelation to him of the city's fate and the advice that I had given to him on that occasion that had resulted in the massacre.

Oddly enough, he did not draw my attention to this fact. He stood at the door and let me go on. When I had finished, he came to my side and squeezed my hand.

'Do your work here at the college, Kallias,' he said. 'You have served me well, now and again. I am always conscious of the fact that it was your counsel which diverted Sybaris from a fate which has always haunted me. For that destruction which you spoke of was at the back of my mind when I first called you here from Elis. Now we are free of it, thanks to your device of using the abandoned village as a substitute. No matter how hard Pythagoras works, he will never come up with an idea which matches that for sheer ingenuity.'

Caught in my own snare I had to let him go, all my arguments confounded.

As the city successfully withstood the siege, Telys' popularity rose to the point where the statue of Apollo was removed from his temple and Telys was installed there as Third Gnomon, in its stead, an act of unforgivable sacrilege.

The curfew had been relaxed on those days when it was known that the besieging army would not attack, because it was not numerically fortuitous to do so. I was taking a stroll with Leogoras and Chero in the south-west quarter, close to the old shrine of Bes, and I took time to go inside. The statue of the obese god was on its side, and a chamber was visible beneath. Leogoras told me that everyone in Sybaris had known that the food, drink and money went somewhere below, and was regularly cleaned out, but no-one had ever had the temerity to claim that this had not been in the good service of the god. Now Bes had been abused, and his stinking treasure-house robbed. I was reminded of my first visit to the shrine with Telys, and how he had exhorted me to take notice of the cult of Bes and see the god as a representation of the city.

There was a man down in the pit beneath the altar. He was up to his knees in rotten food, feeling around for coins. I was surprised that the level of the sludge in the pit was so low, having seen the volume of food and drink poured down the throat of the statue. When I shouted down to the wretch who was wading through it all, a cloth tied around his mouth and nose, and asked him if there was an outlet, he nodded and pointed to a corner of the pit. I tossed him down a few coins and hurried away to the clean air.

'You're thinking that it's time to get out of Sybaris?' Leogoras asked as we headed across the agora, passing the children who were playing in and out of the posts of *The Holy Tetractys*. 'Don't imagine that we could get out that way. There's only one approach. Be bold. Walk out.'

That evening we continued our walk to the Temple of Poseidon and the tomb of the Sirisian's sea-monster, now defaced, then went back along the Avenue of Olympia, past the luxury shops and the stoa, where entranced girls were singing streams of random numbers in high, delirious voices, then made our way through the north-eastern quarter towards the gate which led to The Road to Prosperity. We had heard that Milo's engineers had been constructing an enormous new engine, and we wanted to take a look at this machine.

It was essentially the old style of ballista, with a cable strung against a thick bough of seasoned yew, but on a much larger scale. It had been placed at one full stadium from the walls, a greater distance than usual for stones fired from such an engine to travel. While we watched, a team of transport horses pulled a long wagon which carried a covered load up to the side of the ballista, and cranes were lowered. By now the light was fading, and the engineers paused in their work so that the waggon could be unloaded in darkness. Later on we returned and saw great activity at the edges of the working area around the ballista, and strange, elevated shapes reflecting the firelight, but it was impossible for us clearly to discern what was going on.

A high state of alert was ordered that night, and when dawn broke most of the citizens of Sybaris were to be found on the walls, including *The Third Gnomon* himself.

TWENTY-SEVEN

The greatest feat of military engineering of those times was considered to be the building of the bridge of boats across the Bosphorus by the Samian architect, Mandrocles. This structure enabled Darius, the Persian king, to conquer Thrace and Makedhonia, and that had been an objective which any man could have guessed; but the purpose of the machine which was revealed on the back of the ballista by the rising sun was not so easy to arrive at by speculation. It appeared to be a dart made out of a hollowed tree, with wings of cloth stretched over a frame. On the stern of this strange vessel were two parallel poles supported by slim stanchions. At first glance the machine did not have any function of war, the front of it being a spoon shape. We surmised that as it was made of timber it could not have been designed to carry fire; unless, of course, the idea behind its design was that it should be a giant flaming arrow which would be fired deep into the city.

When the Kroton engineers made preparations to fire the ballista, winding back the cable, we were interested to see Milo himself limbering up beside the machine. An engineer climbed up on to the dart and attached a satchel to the end of one of the poles, then got down. While these preliminaries were taking place, the entire army of Kroton was marched up regiment by regiment and positioned on the plain so that the men could witness the event.

As the birds sang their welcome to the new day, Milo climbed up on to the ballista and took up a position between the two poles, one hand on each, his body side-on. Drummers drawn up on either side of the engine beat out a slow roll, which came up to an intense pitch then stopped dead. The ballista was fired and the dart shot upwards at an angle, the cloth wings trembling.

On the stern of the dart Milo began to perform a routine of marvellous gymnastics. The motion of the dart through the air did not affect his balance at all, and he twisted, turned, span and flicked his hands from one bar to the other, as if they were firmly positioned on the ground. Everyone who was watching could hear his chuckles of joy as he flew through the air performing these wonderful acrobatics.

The citizens of Sybaris could not help themselves cheering at this superb display. On the plain the army of Kroton beat their swords against their shields in a thunderous applause as Milo shot up, nonchalantly tossed the satchel down behind the western gate as the dart began to pass over it, released his hold on the parallel poles and dropped safely into a ship's sail, which a band of Kroton seamen had crept up to the walls with during the excitement and were now holding out to catch him. They then raced out of bow-shot in triumph.

All this I saw with my own eyes, as did all the soldiers of Kroton and the population of Sybaris. When the dart crashed into the north-west residential quarter it did little damage, but the contents of the satchel proved to be far more destructive. *The Flight of Milo* has become part of legend, exceeding the fame of Mandrocles' bridge of boats or, some might say, even the wooden horse at Troy, but it was the strategy behind the deed that mattered, for the satchel contained the last wills and testaments of all the *azygous plutos* exiles, leaving their total estates, wealth and property, including their businesses to the coffers of the Orphipythagorean seminary in Kroton, 'in order that the great work of reforming the nature of human civilisation should proceed with sufficient funds', so stated a clause common to every document, obviously dictated by Pythagoras.

These forgeries had been reproduced many times. As the satchel fell through the air, the fastenings were designed in such a way that they were torn open and the contents scattered over a wide area, falling into the hands of the Sybarite people in general.

*

Before the end of that day, rebellion was astir in the city.

I did not see the beginning of it, because shortly after noon I was called to the old wooden Temple of Hera in the north-western quarter, where the statue of the goddess was bleeding from its mouth, eyes and ears. As I trembled at the sight the flow increased, then *The Third Gnomon* himself entered the temple and stood by my side looking grave, the blood washing over his feet.

'How did you manage this, Kallias?' he asked. 'I've had enough tricks for one day.'

'Hera is affronted by Milo's flouting of natural law,' I told Telys. 'For a man to fly is an hubristic act of the first magnitude, though I know it was Pythagorean geometry that was behind it.'

Telys gave me a quizzical look and paddled towards the temple entrance.

'Stop the old b-b-bitch bleeding will you?' he called as he went cautiously down the steps, which were running with blood. 'I know that you've got a gang of your students down there pumping the stuff up.'

My denial was not heard as he hurried away. I followed him to the temple of Apollo, where he fetched a ladder from behind the god's throne and climbed up, drawing it up after him. When he sat in the great chair, dwarfed by its size, his madness was pitiable.

'There are no gods,' he shouted down, 'nor are there numbers.'

Then he fell into a silence, his eyes on the entrance. People were coming in. They made no noise as they filled up the space before Apollo's throne. Some of them had come from the temple of Hera, and had her blood on their hands and feet.

I looked up at Telys, pleading with my eyes that he should remain silent, but the man had to speak.

'Do you want to ask for something?' he cried.

The crowd stared up at him, amazed at his audacity. Each one knew that all fear of Telys had gone from the city, and what sat on Apollo's throne was no more than a powerless man.

'What do you expect me to do? Milo flies, Hera bleeds . . . what should Telys do? What magic have I got?'

Men at the front of the crowd knelt on the floor and allowed others to climb on their backs. I begged them not to do this, hoping to prevent any sacrilegious bloodshed in the temple, but they were deaf to my efforts. Still in silence they climbed upon each other, until a human pyramid was made.

Telys remained where he was, watching. As a hand came towards his ankle he swung his leg away.

'Nearly,' he said.

The crowd suddenly cried out in one voice, a noise so charged with indignation and insult that it made my heart leap to hear it.

Telys drew his feet up on to the seat of the throne and squatted there, hunched forward, his eyes bright.

'Now, that's music to my ears,' he shouted as the first man clambered up on to the level of the throne. 'I hope the gods can hear it as loudly as I can.'

I knew what he was going to do before he did it. As he perched on the edge of the huge marble throne, I was minded of a fledgling who stuggles from the nest and prepares to fly for the first time.

With no further word, he leapt forward and fell into the crowd.

Within moments he was beaten to death.

The end of *The Third Gnomon* was an act of sacrilege, but it had the effect of expiating Telys' heinous sin of usurping the god's place in the temple, thus it could be forgiven. Also it began the final phase in the city's life, fulfilling the Delphic Oracle's prophecy which had been scorned by those who had sought it: 'All happy, thou Sybarite, all happy shalt thou remain for as long as thou honourest those who live eternally, but when it comes to pass that a mortal man is held in greater awe than a god, then war and civil strife shall come upon thee.'

But what of the man who was held in awe by the usurper? In my view it had not been Telys, that opportunist lawyer, who had sat on the throne of Apollo, but the man who had manipulated him, a man as beautiful as the god, as clever, as bright, but not, I hoped, as capable of rising relentlessly through dawn after dawn.

Pythagoras should have been the victim of the mob, the sacrifice upon the altar of their disappointment.

The death of Telys and the miracle of the bleeding goddess wrought a change amongst the Sybarites: sense began to prevail, and a new awareness of the need for honourable action in the war moved the population. The excesses of the numbers cult declined back into their breeding-grounds – the counting houses – and there arose a military spirit, inspired by the conduct of Milo's army and its daily demonstrations of discipline. There was a feeling current in the city that an opportunity had been presented for Sybaris to reform and purify itself. This was not dependent upon Milo lifting the siege – a matter of honour being at stake here, vengeance for the thirty ambassadors – but more on the new sense of manly pride which had appeared. Taunted by Milo, stripped of their venal hopes of unearned wealth, the people fell back upon their basic sense of self-preservation, an instinct that must always be reinforced by valour as much as guile.

I kept my ear to the ground, always listening for information which might help me to divert the city's destiny. Leogoras and Chero had become less reliable as sources of news once they had gone to work at the liquid fire factory. They seemed to have moved away from me, their allegiances turning to their co-workers. In the case of Leogoras this caused me great heartache, as I loved the man, but I could see that too many ideas had been discredited for him to remain of his old mind. He had, by his own confession, become a Zoroastrian vitalist, converted by a group of Medes who had been impressed as forced labour and slaved alongside him at the vats.

TWENTY-EIGHT

To show respect for the death of Telys, Milo declared that his army would observe a truce during funeral games, which he arranged to take place on the plain of Sybaris. Athletes were invited from all over Greece and Greater Greece, but Milo let it be known that he would be competing in every event, thus setting the standard.

While the invitations were sent out and replies awaited, Sybaris enjoyed a respite from the siege. It was now full summer, and the city was hot. All the food which came into the markets had to be brought by sea, because Kroton's army was camped on all three sides of the land-facing walls and Milo had not extended the conditions of the truce to cover a free traffic in goods during the period of funerary observations. Water was becoming scarce because both the Kratis and Sybaris rivers were low, all the snows having melted in the mountains, but also the supply was being reduced by Milo's engineers, who were draining off large quantities into dams and cisterns. Drynios, the mercenary general, who had been left as the only authority in the city after Telys' death, protested to Milo that interfering with the water supply was not in keeping with the spirit of the truce, but he gained nothing. By the time that the replies to the invitations had all come in, most of them declining because the athletes could read between the lines that this was to be Milo's show, the city was starting to suffer drought.

Drynios was a resourceful man who had been in many tight spots. He ordered that ships should be sent to every neighbouring city to bring back water. When these vessels appeared at the ports of Sicily and Italy they were turned away, the name of Sybaris still being hated for her past success. The masters of the ships made landfalls wherever they could to find water out in country areas, but many fell prey to pirates and robbers or were taken for invaders, so little water got back to Sybaris.

On the day before the funerary games were due to begin, Drynios came to my house and said that he wanted to talk to me.

My respect for this old soldier had gone up since the death of Telys. He had many qualities which were, at first, hidden behind a screen of apparent misanthropy. With his shock of frizzy white hair, big, beaked nose and small, skinny body, he looked like an eagle-chick.

'Two things,' he said. 'One: I've had a message from Milo, asking if you will agree to officiate as hierophant at these games. Make up your own mind about that. Two: and perhaps you'll have to take the first into account when you think about this. I've decided to go. There's nothing more I can do.'

I knew that Drynios had worked hard to find a diplomatic solution to the war. He had even managed to persuade the citizens to offer thirty old men to Milo in compensation for those who had been killed in the surrogate Sybaris. They had rounded up some very ancient grandfathers and a few younger men on their last legs with disease who had been willing to submit to this on condition that their families received large benefits, but Milo had rejected the offer because all the man had been of the poorest sort and every one of the Kroton ambassadors had come from good family.

'I've paid myself from the treasury,' Drynios said wryly. 'Not an easy thing to do, but honourable enough, given the circumstances. What I've taken is exactly what I agreed with Telys, minus the victory bonus, of course. I noticed documents pertaining to you there, Kallias,' he continued, his eyes fixed on me. 'You will have to decide for yourself what should be done about your contract.'

I told him that I had fulfilled all the conditions and would expect to be paid, if there was anything left.

'Then you'll have to pay yourself, like I have done,' Drynios replied, 'because there's no-one else to do it. When I go – which I intend to do tonight – the people will turn to you as leader.

Once, this had been my ambition. But to be given power over a doomed city is not the same as becoming leader of the richest in the world.

I asked Drynios not to desert Sybaris, telling him that none of the Greek cities in Italy would be safe from Milo and Pythagoras should they conquer Sybaris and get their hands on its wealth. He was not impressed with my arguments.

'Those are considerations for a king, not someone like me,' he said. 'I want to get back to my farm before the grapes start to rot.'

When I mentioned the possibility of an alliance which Sybaris could offer, backed by large payments of money for military assistance, he just laughed.

'No-one will lift a finger to help Sybaris,' he told me. 'She had too much, and she wouldn't share it. People don't like that.'

He left that night.

Once it was known in the city that Drynios had fled, I was approached by representatives of the people. These were all ex-students of mine, hand-picked by the men of low birth who were now running Sybaris on a street-corner basis. This fragmentation of authority pleased no-one. It had risen because Drynios had been unwilling to take on the full powers of a tyranny, and all the old forms of council government had gone with the *azygous plutos* when they had been exiled.

The choice put to me, therefore, was to become tyrant or to flee like Drynios.

There was no other person I could talk to about this except Nonios. She did not attempt to dissuade me from taking on the power of tyrant, but she did advise me not to officiate as high priest at the funerary games. The slaves had picked up rumours from the streets, she told me, that I would be lured to the fields where the contests would be held and murdered.

So I made a proviso: the ceremonies for the games must all take place in the temple of Apollo within the walls of Sybaris. The shorter rituals at the beginning and end of each contest would be held on the walls within sight of the competitors.

Milo's answer was to scoff at my fears, but he accepted. He did ask that all the participants in the various events should be allowed to enter Sybaris for the opening and closing ceremonies at the temple. When I studied this proposal with Nonios, she advised me to ask for lists of names of the athletes. These were provided, and I saw that every one came from Kroton, numbering several hundred.

Nonetheless I went ahead and agreed. On the day of the ceremony I paraded the whole of Sybaris' army in the avenues and allowed the detachment from Kroton in under heavy guard, insisting that they come unarmed.

Nothing untoward occured, and the ceremony was conducted to the satisfaction of all. In his speech Milo said that it was a great pity that not one man in Sybaris was prepared to be a competitor in the games for its dead leader, but that was not a matter for mortals to comment upon. The shame, he said, would be in the minds of the gods. It was they who saw most clearly what value was put upon human vitality and health.

In the toils of my own changes I had not noticed how the temper of the city's manhood had altered, and this veiled insult from Milo was enough to bring out the new Sybarite. Immediately after the ceremony and the departure of the contestants from Kroton, I had to receive a deputation from the wards of the city, humble men who had previously admired only the careless luxury of their superiors' lives, who now wanted to show Milo what they were truly made of.

I counselled against it, having seen Milo in action in Kroton with the *azygous plutos*, and before at the Olympic Games in Elis, but they would not retreat. Lists of names were given to me, and these had to be reduced before I could submit them. To allow everyone to enter would have made the contests impossible to hold, there were so many who had put themselves forward.

Upon Nonios' advice I had to negotiate one further point with Milo: that hostages should be provided for every Sybarite who left the safety of the walls to compete in the games. I had anticipated a furious reaction, but none came. He agreed, and even proposed that for every Sybarite he would send two hostages.

*

Men do not become fit when cooped up in a hot, thirsty city under siege. Our contestants had insufficient space to train, and there were no atheletics coaches available. When we gathered on the walls for the first foot-race, ten stadia up and down a track running parallel to the western wall, I made sacrifice to Herakles with a white oxen to signal the start. As the blood gushed from the beast's throat the runners set off, Milo immediately sprinting to the front and barging the other competitors aside with his elbows. He won easily, great thighs flashing up and down the track. This was the outcome of all the events, until by the stone-throwing everyone was so embarrassed for Milo that they could hardly watch. It did not stop him, however, and he made a great show of picking up the heavy stone and tossing it lightly from hand to hand before heaving it an enormous distance, twice that of anyone else.

When it came to the last day and the chariot-racing, the hopes for a Sybarite victory increased. Anything to do with horses was their strong point. The best horses and vehicles had been prepared, and the people of the city were looking forward to a change of fortune.

Milo, of course, was the top-ranking competitor from Kroton, driving a team of magnificent blacks. Our most fancied charioteer was Erdos, who was now an acting captain in the citizen cavalry and had been head stableman to one of the *azygous plutos*. He had a team of greys which he had groomed and decorated until they looked so beautiful, so like the old style of Sybaris, flamboyant gold trappings, silver reins, gilt flowers and jewelled diagrams on the chariot, white plumes and clouds of spun sapphire everywhere, that the crowds on the walls wept to see him go out.

For this event I had agreed to leave the city and watch at the finishing line, Milo having sent two of his own sons as hostage to encourage me. He knew how important this race was to the morale of people in the besieged city. If he was victorious again, it would be easier for him to crow and humiliate me if we were face to face.

When I got there, I found Pythagoras amongst the crowd which had gathered around the waiting chariots. He bowed to me with one of his facetious smiles, then held out his hands.

'How should I treat you, Sphinx, old friend?' he said sweetly. 'As tyrant, priest, or as one who was once my bosom companion?'

I did not take his hands, which told him which role I preferred least.

'Your man Erdos looks very fast,' Pythagoras continued, 'but if you compare him with Milo, then he doesn't come up to the mark. His horses are not in the peak of condition.'

Milo appeared in the confusion of horses and chariots, driving up to where I was standing with Pythagoras and Nonios, who had accompanied me. Around us the air was thick with dust and dung as the high-spirited animals felt the excitement of the forthcoming race.

With Milo's four horses standing directly in front of me, I looked past their gleaming black heads and rolling eyes to the chariot where Milo should have been. He had gone. Then Nonios was by my side, her arms gathering in the foaming mouths of the four horses to kiss.

'Brothers, sisters, greetings,' she said, tossing her tail of coppery hair. 'It is good to see you.'

Then I heard the voice from the chariot. It was the god Hades, wearing his helmet of invisibility. As he spoke, I saw my Nonios transfigured into a fifth black horse, which was not harnessed to the chariot, her leather sling hanging from her mouth.

'The eel-writing was mine,' Hades said. 'The meaning of it you should know by now. As patron of the rich I have done all I can for Sybaris, pleading her case with Zeus, but he wants an end to the city because he is jealous of her wealth. So she must perish.'

A sheep and a knife were thrust into my hands to make the sacrifice which would start the race. I cut the animal's throat without looking, my eyes on the empty chariot which filled with Milo as I felt the sheep shudder between my knees.

The chariots set off around the circuit to the cries of the crowds.

'There's a loose horse,' Pythagoras said.

Milo had gone to the front straight away, and was driving his blacks towards the first bend. Nonios in her transformed self was galloping across the circuit, kicking and whinnying.

The four blacks had retained their spirits as the team of Hades and turned their heads towards her, ignoring the efforts which Milo made to bring them under control. As the chariot entered the bend he could not manoeuvre it into a good line of approach and it went up on one wheel, then turned over.

The rest of the field tore past the fallen Milo, who was forced to shelter behind his broken vehicle once the horses had come to rest. When the jockeying for position had sorted out the leaders after Milo's crash, I saw that Erdos was in the lead and that Nonios had disappeared.

Pythagoras noticed me shielding my eyes and searching the plain away from the race.

'She'll be back,' he muttered, then left to console the fuming Milo.

The victory of Erdos in the chariot race put new heart into the Sybarites. They saw it as a confirmation of their old skill with horses.

It was unfortunate that the siege had got to the point where the city could no longer sustain all the animals kept within the walls, and I was having to contemplate a general slaughter to reduce the drain on our supplies. Under the circumstances this was unthinkable. To do that would destroy the new spirit of the citizens, but not to meant that we would have to take the military initiative and attack, which I knew would be hazardous.

I shared my thoughts with Nonios. A sense of despair was not inappropriate for me at this time; after all, Hades himself had declared Sybaris to be condemned to the fate which I had knowledge of, and the buoyant mood of the people was more of an irony to me than an encouragement. Through her magical powers I knew Nonios to be partially divine, but that did not make her any more helpful.

She could not give me any hope. It was her opinion that all the damage had been done by Sybaris' past vanity and favouring of Hades through Bes. Telys had been a tool of the gods to weaken the city, now I was to be the hammer that would smash it.

'How am I to behave?' I asked her.

'Conduct yourself like a man,' she said, her eyes green above her veil, 'and honour your destiny.'

Love for any woman, mortal, nymph or goddess, comes in its own time and goes in its own time. Those who make promises that it will last for ever are fools and liars. The gods never give such guarantees, and mortals are deceiving themselves when they believe that they can be more constant than the Eternal Ones.

When I felt my love for Nonios declining, I knew that it was part of the process by which Sybaris would be delivered to its fate. She did not resent my coldness, nor the deliberate philandering which I began, to free myself from her. Instead she withdrew into the temple of Hera and became solitary, only seeing me when I went there to perform ceremonies.

My new companion during the time was Erdos, the victor of the chariot race. He was now a hero, and every house was open to him. With what time was left to us I sported with Erdos, appointing him as general of the city's cavalry.

The shortage of water drove me to decide that the military conclusion had to be precipitated. Milo and Pythagoras remained camped on the plain, sweating it out in the heat, but with a constant supply of fresh water from the two rivers. Their engineers had progressively reduced what flowed through to the city by building dykes to divert water into reservoirs.

On the day that the Sybaris river dried up completely – the Kratis having done so several days before – I ordered Erdos to prepare for a full-scale cavalry sortie from each of the three gates facing the encircling enemy. The horses would be able to get across the dry beds of the rivers, and our forces could break through the lines of the encamped Kroton army and turn to drive them up against the city walls, where they could be assailed by archers, ballista and engine fire, then infantry coming out of the gates.

Erdos was enthusiastic, seeing this as an opportunity for great glory and the rebirth of his city.

'No-one will ever mock us as effeminate libertines again,' he said, his eyes alight.

'No,' I replied with a heavy heart, 'I don't believe they will.'

TWENTY-NINE

In spite of the success of Pythagoras' ruse whereby Milo had showered the forged wills of the *azygous plutos* over the city, the actual treasure had remained where it was, intact, because the common people of Sybaris yearned for a proper authority to declare that it was right that they should be made rich. For a Sybarite to be a looter offended against all respect for wealth, and theft was not seen as a good foundation for a new plutocracy of the many. Also, the charisma of being a legitimate *azygous pluto* had survived everything that had happened.

I decided that I would give the people what pleasure I could and asked Nonios to help with the distribution of the treasure, which had been stored away in warehouses close to the Scythians' barracks. I had it transported to the temple of Hera and broken up into lots. It was handed out to the citizens after a ceremony dedicated to Hades, lord of the rich and the dead.

For my part, I did not take even what the city owed me.

That night was given over to celebration. I did not take part, thoughts of the future battle weighing me down.

A messenger came while the streets were still full of roistering. He had been sent by the officer at the western gate with a written request from Milo for a parley. Not wanting to meet with the enemy during the last festivity which the Sybarites would ever know, I declined but said that I would be prepared to attend a meeting in seven days, which was the length of time I estimated the revelling would last.

Towards dawn Nonios came to me, distraught. As instrument of Hades and Aphrodite and nymph in nature, she had taken to the streets with the crowds. I could see that her feet were raw with dancing, and she stank of wine.

A man had ripped her veil away at the moment of orgasm and gone into a frenzy of horror, she told me, and the crowd had chased her away as a witch. I bathed her and put her to bed in my own chamber. As she lay on my pillow I asked her why she kept the harelip, when the power to remove the blemish was hers, and always had been.

Her reply was inaudible, said with her mouth pressed into the pillow. Then she was asleep and I left her. When I returned some time later she was gone, but the pillow had turned to stone, and in it was the impression of Nonios' face, without the harelip. I sent out for a sculptor who worked in clay, and got him to make a cast. When I went to my chamber to look at it I found the sculptor quivering in a corner, his face covered with his hands and the cast broken on the floor.

The sculptor could not recover his senses, and I had to have him removed. As he was taken away he kept moaning one word: light, light. Once he had gone I locked the door of the chamber and did not sleep there again, forbidding anyone to open it upon pain of death.

It was this event which made me shake off my despair and begin to make arrangements for leaving Sybaris. I had continued Telys' policy of preventing people from deserting the city during the siege, and all those who wanted to go had to submit to examination. There was already a trade in progress whereby people escaped on the water-ships, hiding in the empty jars. This was controlled, and no-one left in this way without me knowing who he was, or who had arranged it.

I contacted Leogoras and Chero and proposed that they should leave Sybaris, taking Leogoras' family and Nonios with them. This they accepted without further question, but Nonios sent me a message to say that she no longer had any need of my interest in her welfare and she would, in future, look after herself.

On the evening before his departure Leogoras asked to see me, and we met at his dwelling, his wife and children sitting out in the courtyard while we talked inside. He was thinner now and had lost his countryman's lustre, his time in the pitch and oils factory having dulled his skin. But his eye was still as bright, and he spoke with all his old energy and firmness.

'To think that it all began in my vineyard,' he said ruefully, 'but I suppose if it hadn't happened there it would have started somewhere else.'

I told him that it was a mistake to imagine that I had brought the fate of Sybaris to the city. Telys had already sensed what was in store, and I had only confirmed it for him.

'But it looks as though the gods are now on the side of Pythagoras, who is their enemy,' Leogoras said, tugging at his hair, which was now streaked with grey. 'I don't understand.'

'Pythagoras is being used, but he doesn't realise it.'

Leogoras let me know with a sidelong look that I had seen many times before, that this answer was not good enough.

'What for?' he asked. 'Where can all this lead?'

In his simple way Leogoras was only putting questions to me that I had asked myself over and over again. Why must Sybaris be destroyed? If Zeus owns everything, why is he jealous of wealth? Is there a limit, as yet unseen, beyond which human wealth becomes hubristic? If so, will the fall of Sybaris reveal it?

I told Leogoras that I had received so many signs and communications from the Eternal Ones on this matter that it had made me certain of one thing: that the fate of Sybaris was of great importance to the spiritual life. Whatever happened would be by design and not chance. All would be to the good.

With that I embraced him and took my leave, glad that he would survive.

Chero, I never saw again. He had been living in the Tyrrhenian community for some time, one that had become increasingly unpopular because the Sybarites believed that it was the duty of their old trading partner to come to their aid. But nothing came from Rome – not even a word of support. My own view was that the Tyrrhenians had come to an understanding with Pythagoras. Once Sybaris had fallen, then the trade which she had enjoyed would be taken up by Kroton at lower prices.

I heard from the water-ship on which Chero had been due

to sail that he had not turned up. Whether he had decided to stay and prove that at least one Tyrrhenian was mindful of the debt of honour which his country owed, I did not know, but it was a decision which I thought at the time would have become him.

The celebrations which followed the share-out of the *azygous plutos*' wealth went on longer than I had anticipated. I had assumed that the people would begin to sense the destiny which was at work all around them. They had plenty of evidence and warning by now. But where there was not water, there was wine. Where there was no future, there was the present. The festivities dragged on and on, each night made restless by the cries of revellers. And I sat and let them play, hardly seeing anyone, keeping to the city hall.

Finally they were exhausted. The streets quietened. I waited for two days to give everyone time to recover, then sent for Erdos and told him to prepare the attack for sunrise the following day.

Then I sent word to Pythagoras and Milo that I would meet them as requested.

The Long-Haired Samian was at his most radiant when we encountered each other in Milo's tent. I had come alone under cover of night, dressed like a low-born man. In contrast, he was clothed in gold, his hair dressed with roses. In his beauty he resembled a god, but I hated him and could not hide it.

'Have some charity, Sphinx,' he chided me. 'Soon it will all be over, and you will need my friendship.'

I retorted that I did not expect to have any friends by the time the whole thing had finished; which made him laugh.

Then we got down to business. When all was arranged I left, refusing to dine with them. As I walked through the darkness towards the city walls I was awed once again by the sheer size of Sybaris, its great mass pale under the stars.

Could it ever be destroyed? I asked myself. There is so much of it.

The army of Sybaris, once gathered, was a great host which outnumbered that of Kroton three to one. Erdos marshalled the cavalry in the avenues behind the three land-gates, the numbers spreading back towards the centre, horses packed into every street and side turning.

The mood was one of silent gaiety. Some kindness of the gods had made these one-time warriors feel invincible. They observed good order, controlling their mounts in preparation for the opening of the gates. The signal for this was given from the eastern wall by a trumpeter who took his cue from me.

The sun, which was rising out of the ocean, as the musician put his instrument to his lips, was as red as blood. The trumpeter looked at me, knowing that I must give the order soon.

I waited, hoping to receive a sign that what was ordained need not to pass.

But the sun-god gave no sign.

I told the trumpeter to blow, my soul withering as the notes hit the air.

The three gates were opened. As the Sybarites poured out they raised a great cry and spurred their horses into a headlong charge against the lines of the encamped enemy, knocking down the tents and overturning the siege-engines as they went through to turn and drive the army of Kroton up against the city walls.

Once the Sybarite cavalry had passed through, Milo's soldiers formed into lines behind the bagpipers. They had learnt well the tune that I had given to Pythagoras, and as the horses of the Sybarites heard it when they galloped in for the second charge, they slowed down and began to dance.

The momentum of the attack was lost. With the notes of the bagpipes wailing over the battlefield and the horses prancing this way and that, the soldiers of Sybaris were pulled from their mounts and butchered, and the city's open gates seized before they could be shut.

Once the battle was lost I left the walls and hurried to the temple of Hera where, as agreed, I had placed a marked waggon containing my baggage and treasure. Milo had told me that there would be no sack of the city in the usual military sense, only a systematic demolition of defences and garnering of valuables by orderly squads. There would be no rampage, no letting the men of Kroton loose to do their worst.

I had made the condition that I should be well clear of Sybaris before the army began exterminating the people, as I knew from the prophecy must happen. But as I left the city I passed the Tetractys and saw a structure being raised over the ten posts: a long frame which had a hundred sharpened stakes on it that could be winched back and sprung. I had no doubt that it was a killing machine, designed to do mathematical mass slaughter. As I reached the gate I heard the crash of the mechanism and the screams of the first batch, and I thought that I heard my name being cursed over and over again by the dying.

With my head bowed I rode out.

My escort stayed with me until the end of the covered way, then I continued alone along the Road to Prosperity. When I reached the turn-off for Telys' villa I took it and drove up to the vineyard. It had been my intention to climb the oak and remain there for the time that it would take for Sybaris to be brought to the ground, for that I knew to be its fate. But the tree had been cut down, and sitting on the stump was the female slave whom I had taken in my lust after the inner scene of Herakles.

At her breast was an infant which she presented to me as my child. It was a boy and, as yet, unnamed. When I asked who had cut the tree down, she told me that a goddess had come and felled the oak with a single stone from a sling.

'Did she have a harelip?' I asked.

The woman told me that the mouth of the goddess had been as firm and pure as the crest on a drift of snow. After the goddess had brought the oak down, she had helped the slave to be delivered of her baby, told her to wait there for me, then thrown a leg over the tree and ridden it into the sky.

The slave's name was Bekela. I put her and the child into my waggon and drove deep into the hills along small tracks as far as I could before nightfall, then unloaded it and hid my baggage and treasure, returning to watch over the waggon in case Pythagoras had had me followed.

No-one came. On the following morning I went ahead on foot until I found what I was looking for: a secure, high place where I could hide the waggon. It was a deep flat-bottomed gorge, which opened out to the east just below the summit of a hog-backed mountain. From the end of the valley I could see over the plain to Sybaris.

It took all the daylight hours to get the waggon up there. By the time that I had it in position, both Bekela and I were exhausted, and one of the horses had been lamed. But I knew that my decision had been right. From my vantage-point I could already see people who had escaped from Sybaris coming towards the high ground, and the pursuing Kroton horsemen who harried them. Along every road and track, wretched families who were still hanging together in the last stages of fatigue and despair were cut down by Milo's troops.

If any of these citizens had caught sight of me, they would not have kept quiet about my identity. I knew that they would blame me for the fate of Sybaris, not knowing that it had been settled by greater powers than mine. As the betrayer of the army, they would hold me responsible and do all they could to bring about my death.

I got Bekela to cut my hair and beard, also to bleach them both with the juice of the orphax plant which grew on the mountain. My skin I darkened with walnut, and I drew some simple designs which Bekela painted on to my cheeks and upper body and arms to look like tattoos.

As I adopted these changes, gazing at myself in a mirror, my eyes often went to the distant city. Day after day smoke rose from the towers and roofs and made a pall over the plain. More refugees appeared in the foothills, only to be hunted down by the Kroton cavalry, which now treated the pursuit as sport, blowing horns and using hounds.

Then, after many days, I saw the vista of Sybaris' suffering alter. Ships of all sizes and shapes came from the north, east and west, crowding into the harbour and sea-roads. At the same time convoys of wheeled transport arrived from Taras in the east of Italy, Metapontion and Siris, others from across the Ionian Sea, strange vessels from Kerkyra and Epeiros, and fleets which came up from the Greek cities in Sicily, all sailing without obstruction in waters previously not open to them.

It was not until later that I learnt what had been going on.

Pythagoras had been auctioning the city. In the assembly room of the city hall where I had first met the *azygous plutos*, all the temples, houses, buildings, stone, timber, furniture and slaves had been sold off to the highest bidder. Once a sale had been agreed, the buyer would be given a detachment of engineers and labour to break down the structure and load it on to his transport. In this way all the great temples and their statues were demolished, the paved avenues ripped up, the mansions of the rich taken down, the bridges being left until last. Foreigners bought the walls and gates of Sybaris, her roofs and foundations, her total habitable soul. Everything was sold off to the scavengers, and the profits which Milo and Pythagoras made were immeasurable.

None of these business details were apparent to me as I saw the piecemeal destruction of Sybaris begin. I could not conceive of the sale of an entire city as if it were a dead man's furniture. As the traffic flowed to and fro, I believed that I was watching the beginnings of an empire, these new connections with hostile cities and provinces written across the plain of Sybaris like a master-plan on Pythagoras' table.

This is how I spent moons of guilt, high on the hog-backed mountain from summer into autumn, watching Sybaris being taken down. I aged beneath my semblance of age, until no disguise was needed. Each cart full of stone carried off; every ship-load of timber and goods leaving port, was registered by a wrinkle, a lessening of power, a new ache or pain in me. As I watched the great temples come down, parts of my spirit seemed to collapse with them.

When every stone of Sybaris had been taken down, the army of Kroton began to dig channels. At first I thought that these excavations were mass graves for the thousands of dead in Sybaris, but as the work progressed I was able to discern the triangular form which the channels made, and how they linked up with the course of the two rivers, the Kratis and the Sybaris.

There came a morning when the army of Kroton was divided into two parts: one gathered at the Kratis river, and one at the Sybaris, where the points of the triangle were closest. I saw two ceremonial processions approach as all the soldiers began to dig. By the time that the channels of the triangles had been cut through to the rivers, Milo and Pythagoras had presided over the breakthrough with trumpet fanfares, and, I imagined, speeches of congratulation to their engineers.

When the brown waters poured down the channels I saw horsemen galloping along to keep up with them, and heard the great cheering of the army. What are they going to grow? I asked myself. What crop needs so much water?

The flood poured down the channels and joined together where the western gate of Sybaris had been, then spread out to submerge the site of the whole city, draining into the lagoon so the sea turned brown.

Sybaris had gone.

What this performed upon me I can describe only as my own inundation. At last I saw the fulfilment of my inner scene in the oak, when Herakles was stuck in the bed of the river and rose to be throned in water. A bird had brought a fish which was consuming itself and dropped it in my lap. Now the city was under water, the fish had had the price of my worth, and what was enthroned was the will of the gods to which all men must submit.

Is this truth? I asked. If so, can it be worth anything?

It was while I was in the toils of this blasphemous despair that the Durva came.

THIRTY

The Durva had had me under observation from the time I had returned to Telys' vineyard. They had followed me up the mountain and watched every day as I sat on my perch overlooking the plain, brooding over the fate of Sybaris.

Once the initial shock had died down and I had got control of my fear – their warlike dress and paint was still as repulsive as I remembered it at the Grotto of the Sacred Eels – I remembered that I must keep my full disguise intact. But as I got ready to plead with them as a poor refugee from the wars of their enemies, they prostrated themselves in front of me.

I had a clear memory of their strange behaviour at the grotto, and I noted that their buttocks were similarly unclad, though this time they were lying face down in the grass, so I did not rush to the conclusion that they were abasing themselves. Shortly afterwards, they demonstrated their veneration in other ways, singing and praying.

We did not share a language. There was no-one who could translate into words what necessary understandings had to take place. Bekela was afraid, as well she might be, the Durva having a terrifying reputation for cruelty against all Greeks, free or enslaved, and I needed to knew what I was being worshipped *as*. The tortures committed upon the young Sybarite men who had gone to treat with the Durva came back to mind, also the story of the dead warriors astride our dead horses, petrified in the grotto.

All this made a mix of many possibilities. When the Durva produced baskets of food I had to signal to them that I was not hungry, not being prepared to take the risk of eating anything which they had prepared until I was sure that they were genuinely hospitable. There are peoples in isolated places who honour their sacrificial victims with gifts before taking them to the altar.

So we had a strange day; sitting in the sun, the baskets of food between us, the sea breeze coming from the coast in its new purity, now the stench of corruption and burning from the city had gone. I looked at the Durva. The Durva looked at me. We smiled, we gestured, we made it plain many times that there was peace between us. But we could get no further until I knew who I was to them.

My aloofness troubled the Durva, and they began to enter into many debates with each other. I could not help them, because if I revealed my identity as the man who had conjured the silver eels out of the grotto they might kill me in reprisal, but I was almost certain that they revered me as a result of that notable event.

The deadlock was finally broken by a sinewy old warrior who owned few teeth and a bloodshot eye. He stood up and approached me with a snake which he had caught. With a blow from his iron sword he cut off its head, then stuck the wriggling serpent between his buttocks, letting out a cry of terror.

The rest of the Durva took up this wailing sound, then altered it in the backs of their throats until it was an ululation of joy and praise. I had no doubt then that it was as Kallias, the master of the sacred eels, that I was being venerated, and I took the chance of eating the food they had offered.

From this time on there was an increasing amity between us, though theirs was always shown with inordinate respect, bordering upon dread. Both sides took pains to exchange smiles, touches, signs and symbols of goodwill; yet I remained their god, notable, cherished but maintained at a little distance.

All that being accomplished with Sybaris and my prophecy, I knew that the time had come to leave the hog-backed mountain and follow my new, unseen future. When I had arrived at my home after the descent into the lake at Enna, I had discovered that Sybaris had been destroyed during the summer before that spring, so I knew what time must elapse before my return.

Long enough for a god to take his revenge, even if he was only the god of the Durva.

The Durva carried my waggon down the mountain upon their shoulders, singing praise-songs to me. I was apprehensive about this boisterousness, knowing that Milo's forces were still in the area, though in diminished numbers, but I did not need to worry. The Durva host – which numbered 8,000 male warriors – was not an opponent which Milo relished at this point in his triumphs.

On our way to the homeland of the Durva in the southern mountains, the host crossed the old alternative western trade route and came upon a party of Sybarite refugees. Most of these unfortunates took their own lives as soon as they saw who was descending upon them, but I was able to get to one of them, a brown shrimp of a lad, before he could cut his throat. He was hardly more than a boy, and the reason why he had been so slow to save himself from an imagined, atrocious end at the hands of the Durva was that he was blind. When I spoke to him I was careful to use an assumed voice, in case he had ever heard me speak at ceremonies or public functions.

He took comfort from hearing Greek. When the Durva had arrived, his companions had shouted to him to make an end of himself to save further suffering, and that was the last intelligible word he had heard before the shrieking, gabbling tribesmen had filled his ears with horror. When I spoke to him, his face lit up like a soul reborn into a better world.

His name was Tassopholos, and he was a trainer of birds. With his father he had run a stall in the market, which sold thrushes, robins, sparrows and finches which Tassopholos had taught to speak, a labour which took a long time, he told me. His father, who was one of those who had died by his own hand, had invested in parrots from Africa during the heydays of Sybaris, but Tassopholos had not been able to teach them anything. Only the small, common birds responded to his tuition.

That night I let him sleep, watching over him. A sweet emotion had hold of me as I sat there in the darkness while he slumbered in his double darkness, the Durva packed around us in a shallow valley protected from the wind. This boy had been able to turn his mind to his own sad history so deftly, putting aside the death of his father, his city, his hopes. What reason could there be for him to chatter about small birds while such dread memories roared around in his head?

I knew my destiny was not to take him with me to Elis, for I would have remembered him being there. I fell asleep full of regrets, hoping that he would find a better home in the meantime.

No love which I could offer the boy would be safe.

The next day we were on easier terrain, and I rode in the waggon with Tassopholos, whom I had placed under my protection, and asked him for an account of the last days of Sybaris from within.

He had been in hiding until the house which had sheltered him and his father had been dismantled, the rest of the family having been killed in the first days after the defeat. They had lived off their aviary of birds, eating them one by one, then trapping more on the roof, including the carrion-fowl which had gathered in great numbers to feast upon the dead.

In his blindness Tassopholos had only had his father to tell him what was going on. Each day his father would hear stories from other survivors, and pass them on to his blind son. I asked Tassopholos to recount some of them to me, and was pleased to hear that the Sybarites had been brave and put up a resistance to Milo's machine of death and destruction. The boy's favourite story concerned a foreigner, who when faced by a squad of engineers who had come to demolish a house, killed four of them with stones from a sling, taunting the others that he had learnt the skill from the ugliest woman in the world, but she was ten times more beautiful than any of their mothers who were all whores. When Milo had sent infantry to dislodge the man, he had fought again and killed several more, but Milo had had a siege-engine erected in the street to batter the building down with this hero still in it. When all hope had gone and he was cornered, the foreigner had taken out a false soapstone eye, using it for one last shot with his sling, killing the officer in charge of the ballista before being slain himself.

When Tassopholos had been telling this tale his dull eyes had flickered as if some life were returning to them, and his colour had heightened. I could see that as a Sybarite he relished such courage being shown in the defence of his home.

'Do you recall the name of this man?' I asked, my own mind already made up as to who it was, but not which name he had chosen to die with.

'He was called Bucchero,' the boy told me.

When I had been silent for a while, he leant foward and said that he could smell tears.

'You tell these stories well,' I replied. 'Go on with them. Tell me more. I could listen to them for ever. Let's hear about the Sybarites who fought bravely.'

'There were plenty of those,' Tassopholos assured me.

'Then let's hear every one you can remember.'

As we continued our journey, the blind boy told me tale after tale of humble, unknown men who had performed deeds of valour in the streets and sewers of the city, often fighting with chisels and sticks. As I listened I recalled the countless days of my education, when I had had to listen to Homer and his poetry of war between kings and noble heroes, his chanting of their virtues and actions, and how the gods had played their part, in the heavens above Troy. Where had they been when the Pythagorean killing machine with its numbers and plans had rolled through the gates of Sybaris?

'Did your father blame anyone for what happened?' I asked Tassopholos.

'That was not his way,' the blind boy replied.

I grew angry with this answer. But Tassopholos shook his head.

'My father had no interest in anything other than birds. He spent all his time on the roof, or in the country.'

Was he rich? I wanted to know.

'At one time, when he began to import parrots and they became a craze,' Tassapholos replied. 'He made a lot of money, but he lost it all.'

This silenced me. I had a view of this quiet, simple man

living within a narrow compass, his blind son by his side as they pursued the value of birds. Then a brutal mechanism which was a thousand times bigger and more complex than their own lives swept them into its maw. Now the birds still sang, untutored, and here he was, this young fellow, helpless in the world but imbued with hope.

'You did not blame the politicians?' I asked.

'Who were they?'

Irritated again, I mentioned Telys by name.

Tassopholos said that he had never heard of him, and added that he had no knowledge of the man Pythagoras whom I had already mentioned, except as a neighbourhood cobbler who had had that name. Milo, he had heard of: as the winner of the foot-race, boxing, long-jump and javelin in many Olympiads; his name had been a byword.

My world and the world of this bird-teacher had hardly touched. My ill-temper and impatience suddenly melted away as I realised that his ignorance had the power to make me glad.

Perhaps it was those sensitivities of hearing which are enhanced in those without sight and his skill in teaching language to birds that made Tassopholos quick to learn the Durva tongue. As we progressed through the mountains, he was able to tell me many things about the warriors and their customs. When a Durva wakens, he must not speak until he has washed out his mouth. This was because they believed that a mist-spirit called Movrubi, a cousin of Gax, their god of death, entered every sleeper and hid in his mouth every night. If a word was spoken before Movrubi was expelled, then the offender would never sleep again.

I had not noticed that the diet of the Durva was vegetarian, much of it in the form of a compacted grass which each man carried in a bark satchel. This was eaten raw in the mornings, but for their sunset meal they would cook it and scatter various powders and crystals over the brown mess. When I asked Tassopholos to question the Durva about this strange food of theirs, he told me that they would not speak to him about what went into their mouths because that orifice was holy.

Upon learning this, I realised how powerfully their superstitious minds must have been affected when the silver eels had penetrated them and emerged from their mouths, this sacred opening. If I was seen as the magician who had launched the eels against them, then they must have had a choice of two attitudes: to detest me, or to be in awe. On the day that Tassopholos explained the religious significance of the Durva mouth to me I made an experiment by biting an apple and then offering the uneaten part to a warrior.

The warrior did not hesitate for a moment: uttering a glad cry, he snatched up the apple, kissed it, then bolted it down his throat. From that time he seldom left my side, casting fond glances at me, ogling me every time that I ate and holding out his cupped hands like a beggar.

This behaviour made me think that I had acted rashly, encouraging some form of intercourse between us. But the word which Tassopholos picked out as the most common utterance of my new devotee when referring to me was *tsygom*, which he was able to translate as *messenger*.

So many mysteries, so many fears! To be a god is not, by any means, to have company and be understood. What if our behaviour as civilised Greeks appeared in the same light to the Olympians? Our ceremonials and rituals might be equally incoherent and peculiar, nothing but irrational gestures in response to a simple action, such as the sharing of an apple.

The landscape which we were passing through was the best setting for these thoughts; full of trees in fruit, lush pastures, tumbling streams of clear water. Even the air itself had the full gleam of ripe colours, honey yellows, warm reds and bountiful browns. Nuts were strewn by the wayside, shaken down by mountain winds. Oats and wheat tossed in fields won out of the limestone. It was a country of harvest, the reality on which our dream of Elysium is based.

So to be a god was not too great an act of my imagination. I had left the horrors of Sybaris behind, consigning them to a part of my memory which I knew would never be allowed to become the past. It was as much an accompaniment to my life as breathing, but, like breathing, one could forget that it was there while it went on.

Could this be a happiness? I asked myself. This fulfilment

of the cruellest prophecy which was ever granted to me? If my journey through this land of abundance was a reward and a rest from my labours, then I was truly lost in my attempt to read the mind of the Eternal Ones. My happiness had the qualities of their remoteness and star-like forgetfulness, but to grant it to me, the betrayer of a hundred thousand, was no boon. The only way in which I could have endured this ecstasy would have been truly to become a god, leaving the Durva and taking the seemingly easy step to the side of Zeus.

THIRTY-ONE

None of the inklings and pointers to the manner of home life amongst the Durva which Tassopholos' early encounters with their language had given, prepared me for what I would find upon our arrival. I had expected a stony barbarian stronghold far removed from fertile land, as grim and distant as those which I had seen in Makedhonia and eastern Mysia, defensible refuges rather than towns in which to live and enjoy life.

But this plateau, by some freak of climate or fortune, was as green and lush as a lowland river valley. It was protected from the northern winds by high peaks, and two walls of grey cliffs, crested with firs, ran its length, leaving only the southern edge open, and this was only reached up a difficult, winding track, guarded by immense boulders serving as lookout towers.

I was impressed by the good humour of the Durva warriors as they climbed up this long natural stairway, carrying my waggon on their shoulders with myself, Tassopholos, Bekela and the infant inside it. We had offered to climb alongside the rest, but this had been refused. It was their custom, it was explained, that all strangers who were to be guests of the tribe should be carried up the Mynxmahogh Way, this access route having been named after the Durva deity who presided over all journeys, creeping plants and wells. When I pointed out that this custom need not include my heavy waggon, which could have been hidden somewhere in the lower forests, they told me that as it was the vehicle of their new god its proper place would be outside his temple.

At several points along the Mynxmahogh Way my horses had to be trussed and carried also. The Durva never brought their own animals out of the fastness, and always marauded on foot. When I saw my first Durva horses, I saw why. They were huge, bred for pulling heavy ploughs through stony soil when the Durva first retreated to the plateau to escape the Greek invaders. Now, when the soil was greatly improved and deepened, they were still bred this way because this remained as the style of animal which they had long husbanded and admired.

At the top of the Mynxmahogh Way was a great arch built of flowers, and around it gathered the whole Durva people, their ranks thick on both slopes going up from the road. My waggon was set down on its wheels, and, in complete silence, was pulled by all the tribe.

As we went northwards, I looked at the females. The Durva did not take their women on expeditions out of their homeland, so I had not yet seen one. There were many stories about the Durva kidnapping women and girls all along the coast, and always taking the most dainty and decorative, rather than the strong, big-hipped breeding stock which predatory tribes favour. Legends had grown up which spoke of a secret paradise in the mountains, where Durva warriors guarded a host of beautiful captives. It was said that if a man distinguished himself in battle then he was allowed to go amongst them for as long as he was able, and that often these heroes died of bliss. Another story related how the Durva celebrated the main festival of their religion by all the men and women coming in a great congress at a given hour, but I had always suspected that this was no more than a fantasy derived from the celebration of the Persian temple concubines during the Nativity of Mithras, when the women offer themselves to the people. The Greeks have a habit of investing foreigners with the practices which they would like to see in their own rituals, but dare not perform, in case they cause civil disorder.

What I saw in the faces of the women was glowing enthusiasm; but my powers of discrimination had been overwhelmed by my welcome. Whether they were exceptionally beautiful or not, I could not tell, because there were so many of them, and in all their eyes was the heat of adulation.

For the first time it sank into me what it meant to be a god. My days with the Durva warriors had not impressed the full significance of this upon me. Perhaps it is only women who can make a man feel that he is a god and keep him sweetly blind to his mortality.

The Durva love wood. Although surrounded by workable stone, they do not choose to make use of it. I saw outcrops of fine marble along our route, but no sign that any quarrying had ever taken place. When I saw the vast beech, oak and fir forest which clothed the plateau and the first Durva houses – long, single-storey buildings, with fantastic carved ornamentation along the roof ridge, gables and eaves and doorposts – it struck me that stone is not the most natural material for the construction of human dwellings. Wood has greater warmth and can be worked better. What it lacks in comparison with stone is durability, but I was told that there were wooden buildings on the plateau that had stood for 200 summers. With the memory of Sybaris' destruction in my mind, and how ephemeral it had made all the work of men seem to me, wood's quality of a vital stillness, echoing its forest days, had more to offer than the dead weight of imperishable stone. Let that be used for tombs and sepulchres, not for places to live.

The settlement was not concentrated into a small area. Roads branched off the main highway like the bones of a fish, and farms and fields were situated along each of these side-tracks. There were herds of small, light-brown cattle, and I could see flocks of sheep and goats up on the higher slopes. The sheep of the Durva are interesting inasmuch as they have four horns and a fat tail which drags on the ground. These animals had recently been sheared, and when I encountered one close-up I thought that it was a comical creature except for its eyes, which were mean slits of yellow. The Durva make sport out of the fighting of the rams, which is a deadly business. Two of the four horns on each head are straight and point directly in front. Rams, when in rut, could drive their front horns right through the skulls of their adversaries.

Other domesticated livestock that I saw on my triumphal

journey were long-haired swine, black and white swans and red-beaked geese on ponds fed by the mountain streams which ran everywhere from the crests, brown ducks, and Durva dogs.

These dogs were the oddest-looking animals. They were bred for keeping sheep and, with the aggressive temperament of the four-horned Durva breed, they had to be very quick on their feet to avoid the lethal prongs. What had been bred was a dog that moved so fast and was so light on it feet that it was often difficult for the human eye to keep up with its movements. It had an arched body, short legs, a whip-like tail, a head with eyes set on either side rather than forward, and its coat was more like a shell than fur, the bristles laid thickly on top of each other to fend off the horns. When the creature became excited this fur did not rise as with most dogs, but was laid flatter.

We arrived at the bottom of a zigzag length of road which went up through a beech wood. There were clearings on either side with houses, but they had no fields or gardens. I later learnt that the people who lived on the zigzag were released from all manual work because they had been given civic or religious duties. Once their term came to an end, they returned to farming alongside everyone else.

Once into the beech wood, the silence of the great Durva host was suddenly broken as every person began whistling imitations of birdsong. It was a tremendous, thrilling sound, very expertly done, and all the birds in the trees joined in. This was all in my honour, and it lifted my tired heart.

The road through the wood was now paved with slabs of limestone, polished and rutted by use over time. To keep these slabs clear of the growing roots of the trees and disturbance, the road had been made on a platform of wooden piles. As my waggon rolled along this supported avenue, its weight making it give beneath, I reasoned that we must be approaching a place of some importance in Durva life, so much thought and labour having gone into the construction of this approach.

The Durva birdsong grew louder as the trees of the wood became an avenue of high, great-waisted beeches, which had been lopped and trained over to make a vault. When the procession reached a pair of red posts the men stopped, and all the women took over the pulling of my waggon, the warriors standing between the columns of the beeches like saplings, their arms held upwards while they began making a booming sound deep in their chests.

At the end of the vaulted avenue, standing in a green light, I saw the outline of a temple. While studying the style of the Durva houses I had noted how different it was to anything Greek, but the building ahead was a structure familiar to me, having two round columns between square pilasters, and a high porch that had designs and human figures painted upon it.

At first I could not believe my eyes and thought that I was hallucinating, but as we got nearer I saw that it was the old wooden temple of Hera from Sybaris. In my amazement I thought it might be a copy, but the exact replication of the weathered tone of the paint, the patches where the wood showed through, the loss of this hand, this foot from a figure, it was all too precise to be anything but the original.

I had found myself saying 'look, look' to Tassopholos, forgetting the boy's blindness. Here was a part of his city which had survived! When I told him what I could see he was not as disbelieving as any sighted person might have been. To him the temple had always been more of an idea than a reality.

'How did it get here?' he said as the waggon rolled to a halt at the foot of newly quarried limestone steps.

This was a question I hardly dared to think about when I remembered how the buildings of Sybaris had been auctioned, and by whose command. If the Durva now had the temple, then they must have been in touch with Pythagoras.

My legs shook as I climbed down from the waggon and went up the steps of the temple.

The statue of Hera was not on her throne. As I looked at the empty seat and smelt the odours of the ancient timbers, much stronger in this high place and after the agitations that the structure had been through, I saw again the blood of the angry goddess and Telys throned in Apollo's temple, kicking his heels at the crowd.

All this was being offered to me to suffer again, like a dog that must return to its vomit.

When Pythagoras emerged from behind the throne, his hair twined with honeysuckle and columbine, his eyes brilliant as the shafted rays of sunshine which came through cracks in the old fabric, I was not surprised; but the dismay I felt was that of a man who has escaped from one madness to be faced with another.

'Sphinx,' he crooned, 'my god.'

The Durva women had followed me into the temple and crowded all around. To have given vent to my hatred of Pythagoras and the sense of cruel disenchantment that I felt at finding him in the place, might have meant his death, but I could not be sure what he was to the Durva as yet. In his bearing he was as cool and supercilious as ever, and I saw no sign of fear.

'Welcome to your new home,' he said with a charming smile. 'As you can see, the old place travelled very well.'

He bowed, then, with a second smile, feignedly serious and elated, prostrated himself before me. This, I must confess, thrilled me in the most disconcerting way.

Before I could speak, the women followed Pythagoras' example and abased themselves, sighing and whispering.

'What are you doing here?' I whispered, leaning over and taking a lock of Pythagoras' silver hair away from his ear, my fingers trembling at the touch.

'I'll explain later,' he replied in a low voice, his face still pressed to the floor, 'but meanwhile think of me as your high priest.' He paused, then shifted his head, peering mischeviously up at me. 'Don't you think that you should sit on your throne?'

I had already taken a decision that I would never do such a thing. Tassopholos was by my side. I told him to find a means of telling the Durva women that it was a rule in my house that no-one should ever sit, and that would include myself. Pythagoras got to his feet, a protest on his lips, but I ignored him and kept a protective arm around the blind Sybarite boy as he haltingly explained the first temple law. It was not questioned by any of the women, and I believe that it had exactly the arcane flavour which my first pronoucement as a god required. The reason why no-one should sit in the temple was not questioned, but immediately assumed to have validity. In this way I avoided the sacrilege Pythagoras had planned me to perform, but that is not to say that by outwitting him I had not created problems for myself. The temple was to be my home. It was the house of the god, Kallias. I had nowhere else to live. Apart from the disadvantage of there being no domestic appointments and conveniences, no furniture, no bed, I had now imposed a restriction upon myself that was to prove extremely irksome during my days with the Durva.

Pythagoras had prepared the ground for my coming, and it became obvious that he had known my whereabouts from the day I had left Sybaris. He had not only told the Durva where I was to be found and that I was a god, but he had also managed to sell them the old wooden temple of Hera as an appropriate place for me to be housed. I later discovered that the Durva had always admired this building because it was the first that the original Greek Achaean colonists had erected at Sybaris, having driven the Durva out, and it represented the superior strength of the invaders and their gods. From that time onwards the indigenous gods of the tribe had waned in popularity, and the people had yearned for a saviour.

'And that is you,' Pythagoras explained as we walked through the beech wood that evening, with the women flitting through the trees around us.

'What has happened to their hatred of Greeks?' I asked him. 'Why didn't they simply surrender like the other tribes and integrate, if they had such respect for the invaders?'

'They have never liked the way we Greeks live,' he replied, 'especially our idea of a greater world. They have always felt that if they opened themselves up to our influence, then they would be absorbed and disappear. What they do accept, however, is that we are able to communicate with the gods at much more advanced levels.'

I made no comment upon this, not wanting to confuse myself any further. Until I could think my way through the tangle of conflicting ideas about the Durva as enemy and ally, I would have to concentrate upon the designs which Pythagoras had made for my future.

'What is your interest here?' I asked him. 'I had expected

that you would be enjoying your success. Why aren't you celebrating in Kroton?'

'Triumph is nothing to me,' he replied. 'I always move on to the next challenge.'

'But the Durva aren't a problem to anyone. They live up here, and if they were left alone no-one need think about them at all.'

Pythagoras took my hand, a gesture of his which I had once welcomed. In our Memphis student days, he would have kissed it.

'To think resolutely through a world change at the highest pitch, bringing all the best of oneself to bear upon what must be done, is an exhausting task,' he said softly, my hand half-raised to his lips. 'You must remember the long talks we had. How much I needed *contrast*.'

I wanted to withdraw my hand, but I could not. In the gloom of the great trees I saw his beauty glowing again as it had in youth, and I was re-conquered.

'Help me,' he said, kissing my hand, 'I mean no harm.'

It had once been my dream that this man would always be by my side; that we would roam the world together, exploring every corner of it in body and mind, leaving no question unanswered. At this moment, with myself as a god to simple folk and my love as high priest, it was all intoxicatingly delightful. To keep the anger and suffering alive in my mind seemed to be perverse.

'I will go out into the world again, Sphinx,' he whispered, his arm now around my neck as we walked on, rabbits scattering from under our feet, 'but I will always need you as a source of regenerating love. Who else have I ever been able to talk to with the same depth of understanding? No-one has ever taken your place.'

My arm had gone up and on to his shoulder without any order to do so from my mind. It had a will of its own, my arm, and it was the arm of a younger man in a perfumed courtyard by the waters of the Nile.

'Tomorrow I must return to Kroton,' he said, sitting down on a fallen trunk. 'I'd like to be able to stay longer, but I must push on with the next stage. If I can get back up here before I go to Rome, I will.'

I sat beside him, hardly aware of the disconcertment that this caused amongst the Durva women. Pythagoras smiled at their noise and spoke to them in their own language, then turned to me.

'I've explained that the god will sit anywhere he likes outside the temple,' he said with a twinkle. 'Is that what you had intended?'

We talked in the wood until the light went, then on into the night, with only the occasional star visible through the boughs. As we did so, the women melted away to their homes, leaving us wrapped in the reborn past.

Where has all the resentment gone? I kept silently asking myself, unable to keep my eyes off his face. He has used me, and always did. But he cannot do wrong when change flows from his mind like moonlight.

While we talked in that magical place, with the mountain breeze giving the beeches a calming voice, I heard him outline what was to come. In every great city of the Greek world he had planted a part of Sybaris – a temple, a house, a civic building, a part of the port – and these fragments of the once-famous *plutopolis* would be the locus of his antipathy, the point at which he could begin his campaign against the worship of wealth. That is why the city has been dismantled and sold off; to explode its symbolic authority in the first instance, them to accentuate the same tendency to wealth-worship to the point where it would refute itself.

'In Rome they now have the temple of Apollo which once stood in Sybaris,' he told me. 'The effort which they had to make to transport it was enormous. As you know, it was ten times the size of the temple which was brought here, and built of stone. But the Romans wanted it so much! Not in the old Tyrrhenian character, I'd say.' Here he laughed, his long, bared thigh touching mine. 'But all they cared about was that it came from Sybaris, the golden city. They wanted its magic, its associations and allure, and, I suspect, they want to build something on that.'

'Is that part of your design?' I asked

'No,' he replied sternly, his back straightening. 'It is not. I sold them the temple in order to flush their dreams out into the open. The hopes which they have for themselves and the ones which I hold are very different. They want to build a Sybarite empire that is greater than the original, that is as vast as what I have conceived for the Orphic Monad.'

By now I was tired, and my eyelids were drooping. I mumbled a question about the definition of an *Orphic* Monad, this not being part of my understanding of Pythagoras' theology of numbers which I had taught at the Luderma College during Telys' final period.

'Some other time,' Pythagoras said as he stood up and offered me his hand. 'You're falling asleep. Let's get you back to bed. What you might remember is that my thinking never stands still. It is always developing. What the introduction of the term *Orphic* implies is that I have been deeply influenced by your defence of the old religion. There, doesn't that make you feel proud?'

He led me back through the wood to the temple. As I walked by his side, our arms interlocked, I was in a daze. I kept searching for a part of my being he had not penetrated that night, somewhere that would give me the strength to resist him, but I found no such refuge. Pythagoras had repossessed me, and my spirit, once so experienced and resilient from its travels and trials, had gladly succumbed.

Where my spirit led in its new weakness, my flesh followed, and before we had reached the temple steps I had fainted into the arms of the Long-Haired Samian. When I awoke it was dawn, and I was curled up naked on Hera's throne, knowing in the most painful and direct way that I had been used by Pythagoras again.

THIRTY-TWO

All these events had not been foretold. The knowledge that was given to me when I entered the future at the end of my descent from Enna did not extend beyond the fall of Sybaris and my part in it. The auction of the city, my time on the mountain, all that had elapsed since then had not been the subject of any writings which I had found in my room in Elis after coming out of the Narcissus Pool. Between the fulfilment of Sybaris' destiny and my return to Elis – the latter being an integral predetermination of the prophecy, and something which I was compelled to perform or be guilty of breaking my vows as an Iamic diviner – had been a blank, except for four things: one, that I would return to Elis by way of Kroton; two, that I would have my treasure with me, intact; three, that I would be back at my home by the spring after the fall of Sybaris; and four, that I would attempt to take my own life.

It had also been a part of the prophecy, a condition even, that I would be saved by Frakdurma, otherwise I would not have been able to return to Enna and thence to Sybaris, to fulfil what the gods had decided was its fate. But when I returned to Elis next time and, in my despair, submerged myself in the Narcissus Pool seeking death, would it be necessary for me to be saved? The process of divination will have ended, I told myself, and anything could happen.

In my new home, the uncomfortable old wooden temple amongst the beeches, I pondered on this question, and it began to take on a mathematical quality.

I had, in that future time, given all my treasure to the

Temple of Zeus at Olympia, for the service of Demeter, our mother. Also, I had shaved my head, sworn never to eat meat or drink wine again, and released all my children, women, relatives, servants and slaves from any duty which they owed to me.

These were the actions of a live man, and I could remember doing them very clearly. However, each one of them could be seen as part of the funeral and testamentary arrangements for a dead man.

In order to keep track of my calculations in this matter I drew up a chart of the events in the Sybaris divination and my part in it, hoping to prove that I had survived beyond the point where I must re-enter the Narcissus Pool as a suicide.

After the donation of my treasure and the actions which I had taken against myself once I had discovered that I had been the betrayer of Sybaris, there had been the voyage back to Sicily. That had been real and, once again, I recalled it in every detail, also the events in Syracuse and my journey back to Enna, where I had unwound time by pulling up the oval rock and resurrecting the pigs.

But was this a man who had done these things, or a ghost? Had I not brought myself back to life at that final moment when Leogoras ran round the lake in pursuit of Geron and returned to me from the circle? Had I drowned at Enna, and had it all been a dream of death?

Here the symmetry of mathematics was shattered. When I looked at my chart, I realised that I had not known whether I was truly alive or not when I had left Elis that time. The distinctions between the reality of men and that of ghosts have often been shown to be cloudy.

It was possible that I had walked the earth as a shade in order to regain life at Enna. This, I conjectured, might have been the means by which the Eternal Ones used me to provide the volition for Sybaris' destiny.

I could not avoid the alarming implications of these thoughts. If I had been a ghost who had been readmitted to full life, and had not noticed the difference, this was hardly a recommendation for life. Most of my days had been spent in the service of the soul, and I had always known that the divine was superior to the mortal state, but I had believed that between the two was a barrier which the human senses could recognise. If it was not there and no detectable difference existed, then my entire system had not collapsed but vanished like Sybaris.

Only one alternative interpretation could be put upon the events which I saw outlined on my chart: that the Durva were right. I was a god, and had been from the time that I had emerged at Elis after the descent from Enna. That whole adventure, from the time that I had plunged into the lake and encountered Thales, Bes, myself in age, Luderma at her death-feast, had been the making of a new god. Had I not loved a goddess in Nonios? Lain with her? Why had I ever doubted that from the time I had made my descent I had entered into the dominion of the gods as one of them?

These were terrifying conclusions, and I often tore up my charts, only to start again. What appalled me was the thought that if this is what it is to be a god, to feel like this, to know pain and fragility of mind, then divinity is hardly desirable.

Sunk in these meditations I grew cold and listless, then bore up and struggled to unravel every thought and feeling which came to me as god on the one hand and man on the other. I paced up and down the old temple as it creaked in the mountain winds, my chart gripped in my fist, talking to myself while the Durva watched me from the trees. Now they irritated me in their silly, misconceiving ignorance. What were they staring at? A disappointed *being*, man or god, what did it matter? A beggar! They were all better advised to go home and worship the food in their pots, rather than the unhappy denizen of this ridiculous sanctuary.

My misery became so acute that I was ready to flee back to Elis and drown myself in the Narcissus Pool in advance of the terms of the prophecy, but that made no sense, as peace could not be guaranteed. There were so many unknowns attached to that return of mine that to anticipate them in any way was foolhardy.

But there was the present.

I knew that I was alive. I saw, heard, spoke, touched. If I climbed to the roof of the temple and threw myself down, then I would know for certain that everything had been an illusion, or I must live on as the divine diviner and make the best of it. That it would be death which would give me proof of the gods' essential deceit did not worry me.

For three days I thought about this course of action, growing weak through lack of sustenance, as I had no appetite to live, never mind eat.

On the evening of the third day I climbed up to the roof. It took me some time, because I was enfeebled and the only way up was by iron spikes driven into the side of northern rear pilaster. By the time that I had reached the roof and got to the front of the temple in order to throw myself down upon the new stone steps rather than the soft earth at the back, the Durva had become alerted to my presence on the roof, and gathered below.

I sat, straddling the ridge and peering down over the porch. The Durva raised their arms to me in praise, the women trilling and ululating excitedly, as if they had imagined my appearance on the roof to be part of a new ceremony. It was impossible for me to jump under these circumstances because I knew that they would catch me, and that would defeat my whole purpose. The sun went down, the evening star began to glimmer, and still I sat there, doing nothing but glare at my worshippers in frustration. The volume of the women's noise abated somewhat as time went by and I became a less distinct figure in the darkness, but the people would not go away. When the moon rode out from behind the eastern crest and cast a new light on the scene, I heard Tassopholos calling out to me from below.

'They want to know whether you have been waiting for the moon,' he cried. 'What shall I tell them?'

As a man who had once thrown himself into a lake embracing a stone, was I so changed that I would not trust the gods to the point where I could risk flying, or breaking my neck?

I was. It had all been a sham in my mind, this threat that I had made against myself; the playacting of a coward.

Kallias was no longer a diviner.

The gift had been traduced.

I stood up, swaying at the pitch of the porch, my arms held out.

'The moon of my Nemesis is here. Ask them this question: if I fall, will they catch me?'

I heard Tassopholos translate this for me, and the general answer which I knew from its sound could only be yes.

'That is all I wished to know,' I called out. 'Now I'm coming down the same way as I got up.'

This I did, offering no explanation to anyone, then spent the night lying on the floor, with all the fragments of my charts as my mattress.

While I waited for the return of Pythagoras – that being all I now yearned for in this world of disappointment – I went amongst the Durva to see how they lived day to day. This old habit of curiosity of mine had not been dulled by my recent purgings of soul, and I was still able to find pleasure in the various details of their domestic life, but it became clear that this was not reciprocated.

The Durva did not want me in their homes and gardens. Although they fell over themselves to make me welcome, they soon let me know that, as far as they were concerned, a god's place was in his temple and not wandering round the countryside asking irrelevant and inconsequential questions.

This rebuff made my yearning to see Pythagoras again even more acute. Now that my Egyptian love for him had come back and I was his slave again, it did not mean that my mind had stopped working within this infatuation. I knew that I was under his control, and I asked nothing more in my isolated wretchedness, but my mind retained its freedom, and my will was active outside this bondage. What I needed to know from Pythagoras was why he had set me up as a god, and whether my suspicion that it was merely to discredit the old religion was true. My need to know the answers was not on my own account – I was now a lost cause, as far as I could see – but on behalf of my people, the Iamidai, and their great inheritance of vision, and all those who clung to the Olympians for sense and comfort. In spite of all my doubts I did not want to be part of any machinations that would bring down the gods in the minds of men.

*

At first I was so delighted to see him that I did not notice how drawn and anxious he had become.

He had little interest in anything, took frequent naps, would not eat, and often went off into the countryside alone. When I asked him the questions which had been troubling me he seemed to think that they were of no importance but he found the energy to assure me that he had made me a god to the Durva because he now believed that a modified form of the old religion had to be kept going, in order to provide a framework for the great changes which he would be initiating throughout the Greek world. Science did not yet have faith's power to soothe. While the Monad would rule the intellect, the Olympians would retain some hold over the heart until a new mysticism had been found to replace it. This would have a much more human face, one such as mine, he told me with an ironic smile, and be based upon the idea of a purified, ascetic life, which would be governed by strict rules. Already he had developed the laws of the Durva temple practice and at his estate in Kroton, his disciples were not permitted to sit in the sacred areas, especially the fields of sacred beans which surrounded his house. These beans had to be planted each year, not to be harvested, he explained, but so they could shoot, flower and form fruit which would be the new seed of thought for the future.

'My disciples had taken to the practice of sitting in the field and contemplating the beans during each stage of their growth,' Pythagoras said to me as we lay side by side in the warm sun which flooded the painted porch of the temple. 'Some of them had gone even further. Once a bean had been planted, they simply sat and stared at it until the tip of the shoot appeared, then they would celebrate for a few days but return to the bean and sit down again to wait until it flowered, then another celebration, then back again to await the formation of the fruit. In this way they have been wasting their time, and I've had enough of it.'

I asked him, as gently as I could, why these disciples had such a marked interest in beans.

'A principle of my new mysticism is derived from the Orphic tradition, whereby all things are invested with a spiritual identity. You, at one time, I remember, inclined towards that when we used to argue about the true function of the pyramids.'

I could not recall this, but I conceded that it was possible for me to have held those views at some time during my student days.

'Vegetarianism is all very well as a means of dietary religious identification,' Pythagoras went on, 'and it serves its purpose in separating the Pythagorean mysteries from temple practice, with its emphasis upon sacrificial bloodshed. But I have discovered that some element of symbolic flesh is needed in our ritual structure, or it lacks credibility. After all, flesh is a fact of life, so is sacrifice.' With a short sigh he put his hands behind his head and squinted at the sun through his long lashes, then continued: 'In my wisdom, which I still defend, I decided that it would be best if the bean should become the soul of the dead, as it were.'

'Surely to eat the soul of the dead is an offensive idea to anyone who has religious feelings?' I said, shocked.

'They are not allowed to eat beans,' he informed me.

'But you said that there are fields of beans which you have planted in Kroton.'

'There are, but not for the table.'

I confessed to him that I was confused. Why cultivate a crop that would not be used?

'To resurrect the dead,' Pythagoras said, his slender forefinger to his lip like a maiden thinking over a proposition. 'That is what people want from religion, as you know. If one can show this being achieved in a natural way – what is more natural than a bean? – then much of the haziness can be removed from spiritual matters. Take the bereaved into the field, find a bean and point to it, say 'There's your lost one, flourishing.'

Oh, how my heart nearly stopped to hear him talk this way! It was as if we had been flung backwards in time to the chamber that we had shared in Memphis by the river and the endless discussions which we had had through many a night, until the sun rose.

'You grow fields of beans to bring the dead of the human race back to life?' I said, my voice wavering.

'I knew that you would see straight into the centre of what

I had intended,' he replied, kissing my cheek. 'How we used to wonder where the hordes of the dead gathered. In the air? In the sand? We never worked it out, did we?'

'You have noticed that the Durva grow several types of bean,' I said to him. 'Is that why you came here?'

He got up and left me, taking the path to the higher ground behind the temple. A while later I saw him against the skyline, his hands clasped behind his back, hair flowing in the breeze as he walked his thoughts up to yet another unimaginable height.

To have dwindled down from a god to a burnt-out diviner, and thence to a mere man in love with a superior mind which he knows is not in love with him, is a humiliating decline to anyone who marks the stages of it; but I did not. My body did, however, and soon I was in the grip of a malady which shook me for days. Bekela nursed me through it, keeping me screened and away from Durva eyes, and though I often called for Pythagoras to come to me, he refused, or was not told. When he did visit me it was at the end of my sickness and the worst was over, but I had been left very weak.

'I thought it wise to keep away until I had done all the thinking that I had come here to get through,' he said, stroking my brow. 'It is becoming more and more difficult for me to work in Kroton. Too many distractions. Too many disciples always knocking at the door. But up here with you, Sphinx . . .' He paused and smiled, the corner of his pale lips lifting in the way that had always reduced me to sensual wonder, '. . . everything falls into place.'

There was a note in his voice which told me he was going soon. I challenged him to admit this, and he told me that it was so.

'I cannot leave Kroton for too long these days,' he said, his eyes on the ground. 'If I do, then my enemies come out into the open and begin criticising me in public.'

'I didn't know you had enemies in Kroton.'

'Every man active in public affairs makes enemies, as you know,' he replied, with a spurt of irascibility. 'Do you imagine that all the changes which the infusion of Sybaris' wealth has made in the city have been good ones? As I said to Milo, it has to be controlled. One can't just multiply Kroton's treasure by a thousand and expect everything to go smoothly. The Tyrrhenians want to get their trade restarted, but the merchants in Kroton are so rich already that they're not interested. The soldiers have gone back to their farms with their loot, and it's enough to keep most of them for the rest of their lives.'

'I see . . .' I ventured, watching him closely. 'You sound ill at ease with all this.'

'I must have time to reorganise. But I can't have Kroton becoming a lesser version of Sybaris.'

'Then why did you destroy it so completely?'

He said nothing for a while, staring at the toes of his shoes.

'To keep religion alive as a force,' he said eventually, 'so I could have something to change rather than reintroduce. If Sybaris had been allowed to continue floundering its way towards godlessness, and it had found a way to survive and keep its wealth intact, the future would have been unthinkable. It had to fail. That is why I worked so hard on Telys. I was deceitful, I know, and I made use of you, but it was to keep the spiritual dimension alive in civilisation that I did it. Even now, I don't regret what happened to Sybaris, and I would do it again.'

'Are there people in Kroton who do regret it?'

He looked at me, and in his eyes I saw the answer to my question. For the first time in my life I felt sorry for this beautiful, brilliant man. His crimes against me had long fallen into the shadow of forgetfulness, and such was my desire for him that I had forgiven his annihilation of a city which had become part of my life, a city that had seduced me from that all-important prerequisite of a diviner's work – his necessary distance from the client.

But while I had allowed Pythagoras to redeem himself because I loved him, others had not.

Sybaris was being mourned.

THIRTY-THREE

Pythagoras slipped away that night, leaving no word when he would return. This arbitrary coming and going of his hurt me, but I remembered how he had behaved in the same way as a younger man.

It was harvest time for the Durva; as their god, I had many functions and duties to perform. I tramped around sheaves of corn, accepted thanks and libations of new wine, blessed vegetables, execrated pests, embraced industrious draught animals, read weather signs; all these were simple enough tasks for an experienced priest, but dealing with my failures and disappointments was another matter. As a diviner I had always the gods to blame, but now I had to find explanations for my inadequacies as a god, and that became an artist's work. As I lied and counter-lied my way through the death of infants, the appearance of leaf-mould upon cabbage, a horse's burst blood-vessel, every minor obstacle to a smooth, harmonious pastoral life, I almost became a poet.

My wit and resourcefulness carried me through, but not without some censure. My worst moment came when the Durva headmen arrived at the temple one morning with a naked man bound with ropes. He had been painted with black lines all down his body, and his hair, which had grown down to his waist, was stiffened with resin so it stood out from his head, giving him a wild, ferocious appearance. This captive was quite old, fifty summers by the look of him, but he was hard and lean, his body burnt by the sun and wind.

When I got Tassopholos to question the headmen about the identity of the wild man, they told him that he was their previous god, the one whom I had ousted. He had been living in the high mountains, but had been kept under watch from afar.

Now he was needed for the harvest.

I did not need to make too many enquiries concerning the use to which the wild man would be put. He was clearly terrified of what he knew was about to happen to him. Around his mouth was a green stain, and I later discovered that he had been stuffing himself with *aranata*, a herb which grows on the sides of mountain streams. This plant is an anaesthetic.

Here was a moment when I needed Pythagoras to be at my side. The wild man had been prepared for sacrifice, his genitals shaved, his heart sketched out on his chest in charcoal, and he was being delivered to me trussed and ready for the altar.

But if this was last year's god and he had to die, what was in store for me at the next harvest? What had been Pythagoras' arrangement with the Durva? Had their whole religion been altered when the temple of Hera had been brought up from Sybaris and I had been installed? Evidently not, if I was being asked to sacrifice this poor fellow as part of their old harvest ceremonial.

Tassopholos was trembling from head to foot, the smell and sounds of the wild man who was being held directly in front of him communicating the dreadful fear of death. I put a hand on the blind youth's shoulder to comfort him, and whispered in his ear that he must be steady.

'Tell them,' I said, taking a deep breath, 'that, as this will be the last sacrifice of this nature, the high priest has gone to the coast to bring back a golden jar in which the blood can be kept for ever. In this way the Durva will not lose the continuity of their lives, because the old warship will be poured into the new warship, which is how it must be if the people are to remain strong.'

This was a difficult piece of translation for Tassopholos, and it produced a lot of lip-pulling amongst the headmen. When they replied, I could see a hot, hectic gleam in many of their eyes.

'They say that all this makes sense,' Tassopholos told me,

'but the blood can be kept in a bucket until Pythagoras gets back, and then poured into this golden jar afterwards.'

The wild man's eyes were pleading with me to help him. He tried to fall to his knees but the headmen held him up, fiercely jerking him back to his feet.

'Tell them that I can make the sacrifice only when the correct altar has been installed in my house,' I said to Tassopholos. 'Point out to them that when they bought the temple from Sybaris, they should have been careful to specify that the altar should be part and parcel of the sale. Without the proper altar I cannot undertake such an important sacrifice. When the high priest returns, we will ask him what has happened to the altar. If it was sold to someone not too far away then we can send for it, but if the records have been lost, or no-one knows where it is, then someone must set out to look for it.'

As Tassopholos stumbled through his translation of this spontaneous and inspired proposition of mine, the mouths of the Durva headmen began to hang open. By the time it was completed, their shoulders had slumped and all the heat had gone out of them. When they turned to go, I told Tassopholos to let them know that I would guard the former god in the temple until the altar had been found, but they ignored this when it was translated for them, dragging the wild man away with them.

The next morning I noticed eagles, hawks and carrion birds circling over a buttress of rock further up the slope. I climbed up, passing men and women who gave me covert, surly glances, and viewed what I had already guessed to be there.

The wild man had been staked out face down, and his heart had been cut out through his ribs, his lungs pulled out to lie like red wings on his back. His resined hair had been pegged to keep his mouth and nose in the earth so he would eat it as he suffered his death throes.

It was so reminiscent of my inner scene with Herakles at Sybaris that, for a flashing moment, I felt my gift return, then it faded.

As I returned to the temple, I knew that my days as the god of the Durva were numbered on two accounts: they did not want to worship me any longer, and I did not wish to serve them.

Pythagoras returned not many days after. He arrived at night, exhausted, and slept until noon the following day. When I saw him in the light I realised that the man was under a heavy strain. All the brilliance had gone from his eye, his skin had gone sallow and lined, and his movements were lethargic. When I asked him how he was, he replied that the journey had tired him, but he had made no recovery by evening, sitting with me in the woods, his tongue too numb to wrap around a word. I could not avoid telling him the story of the wild man.

'None of this matters,' he said. 'We have to leave here. You can see that for yourself.'

'But will they let us go?'

'I'll find a way. If you had heard me persuading them to buy the temple and accept you as god, then you wouldn't doubt that I'll be able to talk them into letting us go. All one has to do with the primitive mind is cover the important points.'

I asked him where he would go. He told me that we must travel to Kroton, where he needed my help.

'To do what?'

'To defend what we did to Sybaris.'

'*We* did?'

'You were as much a part of it as anyone else. If you had not given Milo's bandmasters the tunes to make the horses dance, then the city would never have fallen.'

My laughter must have sounded strange in those night-owl-haunted woods, blending with their mournful hootings.

'Why should I agree to this?' I said. 'As far as Sybaris is concerned, all I will take responsibility for is the prophecy which I was paid to make. That is something I have done for many cities. What happens afterwards is out of my control. If it wasn't, then I would have more wars and disasters to my charge than Zeus.'

'You will do it because you have to,' he said quietly, 'or I will leave you here. How long do you think your godliness is going to last with these people? They're already reverting to their old ways, and that included an envious hatred of all Greeks, one that I managed to persuade them to suspend when I arranged your apotheosis. But they obey the high priest first, the god second.'

I kept silent for a while, repelled by the ugly hypothesis behind what he had said: that it is priests who control gods.

'For what reason would you like me to accompany you to Kroton?' I said, when I had recovered enough poise. 'Because I love you or because I fear you?'

He smiled, that effusion of unique magic of his shining through the hatchings of new lines around his mouth; his tongue darting out to wet his lips.

'Still the novice, aren't you?' he chuckled, tapping me affectionately on the cheek, his head held to one side. 'Dear man, don't you yet understand that fear and love are the same thing?'

Pythagoras' ruse to extricate us from the Durva was of such intelligence and subtlety that it dealt the death-blow to my faith in anything but his mind. I could not envisage any power in the universe that could be so supple, so devious, and yet so illuminating. That it was devoid of love was something that I regretted, but I had reached that point in my examination of myself where I had come to view love as an inferior emotion, which thrived upon weaknesss and dependency. Pythagoras was now effectively my god, and the laws which governed his existence transcended those which ruled mine. He was the only free spirit in a chained universe, a hero as bold and expedient as Odysseus, but a hundred times more resourceful, a thousand times more gifted.

Over three long days, with extraordinary patience and the sweetest of temper, he charmed the headmen of the Durva into believing that I had been summoned to Olympus to attend a meeting of the gods.

When the chief, a shrunken old man who sat wrapped up in a bearskin, was advised to ask for some form of hostage against my return, Pythagoras showed he had been able to anticipate this demand.

The means by which he calmed the suspicions of these primitive people was to weave them a new religion out of the torn fibres of the one that they had come to doubt. God's son, he told them, would remain behind with his mother. This child was not only the inheritor of my divinity, but had also been born of a virgin. When the Durva gave Bekela glances full of disbelief and made angry sounds, Pythagoras added that the mother had returned to the spirit world once the child had been born, leaving strict instructions that he was to be taken to the Durva by his father, the god, and a wet-nurse, Bekela.

Here the chief struggled up from the bearskin and pointed a trembling finger at me. If the child had been born of a virgin, then what was my function in all this? he wanted to know.

Pythagoras gave no sign of being unprepared for this question. His answer was that I was not only a god but also a *demiurge*, which meant that my creative power was general rather than particular. I did not spend my time impregnating women, because that was below me. From there he went smoothly on to appoint Tassopholos as high priest in his absence, filling the Durva with dread of the boy when he described his blindness as being that of one who does not need to look at the world, because all is known to him through darkness; and to appoint ten disciples who would come under the jurisdiction of the high priest, and whose duty it would be to guard the body of the child and carry out his wishes.

As I listened to Pythagoras' musical voice beguiling the Durva, I was suddenly aware that a new religion was being created on the hoof.

As the questions began to come thick and fast, Pythagoras invented his replies from sheer inspiration, adapting foreign forms and concepts which I had heard of before from other places, and fitting them into his manifesto, building up a body of principles and practices that swelled like a bladder being blown up. Even when it seemed to me that the mystery which he had created had been filled to bursting, he continued to cram myths and rituals in, until he had exceeded all understanding. Then all that was left was to believe.

When it was finished, the Durva sat around him in a state of trance-like exhaustion, scarcely able to summon up the will to leave his presence because they yearned for still more.

He had had an answer for everything. He had moved the truths of religion around with the ease of someone rearranging furniture in a doll's house. What could be denied such a man? Not godhead, certainly. He was more able to manipulate that authority than any of the dim, uncommunicative deities who had plied me with visions of obscure meaning. What Pythagoras lacked in mystery and command of the natural powers, he made up for with the creative intelligence of his genius. He knew what was *there*, the harmonies, the strength, the way the world worked.

Two days later the Durva pulled my waggon down to the beginning of the Mynxmahogh Way, then a force of warriors carried it down the pass as they had carried it up, on their shoulders.

Inside it was my treasure, and little else. Tassopholos, Bekela and my son had been left behind. As I thought about the child, I realised how Pythagoras had forged a protective shield around the infant: the boy was so innocent, not yet being able to speak, that he would make no mistakes. By the time that he had the use of his tongue and mind he would, to all intents and purposes, be a Durva and have their understanding of themselves. To be a god with those insights meant that there was some hope of a future for him.

It was in the supervening mood of sorrow that I had conversations with Pythagoras during which he came closest to any admission of ordinary human frailty.

As the waggon bumped and lurched down the track through the forest, I said: 'If you had stayed in Eygpt and learnt everything which they knew, then, perhaps, you would have been happier.'

'I did not set out to be happy,' he replied

How could any man not set out to be happy? It was the only trustworthy instinct in mankind, though often abortive in its results. I put this to him.

'By the time I arrived in Memphis I already knew how the laws which govern reality are set in immovable truth; that they are consistent; that they have harmony,' he said, the long reins wrapped around his fingers, 'and I also knew that they did not cover my happiness. Once I knew that, then happiness had to be excluded from my considerations, otherwise I would lead a life of negation.'

My silence was testimony to my feelings. He glanced at me slyly.

'The structure is not there for us to enjoy,' he said, jerking on the reins as the horses stumbled, 'but for us to fit in with, as much as we can. That way, life is more in the flow of things.'

'Am I in the flow of things?' I asked, holding on as the front wheel beside me rose up over a boulder. 'Who gave me my gift?'

'What gift?' he said. 'I am not aware that you have one.'

'My inheritance from the sons of Iamos. The power passed on in the family blood to prophecy.'

'Oh, that,' he scoffed. 'Did you ever possess it? Who will ever know? Who can be interested, when the potential for fallacy is so great? But the laws, the hard, immovable laws which are my prophecy, the laws which work, which fit into each other, which have form . . .' He paused, scrutinising my face for a reaction. 'They are something to love without a hope of happiness, and they are everyone's inheritance on this earth.'

Rage suddenly rose up in me. I saw my son, sired by me in a frenzy upon a slave, but still my son, my blood, held on the temple steps, that weatherbeaten, dilapidated, creaking old house. When the time came for him to have need of me, I would not be there. This absence of mine had more force than all the laws of nature which could be uncovered.

'And if a child is born, what are those laws to him? He can live his life without any knowledge of them at all,' I blurted out. 'That is probably happiness. But you wouldn't know that, would you, not ever having had the heat to engender a child.'

He leant forward, his elbows on his knees, looking for all the world like a tired farmer coming home from market. When he spoke it was in the accent of his native Samos, a sound that sent a flame of sensual memory up my spine.

'I do have a child, and he has always been with me; not like he's with me now, but in my concerns,' he said, his eyes fixed on the ferns which were being trampled under the horses' hooves. 'You are my son.'

THIRTY-FOUR

My cry of horror frightened the horses, Pythagoras had to stand up to control their rearing, operating the brake with his foot. He yelled at me to get down and hold their heads until they calmed. As I did so the waggon tipped to one side, and I fell into a thorn bush, having to tear myself out of it at the cost of deep scratches over my face and arms. When I had seized the horses by their bridles and held their heads down, Pythagoras descended from the seat and took my face in his hands.

'What a mess,' he said, tracing a scratch that went across my upper cheek, 'that could have taken out your eye.'

'You're not my father!' I ranted, thrusting the bridles into his hand and stumbling away.

'I am,' he declared. 'It's a simple story.'

'Not to me!' I raved, pushing deeper into the ferns to get away from him.

He shook his head and turned, leaning back against the horses which had now bent to graze.

'I came to Elis to study under Manastios, when he was arch-priest and headmaster at the school of divination at Olympia. I was barely twenty summers old when I met your mother.'

I groaned as I imagined the glory of that youth. How could any woman have resisted him? But in all his affairs and conquests over the years, why should my mother be the only female to conceive by him? It made no sense and, besides, there was something about his very beauty that was sterile. It could not be repeated, and certainly was not in me.

'It may be that you had my mother at the time I was conceived,' I shouted, 'but my father must have had her as well, because I know that I'm his son.'

Pythagoras laughed and folded his arms like a man who knows that he has a long wait in prospect.

'You will come to terms with the knowledge, Kallias,' he called after me as I blundered out of the ferns into the shade of a clump of trees. 'What you mustn't do is avoid all the implications.'

I flung myself down on the dead leaves, fighting to keep these implications from entering my mind. If I was not my father's son, then his blood did not flow in my veins. It was that blood, the blood of Iamos, the founder of Iamidai, that had given me my powers of prophecy and divination. To be Pythagoras' child meant that, should this be generally known, every inner scene, every vision, every communication that I had ever received, would have its authenticity doubted. I had been respected because I was of the kin of Iamos and the inheritance had flourished in me, but once it got out that I was the bastard of Pythagoras, for all his reputation and status, my standing in the world would crumble. People would not say, 'There goes Kallias. He's fallen on hard times, but he used to be the best Iamic diviner in the Greek world.' What they would say is: 'There goes that fraud, Sphinx, who's fooled us all for years. Every vision he's ever had has been spurious.'

All I had left of my old freedom and pride was tied up in the past, the notable successes in Arkadia and Athens, my triumphs as far afield a Chalkidike, Troad and Knidos; everywhere that I had worked people had cause to respect my skill. Now it would be washed away, all this goodwill, and I would be left with the misery of my role as the betrayer of Sybaris.

'Is it such a bad thing to be my son?'

Pythagoras was standing over me, his hands on his hips. When I looked up the length of his body and remembered everything that had happened between us, I shuddered, then retched.

'Oh, that. What is it, after all?' he said dismissively. 'If there is one myth that is more pernicious than all the others put together, it is purity. The same instincts are implanted in all of us, but without guidance about what we should use them for. Don't be ashamed.'

'You knew who I was . . .' I said, but could not go on with the rest of the accusation.

'That is what people seem to want from me. You were no different. Why should I deny you what I gave to others? It leaves no marks. It is meaningless, except as an expression of harmony. Without it there would have been no unison between us, our ideas being so opposed.'

I put my hands over my ears and screamed, then got up and ran with my head down towards the nearest tree, intending to brain myself. Pythagoras reached me in time to prevent this, pulling me to the ground, now laughing as if my agony were a romp.

That is the last thing I remember. I must have fainted with the force of my shame. When I awoke I was in the back of the waggon, my arms firmly tied to the struts, my head cushioned against the wooden side, reduced to the condition of a sheep on its way to slaughter. I could see Pythagoras' back as he drove the waggon along level ground. I must have made a sound as I woke, because he turned to look at me.

'You had a nosebleed,' he said jovially.

I had nothing to say to him; my mind was so full of self-reproach that his existence barely registered. Whatever had been done, whatever mistakes and errors, had been my fault. My insolence, my pride, my making of my own laws within my passions, had led me to this nadir. To blame Pythagoras was pointless. He might have sired me but, in truth, he was no more my father than the breeze. To have him removed from my conscience in this way made me light in the head. I even sang a little to myself. Nothing would ever matter to me any more.

'I'm glad you're feeling better,' he said, peering from over his shoulder. 'Now we can forget the whole father and son business, and make some plans. What's that you're singing? It's one that I haven't heard before. It would be good with a harmonic accompaniment on the lyre in perfect fourths . . . no, perhaps fifths. Sing louder so I can hear the words!'

Not in any obedience to him, but to liberate the demons

from my soul, I raised my voice and sang the hymn which I had made out of the writing of the silver eels:

The face looks on thee
        through the mask.
turn not away
        to hide thy endowments.
It is hopeless.
        Watch the gecko lizard . . .

Then I saw the gecko blazing on Pythagoras' back, its legs thrust out in spokes of smoking fire. There was a commotion at the front of the waggon, a wild neighing of horses and a stench of gases.

The waggon began moving quicker over the ground, Pythagoras wrestling with the reins in one hand as he tried to dislodge the gecko with the other. I could not see what was happening, nor could I stand up to look, but I could hear a mighty team of horses pulling us faster and faster down the slope. Through a crack in the woodwork I could see the haunches of one of them. Our animals had been chestnuts. The hide which I saw flexing over a mound of pounding muscle was black, foam gathering on it like surf on the edge of a raging sea.

They were the horses of Hades, and I knew that Nonios could not be far away. Pythagoras was now in a panic, rubbing his back against the waggon-arch in an attempt to get rid of the burning gecko, shrieking at the mad horses now in our harness.

Encouraged that help had come to me, I continued singing my hymn, beating my feet on the shaking boards; then we slowed down, and sunlight poured back through the cracks. I heard voices and Pythagoras got down, the gecko still clinging to his back, but now it was a cool green, issuing a trail of silver slime as it crawled through the top buttonhole of his collar.

The covering was drawn back from the rear of the waggon, and Nonios looked in. She was as I remembered her, her sling round her fist and her harelip in place.

She smiled her terrible smile and said: 'We will leave you

to suffer many tribulations in our service, but not the worst of the Long-Haired Samian's fantasies. His theories are all very well, and his audacity and ambition will enlarge the scope of the world, but he is, and has always been, impotent.'

Before I could cry out my gratitude, she had gone. I saw Pythagoras climb back on to the seat and whip up the horses. When he turned and told me that he had stopped to piss, I kept my own counsel, my eyes on the mark of the gecko scorched on his back.

My past had been salvaged.

From that time on, I have never doubted the value of what I have been, no matter what imperfections were attested. Although my Iamic gift has never returned to me since Nonios' appearance on that hillside, and its withdrawal has left me stranded in a colder world, my own history has retained its value.

In order to prepare me for our ordeal in Kroton, Pythagoras brought me up to date with events which had happened there since the fall of Sybaris.

At the time of the victory, the people of Kroton had been proud of the army's achievment. The popularity of Pythagoras and Milo had been boundless, rising to a peak of fanatical adulation when the low-born discovered that they were to benefit directly in the plunder, break-up and sale of the defeated city. Once it had been known that Sybaris was lying helpless on the northern coast, droves of citizens from Kroton had taken to the road and ships in order to be first in the queue for shares. Most of these had been sent back to await the organised distribution of Sybaris' wealth, but one citizen, a merchant called Boupalos, who had taken his entire fleet of seven ships up to Sybaris to load them with spoil, was not one of those whom the army sent back. Instead he was given several contracts to transport material and stores up and down the coast for buyers at the auction, it being forgotten in the excitement of the great triumph that this was the man who had been given the task of caring for the *azygous plutos*.

These Sybarite exiles had, not surprisingly, never attained the high standard of fitness required by Milo for his army. When the invading force had marched out of Kroton to go north, the *azygous plutos* had been sent to a small island under guard, and Boupalos had been awarded the contract to keep them supplied with food and drinking water.

When the news of the fall of Sybaris had come through, and the promise of such rich pickings became generally known, Boupalos had ignored the existence of the *azygous plutos* on the island and joined in the rush. This had coincided with bad weather, and no ship had called at the island for over fifty days.

Upon his return, Milo had wanted to invite the exiles from Sybaris to a feast of celebration. He had sent a messenger, who had come upon a scene that was so dismal and grim that he had turned round and come back, knowing that he would have been unable to keep his wits intact if he had stayed.

The starving *azygous plutos* had started to eat each other, having formed themselves into a democracy based upon the drawing of lots to decide the next victim. The more they ate, the less of them there had been to spread the risk of being next, and the democracy's lot-drawing had become intensely competitive, the *azygous plutos* enthralled by this fatal form of gambling. But the game was honoured. No strong man had emerged. There had been no reversion to barbarism. The rule of their one law had been maintained. Even in the madness which arose amongst the dwindling numbers, the lot-drawing remained holy. When the messenger arrived on the island, he had been asked to wait for a whole day while one of the demented *azygous plutos* took his straw, approaching the fatal basket from the opposite end of the island, crawling on his belly.

Milo had consulted Pythagoras and they had acted swiftly, the survivors being brought back from the island to be tended by the best physicians; but it was too late. The last of the *azygous plutos* had become so crazed that they had no interest in living without their ultimate test of nerve, and they had continued it while confined in hospital, the victims happily submitting to the knife when there was no reason to do so any more.

There had been a public outcry over the treatment of the *azygous plutos*. Boupalos, the merchant who had been charged with supplying the island with its necessities, was tried, condemned and executed. Milo and Pythagoras had still to contend with 138 remaining mad Sybarites, who were being kept in a military barracks which had been converted into what was effectively an asylum for the insane.

At the time of Pythagoras' last journey back to Kroton after visiting the Durva, this building had caught fire. Not one of the *azygous plutos* had survived, because instead of running away from the flames, they had run towards them and perished to a man.

'And I am blamed for this,' Pythagoras said gloomily when he had recounted the story to me.

'Well, the solution to the problem did have a certain mathematical neatness,' I pointed out. 'Anyone on the outside would have to wonder whether you had had a hand in it.'

'They set fire to the place themselves,' he replied with a bitter sigh, 'But what does it matter? Milo has decided to make me a scapegoat. All the sympathy for the Sybarites, which has only emerged since everyone has shared out their wealth, is going to be used to destroy me.'

'Then why are you going back?' I asked.

'To fight, of course!' he snapped back at me, his eyes glittering. 'Milo doesn't have the mental resources to defeat me in court. No lawyer of his will be able to prosecute me without being made to look foolish. Can you imagine it? Pythagoras, the master of argument, being beaten down by a dunce?'

'No, but everyone can be beaten down with a club,' I said, shaken by the news that Pythagoras' position had degenerated so far in Kroton that he was actually to be put on trial. 'Milo must have plenty of evidence that you masterminded the destruction of Sybaria, because you planned it together.'

'Did we?' he replied, guiding the horses to a level place beside a stream and getting down. 'I thought that it was the gods who decided what would happen to Sybaris, which is where you appear on the scene.'

'Me?' I cried, hurrying to keep up with the logic of what he was saying. 'What do you mean?'

He bent down to drink, then rocked back on his haunches and looked up at me, drops of water sparkling on his chin.

'You will be my principal witness,' he said, 'because you

can swear that it was the destiny of Sybaris to be destroyed, a destiny set out by the gods and revealed to you before it happened. As that was the case, then how can I be blamed? All I was doing was carrying out their orders, which you had passed on to me.'

'Why have you waited until now to tell me this?' I demanded.

'Because you wouldn't have come willingly,' he replied.

I got down and knelt beside the stream, sucking up the cold water without using my hands to cup it. The shock of the icy draught as it struck my stomach made me fart loudly.

'I'll need better testimony from you than that, my son,' Pythagoras said, whipping me lightly across the shoulders with the end of his girdle. 'With Kroton only two days away and the trial due to begin on the fourth from now, we'd better do some rehearsals of evidence.'

The lightheartedness of his mood was hateful to me as I squatted there, dully staring at the stones on the bed of the stream. I saw the grey shapes of trout as they flashed back to their holes after the disturbance which my drinking had made. Once in position, they pointed their noses upstream and held themselves ready for any food which might be brought down by the current. The slow waving of their fins and tails had the effect of calming the tumult in my mind. Like the trout, I must think my way through danger and preserve myself.

'If you are to stand trial,' I said quietly, 'why are you not in prison?'

'Oh, I was,' he replied, 'but it was not difficult to liberate myself.'

'You escaped?'

'The prison does not exist that can hold me.'

'When you go back to Kroton, therefore, it will be as a felon?'

'No, no,' he said, tossing a handful of small stones from the bank into the stream and scattering the grey ghosts of the trout, 'I will return simply as one who is above that kind of law. To acknowledge chains and fetters of any kind, body, mind or soul, is not the way of Pythagoras of Samos. The people will understand.'

I pointed out to him that the defence that he was going to

make was based upon the premise that all men are imprisoned by the destiny decided for them by the gods. For the first time in our long and embroiled relationship, I saw that I had made him think. It was only a moment, a blink of his eye, a touch of his fingertip upon his cheek; then he responded:

'That imprisonment is one that all mortals share. With the support of my followers, and the attested proof of your prophecy, I will demonstrate to the judges that I was not an instrument of the gods. You were the messenger. I was the one who sent the message. Who can put the gods on trial?'

So it was out at last.

Until now he had been foxed by his own intelligence, unable to see where his genius was leading. The praise of his disciples over the years had rotted his soul. When they had said that he had a golden thigh, he had never denied it, but from that day on he had kept those limbs covered. But there were men and women all over the Greek world who knew that it was a falsehood. When they had said that he could fly on a javelin, write on the moon, kiss bears on the mouth, he had not denied these false charms, because they fed his mystery.

The creation of lies had run in parallel with that of his discoveries in truth.

Truth to this man was a wardrobe full of clothes. Once dirtied, they could be washed. What guided him in his ambition must be a compulsion beyond science or religion, beyond god or man.

I feared it must be the void.

THIRTY-FIVE

When we arrived at his farm not far to the north-west of Kroton, Pythagoras' disciples were overjoyed. There were several hundred of them, mostly youths of good family, and it was obvious to me that they still adored him. But their welcome had an underlying desperation.

Since Pythagoras' escape from prison, they had been unable to leave the estate. Crowds of ill-wishers had come out from Kroton to rail against them and imprecate the person of the leader whom everyone had once venerated. The house and farm buildings had been searched by Milo's soldiers every day, looking for Pythagoras. These myrmidons had not hesitated to abuse and assault the disciples while they had hunted. Many of the youths bore cuts and bruises from the beatings which they had recieved.

Their delight in having Pythgoras back amongst them was pathetic at first, their harassed, worried faces lighting up as he walked through the gardens, touching each youth on the head in blessing. I could see that none of the plunder from Sybaris had ended up here. There was little furniture. Everything had a spare, frugal character, beds laid out on the bare earth, the wooden bowls worn thin with scraping.

Once the excitement of our arrival had subsided, the disciples became concerned for Pythagoras' safety. He assured them that there was no need to worry. He knew that he had been recognised along the road. Milo would be sure to know that he had come back by now. Because his return had been of his own free will, he was sure that Milo would allow the trial to proceed in the proper manner and the bullying would cease.

The disciples looked doubtful about this. They had borne the brunt of Milo's displeasure and witnessed the mood of the city's mob. The worst of the agitators strutted about in raiment stripped from the backs of Sybarites and cried, 'Remember Sybaris!'

But the disciples could not shake the confidence of their master. He had entered into a frame of mind whereby his own authority was as powerful in the outside world as it was in his head. Once back amongst those who worshipped him and fed upon his ideas, he believed himself to be beyond the reach of his enemies. The more the youths were perturbed, begging him to take heed of their warnings, the more he disdained the danger.

In the tumult of his homecoming no-one took much notice of me. Some of the youths remembered the night at the house of Phalanthos and the practical joke that had been played, but it was no time for comical memories now. Upon Pythagoras' instructions I was treated with careful respect. He explained to them that I was not only the head of the Orphopythagorean Mission to the Durva, but also the most important witness at his trial.

We had arrived in the early morning. When the heat of the day came I asked to be allowed to rest, leaving the disciples to enjoy their reunion with their master. He was, by then, in a fine humour; completely sure of himself again. The youths had bathed him and put a garment of soft yellow on his back, twining late blue daisies into his silver hair. When I left them he was talking about the different pitches of sound made by anvils of varying weights when struck by hammers, something he had noticed that very morning as we had passed a large blacksmith's shop on our way to the farm.

When I awoke it was late afternoon. The window of the room faced west. In the glare I could see movement on the road which passed nearby, the shine on metal, and hear the low sound of many voices. I shielded my eyes, and made out ranks of armoured men, their shields on their backs, restraining a crowd.

While I was looking at this ominous sight, the door opened and Pythagoras entered.

'They've brought the trial forward,' he said blithely. 'No matter. I'm as ready as I'll ever be. Do you want to run through your evidence before we go?'

I asked him if he had heard from Milo.

'No, but he's sent an escort,' he replied, gesturing at the scene on the road.

'Have you spoken to the officer?'

'I don't discuss these things with inferiors. The trial is called in the name of Milo's justice. He will be the principal judge, so he said. I'm not prepared to argue the toss with underlings along the way.'

The sounds made by the crowd became more voluble, and I saw the line of soldiers waver as the people surged forward.

'They're angry,' I told Pythagoras. 'I don't think the trial has been brought forward at all. I think it's been cancelled in favour of a rougher court.'

'Milo would never throw me to the mob,' he told me serenely. 'Think of everything we have achieved together. I'm the custodian of the man's soul.'

As he spoke, the crowd began to chant 'Remember Sybaris!' and heave against the cordon of soldiers. It gave way, and people came running across the field towards the house.

Pythagoras saw what was happening and left the room.

Through the open door I saw him fleeing across the courtyard.

I stayed where I was. Once the crowd had spotted their quarry in his yellow, they gave chase and had no thought for anyone else.

I clambered up to the roof to watch the death of Pythagoras, my greatest love and influence, for I was certain that his moment had come.

Beans had been planted all around the house, filling the adjacent field. In keeping with their esoteric practices, the Orphopythagoreans had not harvested them, but left the fruit to hang on the withered plants. I saw the yellow robe of the master as he ran through the middle of the field to the east, his trail sketched lightly through the trampled beans. A wind had blown up from the sea, sending ripples across the surface of the tinder-dry crop.

Men in the crowd had picked up brands from a fire that had been lit to burn rubbish behind the disciples' dormitory. Some cast them into the edges of the beanfield and flames took hold, fanned forward by the wind.

Pythagoras kept running, a flower of fresh yellow in the drab table of the beans. No-one was with him now.

If he had been watching someone else in the toils of this nemesis, he would have been calculating the speed of the runner against the speed of the onrushing flames and working out how long it would be before one overtook the other; but I am not made of such stuff, and I looked away.

In the aftermath of Pythagoras' death it was discoverd that many of the disciples had escaped, though some shared the fate of their master. I had expected to die also, but once I was found and brought to the officer in charge of the troops, he first apologised for what had happened giving as an excuse the volatility of the people of Kroton *these days*, then assuring me of my personal safety. He had already put my waggon and treasure under guard, and had orders to conduct me to the harbour, where a ship was waiting to take me back to Elis.

I saw no reason to enter into any dispute over these arrangements, and submitted to them without further ado. When I reached the ship and went aboard I was given a packet bearing the seal of the city of Kroton, which contained three and a third talents of gold which, so a note from the treasurer informed me, was the amount outstanding after the successful completion of my contract with Sybaris.

The ship was a merchant vessel bound for Miletos, the old trading partner of Sybaris on the coast of Caria. The master intended to sail first to Elis, where I would disembark, then go to Kydonia in Crete to pick up a cargo of soft copper before proceeding across the Aegean to Miletos.

Such was my melancholy and the change in my world that I asked him to alter his itinerary and sail directly to Crete, then Miletos. I knew that the prosperity of that great port would have been sorely affected by the disappearance of Sybaris. There would be a form of mourning going on, a sadness in which I could lose myself before returning home. When we reached Miletos, I saw how right I had been in my guess. The hair of the people was still growing out of an obsequious shortness, and many still had ash smeared upon their foreheads as they went about their business, or what was left of it since the demise of their long-established customer.

I stayed amongst the Milesians for the worst of the winter, keeping my identity a close secret. While I was there I had an experience that still ranks as the strangest of my life; even superseding my descent from Enna, which should have prepared me for it,

A play about the fall of Sybaris was put on at the theatre in Miletos, and I went to see it. The writer of the piece was a man of meagre skill when it came to creating character, and his grasp of storytelling was feeble. But he excelled in vituperation and the higher forms of cursing. When he loosed the full force of his spleen upon the audience, they perked up out of the tragic trance which his style had induced in them, and took notice.

The villain of the drama was not Milo or Pythagoras. It was Kallias, the diviner. This part was no less than a personification of evil, drawing on all the actor's skills to achieve my quintessential badness. I was a liar. I was a cheat. I was heartless. I was a profiteer. There was not a good word to say for this man.

I sat there in that dismal theatre, dampened by a mist, glad that the auditorium was three parts empty, and watched Kallias pacing here, and there, plotting, scheming, rubbing his hands, having his visions, laughing like a demon, and I laughed along with him at the absurdity of it all.

I laughed so loudly that people turned to look at me. I would have left, except that I wanted to see what punishment Kallias would receive.

But the playwright failed to come up to the mark. At the end of the ninth scene Kallias made an exit and was not seen again, the only subsequent mention of the character being that he had fallen ill with a veneral disease. No doubt it was the fear of being prosecuted for blasphemy that had made the author draw back from consigning a priest of the Greater and Lesser Eleusian Mysteries to a more savage retribution. Hell, perhaps?

*

When the cuckoos began to sing in Miletos, I knew that it was time for me to go home. Rumours had been going round that Kallias, the betrayer of Sybaris, was hiding somewhere on the coast, but there seemed to be little interest in finding him. Darius, the Persian king, was probably my benefactor here. His relations with Miletos and the string of Greek trading cities along the western coast of his dominions had degenerated since his invasion of Scythia. Rebellion was in the air, and this was of far more importance to the well-being of the Milesians than rooting out a fugitive, no matter how heinous his crimes were.

I had spent much of my time writing the notes which I knew must be found in my room when I would return from the Narcissus Pool. This had occupied my winter days in Miletos, becoming a passion as I struggled to recall them. I had not taken the wax tablets with me to Sicily to rejoin the present, but had committed the details to memory. In order for the full terms of the prophecy to be achieved, the notes I carried back from Miletos must coincide with those I had left behind in my room. Once I had put them side by side and seen them tally, I would have the ultimate equation of the fate destiny and nemesis of Sybaris worked out. I hoped that this harmonious correctness would satisfy the gods. They would see how I had carried out my duties to the letter, and spare me.

I negotiated a passage on a ship going to Chalkis in Euboia, and from there I travelled overland to Megara, avoiding Thebes, where I was too well-known not to be recognised, bypassing Corinth for the same reason, then crossing the hills and plains of Argolid and Arkadia until I reached the eastern border of Elis. By then I was so darkened by the sun, my hair and beard grizzled and thinned by salt, wind and worry, my limbs so attenuated from walking alongside the three asses which carried my treasure, that I was sure no-one would be able to recognise me and I would be able to get back home without an outcry.

But I was soon confronted by a horseman, the first Elean to see me since I had crossed the border. He was an oldish fellow, a farmer by the look of him, having that inquisitiveness which the land teaches. First he stared at my two slaves to estimate their value, then the asses, finally giving me a searching look. I had my cloak held up to my mouth, my hat pulled down over my eyes, but his finger went straight out and he shrieked, 'The Sphinx is back!', wheeled his horse round and galloped off in the direction from which he had come.

The rest of my journey was a punishment worse than any devised by the gods. I was vilified, spat at, mocked, and humiliated by my own people. Because of my noble blood and my ancestry, and my status as a mystagogue and hierophant of the Iamidai, I was not attacked or robbed, but every other form of assault was practised upon me. I was denied food and drink, my slaves beaten, my asses stoned. As these iniquities were performed upon me, my persecutors cried, 'Remember Sybaris!' as if they had been citizens themselves.

When I reached my farm, it was deserted. Food and drink had been set out on the table, my room had been cleaned, my bed made up, but there was no-one to greet me. It took several days before my family, servants and slaves crept back to the house. Even when they had joined me they did not speak, but moved around like timid ghosts, eyes averted as if they could not face my shame.

Soon I began to weaken, to need the comfort of my family. All that I had to offer was the fruit of my greatest act of prophecy, my fee, sufficient to build a fleet of fighting ships or buy land double that which I owned already. I showed my sons the ten talents of gold stacked on the table, two-thirds of it stamped with the seal of Sybaris and one with the seal of Kroton. I showed them the two sets of wax tablets, my notes, which proved beyond any doubt that I had prophecied true and according to my vision, but they dumbly refused to read them. When I became enraged at their silence and threatened to disinherit them, they opened their mouths for the first time and begged me to do so.

I began to despair, and the Narcissus Pool drew me. It was a truly Pythagorean temptation, mathematical in its offer of a completed, harmonious equation: that my own vision, my greatest prophecy, should also mean my death.

The attraction towards the Narcissus Pool was so powerful that I wondered whether Pythagoras had died in the beanfield or not. While in Miletos I had heard rumours that he had escaped astride the magic spear that Abaris the Hypoborean had given him and taken refuge in the Temple of the Muses at Metapontion.

But although I had looked away as the flames approached the Long-Haired Samian through the dried-up beans, I had not stopped up my ears. I had heard his screams.

No other man could have produced the sounds that Pythagoras did when he was being burnt to death.

His screams were not of agony but frustration.

I resisted the pull towards the Narcissus Pool, reasoning that if I did not venture there then the ambiguity of whether I would be saved or not if I tried to drown myself could be avoided.

But my need to go got stronger. It became an unbearable yearning, then a command from within myself.

As a precaution I sent for Frakdurma, my old slave, so he could accompany me and perform a rescue should I attempt suicide, my despair having become very deep. Frakdurma had been posted to a distant hill to watch sheep. I sent one of my bastard sons to get him. When the boy reached the shepherd's hut, he came upon three wolves gnawing at the carcass of my old slave.

When the boy disturbed them, the wolves retreated to a nearby rock. One pressed its face into the stone: another chiselled letters with its nose; the last snarled as it wrapped a leather sling around its paws.

The boy has my prophetic blood in his veins. I had no cause to disbelieve his story.

When I went up to the hut to see for myself, there I found 'REMEMBER SYBARIS' cut into the rock and wolf-droppings flecked with gold.

The three wolves were Herakles, Pythagoras and Nonios, I believe. Which means that the Long-Haired Samian has been made divine. That the gods should embrace a man who spent his time on earth tormenting them seems unfair, but it is no surprise to me.

I did not bother to go back to the house. It is clear what I must do. Everything must be fulfilled.

My reflection looks up at me from the water of the Narcissus Pool. I see an old, careworn man, but the despair has gone. What I must do now needs courage, and I still have that.

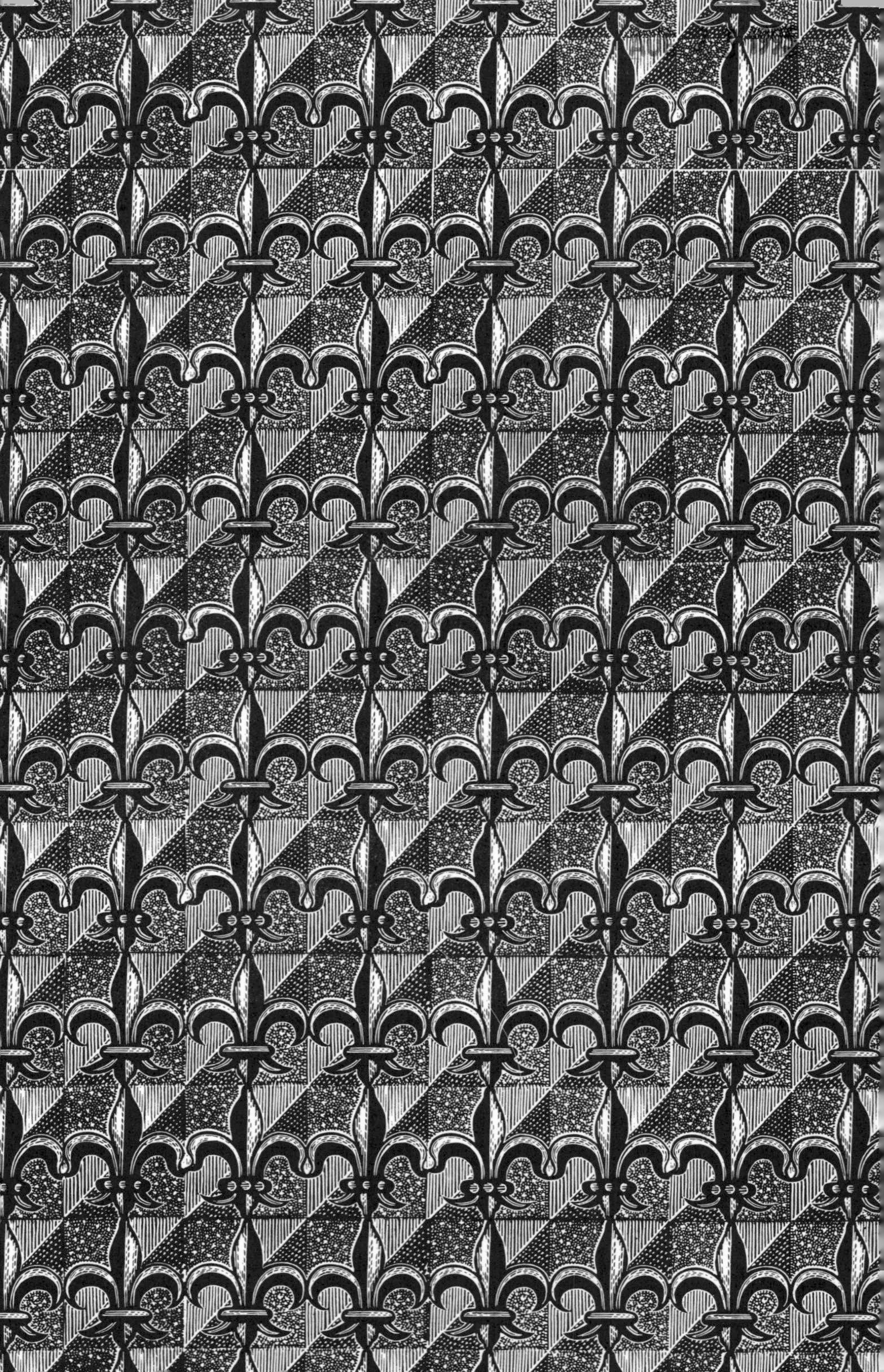